Praise for *Finder*

W9-BPK-531

"Fergus Ferguson, a professional repo man in a space-faring future, chases a stolen spaceship to a backwater colony, incidentally becomes the catalyst for a civil war, and draws the attention of dangerous alien neighbors in Palmer's riotous sci-fi debut." —*Publishers Weekly*

"Wicked, fast-paced, and fun. This is a total romp, and I loved it." —Elizabeth Bear, author of *Ancestral Night*

"A nonstop SF thrill ride until the very last page." —*Kirkus*

"Passionate, powerful, and brimming with humanity." —Julie E. Czerneda, author of *The Gossamer Mage*

"Palmer, a Hugo Award winner for her short fiction, has created a pulp-style space opera debut complete with aliens, stinging space roaches, and lethal spores . . . this will please anyone who embraces outer-space yarns." —*Library Journal*

"Palmer tells a fluid, funny, thrilling tale. . . . The fight scenes and feats of derring-do might recall hard-edged passages from Richard Morgan. And there's a kind of Hitchcockian *North by Northwest* feel to the way fate and misunderstandings impel Fergus's actions." —*Locus*

"The dialogue snaps and crackles, the blend of real-world science and sci-fi tech is inventive, and the motley cast of characters both helping and trying to thwart Fergus in his mission are truly memorable. The deft worldbuilding and complex character motivations only make it more satisfying—there's really no reason a novel this funny needs to be this well thought-out, but it's all the better for that." —Barnes & Noble Sci-fi & Fantasy Blog

"*Finder* is a joy for lovers of lightning-fast plots and engaging reads." —Washington Independent Review of Books

DAW Books proudly presents
the novels
of Suzanne Palmer

<u>THE FINDER CHRONICLES</u>
FINDER
DRIVING THE DEEP

FINDER

Suzanne Palmer

DAW BOOKS, INC.
DONALD A. WOLLHEIM, FOUNDER
1745 Broadway, New York, NY 10019
ELIZABETH R. WOLLHEIM
SHEILA E. GILBERT
PUBLISHERS
DAWBOOKS.COM

DAW Book Collectors No. 1819.

Published by DAW Books, Inc.
1745 Broadway, New York, NY 10019.

First Mass Market Printing, March 2020

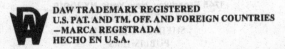

DAW TRADEMARK REGISTERED
U.S. PAT. AND TM. OFF. AND FOREIGN COUNTRIES
—MARCA REGISTRADA
HECHO EN U.S.A.

PRINTED IN THE U.S.A.

To Laurie—for the dare.

Chapter 1

◆—◆

Above the airlock, in at least twenty different human and non-human languages, a faded sign read, *Management Not Responsible For Losses Due to Depressurization or Alien Interference.* Fergus Ferguson considered, not for the first time, whether the life choices that had brought him to this place had been entirely sound. Here he was in yet another unreliable tin can, far from anyone and anything familiar, in a half-devoured solar system on the edge of the galactic spiral arm. He always could have stayed home and raised sheep with his cousins.

Closing his eyes, he tried to imagine living his entire life on a single hillside when he could barely stand to stay on one planet more than a few months at a time. Even his dream—apprenticing himself to a Tea Master on Coralla, spending the rest of his life in peaceful contemplation on those perfect white sand beaches—was almost impossible to imagine actually doing. *I have,* he thought, *made a decent career out of chasing things and running away.*

And Cernekan was somewhere he'd never been before, somewhere new. There was always that.

The car's ventilation system choked out wheezing gasps of stale air in between death rattles. Fergus's feet were sweaty inside his magboots, and the seat's safety harness, built for smaller bodies, pressed relentlessly down on his shoulders through his exosuit. What starlight graced the interior of the cable car was little more than thin, angry half circles in the distance where the glare managed to steal around and through the narrow gaps in the sunshields.

The cable car lazily spun its way along the cable as Fergus clutched his worn travel pack to his chest. The dark rock ahead of them wobbled erratically in space, a convincing illusion when the car felt mostly stationary. Only the faint downward pull toward his seat confirmed his opinion of who exactly was the body in motion.

Craning his head around as best he could in the iron grip of his seat's safety harness, he glanced out the pitted window, wondering how far the cable car still had to go. He sighed; the car was barely halfway down the line.

Turning back, his eyes met the sharp gaze of the old woman sitting on the bench opposite him, his lone fellow passenger. Her exosuit hood and face shield had been folded back, much like his own. She was tiny, with bone-white hair and sharp, almost violet eyes that were unusual in a typically wan spacer face. The bulky arms of the seat harness engulfed her, as if she were slowly being consumed by the car itself. *A grandmother-eating bench*, he thought, smiling at the ludicrous thought. *The bane of little old ladies in space.*

Space aged people quickly, especially out here where radiation shielding, vitamins, and decent medical care were phantoms at best, and the woman was not so much shrunken as gnarled, like her body had been distilled down to the bare but formidable essentials for survival. Fergus had to believe she'd already far exceeded the typical life expectancy of the junk merchants, rockcrappers, and fugitives that made up the human population near the Gap, where stars thinned out to nothing between the galaxy's arms.

Her side of the small car was filled with crates, tucked behind portable webbing to keep them from drifting. With the jostling of the car along the uneven cable, he could only imagine the damage they'd do to anyone trapped helplessly in their seats if they weren't secured. He wondered what was inside—a thousand knit children's hats, teddy bears, or awkwardly sized blankets crocheted from spun recycled plastics? He caught her eyes again, and by the slow deepening of her expression, he knew she had not missed his idle stare.

"I'm sorry," he said, trying to cover his rudeness. "You reminded me for a moment of my mam—my grandmother."

"Are you implying that I'm old?" she said.

He blinked, nonplussed. "Um . . . I . . ."

The old woman cracked a smile. "I'm guessing you're not from Cernee. Where you heading?"

Surnee? Fergus wondered for a half second until it clicked: *Cernekan.* "I'm heading to Central," he answered. "Is it always this bumpy?"

"Gets better from Mezzanine Rock," she said just as a huge jolt threw them both upward against their harnesses and was slow to return them. "Lines are smoother farther in."

Central was the aptly named ring station at the center of the settlement, surrounded by a halo many hundreds of times its diameter of hollowed-out rocks, scavenged dead ships, and a haphazard collection of building-sized tin cans. All that space trash was tied together with hundreds of crisscrossing cables known collectively as the lines and kept stable by a small army of autorockets that nudged and pulled as needed. First chance he got, Fergus was going to rent himself a one-man personal flyer that could get around freely between the lines.

Their thin sliver of sunlight vanished as the car crept into the shadow of a smaller rock. Half a heartbeat later, the already-dim lights in the car flickered, and there was a thud as if something had collided with the car.

The old woman twisted in her seat to look out the window. Pulling a handheld out of a pouch in her exosuit, she tapped at it, then held it up to her face. "It's me," she said. "May be trouble on the line to Mezzanine Rock. No idea, maybe nothing. Stay sharp, and kee everyone in. I'll check back in when I get to the en the line."

She slipped the handheld back into her exo

bony hand emerging again with a small tool. By his count, it took her fewer than seven seconds to pop the in-transit safety lock on her harness and float free.

"Um . . ." Fergus asked. "What's going on?"

Before she could answer, the air handlers gave one last coughing wheeze and went silent as the lights in the car quit for good, leaving them both in pitch darkness.

He heard a few snaps, then jumped as something lightly touched his arm. "You wearing gloves?" the old woman asked from somewhere directly in front of him.

"Yes?" he said.

"Then hold out your hand."

She really did remind him enough of his maimeó that it was automatic to comply. A squiggle of glowing green goo appeared in the palm of his glove.

"Rub your hands together, but try not to get it anywhere other than the palms," the old woman said. "Don't lick it or touch your eyes. Either one will make you wish you were dead."

"I'll try to remember," he said. He held his hands up, turning them from side to side. It was a limited but surprisingly adequate light source. He could just make out the outlines of her face by the light. "That's useful. Thank you."

"Don't thank me yet," she said. "It also makes you an easier target in the dark. If you have to hide, close your hands into fists."

"Are we in danger?" *But I just got here,* he thought. *Even my luck doesn't work that fast.*

She floated over to the instrument panel at the front of the car, one hand gripping the panel as the other worked at the controls. "Dead, I'm afraid," she said after a few moments, then launched herself back toward the center of the car.

"A mechanical fault?" he asked.

"Backup instrumentation is down. It's a self-contained, separately powered system," she said. "Proximity detectors and external sensors are offline, as are all the security cameras. Best guess is an EMP mine, probably slapped on the car as it left Blackcans. We're dead midline and blind. Unless I'm mistaken, you're in the wrong place at the wrong time."

"I often am," Fergus said. He cupped one hand, used the light to look at his own seat harness lock.

The old woman was back in the center of the car and was going over her crates one by one, unhooking the webbing and pushing it aside. "It's also possible that hub control has deliberately shut down the system because the Asiig are doing a flyby," she said. She opened a panel on each crate, did something within that he couldn't see, then closed it again. "You know about the Asiig?"

"Not much, and more than enough," Fergus said, remembering amorphous childhood nightmares. It hadn't occurred to him until just now who Cernee's nearest neighbors across the Gap were. "They do 'flybys'?"

"Once or twice a standard," she said.

Out here, a single solar orbit took nearly fourteen Earth years. It was his good luck that most—though not all—human settlements stuck to old home time references.

"If it's the Asiig, you want to keep your head down and stay hidden," the old woman continued. "If you're out in the open, you might get taken."

"Great."

"Still, I don't think that's the problem," she said, tapping at the display panel on the left forearm of her exosuit. "No alert has gone out."

He watched as she finished with the last of her crates. She snapped a pair of goggles down over her face, and clouds of shock-white hair puffed out around them. She grabbed hold of the window frame and peered out. "Ah," she said. "Something's coming down the line towards us. Minimal heat signature."

"Another cable car?"

"No. Hand spiders. Around a dozen." People free-riding the cable. "If they see you're not one of my people, there's a chance they might let you go," she added, "but I wouldn't count on it from that pestilential den of half-wits."

Obviously there was a lot more going on here than he understood. "You know who's out there?"

She gave a short laugh. "Yes. They've been coming after me for standards now. Haven't caught me yet."

"They're after *you*?" He pointed at her crates. "These aren't all full of teddy bears, I gather?"

She floated back toward him, pale green phantom hands in the dark. "Lichen," she said. "I'm a lichen farmer. These cases are a quarter-standard's worth of produce."

"So . . . these 'half-wits' want to steal your lichen?"

"Not really, no," she said. "Hard to believe, respectable elderly woman like me, but they seem to find my existence a matter of personal offense."

"Really? That doesn't sound reasonable of them."

"It doesn't, does it?" she said. "If you're of a mind to take some advice, I suggest you let me get you out of that harness, and you get your suit sealed up. It's up to you, but after coming all this way to Cernee from"—she sized him up in the green light—"Earth, is it? It seems a waste for you to get yourself dead before you've seen the place."

Not Earth; not in a very long time, he thought, but it didn't matter. "I got it," he said. Sliding a small pick out of a pocket on the front of his suit, he popped the lock on his own harness. Five seconds.

The old woman raised one eyebrow in appraisal. "Now your suit," she said.

Fergus wrangled his travel pack over his shoulders. He could see the old woman fastening up the last few seals on her suit. He turned his cupped palm toward his chest and used the green light to work on his own. "So," he said, "since I seem to be in danger here too, can you tell me more about who's coming?"

"Men who work for a junk warlord named Gilger," she said.

"Arum Gilger?"

There was a pause before she answered. "Indeed. Surprised you'd know that." She must have closed her hand, because she vanished into the dark like a ghost, and he was suddenly keenly aware of the advantage she had over him. That she was also very, very old was no reassurance at all.

Fergus resisted the temptation to close his own hands. "I don't know him," he said. "He and I have some business. That's why I came here."

"What sort of business, if you pardon me asking?"

He answered carefully. "Not a kind he'll be happy about."

"Oh?"

If she knew about Gilger, she could be a source of useful information. And out here, who was she going to tell? "I've been contracted to locate an item not legally belonging to Mr. Gilger," he said, "and secure its return to its—"

"A repo man!" she interrupted.

"More a professional finder," he said. "But essentially, yes."

She appeared at the edge of his light, grinning, holding out a bright gloved hand. "I'm Mattie Vahn. Mother Vahn to most folk."

"Fergus Ferguson," he said, shaking it. "Pleased to meet you."

"Mr. Ferguson," she said, and he liked the old-fashioned tone she said it with. "I suggest you finish sealing up. I'm going to short the airlock."

"You're what?"

"I'm getting out of this trap," she said. "You coming?"

He pulled his goggles up into place from around his neck, swept the lower scruff of his beard aside, and snapped his face shield down. When he looked back at

Mother Vahn, she tapped the side of her head, then held up fingers in sequence: three, one, five. He nodded, then set his suit to that comm channel.

The old woman was peering out the window again. "Something's moving parallel to the lines, behind the spiders," she said. "I only spotted it because it just crossed in front of the lights on Beggar's Boulder. It's either junk, or . . ."

"Or?"

"Or something meant to hurt us," she said. "You set?"

He checked his seals one last time; the status light on his suit display was green, all good. He took a moment to consider how far off his expectation of boredom the cable car ride had become. Still, Mother Vahn could be a lucky find—the information he had on Arum Gilger was thirdhand and months old, so if she could improve upon that, it was worth a little side adventure. And what else was his job if not half luck and half improvisation?

"Set," he said.

She'd already wedged open the inner door of the airlock at the far end of the car and popped the lock on the manual override. She saw him coming and pushed herself back, gesturing at what appeared to be an old-style crank. "Pneumatic," she said. "Purely mechanical system. The crank primes the emergency door release. Do you mind? I'm getting a bit old for this."

He swung himself forward. "No problem," he said.

"I'm going to herd my crates closer. Let me know when it's primed; it's best if the crates get pulled out first when the lock opens so we're not in their way when they go."

He looped an arm around one of the car's poles and did his best to anchor himself, then began winding the crank, sending himself into a corkscrew spin he had to stop and recover from every few turns. Mother Vahn hovered between her crates, edging them forward one by one. The spin of the car around the cable made them dip gradually toward the floor, bumping and drifting toward him and the lock. He wasn't sure how he felt about getting sucked out into space, but he was certain he agreed with letting the crates go first.

"So, this Gilger . . ." he said, hauling on the crank. "What can you tell me about him?"

"He's dangerous and mean," she said. "Although most of the cutwork is done by his number two, a man named Graf. Gilger will shoot you in the face without blinking, but Graf's the one who'll laugh as he knifes you in the dark from behind. If you're really going after something of his, watch your back."

"Yeah," Fergus said. No one named Graf had been in his notes.

Resistance on the crank grew until he couldn't budge it any farther. "That's as far as it'll go."

Mother Vahn was peering out the window. "They've stopped moving," she said. "We better leave."

"Hold tight," Fergus said. He hooked one boot around a standing pole behind him, took hold of the crank handle to keep himself steady, and punched the mechanical release.

The howl of the car decompressing was a physical blow as its entire cargo of atmosphere and crates was sucked out into the dark. He closed his eyes. *If I'm going to get hit*, he decided, *I don't want to see it coming*.

It was not the wallop of a crate but a gentle hand on his shoulder that made him jump. He opened his eyes to see Mother Vahn floating beside him. "Our turn," she said.

He looked out the open door at the scatter trail of crates curling in a spiral line around the car. As he watched, the line deformed, straightening itself, and began to stretch away. Tiny green lights flickered on and off among them.

"Homing smartware," she said as if reading his mind, "and tampering self-destruct. They'll either make their own way back to the farm or give anybody who intercepts them a bit of a surprise. They're not my worry anymore—we are. Whatever they've got out there, they're lighting it up."

Out the far windows he could now make out the heat signature of the device and easily a dozen people around it. "Got it," he said, and using his grip on the bar for leverage, he swung himself out into space. The old woman sailed out gracefully behind him.

"Once they realized we've fled, they'll leave, and we should be safe," she said. "Can you get yourself back to the cable up-line on your own?"

He could no longer see her. "Yeah, though it's going to take me a few minutes," he answered. His exosuit had a limited directional push capability, and he used it to stop the slow spin he was in. Then he pointed himself on a long diagonal toward the cable. Once he got moving, he'd keep going until he reached it.

Around them, Cernee was a scattering of distant lights.

"I hate to say it," he said, "but we're sitting ducks out here."

"Ducks?"

"It's a, like a . . ." *Something a very long way away from here*, he thought. "Like a chicken that floats on water? You must have chickens even out here. Never mind. I just mean we're vulnerable."

"No one would dare risk damaging the cable system, not even Gilger," she said. "Only things worse you can do around here are crack a sunshield, puncture a hab, or mess with the sewage bots."

Movement caught his eye, and he found her at last in the place he least expected: pulling herself along the cable car, green glowing lines in her wake. A momentary panic gripped him that he'd been the butt of some trick, stuck out here with a long haul back to anyplace with air. "What are you doing?" he asked.

"I want to see what they're up to. Once I reach the cable myself, I'll get a good quick look at that device, and then I've got a fast spider that'll get us ou—"

A brilliant flash blinded him, fast enough that his goggles couldn't compensate in time, and he flung his arm up over his eyes as tiny suns danced and swarmed in his vision. Pinprick icicles stung his side, and red lights flared all over his peripheral display. *Suit breach!*

It had been a long time, but it wasn't a feeling you forgot. Where a moment ago it had felt like ice, now his skin burned; his exosuit was trying to repair itself, and burned skin was better than a dead body. It was an agonizing few moments before the topical sedative the suit had released took effect and numbness set in. Whatever had torn his exosuit must have been small.

"Well, shoot," Mother Vahn said. "I never thought he'd go that far. Are you alive, Mr. Ferguson?"

"Nothing that won't seal or heal," he said. He blinked, afterimages in his vision from the blast ruining his ability to make out anything. His own fault for not having better goggles. "What was that?"

"Shrapnel cannon." Her signal was fainter. "Hit my suit's power supply. I'm afraid you're on your own."

"Hold on, I'm coming back—"

"Don't, Mr. Ferguson. You need to use whatever juice you've got to get as much distance from here as you can. I found the EMP mine, and it's got a secondary explosive charge. I guess they don't want any evidence."

"But . . ."

"Since I'm unlikely to see you again, promise me that when you go repo whatever it is of Gilger's you came for, you'll give him my love? Preferably with a space boot up his backside, hard enough to kick him all the way up to his tiny brain."

"I—"

"I can see you're not moving yet, Fergus Ferguson. You get yourself out of here now," she said, and again he heard the ghost of his maimeó.

"There's got to be another way," he said. He had a spare air bottle, enough for them both if he moved fast enough, right? "Use your spider, and I'll meet you—"

The cable car blew, a single brief, orange ball instantly extinguished in the dark.

He cried out as he turned his face away. A thin arc of light bent and curved ahead of him, growing and slipping sideways. With horror he realized it was the distant starlight reflecting off the curve of one of the severed cables, which was whipping straight toward him.

Panicking, he thumbed his suit jet too hard and sent himself into a spin. *Bloody amateur!* He swore, trying to restabilize. The cable loomed closer as he spun, and then it brushed past, sweeping over one knee and thigh with enough impact to send him hurtling off in a new direction. He had to close his eyes to keep the wildly oscillating universe around him from making him sick.

At long last, when he got his motion under control, he found he had been flung well out of the cable path and away from Mezzanine Rock. Two of his suit's power cells were offline, and the lone remainder was nearly depleted. When it went, there would go his oxygen and heat, and his life.

Well, shit, he thought. *Now what?*

As if in answer, ahead of him he saw a small green light blinking steadily like a beacon. If he burned most of what his suit had left, he could just catch up to it.

There was nothing else. He'd better not miss.

When his lazy spin pointed him the right way, he hit his jet again. It was just beginning to splutter and die when he reached out and, like a man clinging to flotsam after his oceanship had gone down, wrapped his arms around the homing crate.

"I don't know where your lichen farm is, Mother Vahn," he said out loud to the dark and the stars, "but I hope it's not too far, and I hope you've left a key under the mat."

He turned on his gloves' mag-grips to fasten himself securely to the side of the crate, then set his suit to maximum oxygen conservation. Immediately he began to feel drowsy. His last thought as he drifted off was that if he survived, he was going to find Arum Gilger. And when he did . . .

He had a job to do—always and only the job. Get in, look around, do what you need to do, and above all, try not to make it personal. But now it was much more than that.

Chapter 2

◆━━━◆━━━◆

Fergus's first fully formed thought was that he was unpleasantly cold, followed by a detached curiosity as to whether that was because he was now a frozen corpse stuck to a crate of lichen floating through space. *Can you be uncomfortable*, he wondered, *and dead at the same time*? If so, that seemed unfair.

His fingernails cut half moons into his palms, and he forced himself to loosen his fists. It was a long, formless moment before he connected fingernails on flesh with *no gloves*, then no gloves and cold all over with *naked*. His eyes popped open into searing light.

"He's awake," a woman's voice said.

There was some gravity, probably from spin. His hands splayed out on the floor beneath him—cold, rough-textured, unyielding—and still blinded, eyes streaming tears, he tried to sit up. A hand shoved him roughly back down. "Question time. We'll know if you're lying."

Only if I'm very bad at it, he thought. The light dimmed, and he could now make out the pale blobs of his arms and legs, and was glad to know he'd been left his undershorts, if nothing else. "Okay," he said. "Ask away."

"Where's Mother? How much is Gilger paying you? Who do you think you are? Who sent you? Where are you from?" The questions seemed to come from all around him at once, women's voices rushing over themselves like a disorganized echo. He shook his head, made an effort to see and understand. Blurry faces surrounded him. He focused on the one front and center. The woman was so similar to Mother Vahn that as soon as he'd discarded (more firmly this time) the "dead" hypothesis, he realized he must be at the Vahn farm.

Nearly identical, yes, but not *quite* as ancient-looking. Daughter?

Then he took in the rest of the faces. The similarity went beyond family resemblance and into the uncanny: they might well have been the same person except for their clothing and the span of their ages. *What the hell?* he thought. *Clones?*

He didn't know cloning tech was that good.

The youngest of the Vahns was holding a giant pitchfork, braced and pointed in his direction. She had the expression of someone contemplating the joys of immediate violence.

The light flared again, emanating from a square hatch set in the floor not fully shut. It lasted just long enough to make his eyes water. *Rotation*, he thought; the brightness must be the intervals when they faced the un-shielded star outside.

"Please," he said, and that seemed to be enough for them to let him sit up. "I only just arrived here today, and I met Mattie Vahn on the cable car just before it was attacked. She saved my life. I couldn't save hers. I'm sorry. I am not your enemy."

"So you say," a middle-aged Vahn said. "Prove it."

"And how do I do that? We barely spoke before the car was attacked. She told me about her farm, and she gave me some glowy goo—you have my suit gloves, you at least can verify *that*."

The woman in front of him glanced back at two of the others, a perfectly matched set. "Macie? Minnie?"

One of the twins nodded. "That's true."

The woman turned back to him. "Is Mother really dead?"

"Yes. I'm sorry," he said.

After a long silence, the woman let out a long, un-steady breath. "Tell us what happened."

"Can I have my pants back?"

"No." The young woman holding the pitchfork shook it in his direction.

Moving with deliberate care, he pulled his knees up to his chest and wrapped his arms around them, hoping to conserve at least some body heat. He told them about boarding the cable car, his conversation with the old woman already on board, and the events from there as best he could.

"Why did Mother stay at the car after you exited?" Pitchfork Girl asked.

"She told me the attackers wouldn't risk damaging the cable system. She wanted to see what they were up to and thought she could still get out in time," Fergus said. He vividly remembered the brief glimpse he'd had of her before the cannon went off and the bright green lines on the outside of the car beside her. The memory snapped into focus. "Uh, and also, she may have been writing an obscene message on the outside of the car in glowing goo."

The lead woman put her hand to her forehead. "That'd be just like her," she said. "Did she say who attacked you?"

"She named Arum Gilger."

"Did you see him or the faces of anyone who attacked you? Any identifying marks on their suits? Color stripes?"

"No, nothing," Fergus said. "I could hardly make out the silhouette of the cannon, much less anyone with it. They stayed dark until they got where they wanted to be, which was only as close as they needed to fire."

"Damn," Pitchfork Girl said.

"I'm sorry," he said again.

"And you? What's your name?" the lead woman asked.

"Fergus Ferguson."

"You're not local. Why are you here?"

Telling one little old woman alone in a cable car hadn't seemed risky. But a whole family of strangers? "I pose you no threat," he said.

"Yes, well, Mother is dead, and you're not," Pitchfork Girl said. "You have to answer better than that."

"Look, I'd rather not—" he started to say, then found the fork wavering centimeters from his face. *Hell.* "I came here looking for something that was stolen. If you let me go do my job, I think you'll find I'm going to cause this Mr. Gilger a great inconvenience."

"Seems like he's the one who *inconvenienced* you," she snapped.

"I assure you I'll do better," he said, stung.

"Mari," the lead woman said, "put the pitchfork down and give Mr. Ferguson his pants back. I'm not worried about him trying to escape, and I'm sick of watching him shiver."

Mari bobbed her head. "Yes, Mauda," she said, then reached behind a crate and flung his pants at him.

He caught them and stood up, grimacing at the pain from his injuries, and slipped them back on. They were so cold he wondered if they'd put them in a freezer. Ignoring the chill as best he could, he sat back down on the floor, willing warmth back into his body. "What do I have to do to get my socks back?" he asked.

"Gilger and his crew have been after us for a long time," Mauda said, ignoring the question. "We've managed to avoid him up until now, and here you are. Maybe that's a coincidence, and maybe Mother was showing off to impress you—for all her years, sometimes she was the biggest kid of us all. But we've been in a stalemate for a long time, and the only thing that's changed is you. We need to know you're not a danger, and that you're not working for Gilger."

"I work for myself, one job at a time," he said. "I didn't know anything at all about any of you until I got bored and started talking to your Mother Vahn on the cable car."

"And now?"

"And now what?" he asked. He took in their faces, a mix of anger, grief, and . . . hope? "I'm angry about what happened too, but I don't know any way to help you beyond doing what I already came here to do. I'm not the law, and I'm not a soldier. I'm only one person, and a half-frozen one at that."

One of the other women groaned. "He's useless," she said. "What good is a hulking, stupid Earther against Gilger and Graf's fighters anyway? We're wasting our time."

Without turning, Mauda waved one hand. "You can leave, Meg. I'm sure you have better things to do."

"Don't we all," Meg answered. She opened the hatch in the floor the rest of the way. Whatever was outside the hatch was so bright, Fergus couldn't make out any details before the woman had climbed down through it and slammed the hatch shut after her.

It was Mauda who spoke again first. "Mr. Gilger is hard to inconvenience," she said. "What do you know about him?"

"A bit of his history and where his territory is. That he's a scrap merchant operating between here and Crossroads, running salvage with a small crew." Crossroads Station was another settlement in the same solar system as Cernee, closer to the sun by three gas giants and a lot of rubble. Fergus had been to Crossroads a half-dozen times before, but until this job he'd thought it was one of the farthest things out in what could barely still be called "human space." Cernee had a more extensive footprint, but Crossroads had the advantage of sitting near an active jump point, which was how Fergus had arrived in the system; passive FTL travel wasn't tied to specific points in space but was a much slower ride. "Mother Vahn mentioned his second-in-command, Graf, and that he's in some long-running feud with you."

Mauda sat down cross-legged on the floor in front of him. Mari leaned against the wall, one foot resting on the fork.

"About the salvage, that's true, but Gilger pulls in stuff that's hard to believe was acquired legally," Mauda said. "Rumor is some of it still has bodies inside. He's got three rocks and a can all to himself just past Humbug, about thirty degrees up the Halo from us. His crew used to be small, but it's tripled, maybe more, over the last standard. Also, he somehow got his hands on a fancy cruiser that's faster than anything else around here. He likes to buzz the rockcrappers when he's bored or drunk."

"That cruiser," Fergus said. "He's got just the one?"

"One's more than enough."

"And it's about forty meters long, rounded nose, jump engine on an underside fin, blue stripe down the side?"

"That'd be it. You've seen it?"

He weighed what they'd told him and made a decision he hoped he wouldn't regret. "Not since it was being built," he said. "But I came here to take it away from him."

Mauda leaned forward and put her chin in her hands, staring at him intently. "That, Mr. Ferguson," she said at last, "would definitely get you your socks back."

They did return his socks, and his shirt too. Mari—she of the pitchfork—seemed disappointed with that largesse. Still, it was understood that their interests overlapped.

Mari threw open the hatch. Through it Fergus could see the ends of a narrow ladder snaking down toward . . . nothing? He did a double take, then saw the thin metal catwalk below and stars beyond it. Mauda went first, and he lowered himself down behind her, disoriented as his feet headed toward space and his head emerged last from the solidity of the room above. The other women followed.

The lichen farm was a large wheel spinning edge-on to Cernee's distant sun, and from here he could see that it was one of a series. Past them all, the glittering surface of one of the massive sunshields filled the view to their right at a sharp angle; they were just outside its shadow. *Makes sense for a farm*, he thought.

Artificial gravity systems were expensive and used a lot of energy. It was easier and much cheaper to use spin to achieve a similar effect, but unlike on a planet, where gravity always pulled you down toward the center, spin pulled you outward. A lot of habs were cylinders with a single layer of living spaces around the outer diameter and a gravity-free open tube running up the center that connected everything. Wheels were similar, although rather than being one fully enclosed structure, they were multiple units connected to a central spindle by hollow spokes, which eliminated the need to heat and cycle air through spaces where the spin was slow enough to make it less useful. Line up a bunch of wheels along the same axis, and you could adjust the rotation of each individually, giving you variable gravity or, as Fergus expected was the advantage here, different light-dark/heat-cool cycles.

There were only a few ring stations in Cernee, which combined the architecture of wheels around a central cylinder, on a much larger scale.

This was the first time Fergus had been in a wheel where the outermost surface—the basement floor, as it were—was transparent. The farm's catwalk ran along the outside edge above thick, transparent xglass that formed the outermost shell of the wheel, like an inside-out greenhouse. A slight blurriness to the light coming through suggested the presence of a thin gel shield to catch fast-moving particles and absorb some of the solar radiation.

The lichen grew overhead like a thick ceiling carpet, a patchwork of blues and greens bathed in the stark light. If Fergus stretched his hands up, he'd just be able to brush the lichen with his fingertips; given how he towered over the Vahns, he expected they had to use ladders to harvest it.

Once they'd spun to face the sun, Mauda began to walk the narrow path at a pace that exactly matched the spin so that the sun stayed directly underfoot, throwing their shadows upward.

"Mother was on her way to meet one of our regular

buyers at Central," she told him. "Now that all the crates have found their way home, we need to arrange another meeting. We grow a modified lichen, freeze- and rad-tolerant with boosted nutritional value. Compact, grows fast, keeps forever. A lot of rockcrappers and deep spacers live off it and little else."

"How does it taste?"

The faint trace of a smile ghosted across her face. "If you have nothing else to eat, it tastes great," she said. "Also, we grow many flavors."

"Yeah?"

She pointed at a blue patch overhead, then at green and purple, then at other shades in between. "Those'd be Ew, Ick, Blech, Yeegh, and Guh," she said. "Want to try one? I recommend the Guh."

"Do you?"

"No," she said. "Here we are." She stopped at another ladder beside the path, then ascended to another section of the wheel's interior. He followed her up, relieved to go back inside solid walls.

Although claustrophobically narrow, the interior of the wheel was clean and well lit. Mauda led Fergus through the halls as Mari stomped along close behind him. The pitchfork was nowhere in sight, but the menace of it shone brightly on her face every time he caught her glare.

They passed several more women in the tight corridors, including one carrying an infant. He found himself thinking about cloning again. "Are there many of you living here?" he asked.

Mauda made a noncommittal gesture. "Just family," she said.

As they walked, Fergus glanced down at his shirt. It had several tears in it from the shrapnel cannon and a large bloodstain eclipsing the faded yellow umbrella of the Kuan's Café logo. It had been his favorite shirt, and he felt his grudge against Gilger increase. "My pack—" he started to say.

"It's safe," Mauda said.

"Where are we going?"

"There's a family meeting. We have a lot of talking to do."

She turned to Pitchfork Mari. "Can you take him down for some food until we're ready for him?"

Mari crooked one finger at Fergus. "Come, Earthman," she said. She led him a quarter turn around the wheel and then into a large dining hall. There were a half dozen women and two small children in there. All conversation died as he entered.

Mari pointed at a pot on a side table. "Bowls and spoons are next to the pot. Help yourself. Stay here until I come back for you or else."

She stomped out again.

Fergus smiled anxiously at the women, picked up a bowl, and ladled out a small portion of soup. Then he crossed to the empty end of the big table in the center of the room and sat down. "Hello," he said.

No one answered. Giving up, he dipped the spoon into the bowl and took a tentative sip. It was less licheny than he'd feared and warmer than he could have hoped, but he ate in uncomfortable silence as the other Vahns stared at him.

It was the youngest girl there—Fergus guessed she was about five standards old—who broke the ice. She got up, walked the length of the table, and set down her bowl with a sloshing thump beside him. Frowning, she reached out to touch his beard. "You're funny-looking and have weird red hair all over your face," she said.

"Mella, no!" one of the other women said, her eyes wide with horror.

Fergus smiled. "I am, and I do," he said to the girl. He pointed at his own chin. "This is called a beard. I was born on Earth, which is a planet very far away from here. Do you know about Earth?"

"Yes! It's near Mars, right?" the girl said. "Mari and Arelyn talk about Mars all the time! I'm Mella."

"I'm Fergus," he said. "And yes, Earth is very near Mars."

Mella sat down. "Mari never talks about Earth, just Mars, Mars, Mars, boring Mars! Did you have to run away because of the giraffes?"

He blinked. "What?"

"Giraffes. I have a picture book."

He laughed. "There aren't any giraffes anymore," he said. "At least, I don't think. But even when there were, I'm pretty sure they were friendly."

"They didn't eat kids?"

"No."

"Oh." She took a long slurp of soup and looked disappointed.

The other child came over and sat down next to Mella. "Tell me about Earth too!" the new girl demanded.

"It's been a very long time since I've been there, and it's a very big place," Fergus said.

"Did you live in a wheel?" Mella asked.

"No," he said. "I lived on an old farm on the side of a mountain. Mountains are like giant rocks that stand up tall on the surface of planets. My grandparents were born in a small town named Kilcreggen, which was flooded over when the oceans rose and the lochs merged together and everyone—"

"What's an ocean?"

One of the women laughed, and then another. Although conversation didn't start up again, they were now looking at him more in curiosity than fright. So he did his best to explain using the soup bowl and a hunk of bread, and the girls both asked questions, and then the other women did too. By the time Mari came back to fetch him, everyone was laughing and talking loudly and a wasteful amount of soup had gone tepid.

Mari glared at him suspiciously. "Put your bowl in the wash over there," she said.

Fergus stood up, wiped his chin, and picked up his bowl. His was empty; he hadn't realized he'd been that hungry. "Maybe someday you'll get to see mountains and oceans and birds for yourself," he said to Mella as he slid it into the washer.

Whatever warmth he'd earned from the room evaporated in an instant. Mari gave him an odd, cold look. "Time to go," she said. *"Now."*

She ushered him out of the room. "The family is ready to talk to you," she said.

"Sort of a key witness thing?"

"More like an Exhibit A thing," she said.

"Oh."

Judging by the curve of the floor, they'd gone another third of the way around the wheel when Mari stopped in front of a large door. Fergus could hear arguing on the other side. Mari rolled her eyes, then knocked loudly and counted to three. Opening the door, she shoved him in ahead of her.

Around a dozen women, all very much Vahns, were sitting in a semicircle of chairs in a large room with faded off-white walls, one of which had a drawn-out scrawl of some child's art that had either escaped notice or survived attempts to remove it. There were a few empty chairs left, plus a solitary one in the center. Mauda was standing. "This is Fergus Ferguson," she said. Mari leaned against the wall by the door.

Another woman only slightly younger than Mauda leapt to her feet. "This man should have been spaced the moment he showed up here, not led inside and fed!"

"I don't believe he's our enemy, Muire," Mauda said.

"Who said you get to be the judge of that?"

"Mother did when she named me second-in-charge," Mauda said. "Can we move on?"

"And Mari? What do you think?" The woman looked at Mari, who seemed surprised to be asked.

"Yeah," Mari said at last, the words reluctant at best. "I don't think he's here to hurt us. Intentionally."

Defeated, the woman sat down, glaring across the room at Fergus as Mauda waved him toward the seat in the center. He sat, keeping his expression what he hoped was neutral and harmless.

"Your name is Fergus Ferguson?" one of the other women asked. "Your mother had a sense of humor."

"Yes," Fergus lied. He got that a lot, but the truth was he'd never in his life heard his mother laugh and could barely remember her smiling. The years she'd spent staring out over the inland sea that had once been the home of her parents and grandparents, obsessing about a heritage lost to her, had drowned whatever joy she might have had. She'd tried to pull him down into that same bottomless grief, and no matter how far away he got, he still felt the overwhelming need to escape.

"Please tell everyone what happened in as much detail as you can," Mauda said.

"Um, okay," Fergus said, pulling his thoughts back out of the past. "I jumped in-system at Crossroads Station and caught a ride on a freighter from there to Cernee. It docked at Rock Five, and then they dropped me at Blackcans by shuttle on their way to a hab named Footstuck. From there I got on the first cable car to Mezzanine Rock. Mother Vahn was the only other passenger, and she and her crates were already there when I boarded. There were a few other people waiting at the cable terminus, but no one else got on—I assumed at the time they were waiting for someone. Is it possible there was general knowledge that the car would be attacked?"

"Mother was well liked in Cernee. We don't make trouble, and we contribute regularly to the settlement emergency food stores. A rumor like that would have reached us," Mauda said.

He told the rest of the story up until when he'd attached himself to the last of the homing crates in the hopes that it would carry him to safety. "I woke up here, and you know the rest," he finished. "My apologies for what might be an intrusive question, but what's Gilger's argument with you, anyhow? You don't seem like a threat to him or that you have much he'd consider worth stealing."

"He's a Faither, at least nominally," Mauda said.

"Right. And they believe clones are soulless abominations," Fergus said.

Several of the women scowled, but Mauda nodded. "I wouldn't say he's devout except when it's convenient. Graf, on the other hand . . . he'd probably have already killed us all if not for Gilger's restraining hand. It may be that Gilger has finally become powerful enough not to care about repercussions."

"If that's true," he said, "given that Gilger has the tech to take out a cable car and he has an armed ship, why hasn't he just attacked your farm directly and been done?"

"We're part of what's called the Wheel Collective," Mauda said. "There's an even dozen interconnected wheels here and a stationary hab named the Hangar. Eight of the wheels are our farm, and the rest are home to Mr. Harcourt and his crew."

"Who?"

"Mr. Harcourt is a weapons dealer. Openly attacking the Wheels would mean starting a war with someone who can and will fight back. Gilger hates Harcourt as much as Graf hates us. No one has ever figured out why, including Mr. Harcourt, but Gilger knows he can't afford to take him on."

"What about your Governor?"

"How do you think any politician makes life out here pleasant?" Muire interjected bitterly. "We're farmers; he's out of our price range."

"We haven't had much direct interaction with Cernee's government," Mauda added, her eyes on Muire, "although Mother had some confidence in the integrity of the Governor and Authority. I don't know enough to have an opinion of my own."

Fergus leaned forward in his seat. "Even if—*when*—I take Gilger's ship away from him, he's not going to leave you alone, and from how you describe him, he's still going to have a lot of resources to come after you. As much as it pains me to say it, I think you should think more about your survival than revenge. With Mother Vahn gone, that's the end of your farm sooner or later anyhow."

"And how do you figure that?" Mari stood up.

"Look, no offense, but everything I've heard says cloning is best as a one- or two-gen process because of pattern integrity degradation. With the original gone—"

"We're not—"

"Mari!" Mauda snapped, and the younger woman retreated to her chair, folded her arms across her chest, and chewed angrily at her lower lip.

Not clones? Fergus wondered if that's what she had been about to say, but there was no other explanation he could think of that didn't fall solidly into the realm of fantasy. That Mother Vahn might lie to her family about their origins was disappointing, but it was the only plausible explanation. It wasn't, however, his job to puncture those fictions, nor to track down the truth.

"The long-term survival of our farm is our concern, not yours, Mr. Ferguson," Mauda said. "A few minutes' conversation on a cable car doesn't make you part of the family, or even, to be blunt, a friend. It suits our ends to give you back your things and let you go about your business taking Gilger's ship away from him. You should be grateful for that."

"I am," he said.

"Aside from wishing you sincere luck with that, our purposes and paths diverge. You will have to find your own way around Cernee without help from us." Mauda pursed her lips. "If that sounds heartless, it may be some small comfort to know I'm not in much different straits myself despite having lived here my entire life."

"How so?" Fergus asked.

"While you go about your business with Gilger, I need to get our lichen crates to Central to conduct ours. None of us besides Mother have ever been far from the Wheels. She handled all our dealings with the outside world, especially once Graf arrived and got interested in us. I have the most experience off the farm, but even that's limited. I don't suppose you have much sympathy, as in your line of work you must be adept at learning your way around unfamiliar places, but for me this is not a natural skill nor a responsibility I look forward to."

"My original intention when I arrived was to start at Central," Fergus said. "That hasn't changed."

"So?"

"So I am good at getting a feel for things. I also owe Mother Vahn a debt for getting me out of that cable car. If you'd like me to accompany you to Central to help work your deal and then part ways there, I'd be willing to do that. And it might be safer to have a second pair of eyes out."

"No, Mauda!" Mari said from across the room. "If we need to send someone else, I'll go with you."

Mauda frowned, considering for a long minute. "I'll take you up on that offer, Mr. Ferguson, if there are no other strings attached."

"None," Fergus said, "though if you want to point out any landmarks on our way, I'd be grateful."

"Mauda!" Mari said.

"No, Mari. It's not safe out there for you." Mauda surveyed the room. "If there are no other objections?"

When no one had anything further to say—though Muire clearly had much she wasn't willing to, and Mari looked like she wanted her pitchfork back—Mauda turned back to Fergus. "Thank you," she said. "I'll ping our buyer and set up a new meet, then."

He stood as everyone else filed out of the room. Muire and another woman were deep in argument, casting suspicious glances back at him as they crossed through the door. "Let me show you to a room where you can rest while I set up the meet," Mauda said.

He nodded. "That and a chance to clean up would be much appreciated."

Mauda led him around the wheel back the other way and up a ladder, Mari following silently behind them. She opened an interior door to a small, plain room with a bunk, wash basin, and mirror. "Will this do?" she asked.

"This is fine, thank you," he said. He stepped in and sat on the soft mattress.

Mauda closed the door, then moments later Mari opened it again. "Don't wander," she growled, then slammed it shut.

Fergus's pack sat at the foot of the bunk. He let out a low breath and hauled it up next to him. He rarely needed much, but a change of clothes was remarkably high on his short list at the moment. His leg where the cable had hit bore an angry red puckered caterpillar that ran from the back of his knee down across his ankle; he'd have to check his exosuit to see if it had been able to fully self-mend. *If it hasn't,* he wondered, *where will I find another one?* Out here along the Gap, exosuits were expensive, and he hadn't met one yet that hadn't left his larger Earther frame with a colossal wedge-up.

Once he had changed, he lay down on the bunk and stared at the ceiling, resisting sleep long enough to sort through the day's events and impressions. Until the job was done, information was everything. Idly he wondered if the door was locked, then decided he didn't care; he wasn't afraid of Mother Vahn's strange family, not even Mari. Closing his eyes, he put his hands behind his head and let himself drift off.

Chapter 3

◆

H e slept just long enough for the aches of the cable car escape to settle in. Forcing himself to his feet, he found the fold-out lavatory funnel and took care of immediate business. Done, he let some water from the single tap into the adjacent basin and washed his hands and face before stripping off his shirt. He did his best to clean the rest of himself up, taking care to examine each cut and burn.

When he was finished, he wrung the towel out carefully over the water reclamation drain, then pulled his spare shirt on. *All in all,* he thought, *way better than dead.*

There was a knock on the door, and it slid open a crack. "Mr. Ferguson, are you ready?"

"Yes," he said. He opened the door the rest of the way. A middle-aged Vahn woman smiled anxiously at him and waved him down the hall.

She led him back to the conference room. The chairs had been pushed back against the walls and fastened, and a table had been brought into the center of the room. An elderly but serviceable display was projecting an annotated 3-D map of Cernee into the air above the table. *Now that's useful,* he thought, and stepped in to study it.

Mauda was at the far side of the table. "A Cernee-wide bulletin came through from Central this morning," she said. "The broken cable punctured a section of Rattletrap before it could be pulled back and secured."

Fergus winced. "How bad?"

"At least thirty dead. Rockcrapper families, mostly. Right now they're asking for information or witnesses. There's rumor of an impending security lockdown while they investigate."

He rubbed his face. "That might make things harder."

Mauda slapped something down on the table and flicked it toward him. He picked it up and turned it over, then raised his eyebrows in surprise. "Anderson Anders?" he said.

"I assumed alliteration was your thing," Mauda said.

It was a Cernee ID chip. "How did you get this?"

"Helpful neighbor," Mauda said.

Oh, right, he thought. *The arms dealer.*

"If it comes up, you came here from Crossroads Station and are helping us out as a favor to Mr. Harcourt," she said. "If we're lucky, no one will look at either of us. We've got a permanent shipping card for the lines, and we're well known, but there's no way to disguise the fact that you're not a woman." She waved one hand dismissively up his length, stopped at his beard, then shook her head in despair.

"I expect not," he agreed.

She turned to the display, pointing out virtual objects. "The Wheel Collective's line connects to the near side of Blackcans. You and Mother Vahn both got on the cable car at the main platform there. With the Mezzanine Rock line now broken, we need to take a different route to Central."

She pointed to the next line out of Blackcans, and it lit up purple at her touch. "This line goes to Leakytown and then to Mezz Rock. That's the most direct way now."

"May I make a suggestion?" he asked. He touched a different sequence of dots, moving the purple line over. "We should go from Blackcans to"—he leaned in to read the labels—"EmptyRock, from there to Bugrot, Bugrot to here, then here, and then from there to Central."

"That takes us nearly a third of the way around the Halo," she said. "Why would we do that?"

"Caution," Fergus said. "If Gilger is out to get you, he's going to know you're in disarray now and that none of you know your way around Cernee as well as Mother Vahn. He may see it as an opportunity. His best bet to get at you is the next time you take your crates out. With the Mezzanine Rock line down, he can make a pretty good guess which way you'll go instead. I'm suggesting we pick a less obvious route."

"And if he doesn't intend to attack us after all?"

"Then we've wasted a few hours and nothing more."

Mauda pursed her lips, then nodded once, conceding. "You may be right. We'll take your route."

"When do we go?"

Reaching under the table, she pulled out his exosuit and thrust it into his hands. "Right now."

The lichen crates had been staged on an enclosed platform on a central hub, ready to be hooked up via spiders to the Wheel Collective's line. The hub itself wasn't spinning, leaving them all free-floating by the time they'd passed from the last Vahn wheel out onto the platform. Mari was there and suited up to help get them sent off.

"It's hand spiders most of the way," Mauda said. "We'll have to recharge at Bugrot and again at NoMoar. Then we can take a car the last leg into Central. How's your exosuit?"

Fergus had inspected it at length and been unable to find anywhere the thick, flexible smartfabric had been damaged. "It's better than new, I think," he said. "Thank you. Beautiful work."

She waved a hand, dismissing the compliment, but a smile lingered briefly on her face. It bothered him that he could never tell if he was going to say the right thing or not, but he supposed it didn't matter except to his pride. This trip, for him, was one way, and he wouldn't be coming back to the farm to get a second try at figuring these people out. *And they probably won't give me a second thought once I'm gone, either,* he thought.

"I'm setting my suit comm to channel one-seven-one," Mauda said, pulling up her suit hood, her transparent face shield still open and up. "If you see anything, give a shout. Otherwise I'll see you on Blackcans for the next hop."

Fergus tucked the ID chip into the wrist of his glove, where he could easily pass it over scanners without un-suiting. He toggled his comm over, pulled his hood up and faceplate down, locked it, and then checked all the seals. His bottles and powerpacks were fully charged. "I'm set," he said.

The spiders were a quartet of heavy wheels that clipped onto the cable and crawled along it until told not to. A handle with controls along the thumb rest was slung be-neath them. He'd used them before, but each settlement had its own version, and Mauda had to show him how to connect them to the line.

"Depressurizing the bay," Mari announced. "If you're not ready, too bad."

He kept one hand on the wall bar, his magboots keeping his feet firmly on the platform as the air was sucked out of the bay into storage tanks. The wide doors opened onto space.

Mauda clipped herself ahead of the lead crate, waved to her kinswoman, then shot out into the inky dark. The crates fell in behind her one by one. When the last few were at the platform's edge, he moved his spider onto the line behind them and unmagged his boots.

"Whoa!" he exclaimed as the spider yanked him out into space with a sharp jerk. Before he knew it, he was well out and moving, the distant lights of Blackcans ahead. Be-yond that was the faint, flickering halo of Cernee itself.

He glanced back in curiosity, having been unconscious during his arrival; twelve giant wheels spun in parallel around a single central axis, glinting in the sun. He could identify the part that was the Vahn farm by the blue and green tint. A small, unspun hab hung off the other end with clusters of vehicles docked around it. The Wheel Collective was bigger than he'd expected, but the idea that almost none of the Vahns had ever left made it seem achingly small.

I love what I do, he thought as he sped along behind the line of crates, *but I'm glad I grew up with my feet on the ground and my head in free air. Even if I did run away.* Sometimes memories were even more claustrophobic than space.

Mauda must have seen him looking back. "You told Mella you grew up on a farm," she said to him over the comm. "What did you grow there?"

"Bitterness," he answered, then realized how glib that sounded and added, "Sorry. My grandparents lost almost everything in the floods on Earth and my family never recovered."

"That must have been hard," she said.

"Yeah," he said.

The line slipped behind the sunshield and into Cernee's Halo proper. "I can see Blackcans up ahead," Mauda said. "Ten minutes and we'll be in. I was here a number of times with Mother, and to Mezzanine Rock, but otherwise it's new territory." She sounded anxious.

He finally spotted the hab himself; it was, true to advertisement, three can-shaped habs connected end-to-end and painted matte black everywhere there weren't solar collectors. "Do you want me to take the lead?"

There was a long pause, then at last, "If you don't mind."

"No problem. You'll have to show me what I need to do with the crates when we get to EmptyRock."

"It's easy," she said.

It took several minutes after Mauda reached their platform at Blackcans for all the crates to get hauled in, and him with them. By the time he landed, Mauda had already fed more than half onto a conveyer tunnel that would take them around to Blackcans' inner-Halo stations. Once she showed him how to get them lined up and inserted into the cargo chute, he hauled the rest over and pushed them in.

"Rest for a minute," she said when he'd finished. "The cargo tunnel is slow, and once we're inside we'll want to move through quickly."

He hooked an arm around a wallbar and floated there, catching his breath. The platform was tiny and empty of other people—certainly not the one he'd passed through on his way in from the docks. "You have this all to yourself?" he asked.

"Now we do," she said. "There used to be another hab between the Wheels and Leakytown named Turndown, but it's dark now, floating out beyond the Halo."

"What happened?"

"Spore ticks," she said. "They cut their own line and drifted rather than risk spreading them to the rest of us."

"Oh," he said. So very many bad ways to die in space, but that one was more terrible than most.

"They were nice people." Mauda sighed. "You ready to go?"

"Yes."

They cycled themselves through the platform's airlock into Blackcans. Fergus hadn't had to negotiate the interior when he'd first arrived in Cernee, since the major lines all ran directly into and out of the main platform, and he was immediately grateful for that earlier mercy. The narrow corridors of the public passages were slathered with black paint on every possible millimeter of surface. The only things breaking up the dark monotony of the corridors were the lights, set at varying intervals, heights, and intensities in a cacophony of ill-toned, strobing colors.

"Why would anyone choose to live in this place?" Fergus asked. "It's so awful it's giving me a headache."

"It's also one of the least crowded habs in Cernee, especially for one with six lines into it," Mauda said. "Now you know how they keep it that way."

He was ridiculously happy when they reached the far end of the corridor and the exit, even if that was exactly how the residents wanted him to feel. *They win; they can have it all for themselves*, he decided.

There were two security officers at the blast doors that led to the main platform. They wore black suits with thick yellow stripes along the legs and arms like walking hazard signs. *And maybe they are*, Fergus thought. One guard waved a wand halfheartedly in front of them both and then let them through.

"Authority," Mauda said once they were past. "Don't often see them out this far."

Their crates were queued up behind other cargo, and they waited patiently until at last they could grab them from the cargo chute and attach them to the EmptyRock line. Mauda unclipped a small device from her suit and sent it floating over the crates to Fergus. "They'll follow that," she said, "so don't worry about them keeping up or overrunning you, although if you stop suddenly you may get bumped hard."

"Thanks for the warning," he said. He attached the crate beacon to the head of the line, then placed his spider in front of it. "Can you manage the rest of the crates by yourself?"

"I can handle it," she said.

He got a good grip on his spider and thumbed the go button. The spider leapt into motion again, dragging him behind it like some random piece of flotsam caught in its wake. He looked back to see the first of the crates shoot out toward him as if fired from a cannon and resolutely turned to face forward.

It seemed only a short time later that Mauda's voice came over the comm. "I'm on."

Goodbye, Blackcans, he thought. "Everything look good back there?"

"Fine. You?"

"So far, so good," he said.

The cable was quiescent and safe, diminishing steadily into the distance. Unlike the line out to the Wheels, main lines were made of pairs of cables, each monodirectional. The incoming line was just a half dozen meters to their right. They passed a few individuals heading into Blackcans, then a small, gray pod marked with a white circle. People in gray-and-green suits rode spiders both in front and behind it.

"What was that?" he asked Mauda.

"Medical pod from Medusa," she answered. "It's on the far side across the Halo, out near Sunshield Seven. There are medics all over Cernee, but if you get yourself seriously hurt, try to do it as near to Medusa as you can."

EmptyRock was a captured, mined-out asteroid, and aside from a distinct smell of old oil in the air, it was a vast improvement over Blackcans. Unfortunately, it was also so crowded it was hard to move between platforms, even with multiple routes to choose from. "I hate to say it, but I'm starting to see what Blackcans was thinking," he said.

"Another reason we're pretty happy out on our farm. This . . . is overwhelming. I don't know if . . ." Mauda's voice trailed off.

"This would overwhelm almost anybody," Fergus said. "Think of it as just another deterrent like Blackcans. You haven't been here before?"

"No," Mauda answered. "Mother talked about it, though."

"Are the habs and rocks like individual towns, or are we in someone's territory?"

"The smaller habs and rocks are mostly run by consensus," she said. "A few are either their own little tyrannies or run by gangs. Most of them are loyal to one or another of the 'big five' powers but don't interfere with visitors passing through without good cause; a push in one place is going to make someone unhappy enough to pull somewhere else."

She pointed to two men standing together by the edge of the corridor, watching the crowd pass by. "Blue stripes. That's how you know EmptyRock is one of Vinsic's interests."

Vinsic was another one of Cernee's "powers" and one of the oldest. His territory abutted Gilger's, limiting the latter's expansion in that part of the Halo.

"How long has Gilger been one of the five?"

"Four or five standards, maybe? When he arrived he was just this slimy enforcer from somewhere else that no one paid much attention to, and then next thing we knew he's not only running his own show but he's got an entire operation transplanted from somewhere else to back him up. It would take all the others working together to bring him down, and none of them trust each other enough for that, so he just festers and grows."

"That's too bad," Fergus said. Mauda fell silent, either lost in thought or at the end of what she knew.

A single yellow-striped Authority guard was at the far platform, checking IDs but nothing more. After a lengthy and cramped wait, Fergus and Mauda finally got their crates queued for the line out. Fergus took the lead again.

The next hop was to a large cylinder hab named Bugrot, which Mauda described to him as "an aggressively self-managed independent co-op." The Halo here was thicker—there were lights all around them from habs and tethered rocks—and twice Fergus was nearly hit by someone zooming past the line on a flystick. He wondered how even the small personal flyers made it through without accumulating hapless riders pasted all over their nose-cones like bugs on a windscreen.

"Bugrot's just ahead," he said. "You okay back there?"

"I need to recharge my air soon."

"Me too."

"See you inside, then."

He slowly throttled down his spider on his approach and had the stack of crates down to a safe crawl as he swung through the platform entrance. Unlike Blackcans and EmptyRock, Bugrot was large enough to have an automated cargo system, and once he was off the line the lichen crates began creeping forward again.

Fergus cycled himself through the airlock into Bugrot itself. There were a few people here, enough to make the place seem busy but not so many as to feel crowded. As he turned around to see if there was a recharging station nearby, someone slammed into him from the edge of the platform and knocked him over to the far wall.

A fist crashed into the side of his head, painfully mashing his ear through his exosuit hood, and was coming in for a second blow when he caught it, twisting and sending both himself and his attacker spinning in the zero-grav. People pushed out of their way. Whoever his attacker was, they were much smaller and shorter, and Fergus easily outmatched them in strength if not ferocity. Keeping the captured arm in a lock grip, he grabbed at his assailant's opaqued face shield with his free hand and pulled it away.

Pitchfork Mari.

"What did you do to my aunt?!" she shouted at him.

"Nothing!" he shouted back. "She's bringing up the end of the crates."

"She was in the lead when you left, and you were supposed to go to Leakytown!"

"The plan changed," he said. "I didn't know we were expected to consult you." Taking a chance, he let go of her and floated back, lifting his own mask.

Reaching down, she turned on her magboots and stuck herself to the floor with a clang. "You're a liar," she said.

He crossed his arms over his chest. "Am not," he said. "When Mauda gets here in a few minutes, you can see for yourself that nothing's happened to her. I expect she'll be happy to see you too, considering how far from home you are for someone who's supposedly never left the safety of the Wheels."

"That's none of your business!"

"True, so why make it mine?"

"Not all of us want to spend every minute of our lives on the farm, despite what Mauda says," she snapped.

He shrugged. "Your aunt is only two or three crates out now. You can discuss it with her directly."

Actually it was closer to ten; *I am a liar, after all,* he thought.

Mari glanced out the portal glass. "You can't tell her I was here," she said. "And if she's not at the back of the crates? You won't live long enough to know what hit you."

"Great," he said. "I'll look forward to it. Since you got here, I assume you can figure out how to get home again?"

"I know my way around," she said. "I found *you*." Slamming down her face shield, she merged into the tail end of a party passing through on the people-mover and vanished.

She did find me, Fergus thought. *If she just followed us, I'd like to know how she managed to get ahead. And if she didn't follow us . . .*

There was more to Mari than just a menacing pitchfork, it seemed, though he didn't expect his association with the Vahns would last long enough for him to untangle it.

As soon as Mauda came through the platform airlock, she opened up her face shield and caught his expression. "What is it?" she asked.

"Nothing," he said. "We should talk about ways to get you safely home after the meeting."

"Can't I just go back the same way?"

"Not if Gilger has people watching in Central," he said. "If he knows you got past him, he's going to sit tight on Blackcans waiting for you on the return trip."

"Blackcans has the only line to the Wheels."

"That's why it's a good place for a trap," he said. "But we should get your lichen sold before we worry about it."

"There's a small cafeteria near one of the other platforms where we can get something hot to drink while we recharge," she said. "Bugrot's likely the only decent food we'll find before Central itself."

"Sounds good to me," he said. She grabbed a people-mover handle, and as he reached for his, he saw a familiar suited figure farther down the tunnel, stationary, watching them. Then they turned a corner and Mari was gone.

———

After Bugrot, they didn't linger anywhere longer than necessary. None had the scare tactic ambiance of Blackcans, but despite that, none were any more pleasant. It was a relief when they finally caught a cable car from SpudRock toward Central itself.

Mauda fretted, frequently pulling at the safety straps as if they were choking her. "I've never ridden in one of these before. I can't help imagining . . . I mean, how awful to be trapped in one of these seats, unable to do anything to save yourself? It's just horrid."

Fergus caught her gaze. "Mauda, I may not understand the slightest thing about your family, and I may know almost nothing about Cernee, but I don't imagine Mother Vahn was ever trapped by *anything*. Certainly nothing so petty as a cable car. She was resourceful, sharp, and fast, and she wasn't afraid, even right up until the very last moments of her life."

"I just wish I were more like her," Mauda said.

Fergus stared at her, a virtually identical copy of Mother Vahn. "That's a joke, right?"

She glared back at him. "We are each the product of our environment, and mine has been sheltered," she said.

Fergus shrugged. "No one's life is easy."

"Yours doesn't seem so hard."

He laughed. "Oh, I am a rubbish example! My life is running from one place to another, then running away again, usually just ahead of angry people with guns. My home consists of bags half forgotten in long-term rent-a-lockers in spaceports here and there, scattered across a dozen worlds. Would you give up everything you have—everyone you love—to live my life? I don't think so."

"You chose it," she said.

"I chose to *survive* and not to drag anyone else down with me," he corrected. "It's all I've got."

Mauda said nothing else for the rest of the line, and Fergus was fine with that.

Central was a proper space station with several spinning rings around a massive spindle-hub, wide corridors, and fresh-tasting air. Nothing noticeably rattled or creaked or smelled, and the walls were a crisp white that, after hours in space or pushing through dark, dank habs, hurt Fergus's eyes.

They rented a storage cube near the line docks on the spindle and shoved the crates into it with what little energy they had remaining. Mauda's buyer was waiting in the merchant concourse on one of the rings. They floated, then pulled, then trudged their way up a spoke tunnel from the spindle as the spin gravity picked up. Fergus's muscles felt like stiff jelly. Between their meandering route, crate transfer holdups, queues, and stopping to rest and recharge, it had been nearly seven hours since they'd left the Wheels.

At the entrance to the ring, a large security post blocked their path, checking people in one by one. *And out,* Fergus noted. That meant they kept data on who passed through.

He'd given Mauda back the shipping pass at the docks, and no fewer than three yellow-striped Authority guards looked at it, then her ID, before letting her through. They stopped him, wanded him, passed his ID around, and just as he was about to ask if there was a problem, let him through as well.

No one asked for bribes.

The market took up a full third of the ring, lined with one booth after another selling just about anything a person might want and some things Fergus was sure no one could possibly need.

There were directory kiosks located at intervals along the wall, and with them they found their buyer's booth easily enough in one of several long rows of merchants crammed together on a wide concourse. Fergus lingered at the edge of the booth as Mauda and the buyer haggled. Once an agreement was reached, Mauda presented the man with a verified key for the storage cube and a content certificate from the dock registrar. The merchant, who had the stocky build and clothes of a Sfazili groundsider, in turn handed Mauda a credit transfer pad, and they both thumbed it simultaneously to finalize the exchange.

"That's it?" Fergus asked as Mauda headed back over to him.

"That's it," she said. "Now I just need to get home and figure out how to run a farm and a family. Your part is done."

He held up a hand before she could leave and handed her a small fob. "While you were dealing with the dock registrar, I rented you a flystick," he said. "Have you ever ridden one?"

"When I was a child."

"Take it back to the Wheel Collective directly and avoid the lines. Once you're home, just set it to auto, and it'll return itself to the rental agency."

"I can't afford this!"

"They're not that expensive, and anyway, I can. Don't worry about it," he said.

She reached out and shook his hand. "Thank you. You didn't have to help us, but you did."

"It's a character flaw," he answered. "I have an overwhelming need to try to make myself useful."

Mauda nodded. "It's been interesting knowing you, and I wish you luck with your . . . *project*. I expect we won't meet again."

And with that, she turned and walked away.

After a few moments' contemplation, he headed back into the merchant concourse. It was time to pick up a few things, find a good place to set himself up, and start working on the Arum Gilger problem.

Chapter 4

◆━━━━◆◆━━━━◆

Fergus wandered around Central's extensive merchant concourse for several hours, trying to get a sense of the movement and rhythm of the place and its people. Though not particularly interested in shopping, he did buy a few packs of nonperishable food and a comm code for Radio Cernee, which seemed like more of a gossip and entertainment channel than any sort of real news. He didn't mind; all information was good information. The familiar routine of the job was comforting: slip in, look around, get what he came for, get out, and leave no trace. This was how it should have gone from the beginning.

He checked out through station security as Anderson Anders, reserved himself a seat on the cable car back to SpudRock, then slipped that ID chip deep into a faraday pocket in his pack. From that same pocket he extracted another chip—not a Cernee native one, but a Crossroads ID with the name Liam Langston. Mauda had guessed correctly on the alliteration thing, which spoiled the fun of it just a tiny bit.

Instead of boarding the cable car, he went back to the flystick rental kiosk. Flysticks reminded him of an antique Earth toy called a pogo stick but with a large, maneuverable propulsion engine welded to the bottom and a jack so you could connect it directly to your exosuit systems to control it. The first time he ever saw one, he thought it was a joke. Second time he took it for a ride and was terrified. Third time he didn't give it back for a week.

It had been a while.

So far, only one place in Cernee had seemed like somewhere he could blend in and not hate every moment, someplace not too crowded, not too quiet, not too directly unwelcoming. He took the 'stick and headed back to Bugrot.

Once there, it took him less than an hour to find a room to rent that met his needs: small, out of the main corridors, but with more than one way to and from it. He wondered, as he often did, if he was being too paranoid. But this time he had a better excuse than usual: not too many jobs started with him nearly being blown up and then detained on an improbable clone farm before he'd even gotten his feet on the ground, so to speak.

Bugrot was a stationary hab with no spin gravity. The room's minimal amenities included a small, padded systems console on a flexible stand, a metered air recharger, and a pullout bathroom with suction features. The room was clean, and the air smelled fresh enough that he only glanced at the O_2 panel from force of habit. Various bins, tethers, and stickypads lined one wall for storing belongings. There was also a hammock bag stretched between opposing corners, and after checking the door lock, he pulled himself into it.

He woke up several hours later. Hauling his pack over to the hammock, he unpacked his tool kit into the air around him, checking each item. Nothing was missing, not even the rusty, worn motorcycle key he'd carried with him since he'd lifted off from Earth for the first and only time. Among his things was a small blackbox device he'd had built to spec for him on Tanduou, one of Guratahan Sfazil's moons and his favorite place to buy things no one should be allowed to have. The maker had given him a long technical name for it, but Fergus called it the *confuddler*. Unwinding its leads, he carefully removed the back plate from the room console, wired the confuddler in, and flipped it on. Sitting back, he watched as its only light flickered amber for several long minutes before turning a confident green.

He had inserted himself into Bugrot's console network, burying outgoing data packets in the identities of consoles all over the hab and beyond, sifting out the responses it wanted from the misdirected replies. A few simple queries, and it happily strip-mined the system of all public information it had on Gilger, buried in enough random bit noise that anyone on the lookout for a rise in hits on that name would be unlikely to see it as a direct query from a single source.

The confuddler quietly nulled the masking noise on its end, leaving Fergus a long night's worth of information to go through for anything he could use.

Gilger had originally come here from Baselle—a human Faither colony—about seven standard years ago, but it was almost as if he'd come out of nowhere. There wasn't any mention of him in any of the colony records Fergus could get access to, nor a single mention of his family. In a culture as lineage-obsessed as Baselle, that was striking. Either there was an unprecedented omission in the data stream, or someone in Gilger's family had done something so unacceptable that the family's entire surname had been stricken from the records. Finding out which would cost more time and cred than Fergus could afford and risk the potentially fatal attention of the Basellan security apparatus. It did bolster his hunch that Gilger had been high society, as someone lower class would have been exiled or executed with a perfunctory but explicit footnote, preserving the shame.

Gilger's "pestilential den of half-wits" consisted of his second-in-command, Borr Graf, a small but mean crew of Cernee locals—Fergus had known about those before he'd gotten here—and a lot of muscle from a Basellan exile colony named Luceatos that Fergus hadn't known about. As near as he could tell, the Luceatans had arrived in one massive influx, adding weight to Mauda's impression that Gilger had seemed to rise in power almost overnight. He certainly hadn't gotten there selling old aircans and generator parts.

There was no easy way to infiltrate Gilger's gang. Gilger wasn't going to believe a red-bearded giant he'd never seen before was one of his own people, and even if Fergus did slip into the Luceatan group without Gilger noticing him, the Luceatans themselves would notice. Their home outpost was a Faither penitent colony that believed redemption could only come through death for a righteous or glorious cause. They wore their sins— which ran the spectrum from murder of other Faithful down to being too poor to make the weekly tithe—as tattooed glyphs covering their bodies. How they ended up in Gilger's employ was unclear, although perhaps the leader mattered less than where he led.

At least Gilger's territory hadn't changed much from Fergus's original research. The hub was a rock on the outer edge of the Halo named Gilgerstone. It was set behind three habs, one of which was connected by a long line to Humbug, which in turn connected to Leakytown. Gilger had influence over another half dozen habs, slowly spreading his control in toward the center. On the map, it was an arrow aimed directly at Central itself.

It's good to be clear about your ambitions, Fergus thought.

His hand found the flystick fob in his pocket, turning it over and over as he let his mind drift, hoping for inspiration. An hour or so later he gave up, wondering if Mauda had made it home safely.

Focus, Fergus, he told himself. *Mauda and the rest of her family are no longer any of your concern, and the best thing you can do for them is go about your own business.*

Wriggling free of the hammock, he unplugged his bottle from the room's air recharging unit and left. In Bugrot's small central concourse, he paid a half cred for a map of Cernee and the latest news download. The top story was the Governor's upcoming hearing on the Mezzanine Rock cable disaster, which was described as an accident inquiry.

Accident? Really? He closed it with the remainder of the news unread.

He unchecked his flystick from where he'd stowed it at Bugrot's underside dock, then cycled it and himself out into space. He'd already loaded the map into his suit's memory, and as soon as the visual overlay came up, he aimed the 'stick for Burnbottle, the outermost of Gilger's habs.

By the time he passed Mezzanine Rock, he was moving at a good speed. *If only I had wind in my hair,* he thought, *this would be fun.*

Leakytown came and went. It was an enormous old service freighter with an agglomeration of shipping cans and other space trash attached to it, bigger than even Bugrot. There was an asteroid out past it, too small to be inhabited, already mined of anything worthwhile, and just far enough from the periphery of the Halo not to have been hooked in yet. He slowed his 'stick, inched closer until he could reach one of the old surface tethers left behind by miners, and pulled himself onto the rock. Snapping the flystick's anchor cable onto a ring set into the surface, he pulled his way along the tether until he could make out the rough shape of Burnbottle in the distance.

Through his goggle zoom, he studied the surrounding territory. Burnbottle was a medium-sized can with spin, a small crowd of 'sticks and red-gold vehicles hanging off it in every direction. Traffic moved steadily: the 'sticks, bobsled-sized one-mans, and the slightly larger two-mans coming and going on the exact same approach vector. If the travel corridor was consistent, that meant the untraveled spaces were as well.

If Fergus got lucky, he'd never have to go near Burnbottle, but he filed that info anyway.

Behind that can was the rock Gilgerstone, and below that was a small, shining silver blob that when magnified proved to be a medium-sized private starcraft, its jump engine slung below it on a single outsized fin. The blue stripe and silver hull shone in the starlight like a pearl against black velvet.

Venetia's Sword. Stolen, and now found. "Gotcha," he said out loud, and grinned.

The ship winked at him.

What the—?! Fergus flinched, nearly losing his grip on the bar. When he recovered, he set his goggles to their highest mag and watched, his whole body tensed, until it happened again. Some dark, fuzzily out-of-focus object had crossed between him and the ship, momentarily obscuring it. It took him a few minutes to find it again because it was smaller than he expected and a lot nearer.

Hell.

Now that he knew what he was looking for, he spotted them all over, circling Gilger's territory: sentry bobs. Spheres about twenty centimeters in diameter, they were fully automated, always communicating with each other and a central security system. They had sensors for just about everything on the electromagnetic spectrum plus rudimentary logic and processing capabilities that took cunning to circumvent or fool.

The one that had first drifted across Fergus's field of view was outside the area of Burnbottle, nearly two-thirds of the way to his little abandoned asteroid. He was lucky it hadn't detected him coming in. He'd gotten past worse, but several of those jobs had nearly gotten him killed, and he'd already had more than his share of near-death experiences on this one already.

He unclipped his 'stick and shoved himself off the rock with one foot, letting himself drift unpowered some distance away from the rock before he fired it up. He kept the rock carefully between himself and Burnbottle, taking a winding route back to Bugrot just in case he'd been seen after all.

It was a long float back to his room, trying and failing

to think up a workable approach. Only suicidal ones or suicidally expensive ones, like bringing in his own team of mercs from outside and blasting Gilger's entire encampment to shit, came to him, and his mood grew fouler by the minute.

He came around a curve in the corridor and found a black-suited, black-haired, olive-skinned young woman hovering by the entrance to the rent-a-rooms, waiting. He put one hand to his forehead, closed his eyes, and willed away all the immediate responses that leapt to mind. When he could speak politely, he opened his eyes again.

"Mari," he said. "Did Mauda get home okay?"

"Yeah."

When nothing more was forthcoming—no explanation of how she'd found him again or why she was here—he grabbed a wallbar and brought himself to a halt. "It's been a long day," he said. "Is there something else you need?"

"I want to help."

"No," he said without hesitating.

Her green-brown eyes narrowed. "Why not? I know a lot more about Cernee than you could ever hope to. I know my way around, I know people to talk to, I found *you* again—"

"Yeah," he said. He'd swung past her to his door but hesitated before keying the lockpad. "Rather convenient, how you keep doing that. The answer is still no. I can find what I need on my own and without putting other people in danger. I don't want to be responsible for anyone else. Go home, Mari. Help Mauda; she needs you."

"I'm not just—" she started to retort.

Sirens cut through the air, drowning out the rest of whatever she had been saying. Angry yellow lights strobed the corridor.

Fergus stuck his fingers in his ears to block the brain-piercing noise. "*Now* what?!" he yelled.

"Flyby alarm!" Mari shouted back. Her eyes were wide. "The Asiig. I ... Can I come in? I'm sorry. Please?"

Flyby? The Asiig? Were things not complicated enough already without adding in a visit from the deeply scary aliens next door? Whatever else he might have said, her genuinely frightened expression was enough to make him to relent. "Just until it's over," he shouted over the din and opened the door.

She floated in ahead of him, touched off the far wall, turned, and hung there. He slid the door shut with a bang. The clamor of the sirens was dampened but still bled through, and he wished desperately that the walls were thicker. Pulling himself out of his exosuit, he clipped it and his pack to the ring beside the door. Then he kicked off, grabbed the hammock, and pulled himself in. Mari remained motionless, her eyes taking in the confuddler wired into the console and the scattered tools before finding their wary way back to him.

"So, what the hell is happening, again?" he asked, once the hammock had stopped spinning.

"It means the Asiig are in the area. They come across the Gap every once in a while. Sometimes they just pass by in the distance, and sometimes they park right outside the Halo for a while and scare the crap out of everybody. I've never been through one anywhere other than home in the Wheels. It startled me is all. You know about Radio Cernee yet?"

"I bought a code for it," he said.

"They'll give updates if you're listening. The alerts usually last a few hours, almost never longer than that. When you go out again, you can also set your comm to monitor channel nine-ninety-nine for the alert. It's a public Boolean broadcast, on or off for 'they're here' or 'they're not,' but it carries throughout the Halo and a fair bit beyond. You don't want to get caught out while they're in the neighborhood."

That much he knew. "Any reason for the visits? Anyone know *why*? Like, why now?"

"They watch us all the time," she said. "Either they saw someone they want, or I suppose maybe it's because of Mother."

"What?"

"They took her when she was my age. Got caught off the lines."

"No one ever comes back from them," he said. "Not alive, anyway. That's what all the stories say."

Mari had crossed her arms across her chest, her eyes unfocused. "Not *many* come back. But the few they let go . . . they're never the same again. Mother wasn't. Sometimes she'd tell us she thought they watched her, but I didn't believe her. Don't repeat that to anyone. It'd just give Gilger another reason to hate us. I don't know. It's none of your business."

"So everyone keeps telling me," he said. He pointed. "There's a wall coffee maker and clean tubes, if you want some."

"Thanks," she said. Her hands shook as she coaxed the hot brew out of the machine. Wrapping both hands around the tube, she let out a long, unsteady breath, then looked him in the eye. That hard-edged defiance was creeping back in. "You really think you can steal Gilger's ship?"

"I do," he said. Not that he had any idea how yet.

"Why?"

"Because it's what I do," he answered. "And I'm really good at it. I go, I see, I think, I take."

"Why?"

"Why what?"

"Why are you taking it from him?"

"First, because it isn't his," Fergus said. "He arrived at the Shipyard at Pluto with impeccable credentials, enough to get the use of *Venetia's Sword* on credit for a three-day trial. He took off, and no one ever saw him or the ship again. It took the Shipmakers and me this long to track down who he was. And then they sent me to find him and bring it back."

"It can't be cheap, paying you to do this," she said. "How much is the ship worth?"

"It's not really a matter of value," he said, though the truth was that he was being underpaid at his own insistence; the Shipmakers were some of the few people he could call friends, and they wouldn't let him do the job just at expenses. "For the Shipmakers, these ships are like their children, and they take great care when they sell one to see that it ends up in good hands. And that's the other reason I'm here: *Venetia's Sword* has a class-four simulated intelligence. These things are smart, as close to genuinely sentient as anyone can make them, and it's not just that Gilger stole it. He would have had to inflict gross damage to its mindsystems to take control of it."

"It's just a *ship*."

"And we're just sacks of protein and piss," Fergus said. "You think you're the right one to judge what counts as a person and what doesn't? Because Gilger thinks he can judge, and not only didn't he find this ship worthy of its own identity and existence, he clearly doesn't think Mother Vahn or your whole family are worth theirs either."

Mari stared at him, fury in her eyes.

"I'm sorry," he said after he was sure his point had sunk in. "That's what these ships are and what they mean to their builders, and that's why I'm here."

"If they cared so much, how come they didn't check his credentials better?" she snapped. "See that they were fake?"

"Gilger used real credentials. The legitimate owner of them was found floating outside Crossroads Station about a week after Gilger lifted the ship. Or his body was. It was tagged as an accidental decompression until his IDs turned up back in Earth system as part of a criminal act."

"If it's a criminal act, why don't—"

"Police? Earth Alliance? Do you honestly think any-

one gives a shit what anyone out here in these waste-
lands is doing or has done? No one cares about people
out here, not when there are already more and bigger
crimes than they can deal with going on right within
their cozy reach."

Mari made herself another bulb of coffee, and eventually met his eyes again. "So it's just you," she said.
"What's your plan?"

"I'm working on it."

"Oh, great!" She threw up her free hand, sent herself
into a slow sideways tumble. "So what you're saying is
we've got nothing, no hope of justice, no hope of even
hurting—"

"I said I'm *working* on it." He pointed around the
room at the tools, at the confuddler, at her. "Gilger's got
a lot of security, which makes it hard to get to the ship,
but there's got to be a hole. There's always a hole. I'll
find it."

"Siren has stopped," she said.

He blinked. *I didn't even notice*, he thought. "Oh."

"I should get home. They think I'm over at Harcourt's."

"Then go home."

"Are you going to let me help? At least with information?"

He should've just said no outright again, but that angry stubbornness reminded him of himself when he was
that age. *She's even more like Dru*, he thought, *and you
know how that ended*.

But if it was just information and it satisfied her need
to help, maybe then she'd go back to the farm and stay
safely out of his way? He didn't need another complication on his hands.

"I don't know. Ask me again tomorrow," he said at
last.

She let go of the empty coffee bulb, let it hang there
in the air, and kicked back across the room to the door.
"Count on it," she said, slid open the door, and pushed
out.

He locked the door behind her, rustled a package of dried food out of his pack, then pulled himself back into the hammock. Hanging there, he unwrapped the food bar, smelled it, then let it float away into the room uneaten. Closing his eyes, he willed his mind toward quiet and waited for inspiration.

Chapter 5

◆━━━◆━━━◆

One thing about a hammock in zero gravity, Fergus thought, *is that you can be restless in 360 degrees.* Seeing the same dull beige walls go by over and over began to mirror the repetitive paths of his thoughts, always coming to the same dead ends. Frustrated, he pulled himself free of the hammock and tumbled slowly, pushing off again whenever he got near a wall, trying not to cannonball too hard through the floating field of tools now scattered and drifting throughout the room.

On his fourth pass, a small silver cylinder collided with his foot, and he plucked it from the air, scowling. The ship's doorkey. He turned it on, shining its coherent light beam at the opposite wall. Twenty-meter range. Right now he didn't see any way he was going to get close enough to use it. *It's never that easy,* he thought. *Except that first time.*

The motorcycle key floated past.

It still felt like yesterday that he'd rolled his cousin's Triumph, remnants of faded sapphire-blue paint flaking beneath his unsteady hands, out past the fringes of town, his heart pounding in terror of being caught. *Of going home again.* Behind a stand of alder, he'd filled its tank with petrol stolen from his uncle's shed and started it up. If anyone had heard him roaring across the causeway over the Scottish Inland Sea, no one had come after him. At the time, he had felt like a rare bird flying free at last, a wild thing no longer able to be caged. Later, he'd wondered if it wasn't just that they'd decided an antique motorcycle and some contraband fuel was a fair price to be rid of him.

He'd never stolen anything before then; nothing he'd stolen since had been anywhere near so easy or weighed so heavily on his conscience. And year after year, he kept paying the increasingly exorbitant storage fees for the Triumph, carefully tucked in a tiny, sealed storage unit a few kilometers from the Glasgow Shuttleport.

As with himself, he liked to think of it as *abandoned, with options*.

He checked the incoming data stream, which had slowed to a trickle as it caught new references to Gilger. Most were about the upcoming public hearing on the cable break and the people expected to be in attendance. Even if Gilger went to the hearing, he wasn't going to get there on a ship the size of *Venetia's Sword*. And other than the hearing, Fergus had no way of knowing where else Gilger might go.

I could use a Vahn as bait to lure him out, he thought. *I know which one I'd pick*. There was a small but mean-spirited appeal to the idea, even if it was well outside the realm of anything he'd actually do.

He floated over to the coffee dispenser and got it to squirt him out a fresh tube. Then he parked himself cross-legged mid-room with the confuddler in one hand and the console at the other, trying to fill in the details of Gilger's history—everything he had ever done, everyone he had ever crossed, since the day he'd shown up at Cernee as the new second-in-command of a half-merchant, half-pirate scumlord named Tamassi.

At his height of power, Tamassi had more than half of Cernee's outer Halo under his thumb, kept in check only by Vinsic and the Governor. It hardly seemed co-incidental that just at the time Gilger had decided to go independent, Tamassi's organization collapsed from within. Enforcers had turned up dead or turned on one another, or, towards the end, fled Tamassi's household to work for Gilger directly. Tamassi himself, according to reports, had cycled himself out an airlock sans exosuit in what had been formally pronounced a suicide. A no-table number of people whose circles intersected Gilger's ended up dead that way with no charges ever filed.

Though what info Fergus had gathered suggested that
Gilger had no friend in Central either, at least not at the
top. Security movements over the last year suggested the
Governor was not unaware of Gilger's encroaching arrow.

Gilger's second-in-command, Graf, appeared just as
Gilger's star started burning bright, but he'd remained always in his boss's shadow. Backtracking as far as he could,
Fergus found the man—his thick neck and arms festooned
with Luceatan sin marks—lurking in the background of a
newsbit about a work strike on Burnbottle three days before Tamassi's death. Graf was clearly Gilger's connection
to Luceatos Colony. Gilger was Basellan, and Luceatos
was Baselle's human dump for unwanted criminals and
political dissidents; it was supposed to be a one-way trip,
a hell to neither be escaped from nor remembered in, not
a place to which any Basellan citizen of any class wanted
any connection. Though if Gilger himself had fallen into
scandal, he should have those same marks that Graf did.
There were connections there that Fergus didn't understand yet.

He'd come here thinking that the big players were the
Governor and Authority under his control, Vinsic—a
primary mover of ore and black-market goods between
Cernee and most of the area rockcrappers—and then
Gilger, a distant third.

There were two other people on Cernee's power stage
who hadn't made it into Fergus's research, probably because they weren't actively engaged in the push-pull for
territory and influence that the others were. There was
Harcourt, the arms dealer who lived in the other part
of the Wheels, who conducted most of his business in
Crossroads and farther out and seemed content to leave
everyone else alone as long as they afforded him the
same courtesy. The last was a woman named Ili who
held the reins on medical services and controlled a large
part of Cernee's oxygen generation capacity. Everything
in Cernee was balanced on the precarious stalemate between those five powers, like a room of smiling dancers

with knives up their sleeves waiting for the music to break their way. The rest of the population was strung out around them, trying to eke out its own survival from the many thick bands of rocks and ice that lay between Cernee and the edge of their backwater solar system.

The hearing would almost certainly clarify the power relationships between the five. *I should go,* Fergus thought. He wanted to see these people interacting in their own domain, get a firsthand sense of who they were, what made them tick, what might make them useful. *Then I can just walk up to Gilger, introduce myself, and ask if he minds if I have a peek at his fancy new ship.*

And that, he thought wryly, *is the best plan I've come up with so far.* He pulled on his exosuit and decided to go for the zero-gravity equivalent of a long walk.

The public section of Bugrot was filled with hole-in-the-wall eateries and a market that had none of the magnitude or cleanliness of the one on Central. It maximized the use of the cylindrical structure, with stores and stalls in 360 degrees around the central tube as if it were more hive than hab. Down the centerline of the tube ran a bar with spokes out to the walls to help people navigate their way through. The air was faintly rank with the smell of people but not overwhelming or stale.

Everyone wore their exosuits, hoods up but face shields open. Whether it was standard practice or increased fear because of what had happened to Rattletrap when the cable hit, Fergus didn't know. Suits ran the usual short spectrum of monotony from dark gray to black, but he noticed after a while that the people who seemed most at home all had a similar symbol patch at the center of their upper backs: a black circle with a white asterisk-like star in it.

Others had different patches, although people who were together usually had a symbol in common. One person he saw had three. He wondered if it was a way of deanonymizing neighbors when exosuits were so generic and near-identical, of identifying people to their own.

Dallying through the market, he found a small public lounge and settled into a bright red grippy chair with a fresh download of the local news, keeping half an ear on the conversations around him as he skimmed it. A vid setup at the far end of the lounge was projecting a 3-D drama-opera called *One Star, Bright and Distant* that was entirely produced in Cernee, set in a fictional hab named Proudcan, about a community of poor but honorable rockcrappers threatened by a predatory warlord named Oskin. Confirming Fergus's earlier guess, the Proudcanners all had the same orange-and-yellow pickhammer city-mark on their suits.

The show was compelling in ways he was at a loss to pinpoint or explain. After a while he discovered his handpad had gone idle and shut down on him and nearly two hours had gone by. Embarrassed that he'd wasted so much of the day watching a fic, he slipped his handpad back into his bag, pushed out of the chair, and headed farther along the central bar.

At a tiny niche-café he bought a bag of hot noodles, wound one arm through the greasy netting lining the walls, and hung there with a handful of other patrons. He was prepared for bland disappointment but instead found an intense, rich flavor he could not begin to pin down. *So far,* he thought, *Bugrot is weird, but a win.*

Slurping his noodles, he watched passersby. A young father brought his child through, the girl nearly lost inside a suit at least two sizes too big, and was helping her navigate the central bar through the concourse. He was quizzing her on how to find the emergency exits.

Not long after, a pair of adults came through with a dozen children the same age all holding hands in a long line, singing. A school? The concourse had become quieter; some people watched them pass, smiles on their faces, and more than one was quietly singing along. An unfathomable number of light-years from Earth, and yet wherever there were humans, there was and would always be the equivalent of the town square.

Twice, men in the yellow-striped black suits of Authority passed down the bar. If they were looking for something in particular, nothing they saw seemed to be it, because they moved through without stopping. Whether it was just in his own mind or a combination of news and crowd dynamics muddling together in his subconscious, things felt restless, uncertain. *Not, though,* he decided with relief, *dangerous. Not yet, anyway.*

The noodles were spicy enough to make his eyes water. He ordered a second bag to go and bought one of the café's T-shirts to replace the one he'd ripped in the cable car explosion. The human race had come hundreds of years and tens of thousands of light-years from the humble origins of the T-shirt, but it clung on like some sort of stubborn, cultural appendix across it all, an indelible personal currency of experience.

Who knew? Maybe *Bil's Bugrot Firebowl* would be his new lucky shirt. He tucked it and the takeaway into his shoulder bag and disentangled himself from the café's nets before pushing off back out into the hall. Glancing back, he noticed someone had pried the L off the end of "Firebowl" and wedged it back in between the B and O. He laughed, shook his head, and hoped it wasn't meant as a warning.

Back at his rent-a-room, he tossed his noodles into the smartfridge, pulled himself into the hammock, looped it closed, and tried to settle his mind into a more constructive, relaxed place. Instead his thoughts drifted off once again to Mother Vahn and her family. Mari's parting words, his conversations with Mauda, and visions of Gilger's security perimeter danced through his attempts to think like a drunken marching band crashing a funeral wake. Pressing the heels of his hands against his eyelids, he groaned. How was he ever going to line up all the pieces and players in just the right way so that he could do his job and get out of here if he kept getting distracted?

Eventually he fell into a fitful doze.

He woke with a start, trying to sit up and getting a faceful of hammock netting for his efforts. The seed of an idea had blinked into life. *Crap*, he thought. *Would that work?*

The rent-a-room's doorchime sounded for what he guessed was not the first time. He propelled himself out of the hammock and slid the door open with an almost manic fury.

Mari was out there. She opened her mouth to speak, but he just reached out, grabbed her, and pulled her into the room. "I have an idea!" he said, too loud, still feeling the dream sloughing off him like a summer rain.

"Are you even awake?" she asked. "You look like shit."

"Yes, mostly," he said. "And thanks a lot."

"Okay. Calm down," she said. She slid the door closed and made herself a bulb of coffee, then another one for him. "Think it through. Dream ideas don't usually make a lot of sense in the real world."

He put his face in his hands, squeezing his eyes shut hard, trying to focus. Then he reached out and took the bulb from her and drank it down. "You're right," he said. "Damn. Although . . ."

Mari waited, her expression not a study in patience.

"I think it could still work," he said at last, "but I'm going to need some help."

"Told you. Now go through the whole idea with me, and if it doesn't sound completely crazy, I'll help you," she said. *"Maybe."*

Fergus pushed across the room and snagged the door-key from the small cloud of stuff he'd left there before falling asleep. "I need to get close enough to *Venetia's Sword* to use this," he said. "It's a doorkey, keyed to just me and just that one ship."

She gaped at him. "Seriously? You've got a key to the fucking thing, and you're still moping about how to pull off stealing it?" She reached out and took it out of his hand. "Are you the worst thief ever?"

Fergus snagged it back. "I'm a finder. The thieving

part is incidental. And it's not that simple," he said. "If one physical key was all it took, every pirate this side of the galaxy would have keys, and no one else would have ships anymore."

"So explain."

"If I can get close enough to shine the doorkey on the security interface outside one of the airlocks, it'll send a special coded signal to the ship's computer—"

"You said Gilger killed the computer," she interrupted.

"The computer system has layers," he said. "He has to have damaged it enough to be able to override and/or shut down the ship's higher intelligence functions—its mindsystem—or it would never have let itself be taken outside Earth's solar system. However, if he'd damaged it too much, he'd have left himself with a paperweight in space. Since he got it here and it's still flying, the underlying operational systems must still be functional. So the doorkey will talk to it. It sends a signal straight into the hardwired security subsystem, coded by the Shipmakers specifically for this ship and this ship alone. Once received, it'll send back a coded reply. That's called a *handshake*."

"And what does *that* do?"

"It initiates a security override sequence, but it won't be implemented until I return the correct response to the ship's code."

"And you've got that from the builders, too?"

"No. I have to crack the code myself and send it back to the ship within forty-eight hours or the ship will give an alert that a failed handshake attempt was made and then change the code. And at that point Gilger will know someone is here to take his ship."

Mari nodded. "No problem. Central has a good SI—"

"Can't do it with another computer," Fergus said. "The handshake return is a number of coded items for which the correct answers are nonlogical referential associations."

"Nonlogical referential associations? What the hell does that mean?"

"If I said to you, 'One Star,' what's the first thing that pops into your head?"

"'Bright and Distant,'" she said. "But—"

"But if we weren't here on Cernee but on, say, Mars or Beenjai, or in one of the domed cities of the Zjan System, do you think that's the answer you'd come up with?"

"Not unless people all over the galaxy are watching our show," she said, "and that's a scary thought."

"So that's a nonlogical referential association for you."

"And the builders have given you all of them?"

"Oh, hell no," Fergus said. "They have a system, a complete blackbox into which vast quantities of cultural, historical, scientific, and social information is constantly being fed. Its sole purpose is to produce seed chips for the security system with a selection of random associations."

"That's impossible, then," she said.

"It's not if you've got an excellent memory, a head for trivia, and you've spent enough time with the Shipmakers," he said. "And I have all three." He even had his own small room in the Shipyard, though he rarely stayed long for fear of wearing out his welcome.

He pushed aside a few drifting knickknacks and snagged a cube out of the air, hooking it up to the confuddler. When the holographic interface popped up midroom, he used his fingers to start quickly tracing out a design in pencil-thin blue light.

"What is that?" Mari asked.

"Breaking the handshake code is one problem, but it's not the first problem. The first one is getting it in the first place. And the way to do that is this. *This* is my idea."

Mari squinted at the diagram. "What is it?"

"It's something I need help to build," Fergus said. "There are parts that I can't get. But you know someone who can."

"I do? Who?"

"Your neighbor. Mr. Harcourt. You seem to be friends?"

She tilted her head to one side, raised an eyebrow in suspicion. "Yeah," she said. "He's like an uncle."

"Can you introduce me?"

"Can I? Yes. Will I? Not unless you tell me what this thing is supposed to do."

"It's bait," Fergus said, "and I need to have it built before the public hearing on the cable disaster. Gilger is going to be at that hearing."

"He can't bring the ship into Central. It's too big."

"I only need him."

"He won't be alone. He likes strutting around with his pack of enforcers like he's untouchable. You won't get anywhere near him, and certainly not with *that* thing. He'll be on his guard."

"It's not his enforcers I'm worried about," he said, then had a thought. "You're not planning to go after him, are you?"

". . . No." The answer was slow in coming.

"Look, Gilger has made a lot of enemies all over Cernee and probably beyond. When his shiny new spaceship gets stolen right out from under him, first of all, he loses face. A lot of it. Second, he looks vulnerable. Everyone starts seeing opportunities. He won't last long."

"And what if you fail?"

Fergus shrugged. "I won't."

"With the right weapon, I could turn Gilger and everyone and everything within a hundred meters of him into paste before he ever sets foot in that meeting. Then you won't have any problem stealing his stupid ship no matter where he parks it."

"I'm not interested in any plan that involves destroying part of a space station, nor one that would get innocent people hurt. And that includes you," Fergus snapped.

"You're an asshole." Mari floated near the wall, arms crossed over her chest, glaring at him.

"True. But that doesn't make me wrong."

She threw up her hands. "Fine! So how is this . . . *ridiculous*-looking thing supposed to work?"

"I'm going to tell you, and you're not going to like it."

"I already know I won't like it, because I don't like *you*," she said. "I'm going to make more coffee, and then you can do your best to convince me it's a better idea than mine."

He touched the display cube, had it break out the component schematics, and started furiously adding and updating. "Okay, but try not to kill me before I'm done explaining."

Chapter 6

Mari insisted that he change exosuits. His own was perfectly fine, but she was worried that the other Vahns might recognize it when they headed back into the Wheel Collective to see Mr. Harcourt. So he spent too much cred to rent the tallest suit he could find in Bugrot, which was still determined to ride as far up his backside as it possibly could. "This is *not* comfortable," he complained, bending one knee and trying to pull the offending suit material back out into neutral territory.

Mari snickered. "What about *your* suit?" he griped, irritated.

"My own suit is back at Mr. Harcourt's," she said. "I swap it for one of his spares whenever I go out on the lines."

"And he doesn't mind?"

"We have an arrangement," she said. "I don't go out that often, but without Arelyn around—"

"Arelyn?" he asked. The little girl in the Wheels cafeteria had mentioned that name too.

"My best friend. Arelyn Harcourt. She went off to university on Mars six weeks ago. Mother knew, but Mauda doesn't yet. When she finds out . . . I don't know what she'll do. I can't go back to living my entire life inside the Wheels." Mari met his eyes. "You have something judgmental to say about that?"

"Nope. I ran away from home at fifteen. Mauda should just be happy you come home again. And at least your family would miss you if you didn't." He made one last futile attempt at a suitectomy. "Let's go before this thing cuts off all circulation to the lower half of my body."

They took the central passage down to the end of Bugrot, rented a pair of 'sticks at the flystick kiosk, and flew directly to Blackcans.

"Harcourt doesn't like to have visitors coming at him from free fall," she'd explained when he'd suggested they just go around and skip Blackcans entirely. "It makes him twitchy." A twitchy arms dealer was a convincing argument. They turned in their 'sticks and made the trek through Blackcans to pick up the Wheels line on the far side.

Landing at the Wheels, Mari swiped an ID at the main airlock and cycled them both into Mr. Harcourt's side of the collective. There were two very large men waiting for them. Briefly Fergus wondered if he would have any chance of stealing one of their exosuits in a fight. *You'd have better odds of heading back out into space with no suit at all,* he told himself.

A third, more Cernee-sized man appeared and stepped forward. He was about Fergus's age, thickly built, and dressed in a simple black tunic and pants that were too unwrinkled to seem casual. "Mari," the man said.

"Bale," she answered, matching him cool for cool. "This is Fergus. He has a proposal for Mr. Harcourt."

Bale tilted his head to one side, revealing the jagged line of a scar running along the underside of his chin. "Fergus, eh?" he said at last. "What's your business here?" Still not friendly.

"I wish to purchase some parts and equipment."

"For what?"

"It's complicated," Fergus said.

"You hot?"

"Um . . ."

"Bale means are you carrying any weapons," Mari said.

"Not on me."

"Take your exosuit off."

Fergus couldn't think of a single thing he wanted to do more, so he unfastened all the seals and, grunting with the effort, managed to peel the clingy exosuit down and off.

The two hulking enforcers patted him down and wanded him from head to toe. One found his databall and held it up for Bale, who shook his head. The enforcer handed it back to Fergus.

"The Fireblow, eh?" Bale asked, eyeing his new T-shirt. "You ate there?"

"I did."

"Did you finish it?"

"I did."

"Regret it?"

"Not yet. I got a second bowl for takeaway."

Bale nodded. "You may be all right," he said. "Pick up your suit and follow me."

Mr. Harcourt's part of the Wheel Collective was a whole different world from the Vahn farm. They walked over plush carpeting, and brass handholds and paintings adorned the walls. Fergus tried not to tally the value of the art—*Here as a guest, need his help, not here to repo anything*—as he followed Bale and Mari up along the curving corridor to a medium-sized room.

It was a study of some sort. There was a large sofa and two armchairs, a console, bookcases containing remarkably book-like items, and on the far wall, a gas fireplace behind thick glass. Fergus stared for a moment until a man unfolded himself from one of the armchairs and stood. He was almost as tall as Fergus and dressed in an impeccable business suit, his skin a rich brown, black hair trimmed close. Following Fergus's gaze to the fireplace, the man shrugged. "It burns off excess gases from our reclamation furnaces," he said. "Pretty enough, but stinks like hell if you open the seals. Now who are you?"

"Fergus Ferguson," he said, and the man chuckled.

"I'd make a comment about your mother having a sense of humor, but . . ."

"But Myrtle already made it," Mari said from the doorway.

"That figures. So, if you've met Myrtle, you must be the man who rode in on the lichen crate?"

"Mari's told you?"

"I keep a close eye on my front yard."

Mr. Harcourt seemed entirely relaxed, and something about the confidence that radiated from him shook Fergus's own; he had to force himself not to fidget. He'd dealt here and there with any number of rebels, black-marketeers, assorted con men, and more than a few petty criminals, but men of power? Professional arms dealers? He didn't like not being just another anonymous face.

"Fergus has a plan," Mari spoke up.

"A plan to do what? What's your business?"

"He's a finder," Mari chimed in again before Fergus could speak.

"Oh? And you are here to find something?"

Again Mari beat him to it. "Gilger's spaceship."

"Oh." Harcourt's eyebrows went up. "Is this so?"

"Yes," Fergus said.

Mari held up her wrist, where a small light on her comm was flashing. "I guess recess is over," she said. "Mauda wants me home. Do you mind?"

"No, certainly not, Mari," Harcourt said. "Give my best to the aunt flock."

"Will do." She looked at Fergus. "And you?"

"Give them my best as well?"

Mari shook her head. "No, I mean, do you think you can explain your extraordinarily idiotic plan in such a way that it makes any sense?"

"I'll try my idiot best," he said. "Can I assume you'll be in touch?"

"I know where you live," she said, and left the room.

Harcourt contemplated Fergus for a moment, then nodded slightly. That must have been a signal, because the enforcers left, and Bale followed after a moment. They were alone in the room.

"Not too many people Mari trusts," Harcourt said, "much less likes."

"I don't think she trusts me," Fergus answered, "and I'm entirely certain she doesn't like me."

"Do you remember being nineteen?" Harcourt asked. The man's accent was a little bit Cernee, a lot something else, something familiar, but Fergus couldn't place it. "Trust me, if she hated you, everyone this side of the Halo would know it. As for Arum Gilger . . . I maintain a careful neutrality with him. You need to be aware of that. I also want to be sure to explicitly clarify that my neutrality is not out of any fondness for Gilger." He stood and walked over to desk, took out some tubes of amber liquid, and handed one to Fergus. "Scotch. I'm assuming that's to your taste?"

"When anything is," he agreed.

"If I took on Gilger directly, the damage he'd do to me before I was done with him would be significant, and he'd head right here to the Wheels to do it. For my own safety and that of the Vahns, I leave Gilger alone, and he is mostly smart enough to recognize the value in staying away from me. That said"—Harcourt took a sip of his scotch—"Mother Vahn wasn't just a neighbor but a good friend and a damned good advisor at times. Someone taking away Gilger's spaceship would make me a happy man."

Harcourt's comm chimed, and he raised an eyebrow. "Excuse me a moment, Mr. Ferguson," he said, and he stepped out of the room.

Fergus sat in one of the armchairs and took a tentative sip from his bulb of scotch. That old familiar warm burn in his throat made him smile. If Harcourt's scotch wasn't the real thing, it was the closest thing he'd ever encountered outside of Earth's system. He took another sip. In fact, it reminded him a lot of a particular Martian distiller—

Harcourt's accent clicked. However long he'd been here at Cernee, it wasn't enough to cover up his Ares roots. Fergus had spent more time in and out of the domed cities of Mars than anywhere else since leaving

Earth. He wondered if they'd ever unknowingly crossed paths.

The door slid open, and Harcourt came back into the room, his face grim.

"What happened?" Fergus asked, rising out of his chair.

"Minnie Vahn took it upon herself to go to Blackcans for a few supplies while Mauda was sleeping. One of my crew went with her—Roale. She's worked for me since she was barely a teenager. Someone caught them both just inside the platform airlock. Knife. No witnesses. It has the signature of Gilger's man, Graf, all over it."

"Shit," Fergus said. Had he met Minnie? He didn't know. "Why the hell is Gilger so intent on wiping out a bunch of lichen farmers? They can't possibly be a threat."

"It's Graf who cares," Harcourt said. "Cloning is an abomination to Faithers because clones cannot have souls. And they're independent women on top of that. It gets under the skin of the Luceatans like a little sliver of glass in the sole of your foot, reminding you it exists every time you step outside your door. That Gilger has let it go this far means he's not afraid of consequences, which is bad for all of us. I still can't afford open war, Mr. Ferguson, but I'm interested in hearing your plan."

"I have to explain a bit first," Fergus said. "I have a device called a doorkey. It sends a coded signal into the ship's security subsystem—"

"—and the ship returns a list of nonsense words," Harcourt interrupted. "We've tried it." At Fergus's look, he shrugged. "You know my line of business, Mr. Ferguson, or you would not be here. I am not a pirate, and I don't prey on the innocent, but I am a businessman in a field with unscrupulous competition and often unscrupulous customers. One does what one needs to do."

Fergus took another sip of scotch. "The nonsense is a return handshake, another code."

"An uncrackable one, at least for any of the computing power I've thrown at it, and that includes at least one class-three I had occasion to borrow."

"I have everything I need to crack it up here." Fergus tapped his forehead. "But I need to get the handshake first, and then I need a little time to work through it."

"But you can't get close enough to the ship," Harcourt guessed.

"Yes. From my preliminary survey, Gilger has at least two dozen sentry bobs patrolling the outskirts of his territory."

"Three dozen, plus fifty zero-heat-emission mines arrayed inside the sentries."

Even if nothing else came of it, that information alone was worth the visit, Fergus thought. "I can't infiltrate his crew for obvious reasons," he said.

"You are one conspicuous bastard," Harcourt agreed. "That's not your natural color, is it?"

"Redhead, born true."

"Huh. That puts us back to: you can't get to the ship."

"Right. So I plan to make Gilger bring the ship to me."

"And this would be the plan Mari so enthusiastically described as 'extraordinarily idiotic'?"

"It would," Fergus said. "Gilger will be at the hearing on the cable accident—"

"He can't bring the ship into Central," Harcourt interrupted. "Even with one main line down, the closest he could get is Mezzanine Rock."

Fergus smiled. "That's as far as I need him to get." He held up his databall. "Do you have a schematics display? Also, more scotch. Blódstormur—am I right?"

"You are. You've spend time on the Fourth World?"

"Off and on, yeah. Although I have enough stuff in spaceport lockers all over the planet that I probably qualify for residency. Or at least taxes, if they caught up with me."

"Don't get me started on that," Harcourt said. "Mars Colonial Authority and I didn't exactly see eye to eye on taxes. Or much else, for that matter."

"As near as I can tell, the MCA exists solely for the purpose of being disagreed with."

Harcourt nodded, and his shoulders relaxed. He held out a hand, and Fergus dropped the databall into it. "Let's see this infamous plan, then." Harcourt touched his comm. "Bale? Bring me the holo cart, if you please."

———

Two hours later, Harcourt and Fergus were sprawled on the couch, empty scotch bulbs on the floor beside them. "You are a sad, stupid madman," Harcourt was saying, tears of laughter streaming down his face. "The things we could have done if I'd had you with me back on the red sands! We'd have been unstoppable. Legends!"

"That's why it'll work," Fergus said. "If we were going to lie, we'd pick something more believable, right?"

"Sir—" Bale interrupted from the doorway.

"What?" Harcourt asked, frowning.

"This list . . ." Bale held up a small handpad. "Is this a joke?"

"Yes," Harcourt said.

"Oh." Bale looked relieved, his eyes darting across the empty bulbs on the floor. "Okay . . ."

"I still need the items assembled and delivered to Mr. Ferguson's place over in Bugrot within the next six hours, and I need it to go unnoticed."

"What?! 'Whatever workshop scraps we have that'll fit in a box'? What the hell, sir?"

"It's a secret," Harcourt said. "Six hours, Bale."

———

Fergus took a short detour on his way back to Bugrot, stopping at a comm kiosk in a hab named Catchcan to send a short but very expensive message to a black market identity broker in Lunar Three. He got to his rent-a-room only a few minutes ahead of Harcourt's people. Four of them pounded on his door, and when he cautiously slid it open, they pushed him out of the way and shoved a cargo sled inside. "Being followed, three Goldies behind us," the leader said. "Can't stop for tea." They were gone without a word before the sled had even bumped the far wall. He shut and locked the door quickly.

The Governor's hearing on the cable "accident" was starting in a little over five hours. Fergus cracked the seals on the top case, pulled things out one by one, and set them carefully loose in the air around him.

The handful of working components had been assembled by Harcourt's chief engineer, and Fergus was impressed by how quickly the man had put them together. He plucked the doorkey out of the air and carefully slid it into a fitting at the back of the largest component. It clicked in and left no gap. Perfect.

A small handpad at the bottom of the crate included notes from Harcourt's engineer. *Range up to half kilometer; farther out, target must be still.*

If everything went right, that shouldn't be a problem.

Fergus floated cross-legged in the center of his room and began piecing parts together. An hour later, a half-assembled machine floated in front of him. Powering it on, he checked the readings on the pad he'd tethered into the back and made a few more adjustments. Everything looked good. Either it would work or it wouldn't, and there wasn't much other testing he could do. And if Gilger didn't play along . . .

Then I'll have to come up with an even stupider plan, Fergus thought, and hoped it wouldn't come down to that.

He emptied out the second crate, all items scrounged from the dead parts bin in the engineer's workshop. The rest of this was strictly art and camouflage but no less important for it.

Some time later his door chimed. He opened it to find Mari outside. She floated in, a small wrapped parcel under one arm, and hung just inside the door as he pushed off back into the debris cloud that was his work area. She looked tired and angry.

"I'm really sorry about Minnie," Fergus said.

"Roale was a friend too." She took the package out from under her arm and gave it a gentle push in his direction. It floated across the room and bapped him gently in the chest. "That's for you from Mr. Harcourt. He said to tell you that even though the parts are on him, he expects to be paid for the suit on general principle."

"I already have an exosuit," Fergus said. Two, if he counted the wedge-master he'd almost stuffed in the recycler when he'd gotten back to his room.

"Not *that* kind of suit," she said. "He said you need to look the part if you're going to sell this to Gilger and, even more importantly, the Governor."

Fergus unwrapped the parcel just enough to check it—as if he knew anything about suits that weren't deep space survival gear, which he absolutely did not—but even he could tell the suit had *style*.

"Well," he said. "I might actually look respectable in that." She opened her mouth to comment, then shook her head and closed it again.

Tucking the suit safely back in its wrapping, he returned to rummaging through the spare parts and junk. His hand closed on some sort of generic relay device sprouting cables like a robot Medusa. Snagging a mini touch-welder, he quickly attached the relay to the top of his machine, then trimmed the cables. Mari watched as he stuck a nut on the end of each and tacked them down in a semicircle so that they looked like they disappeared straight into the body of his machine.

Around the central cylinder amp enclosing the door-key, he had mounted six large coherent-beam spotlights. They were in turn surrounded by dials and readouts that only monitored leaking signal activity between themselves. He turned the spotlights on and off again just to double-check they still worked after all his fiddling. From the front he couldn't make out any of the individual lights in the overwhelming brilliance.

"You're pretty good at the no-grav thing for a dirt-sider," Mari said.

"I left Earth when I was fifteen," he said. "Been a lot of places since then, both in gravity wells and out."

He turned the machine off again, purplish spots swimming in his vision from the light. "So, how does it look?" he asked.

"Like something cobbled together in a junkpile," she said. "While drunk. In the pitch dark."

"It's supposed to look like a prototype."

"Well, whatever. You've got a little more than an hour before Mr. Harcourt comes to collect you."

"Wait, what? He's coming? *Personally?*"

"He said it was to lend you credibility, but I think it's more that he's really, really mad. I wanted to see you try to pull this off, but now you've dragged Mr. Harcourt into your craziness, and I'm not happy about that. It's a good thing you two idiots'll have me to keep you from doing anything truly stupid."

Fergus closed his eyes, trying to recalculate that unwanted complication into his plan. "Look," he said. "There's a good chance this won't work or that Gilger will figure out what we're up to, and then things could get dangerous. *Will* get dangerous. Harcourt can take care of himself, but you don't need to be in this fight."

"I *want* to be in it," she said.

"And that's an even better reason to keep you out of it," he said.

"Why? Because you think I can't take care of myself? I do just fine, and I don't need some ugly dirtsider I've barely met thinking he has to *protect* me."

"Maybe I'm trying to protect Harcourt, Mauda, and myself from someone's reckless disregard for everyone else around her," Fergus said. "It might surprise you to hear that I've known other people just as determined to go out with a bang as you are, and some of them took friends with them when they did. So while you're trying to think up exactly which rude gesture that warrants, why don't you get yourself back home before someone misses you? Like, leaving now."

"You're throwing me out?"

"Yes," he said. "I need to take a shower and put that suit on, and if I'm going to carry off the whole confident entrepreneurial businessman act, I don't need your snide mockery ringing in my ears the whole way to the hearing."

Mari slid open the door and pushed herself out. Half a second later she stuck her head back around the door-frame. "You just do your part," she said. "If you can. If you can't, then I'll do things my way, and to hell with you *and* Mr. Harcourt."

Ah, Fergus thought. *So I'm not the only one trying to keep the wayward Vahn in line.*

Once she was gone and the door was locked behind her, he grabbed the parcel with the suit in it and pushed off for the room's tiny closet and tinier pay-by-the-pint shower. There was a comb and a tiny vial labeled "NANOBLACK" tucked into the top.

When Harcourt arrived with Bale and two others, Fergus had already pulled on the business suit and was checking out his reflection in the mirror. He was so unaccustomed to anything other than his usual loose T-shirt and shorts that the strict, formal cut of the suit—tight across his shoulders, almost suffocating his legs in the latest Sfazili fashion—was almost enough to make him forget about how much his scalp and beard itched. Almost. He tossed the empty vial into the flash recycler with a bit more vigor than necessary.

"That's a better color for you," Harcourt said. "If only you weren't so ungodly pale. Seriously, were some of your ancestors dead fish?"

Self-consciously he touched his beard, feeling the faint grit of the colorizer. "My own mother wouldn't recognize me," he said. Though that wasn't anything new; his last few years at home, she'd steadfastly pretended he didn't exist.

"Machine ready?" Harcourt asked.

Fergus pushed himself to one side of the doorframe, letting them see the fabulously ridiculous contraption floating inside the room. He had already unclipped the doorkey and dropped it into one of the suit jacket's inside pockets; everything else he was willing to let out of his sight, but not that.

"You two," Harcourt said, pointing at his men. "Get that out and under wraps, don't let anyone see it, and don't break it."

"No problem, Boss." One of the crew sailed forward and took hold of an edge, and her partner grabbed the other.

"I've got a small car waiting," Harcourt said. "You ready to go?"

"As close as I can be," Fergus said. He gave his machine one last look, both dubious and fond, as Harcourt's people bundled a tarp around it, fastened the corners, and hauled it out. He swung through the door behind them.

On his way past, Harcourt slapped him on the back. "Try not to worry," he said. "Just don't blow it, or Gilger— or the Governor—will kill us both. And one last thing: don't underestimate the Governor. He's been in charge of Cernee for longer than either of us has been alive, and that wouldn't be true if he weren't smarter than everyone who has ever tried to knock him down. And that's been a lot of people over the years."

"Oh," Fergus said. "Is it too late to give back the suit?"

Harcourt gave a short laugh and didn't look back. "Just try not to die in it. It'd completely ruin the look."

Chapter 7

◆━━◆◆◆━━◆

Harcourt's personal flyer was a four-man about the size of a small old-fashioned automobile, just different enough from standard shape to hint at modifications of the sort Fergus imagined would be useful to an arms dealer. Harcourt insisted on flying it himself. With Fergus wedged in the back, they took off from Bugrot and headed outward first, then "down" toward what Fergus arbitrarily thought of as the underside of Cernee. They slipped back into the Halo through a gap in the lines. There were other vehicles moving through the open channel, surrounded by a thick tangle of cables and ringed by single-dwelling spheres and tiny shops. "The Knots," Harcourt said.

Halfway through the Knots, Harcourt brought the flyer to a stop and waited as another flyer covered in multicolored lights and bright streamers passed by ahead of them, several dozen smaller craft and flysticks with matching decorations behind it. A stiff flag on the lead flyer bore a symbol of three yellow dots inside an oval.

"Funeral procession," Harcourt explained, his voice somber. "One last late tour around the Halo before the dearly departed departs us forever. That's Rattletrap's mark."

In the seat beside him, Harcourt's man Bale cleared his throat. "Seen a lot of those the last two days," he said.

They reached a checkpoint about a third of the way in, slowing just long enough for some unhappy guy in a yellow-striped exosuit to eyeball their vehicle and wave them through.

Docking at Central, Harcourt pulled the four-man

into an empty bay with practiced ease. Once Fergus had managed to unfold himself from the back and smooth down his suit, they took a tube lift straight up into the underbelly of Central's spindle. Harcourt handed Fergus a small verified key. "To the storage unit with your prototype," he said. "It was rented under the Anders name."

"Right," Fergus said, following. "Thanks."

Harcourt grabbed his arm and hauled him forward. "If you walk behind me," he said, "everyone will assume I own you, that I am your *boss*. You walk with me like an equal, and you act like that very expensive suit you're wearing is not just your skin but goes all the way down to wrap itself around your bones. Got it?"

"Got it."

"You nervous?"

"Yes."

"Good. Don't let it show."

People streamed around them, walking with purpose, and conversation was loud, fast. There were merchants standing along the edges of the wide corridors displaying wares to passersby, trying to make eye contact but accosting no one, unlike their more aggressive counterparts in Central's ring, where Fergus had come with Mauda to sell her lichen. The farther in they went, the fewer people were wearing exosuits and the more people were dressed as if they could be walking the halls of government or big business on any major human colony.

Except Baselle, Fergus amended, *because then there would be no women allowed out here in public.*

They passed through three more gates before they were allowed onto the executive ring of Cernee. Gravity was nearly Earth-perfect. One of Harcourt's men stayed behind outside with a growing collection of surly, abandoned minionry, and Bale followed Fergus and Harcourt through the wide doors into a richly carpeted, round room. The back wall was hung with tapestries depicting the construction of the sunshields. There was a single wide table at the front and smaller stepped rows of seats lining the perimeter.

I am the suit, Fergus told himself, and took his seat with entirely feigned nonchalance.

Arum Gilger sat on the far side of the room.

He was taller than the Cernee natives, almost as pale as Fergus himself, his face rounded with a thickness that out here meant he'd been well off for most of his life. As if to emphasize the impression of wealth, he was dressed in gold and bright red. *He's patterned his clothes after Basellan high nobility,* Fergus realized. *Did his family fall that far?* If so—if Gilger had grown up with that much power and prestige and then had it suddenly stripped from him—it could explain a lot.

Sitting shoulder to shoulder with him was a Luceatan in a sleeveless tunic in similar colors. He was the reverse image of Gilger, hard where the other was soft, a razor where the other was hidden edges, all the differences an upbringing in comfortable nobility versus brutal exile could write on a man. His expressionless face and ropy, muscular arms were decorated with Faither glyphs and crisscrossed by scars. His eyes, even from across the room, were dark pits.

"Borr Graf," Bale whispered, following Fergus's gaze as he slipped past to take the seat behind them.

"Shhh," Harcourt hissed.

In another section, a man whose bone-thin face was taken up by a majestically sharp nose and equally dramatic scowl leaned back with his arms crossed over his chest, watching everyone else: Vinsic, the ore trader and another of the "powers." He was thinner than Fergus expected. Vinsic had three men with him, dressed in matching dark blue. If the local news was accurate, nearly a dozen of Vinsic's key people had disappeared over the last half year. Best guesses were predation by one of the other five or internal housecleaning, but regardless of what was true, Vinsic was no longer the unassailable power he had recently been.

Not that you'd know it from looking at him, Fergus thought. There was a hard, cold confidence in Vinsic's posture and body language that was impossible to reconcile with any hint of weakness. He was grateful that it wasn't Vinsic he had to go up against.

Not far from Vinsic's left, a middle-aged, mid-toned woman dressed in gray and green sat with one leg crossed over the other, her fingers interlaced over her knee. Her expression was passive, unreadable, but her eyes swept over the room like knives. *Ms. Ili.*

Gilger was starting to look positively soft.

Nearest the door were three people dressed in white exosuits, mirrored face shields down, anonymous. *Shielders*, Fergus realized from his research. Descendants of some of the original engineers who had built Cernee, the Shielders were the caretakers of the shield systems that formed the sunward-facing outer edge of about 120 degrees of Cernee's circumference and protected the settlement from excessive solar radiation and flare. They also oversaw the distribution of energy to the rest of Cernee over the same lines that were used for transportation. Fergus's understanding of how—or even if—the elusive and eccentric residents of the seven gigantic sunshields fit into the social structure of Cernee was nonexistent, and he wasn't sure the rest of Cernee itself was any the wiser. From everything he'd read, they just wanted to be left alone to do their own thing. It was the destruction of a line that must have drawn them out for the hearing.

The seats behind them all filled in with other people who had come to witness the proceedings, some in expensive suits, some not. Fergus spotted an elderly man clutching a Rattletrap funeral flag in shaking hands, and the raw grief on his face was enough to make Fergus look away.

He was careful not to make eye contact with anyone, but he was keenly aware of more than one set of eyes studying him.

A chime rang. Everyone stood as a woman strode into

the room, visibly armed, dressed in a spotless Authority uniform with no rank insignia except a yellow X embroidered on the stiff upright collar. She was short even among Cernee natives but built like a tank, if tanks were constructed entirely of muscle and disapproval. She stood to one side as the Governor entered and took his seat at the head table, then she sat beside him. Two more people in Authority colors entered and stood behind them at the front of the room, one holding a small box.

The Governor of Cernekan was a man for whom the finest, most exquisitely tailored suit—and his was certainly that—only served to emphasize how utterly nondescript the man wearing it was. Late middle-aged, middle-sized, hair a fine gray, there was nothing about him to suggest he was anyone to pay attention to until he leaned forward and began to speak.

"This hearing into the circumstances of the cable break between Mezzanine Rock and Blackcans, the subsequent breach of the hab at Rattletrap, and the deaths of thirty-seven people, eighteen of them children, is now convened," he said, his voice like glowing red iron. "You may sit."

He didn't seem to be speaking at significant volume, but his words carried to every corner of the room. Everyone still standing took their seats quickly and with a minimum of commotion.

"We recovered the remains of an EMP mine amid the debris," the Governor said. The assistant behind him reached into his box and placed a blackened, warped disk on the table. "The cable car was deliberately destroyed."

"I thought this hearing was to discuss an *accident*," Gilger said. His accent was pure upper-class Basellan.

"We wouldn't want to start off with any assumptions," the Governor replied. His smile did not reach his eyes. "The cable station recorded two passengers: an offworlder whose body we haven't yet recovered, and Mattie Vahn, whose body we have. You wouldn't happen to have any-thing to contribute to our understanding of these events, Mr. Gilger?"

"Mattie Vahn and I had our differences, but I never wished her harm," Gilger said, leaning back in his seat. "If there are those who would accuse me of it, I say bring on the evidence. You'll find none because there is none."

"I assume that statement is on the record?" the Governor asked.

"Why shouldn't it be?" Gilger answered. "Surely the record will also show that the woman attracted trouble. Accidents followed her and her family around. Maybe she was the cause of this unfortunate event as well and finally paid the price for her sins."

As angry murmuring broke out around them, Fergus caught the faint twitch of a smile on Graf's face, quickly buried again.

The Governor held up one hand to forestall any re-plies, then gestured his assistant forward. "The incident timeline?" he asked.

"The cable car was first crippled with an EMP mine, taking down all security monitoring systems on the car," the assistant said. "While the car was subsequently destroyed by an explosion, some of the debris had em-bedded fragments that don't match the cable car mate-rial. Virtual reconstruction shows that those fragments and pattern of damage were localized to the back of the car, suggesting a directed attack from outside prior to the explosion."

"Please share with the room your conclusions as to the cause," the Governor said.

"A shrapnel cannon moved to within range, followed by a secondary explosion, likely an added function of the EMP mine itself. Ms. Vahn and her fellow passenger appear to have already exited the car, but must have been well within the blast range when the explosion oc-curred. We are unable to tell from Ms. Vahn's remains if she was still alive at the time of the secondary explosion, Lord Governor, sir."

"Your confidence in this scenario?"

"Approximately ninety-five percent, sir."

"Do you find it plausible that Mattie Vahn shot herself with a shrapnel cannon?"

The assistant blinked. "Lord Governor, I don't—Are you seriously asking me that?"

"Not really," the Governor said, "although I would hate to overlook any possibilities suggested by our concerned citizens."

"I wouldn't think it plausible, no, sir."

"Then I believe we can say with confidence that this was no accident and that Mattie Vahn and the offworlder were intentionally killed?"

"Yes, sir, that is our conclusion. We returned Ms. Vahn's remains to her family just prior to this hearing for C&R."

At Fergus's puzzled look, Harcourt leaned slightly closer and whispered, "Ceremony and Recycling."

Gilger's voice rose. "Independent verification—"

"I suggest that Mr. Gilger strongly consider letting the Vahns mourn in peace while this matter continues to be investigated by those with the authority to do so," the Governor interrupted. "After all, we have not ruled out anyone as a suspect, not even our esteemed colleagues in this very room."

Gilger raised both hands. "I was conducting business in NoMoar when the accident happened. People will confirm this."

The Governor didn't raise his voice or change his inflection, but the sudden chill in the room was palpable. "The murder of two people, one of whom was a law-abiding citizen, is ample crime in and of itself, but the resulting deaths of thirty-seven more people due to the assault on the lines—which is not just our transportation and power distribution system but a vital part of how we maintain the structural integrity of Cernee—is an abhorrent act that demonstrates a callous disinterest in the well-being of our entire fragile community. Both act and consequence will most certainly be weighed fully against the perpetrator when—not *if*—justice is done."

"If there's no security footage—"

The Governor tapped the remains of the EMP mine on the table. "Authority will spare no effort or expense in gathering all available evidence. I am issuing a blanket warrant entitling them to go wherever they need to go anywhere within the territory of Cernee without hindrance, and to talk to anyone they suspect may have information. I am also offering a reward for any eyewitnesses who come forward. If the guilty party can be determined, there will be no rock small enough for him to hide inside." He surveyed the room.

Most of the room watched Gilger.

"If it pleases Your Lord Governor," Harcourt said, standing.

Bloody hell, Fergus thought, standing up beside him. *Here we go.*

The Governor's gaze fell on them like a hawk spotting movement in an unexpected quarter of grass. "Mr. Harcourt, you have information?"

"I seek to offer assistance," Harcourt said. "More specifically, the assistance of an associate of mine." He held out one hand toward Fergus. "This is Mr. Anders."

"Continue," the Governor said after a half beat pause. Across the room, Gilger's eyes narrowed. Graf's gaze had fixed on them both, his face stone.

Fergus cleaned his throat. "Your Lord Governor, I represent a small sci-tech company based in Lunar Three, near Earth. We have a prototype that we think may be able to help shed some light on the events under discussion."

"What is it a prototype of?"

"Ah . . . it's a bit technical."

"Explain or sit down, Mr. Anders."

"Ah. Yes. As you know, the history of the universe is written in light. When an event happens, the light that intersects that event is changed by it, and the reflected light effectively captures the moment. What we've discovered is that photons, as they interact as both wave and particle with other particles in the interstellar medium, affect and are affected by those interactions. Our prototype, set up between two points, uses a highly focused, specialized light source to read the interference patterns between those points and extrapolate backward over time the most probable interactions that resulted in those states."

He took a quick breath and hoped his voice didn't sound as shaky as it felt. "From there," he continued, "we can recreate the images carried by the original light. In short, under very specific conditions, our device allows us to see back in time. We call it a Light Afterimage Retrieval Device."

The Governor frowned and looked at his tech. "LARD?! That sounds . . . stupid," he said.

"We prefer not to use the acronym," Fergus answered. He clasped his hands behind his back.

"I imagine not," the Governor said.

"It's likely that I'm not explaining the underlying concept well, but our scientists have had success in our limited tests thus far," Fergus said. "I was sent out to find an occasion to test it in the real world, and this seems like an ideal opportunity."

"And how much is this 'opportunity' going to cost us?"

"Nothing, Lord Governor. If the test succeeds, that is payment enough," Fergus said. "If it fails, Cernekan is far enough away from the core multiworlds that any potential damage to our reputation would be negligible. No offense. And it won't interfere with your investigation either way."

"This is ridi—" Gilger started. The woman in uniform beside the Governor began to drum her fingers on the table, and he closed his mouth and glared.

The Governor had not taken his eyes off Fergus. "Mr. Harcourt?" he asked. His expression said: *This better be good.*

"I've had good luck with other tech of theirs in the past," Harcourt said. "When I heard of this device, I thought it was worth a try. My people reviewed the science, and to my surprise and, I suspect, their own, they endorsed it conceptually."

"What's the name of your company, Mr. Anders?"

"SteloFocus Tech," Fergus said.

The Governor turned to his security chief. "Katra, get me a background check on the company and Mr. Anders here."

Well, that expensive call I made from Catchcan just paid for itself, Fergus thought. Everyone waited as she pulled up the info on her handpad, then passed it to the Governor. It would show that the hours-old shell company had a history going back to premigration Earth itself, inconveniently headquartered in one of many places that were now underwater. There were even some planted news archives about SteloFocus Tech's tentative steps toward relocating to the moon.

If it didn't show that, and if Fergus lived, he'd be due a very significant refund.

The Governor read it, pursed his lips, then looked up. "Assuming I allow you to proceed—"

Gilger leapt to his feet. "You can't seriously think—"

"Would you presume to tell me what I can and cannot think?" the Governor asked coolly.

Gilger stared for a long moment before retaking his seat. Hatred came off him in waves. "No, Lord Governor."

"Well, then. Mr. Anders, if I were to allow you to proceed, what would you need for this test of yours?"

"I'll need to set up my prototype with a clear line of sight to where the event occurred," Fergus said. "It will shine a very bright, highly focused beam of light along that path and begin collecting data. It will take somewhere between twenty and thirty minutes. Once the test has begun, though, it's important that nothing large and/ or dense crosses or blocks the light path in any way, as that will invalidate the results. The scattering of the light from our prototype will 'corrupt,' if you will, the local residual data, rendering any subsequent attempt at retrieval impossible."

"So you're just going to shine a bright light from Mezzanine Rock down the line? That's it?"

"That's it."

The Governor was shaking his head. *He's not going to go for it,* Fergus thought. *Damn! I knew it was too far-fetched.*

Gilger stood up again, more composed this time. "Lord Governor, I object," he said. "For one thing, do we trust outsiders to be more thorough than our own investigators? And how do we know this isn't just some scheme of Harcourt's to keep *himself* from being implicated by the evidence? You've suggested weapons were used in the attack—do we need to look outside this very room for the likely source? It would be a fool's risk to let them do this."

"Sit down, Mr. Gilger," the Governor said. He pressed his thumbs against his temples, closed his eyes, and sat still for several long minutes. Around the room, the fidgeting that Fergus would have expected anywhere else was almost entirely absent. Gilger was leaning in toward Graf, his mouth moving slightly as he whispered something to his second, but his eyes never left the central table. Vinsic was watching Fergus intently.

Fergus's mind was a whirling, blank pit. *Don't panic,* he told himself. *The suit would not panic.*

The Governor opened his eyes again. *If he looks toward Gilger, we've lost.*

Instead, the Governor turned back toward them. "I'll allow this prototype test as long as it doesn't interfere with my investigators' work. My technicians and security personnel will attend Mr. Anders for the duration, as I'm sure we're all very curious about this rather fantastical device you've described."

"Thank you very much, Lord Governor." Fergus bowed.

The Governor looked around. "Anyone else have anything to add? Except you, Arum." When no one spoke, he stood. "This hearing is adjourned pending further information. You may all leave. Mr. Harcourt, you and your associate stay a moment."

Gilger paused in the doorway, tapped Graf on the shoulder, and gestured toward Fergus. He said something too low to hear, then swept out of the room. The Luceatan stared at him a few seconds longer before following his boss, as if committing his face to memory.

That can't be good.

The Governor had brief conversations with several departing people, including one of the Shielders, in voices too low to make out. When at last the room was empty of anyone except his security chief, Harcourt, and Fergus, the Governor walked back to the head of the room and sat down on the edge of the table. "What are you up to, Harry?"

Harcourt held out his hands, palms up. "I am motivated by nothing except seeing justice done after losing a friend and neighbor," he said. "Mattie Vahn was a good woman and a good member of the community. She donated half her crop three standards ago when we had the biodome failure and saved a fifth of Cernee from starving until it got fixed. You know Gilger has never contributed a damned thing except trouble and death. We owe it to Mattie to see justice done, and you know it."

"Katra informed me of the murder of Minnie Vahn at Blackcans just prior to this meeting," the Governor said. Katra nodded her head in acknowledgement. "You understand that without proof, I must regard that as a separate and unrelated event? Unless something comes along to tie the two things together?"

"I understand," Harcourt said.

It was nearly a minute before the Governor spoke again, his gaze never wavering. "You are not wrong. Gilger is an ass, and a dangerous one at that. This attack was bolder than I would have expected of him, but the way things stand right now, he'll probably get away with it, and I can't say that I like that outcome. If this plan you're concocting works, I won't have any cause to question the integrity of you or your associate, will I?"

"I would hope not, Lord Governor," Harcourt said.

"Good."

The Governor stood again and looked the both of them up and down. "Nice suit, Mr. Ferguson," he said. "Glad to see you survived after all." Then he turned and left.

Katra stayed in the doorway. "I'll be in touch when we're ready to transport you to Mezzanine Rock for your test," she said. "In the meantime, don't leave Central."

"Where would we go?" Harcourt asked.

"Nowhere I couldn't find you," she said, and with a half smile, followed after her boss.

The conference room was empty. Fergus put a hand over his face. "No one here is at all like what I was expecting. Except for Gilger, which is not to his credit."

"No, I imagine not," Harcourt said.

"Harry Harcourt, huh?"

"Shut up," Harcourt said. "Let's get—"

He was interrupted by a familiar wail of sirens. "*Another* flyby?!" he exclaimed.

"Now what do we do?" Fergus asked.

"I've got a small office suite in the middle ring I use to conduct local business," Harcourt said. "We can check the newsfeeds from there. If the Asiig are stirred up, this could all be a huge waste of time."

Walking to Harcourt's suite, they passed people in the corridors murmuring anxiously to one another and jumping at shadows. Every face they passed bore a hunted expression, from visitors to Cernee locals.

They watch us all the time, Mari had said.

Fergus wanted nothing more than to grab *Venetia's Sword* and get out, and he said as much to Harcourt once they were safely in his suite.

Harcourt opened a cabinet, got out a bottle of scotch, and started hunting for bulbs. "I didn't expect Gilger to lose his cool like that. And the way Graf was studying you? You've made yourself an enemy. And that's without them knowing why you're really here," he said. He found bulbs and set them out on the counter. "If there's any particular C&R you'd like or anyone left at home to send you to, best let me know now."

"No. Just—"

The alarms cut off, the sudden silence almost a noise of its own.

"At least that was mercifully short," Harcourt said. He pulled up the news on the office console and read the summary out loud. "'A single Asiig ship passed Fifty-Rock before turning and heading back out into the Gap. None taken.' That's the closest they've come in a long time."

"Why?"

"Who knows?" Harcourt said. "Maybe some day they'll come take us all. For now, though, they've spared us again."

The console chimed, and Katra's face filled the screen. "Naptime is over," she said. "Get your exosuits on and bring your prototype to Authority dock 16B. Be there in an hour or less. *Both* of you." The connection closed.

Harcourt put the unopened bottle of scotch and bulbs back in the cabinet. "Let's get this over with before any more complications come along."

Fergus had been assured that the Asiig only rarely crossed the Gap, but that made two visits in less than a week. When he got back to his exosuit, tucked up next to his ludicrous prototype, the first thing he was going to do was have Harcourt show him how to tune in to the Boolean public alert signal.

If he never saw that little yellow light appear on his suit's display panel, he'd be a happy man, but he was not going to take the chance that the aliens were done marauding until he was safe and sound hundreds of light-years away from there.

Chapter 8

◆━━━◆━━━◆

Several hours later, under the skeptical eye of Katra herself, one security officer, and two of the Governor's techs, Fergus and Harcourt offloaded the prototype from an Authority flyer onto the platform of Mezzanine Rock. No one offered to help. "We've cleared the platform and nearby corridors for you," Katra told them. "The Governor suggested you would probably prefer a minimal audience due to trade secrets." She spoke those last words as if naming a perversion. "I don't know much about photons and waves and transcripting beams, but I know a rat in the walls when I hear it. You be careful you don't go gnawing on anything I care about."

"I wouldn't dream of it, ma'am," Fergus said.

She grunted, unconvinced. "I'm going to check my perimeter while you get set up to do whatever it is you think you're going to do." She turned to her techs. "You two, stay out here with them and *observe*."

She left without looking back.

Harcourt left Bale and his other man on the platform, watching. Maintenance rings had been pounded into the rock surrounding the opening, so it was just a matter of awkwardness to haul the bulky machine up and onto a smooth area of rock.

To their right, Beggar's Boulder was lit up; beside it, a few lights flickered in the remains of Rattletrap. Past both, up against the backside of the last of the sun-shields, was a dimly lit large hab that was starting to feel familiar: *Blackcans*.

Once the prototype was aimed in the hab's direction, he tethered it down and began powering it up. "Right," Fergus said. "You sure you want to stick around for this?"

Harcourt laughed. "I should be putting as much distance as I can between myself and this madness. And yet here I am. And besides, Katra said I had to be here."

"True. But you could have made some excuse. You don't need to put yourself in danger."

"Right, because otherwise my life as an arms merchant out along the Gap is very low-risk," Harcourt said. "I looked you up, you know."

"What?"

"Mars. I know what you did there. You were a *hero*. And then you just disappeared. I don't understand why you wouldn't be proud."

Fergus sighed. "Because I was an idiot kid. I'd just run away from home, and for the first time in my life I felt like I was free, like I could do anything. I thought I was invincible, and without a single bloody thought about consequences, I convinced other people who should have known better to trust me. People got hurt." *Some worse than hurt,* he didn't add.

"But you succeeded. It was a defining victory for Free Mars. They all knew what the risks were. You've never gone back?"

"Many times, but always under a fake name," Fergus admitted. "I don't want to be anyone's hero, not anymore. Not at someone else's expense."

Harcourt watched him for a few moments, then nodded. "Mars gets under your skin, makes you a different person," he said. "Once it does, you don't really ever escape it."

"Yet you're out here."

"I escaped the Mars Colonial Authority," Harcourt said. "I never escaped Mars. And now my kid is back there . . . Don't you ever feel it, trying to pull you back?"

"No," Fergus lied.

"You will," Harcourt said. "Everyone does eventually."

"Not if—" Fergus started to answer, but then Katra's two techs appeared on the platform's outer edge, pulling themselves up onto the rock not far away. Fergus fiddled with some dials in what he hoped appeared to be a methodical way. When the techs got bored enough watching him to start talking to each other, he carefully slipped the doorkey into the back, clicking it into place.

Good enough, he thought. *Time to do it.*

Toggling his comm over to open broadcast, he cleared his throat. "This is Mr. Anders, recording on behalf of SteloFocus Tech of Lunar Three. I am about to test the prototype Light Afterimage Retrieval Device, Beta Unit Alpha," he announced. "We are in Cernekan's Halo at a location known as Mezzanine Rock, atop Platform C, and we'll be directing our light transcription beam toward a habitat named Blackcans. There was a fatal incident here a few days ago, and we will be attempting to retrieve the afterimage data from it."

One of the techs floated nearer, craning his head over Harcourt's shoulder for a closer look. "What do those dials measure?" he asked.

"Ah . . ." Fergus said. "This one measures the disturbance velocity of ambient particles, and this one shows the correlation between light amplitude and event displacement."

The man frowned. "What?"

"Should we start?" Harcourt interrupted.

"Yes. Yes, we should." Fergus pulled his handpad from his pack.

"And what's that?" the tech asked.

"I'm recording data on the internal functioning of the device for later study by our engineering team," he said.

"May I?" The tech began to reach for the pad.

"I'm sorry, it's proprietary information," Fergus said, turning the screen toward his chest.

"Oh," the tech said. "Well, how exactly does—"

"I'm sorry, but every moment that elapses since the event negatively impacts the retrieval density. I'm sure there'll be time for questions afterward if the test is successful."

"Oh. All right." The tech returned to his compatriot's side and stared glumly out into the darkness.

Fergus powered on the ring of spotlights. The matte-surfaced hab in the distance lit up with a tiny but brilliant white dot. "The device is calibrating itself to the environment, and we should be able to begin collecting preliminary data soon," Fergus said over the open comm for anyone who might be listening. "At this point, it is *critical* that the beam not be interrupted, or we risk corrupting our original data source."

"How long, do you think?" Harcourt asked over their private channel.

"No idea. I just hope Gilger shows."

They stared out after the beam, waiting. "Can I ask . . ." Fergus started to say, then trailed off, not sure he should.

"About?"

"Mari. The Vahns."

Harcourt gave a short laugh. "My daughter was four when we came here on the run," he said after some thought. "I wanted somewhere quiet. Half the Wheels was in ruins, and I had only the bare remnants of a team left, so it was a stroke of fortune that at the other end was a family with kids Arelyn's age, you know? I don't know how we'd've made it if it hadn't been for Mattie Vahn. Arelyn practically lived over there for years, and she and Mari were inseparable. And then they became teens."

Fergus nodded.

"Arelyn's smart. Smarter than me, and not one to back down from a challenge, but also not really one to go out and get into trouble the way I did when I was her age. The Vahns really suit her as extended family. On the other hand, there's Mari."

"More of a trouble-seeker," Fergus said.

"Yeah," Harcourt said. "So Mattie Vahn and I came to an arrangement. Mari started taking on a few small courier tasks for me, showing up when we were doing self-defense exercises, things like that. We wanted her to be able to take care of herself off the farm, because it was obvious she wasn't going to stay put. When Arelyn decided to go back to Mars, explore her heritage . . . well, Mari—"

"Gilger's here," Fergus interrupted, silently cursing the timing. A ship was threading its way carefully between the Leakytown lines in the distance, entering the Halo. Flysticks and one-mans scattered in its wake. Fergus's heart raced at the sight of silver glinting in the starlight. *Venetia's Sword.*

The two techs were arguing about the day's episode of *One Star, Bright and Distant.* No one else on the surface had noticed the encroaching ship.

Gilger's pilot was good. *Venetia's Sword* cleared the last of the Leakytown lines and turned its nose toward the newly opened space between Mezzanine Rock and Blackcans.

"What is that?" Fergus shouted, waving wildly toward the ship. As the techs turned, he shouted over the broadcast channel, "Unknown ship, please change course! You are about to disrupt a vital scientific experiment!"

The techs were talking now, their faces animated underneath their shields, but they weren't on the public channel. *That's okay,* Fergus thought, *I know what they're saying.* Moments later, Katra came up from the platform with one of her officers, took one look at Gilger's ship, cursed, and disappeared again.

Four red lights arced up from the far side of Mezzanine Rock: Authority one-mans, rushing to intercept the ship, too far behind to cut it off in time.

"No!" Fergus cried, letting as much anguish as he could muster fill the word. Harcourt turned his face away, his back shaking with laughter he couldn't quite hide.

The techs shouted into their comms as the one-mans drew up behind the ship. *Venetia's Sword* came to a stop exactly in Fergus's spotlight. The beam beautifully lit up the blue stripe along its side. Fergus held his breath, each agonizing second like hours, until he felt the tiny vibration of a chirp on his handpad. *Handshake.* He had it! He nudged Harcourt with his elbow, and when the man turned, he nodded his head slightly. Harcourt grinned.

Whatever dialogue was taking place between Authority and *Venetia's Sword*, the ship began to move off, but barely at a crawl. Katra had come out onto the platform again. "That ship ruined my experiment!" Fergus complained to her. "It's too late now—all our data is lost!"

"I'm sorry, Mr. Anders," Katra said. "Mr. Gilger claims that he came by to view the trial of your prototype because you'd roused his curiosity during the hearing and misunderstood the direction in which you'd be shining the light. He sends his sincere apologies and hopes he moved out of your way in time. You can be assured that I will be having further conversations with him about this."

"I was quite clear about my requirements at the meeting!" he complained.

"I thought so too, sir," one of the techs said. But his sympathy seemed to be fading already, and both of them left with Katra, no one offering to help bring the device back down.

Once they were alone again, Harcourt switched back over to the private channel. "Now what?"

Fergus took his doorkey back out of the machine and slipped it into a pocket. "Now I need to hole up somewhere quiet and crack the code, then find a way to get access to the ship again. In forty-eight hours or less."

"You realize there's a good chance Katra will confiscate your machine to figure out for herself what we're up to? She's overzealous that way."

"Uh, no," Fergus said. "I didn't think of that. Ideas?"

"None. I can bluster my way around almost any of her officers, but not her."

"Great. Um, who's that?" Fergus said. He pointed.

A small one-man was heading toward them.

"It's not Authority," Harcourt said. After a pause, he added, "Nor is it slowing down. I think we need to get out of here."

"But the prototype—" Fergus started to say when Harcourt grabbed his arm and pulled.

"The driver just ejected. We need to move *now*!"

They scrambled along the maintenance rings back to the platform. "Incoming ship," Harcourt called over the public channel. "Collision course!"

"Get in," Harcourt shouted to Fergus, and together they grabbed the edge of the dock and threw themselves into the envelope.

The one-man hit above them, exactly where they had been perched during the experiment. The force of it turned their tumble through the closing platform envelope into a high-velocity push, and they slammed against the far side. Their comms filled with shouting and the sounds of sirens. The platform's inner doors tried to open but stuck halfway, warped by the explosion, as air from the bay whistled past them and out through the damaged exterior. Through the floor, Fergus felt the rumble of emergency doors slamming shut farther inside the rock.

"Suit still sealed?" Harcourt asked on their private channel.

A few yellow warning lights flared in Fergus's peripheral display, but his suit was unbreached. "I'm good," he said. He felt shaky, and he resented the hell out of the fact that people were trying this hard to kill him before he'd even *done* anything to them yet. "Guess we don't have to worry about what to do with the prototype," he added.

Harcourt's men came flying out into the bay. "Bale, what's the situation?" Harcourt asked.

"Katra is heading back here," Bale replied, offering a hand to pull Harcourt through the envelope opening. Fergus managed to get himself out behind them. "I heard her on the comms, and she's gone fusion."

"I expect we'll be—" Harcourt started to say.

"Danger!" Bale shouted, and used his leverage on a bar to shove Harcourt roughly to one side. There was a bright flash, and the heat sensors on Fergus's suit registered the shot as it passed.

The other man was reacting too, grabbing Harcourt and pulling him into the lee of a pillar. Fergus was dodging on his own, looking for cover, as Bale shot back toward the corridor. Diving behind a rack of fire-suppression equipment, Fergus could now see what had tipped off Bale: small red droplets carried on the current from the air systems toward the return vent.

"Give up, and we won't hurt you!" someone called over the public comm channel.

I know that accent, Fergus thought. There were advantages to traveling as much as he did. "Name your ken!" he called back.

There was a brief silence, then, "I will not!" Several shots accompanied the answer for emphasis, driving them back behind cover.

There were flashes of light around the corner. Harcourt's man pushed over to the wall, then down close to the floor. Bale and Harcourt trained their pistols carefully at the edge of the wall to provide cover fire.

Harcourt's other man peered quickly around the corner, fired a shot, then pulled back.

"Gurne, situation?" Harcourt asked.

"Hit one," the man answered. "Three left. Blue stripes, face shields on mirror. Four bodies: two of Katra's guard and the two techs. Also, they have a hostage."

"Fuck," Harcourt said. "Blue? *Vinsic?*"

"No," Fergus said. "They've got to be Gilger's."

A blue-striped figure moved carefully around the corner, one arm around Katra's neck, the other holding a pistol by her side. He had her positioned as a human shield. Her suit had several burn holes in it, blood peppering the air around them in rhythm with her pulse. "Trade you," the man said. "Governor's pet for yours."

Fergus could see her eyes darting around, taking in who was where. Her expression was one of unmitigated fury.

"Katra?" Harcourt asked.

"Yeah, Harry?" she said. "I'm a bit busy right now."

"How badly are you hurt?"

She shook her head behind her face shield. From where he was, Fergus could see that most of her suit lights were flashing red. *She's not going to make it,* he realized.

The man put his pistol up against her ear. "No more talking. Trade *now,*" he said. "Last chance."

"I don't fucking *do* hostage negotiations," Katra said. She jerked her knees up sharply, pulling the man forward. In his momentary distraction, she managed to wrap her hand around his holding the pistol and squeeze. The pistol fired.

She went slack, the inside of her face shield painted red. The man pushed himself away, trying to get under-cover again as Harcourt and his men opened fire. The man jerked, a small plume of red erupting from his shoul-der just before he disappeared back around the corner.

"Comms are being blocked outside this immediate area. We have to get out of here *now,*" Harcourt said. "Bale, this is your stomp; can you get Mr. Ferguson out of here without anyone seeing you?"

"No problem," Bale said.

"If you can't get him to Bugrot, get him anywhere he can hole up safely and stay with him until you hear otherwise from me. Fergus, you still got your data?"

"I do."

"Good. Let's get out of this trap while we can."

Harcourt did a graceful flip in place behind the pillar and kicked off for the jammed envelope opening, pass-ing through with minimal resistance. Bale pointed at Fergus, then jacked his thumb toward the hole. "Now you," he said.

Shots followed him as he dove after Harcourt, through the envelope, and out. Bale and Gurne came through mo-ments later under another volley of fire. Harcourt was already pulling himself out of sight on the rock; Gurne followed.

Bale grabbed Fergus's arm and kicked off from the wall, pulling him toward the cargo tunnel. "We're going this way," he said. Unceremoniously he pulled him into the chute. "Your public comm off?"

"Yes," Fergus said after checking it.

"Then be quiet while I save your ass."

That seemed a fair bargain, so he shut up and followed Bale, pulling himself hand over hand along the cargo rail through the narrow, grimy tunnel. Suddenly the tunnel widened out and Bale pulled him into a side chute. "Jam bypass," he said. "Hold still and cover the lights on your suit controls."

Fergus did so, and moments later a crate came flying past them down the chute. "That was to test for obstructions, i.e. us," Bale said. "If I thought someone was hiding in here, I'd hope the first crate would spook them into making a run for it and send another one right about now."

Another crate whizzed past.

"How do you know they aren't just normal cargo?"

Bale shook his head.

"Oh, right," Fergus said. "No one else alive on the platform. Now what?"

"Now we wait a bit longer to see if they decide the tunnel is empty after all and go away or come in looking for us."

A light began to play up over the walls of the tunnel. Bale held up a finger for silence, and Fergus waited. After agonizing minutes, Bale suddenly flicked on an extremely bright handlight. The figure in the tunnel threw a blue-striped arm up over his face, and Bale took aim with his pistol and fired.

"Get moving," he said. "No one's going to be sending any more crates in until they clear the body out, but they know for sure we're in here now."

They pulled themselves forward until the tunnel forked, and Bale led Fergus to the left. "The right side heads into a depot; they probably have someone waiting there by now," he said. "Left is a much longer path, but there's an abandoned cut-off ahead."

"How do you know the cargo tunnels so well?"

"Mezz Rock born. Grew up playing in here, gaming the tunnels with my brother," Bale said. He touched the scar under his chin self-consciously. "Not always successfully."

The tunnel forked again, the left side dusty and disused and narrow. Bale went about two body-lengths in and then stopped, paused to do something Fergus couldn't see, then pushed himself through a small, filthy hatch. Fergus followed him and to his surprise found an airlock dead ahead. "Close the hatch behind you," Bale told him, already climbing in.

Fergus did as Bale said, and when the lock had reset, he crammed himself into the small chamber and cycled himself through into a large, dark space. Bale was shining his handlight around inside the room. Finding what he was looking for, he dusted off a small panel and hit some buttons. Dim lights illuminated the faded gray interior.

Something skittered across the floor and walls, disappearing into cracks and corners and shadows. Fergus jumped. "Uh, what was that?" he asked.

"Ballroaches," Bale said. "Most of the old rocks in Cernee have them if they have air. Sort of like halfway between a small cockroach and a spider. They sting. Sharp little fuckers can go right through a suit."

"Not spore ticks?"

"No. Look like them but bigger."

"Great," Fergus said. "Poisonous?"

"Mildly toxic. Burns like shit, and you'll get a welt, but they're not parasites. I wouldn't want to fall into a pit of them, though."

"Is that likely?"

"Down here? Maybe," Bale said. He smiled.

There were several more airlocks leading off the chamber, a row of cabinets covering one wall, and stacked hammocks covering the opposite. "What is this place?" Fergus asked.

Bale flipped open his face shield, folded back his hood, and wrinkled his nose. "Smelly, is what it is," he said. With his hair disheveled and his expression of unguarded, nostalgic bemusement, he looked less like an enforcer and more like a regular person. *A regular person who works out a lot and could probably break you in half over his knee,* Fergus amended.

"It'll take the air handlers a while to catch up; no one's been in here for a long time," Bale said. "This is one of the old emergency shelters, built during the days when the Rock was still being mined. Most of them have been reabsorbed by the settlement, but not this one; the rock spinward from here is porous and unstable, so they've left it alone."

Fergus opened his own face shield and grimaced. *Now I know what decades-old rockcrapper body odor smells like,* he thought. *Guess I can cross that off my to-do list.*

"So miners came here in a cave-in?" he asked.

"Yeah, or to hide during an attack. If you didn't know your way through, the mining tunnels were deadly. If someone was trying to take your rock, all you needed to do was hunker down long enough for them to decimate themselves, then come out and finish off whoever was left."

"That happen a lot when you were a kid?"

"Me? Naw. My grandfather, though, he had tales to tell. He's the one who showed me around the old tunnels, made sure I knew them. Paranoid old gitz. Best grandfather ever."

"Mine taught me to fish," Fergus said.

"To what?" Bale asked.

"Never mind. What just happened? Katra—"

"—wouldn't have done what she did if she didn't already count herself dead. I always said that woman had a spine of titanium." Bale was rummaging through the cabinets, came out with a small box, and jacked it straight into the room's control panel. "Signal's bad this deep in, but I left this booster last time I was here. Hang on while I see if we can get any news."

Fergus hung near the airlock, waiting. *What if this is a setup?* he wondered. He had everything Mr. Harcourt would need to take Gilger's ship for himself; all the man would need to do was keep him prisoner here and make him crack the code. *Then he could just leave my body in this stinkhole for eternity.*

For an arms dealer, Harcourt hadn't seemed a particularly dishonest type. If that was a contradiction . . . well, Fergus was a similarly contradictory thief. Besides, Mattie Vahn had trusted Harcourt; that shouldn't have mattered, but it did.

"Shit," Bale said eventually. "Comms are messed, probably blocked, but I reached a friend here inside the Rock where the local signal is strong enough to get through. Gurne and Mr. Harcourt got away, but there was a lot of fire from rockside chasing them out. Word is there's fighting inside Blackcans; Vinsic must be trying to take control of it."

"Why Vinsic?"

"Blue stripes. That's Vinsic's House color."

"The one who called out to us, though—he had to have been Gilger's."

Bale's eyebrows went up. "Why?"

"I said, *Name your ken*—name your family. It's a Luceatan thing. Sort of means 'Promise on the name of your family.' He and the guy who was holding Katra both had Luceatan accents."

Bale slung himself into one of the hammocks. "You're right. And I didn't even notice at the time," he said. "Here's my best guess: Gilger freaked out about your machine, because of course he's guilty as hell of blowing up that cable car. So he blocks the experiment, but maybe he's not sure he'll get there in time or if you could still pick up something, so he arranges for a dive-bomber to take you and the machine out."

"Makes sense so far," Fergus said.

"The complication is that Mr. Harcourt is there too. If Gilger tries but fails to kill you both, he's got an open war on his hands he can't easily win."

"Right. But the alternative is running the risk I could prove he was responsible for the deaths of Mattie Vahn and thirty-seven people on Rattletrap," Fergus said. "So he frames Vinsic for the attack?"

"Vinsic's been keeping to himself more than usual the last half standard or so. I've seen fewer of his people out and around Cernee, but I didn't really think about it until now."

"Some of his top people have gone missing."

"How long did you say you've been here?"

"About three days," Fergus said. "I read up."

"I guess you did." Bale shook his head. "So maybe he and Gilger have been going after each other and we just didn't know it. Or Gilger wants Mr. Harcourt and Vinsic at odds with each other for some other reason. Either way, I don't like it."

"So far, me neither."

"Taking out Katra is not just the children squabbling in the crèche anymore, that's one of the kids killing Nursie. Whatever chance there was of this getting settled with only a few heads knocked together is gone. This isn't going to end well."

Bale floated close enough to a wall to grab a cabinet. He opened it, sending off a cloud of dust, took out decrepit packs of survival rations one by one, and looked at their labels. Shrugging, he put them all back in. "I need to tell my people that the ambush was Luceatans. If we can get word back to Leakytown, we've got a point-to-point there that can talk directly to the Wheels no matter how fouled up the comms are. Mr. Harcourt will know what to do. You're safe here, but it's hard to do much of anything useful in a cave. And now your weird junk machine is destroyed."

"It's complicated," Fergus said, "but the machine doesn't really matter."

"Then *why*—No, don't tell me. Do you trust me and want to stick with me for a while, or do you want me to try to get you back to Bugrot to fend for yourself?"

Fergus looked around the old room. Prison, tomb, or sanctuary? "You can get me out of here?"

"I can get you out of the tunnels right now and let you go your own way in Mezz Rock, if that's what you want, but it's dangerous. I wouldn't recommend it, but I don't know if you have any reason to trust me beyond my honest face."

Nothing had gone right from the moment Fergus had crossed into Cernee's Halo. *What if I get these people killed? What if they get me killed?*

"Is Bugrot safe?" he asked.

"I don't know. I don't know what's happening out there," Bale said. "Are you willing to wait here at least long enough for me to contact our people and get more information?"

"What if something happens to you?" Fergus asked.

Bale grinned. "Nothing's going to happen to me. This is home. Your call, though."

Adrenaline was pounding through Fergus like a million jittery lemmings on stampede. He didn't like this place at all, but couldn't think of anywhere else to go. And the clock was ticking, counting down the time until his window to respond to the handshake expired. Once that passed, Gilger would know they'd made a fool of him with the "prototype." *I can't spend my forty-eight hours running away. I need Harcourt just as much as he needs me.*

"Okay," he said. "Do it."

"Good. Sorry to leave you bored stuck in here."

"It's okay. I have some things to think through," Fergus said. "But if I need to get out before you come back, tell me which way to go."

"I can drop a map to your pad," Bale said. "Uh, if you get hungry . . ."

"Yes?"

". . . don't try any of the stuff in the cabinets. Gave us kids the shits for a week when we tried it, and I'm sure it hasn't aged its way to better."

"Great," Fergus said. "Be careful out there."

Bale gave a weary thumbs-up, pulled his face shield down, and cycled himself out one of the other airlocks.

Chapter 9

◆◆◆

As soon as Fergus was alone, the abandoned emergency shelter began to feel like a trap. He'd been in tougher places before, but always with information, with an idea of what he'd gotten himself into. He flung himself in lazy circles in the hammock until dizziness made him give up and stare for a long time at what he was fairly sure was the floor. The air systems had kicked in, and whatever particulate dust had been lazily cluttering the stale air now swirled around, slowly drawn toward the vents by whatever paths seemed to involve drifting past his nostrils as many times as possible.

He sneezed at the floor, then made a rude gesture at it before turning himself back up to face the ceiling. Not that it made any difference in the shelter's dismal landscape. *You've never failed a job*, he told himself. *You've never failed to get yourself out of whatever mess you were in. You are all you need. Get over the fear and be useful.*

He pulled his handpad out of his pocket and turned it on. It had decrypted the signal *Venetia's Sword* had sent back.

Moose
Syrup of figs
Ring Me
Tot
McFadden's Row
C'ga A¢
Pluto

And that was the handshake. Seven keys. He had forty-six and a half hours left to find the right response to each one. If he did it, the ship was his. If he didn't . . .

Breathe, he told himself. *Just think about the keys. Let them settle and roll around in your memory. You know billions of useless things; something will stick. And you know the Shipmakers themselves; that can't hurt.*

He laid the pad against his chest, crossed his hands over it, and closed his eyes. Eventually enough dust cleared that he stopped sneezing and fell into a light doze.

Something needle-sharp jabbed him in the neck. Slapping at it, he came away with a small, dark, chitinous thing that leapt from his hand. It hit the wall, instantly got its feet under it, and skittered away. A line of ball-roaches was creeping along the hammock and over his body.

"Gah! Gowan!" he shouted, brushing them off with fast swipes.

Adrenaline and the throbbing pain of the sting kept him wide awake and twitching until Bale finally reappeared.

"What's the news?" Fergus asked.

Bale rubbed one hand over his exhausted face. "Getting you out of here isn't going to be easy. Someone's jamming the public comms all over Cernee—by now, probably all sides are just to level the field—and word is the Governor is going nuts about Katra. Authority is shutting down all the lines in and out of Central. It won't be long before the entire inner Halo is either under martial law or at war. In the meantime, I can't tell what's going on here in the Rock, but I was chased twice. I've seen a few of Gilger's people in their own colors and at least a dozen in Vinsic's. That's an awful lot of stolen or forged suits, if that's what it is."

"Maybe Gilger bought off Vinsic's men? He did that with his old boss, Tamassi."

"You've been here three days?"

"Well, probably four now," Fergus said.

"Ahuh. With the number of them here, either they've got something else going on or they're pretty sure we're not off the Rock yet and they really want us. Want *you*. Locals aren't cooperating just on principle—most everyone here is a rockcrapper or descended from one, and every family has lost someone to raids or hostile takeover attempts. No one's going to give us up voluntarily, but it's only a matter of time before someone points them at the old mining tunnels, hoping they'll come in here and meet a bad end just like in the good old days. We need to get out."

"And Harcourt?"

"Comm signal around the Wheels is fouled just like everywhere else, so we're relying on point-to-point right now. One of our people in Blackcans reported that she saw Mr. Harcourt's ship come in. No one's heard anything out of Blackcans since then."

"That can't be good."

"It's a huge fucking mess, no one knows anything, and it's all just guesses and bad information," Bale said. "None of us ever thought Gilger would try something this big."

Fergus let the man sit and stare into nothing but his own unhappiness for a while, then gently cleared his throat. "If we need to get out of here," he said, "is there a place we can go where we'll be safe?"

"I don't want to be safe. I want to be back at the Wheels doing my job," Bale said, and kicked off the wall for emphasis.

"If you can get me off this rock, I can take care of myself, and you can go do whatever you need to."

Bale thought for a minute. "We have a safe house in Boxhome. It's a ways around the Halo, though," he said. "My brother still lives here in the Rock, so we'll go there first. I need to borrow a suit, because I'm a walking target in Mr. Harcourt's stripes. As for you . . ." He looked Fergus up and down. "I don't suppose you could try to be shorter?"

"Not really."

"Yeah. The more we keep under cover, the better. Got your stuff?"

Fergus finished checking his things, tucked his hand-pad back inside his suit pocket, and slung his pack over his back. "Ready."

Bale pointed at the last airlock. "That way. Follow me carefully; the rock is unstable once we get out of the shelter. Stay away from the edges," he added. "Some places are sharp."

He cycled himself out, and Fergus followed. Bale's handlight threw jagged shadows across the old rock. Fergus turned on his own light to dispel the fear that things were creeping toward him in the dark. He could feel the welt of the ballroach sting even through the many-layered material of his exosuit.

The miners had left behind the pull cable when they'd abandoned this section of the Rock. Suspended from one wall, they could move themselves along it through the tunnels. Several convoluted twists and turns later, Bale drifted to a slow stop. "Careful up here," he said. "We have to go through an old cave-in, then through a safety gate that opens onto a live passage. I'll go first as soon as the way is clear, and I'll let you know when you can come through. When I tell you, move fast. Got it?"

"Got it."

"Okay." The tunnel turned, and ahead of them was a massive jumble of stone wedged into a suffocatingly small area. Without hesitation, Bale threw himself into one of the many dark voids, his feet disappearing as if he'd just been swallowed whole.

Fergus pulled himself forward to where the cable had been bent and permanently interred in stone. He tried to shine his light in, but it didn't seem to penetrate more than centimeters.

On one of those rare occasions when his father had paid him any direct attention, he'd tucked Fergus in bed and told him about traveling as a kid with his own Da, and the time they went to the city of Arles to explore the catacombs. He'd tried repeatedly to impart the level of darkness to Fergus. *Like a cloudy night with no moon or stars, Dadaidh?* he'd asked, and his father shook his head, either angry or disappointed with his lack of understanding, and did not bring it up again.

One hand on the lip of the hole, Fergus turned off his handlight and let the nothingness press in around him. *Like this, Da?* he thought. *Although you had gravity and tour guides and Grandfather for company. How dark is this compared to the bottom of the Scottish Inland Sea?*

"Come now, through the rock." Bale's voice startled him out of his thoughts.

Fergus propelled himself into the hole. It was a thin, twisty tube, but not as ragged as the tunnel he'd left. Pulling himself out the far side, he was bathed in dim light seeping through cracks in the safety gate ahead. "I'm through," he replied.

"Hold where you are. People in the tunnel. When I give the all clear, pull the gate toward you from the left— it pivots, and the lock is disabled—and come through as quickly as you can. Once you're out, try to look like you belong here."

"Right." Fergus brushed dust off his suit, and waited.

"Go."

He grabbed the gate. It swung open exactly as Bale had said it would. Slipping through, he let it close with a soft thud behind him and took hold of one of the many tunnel cables. Bale pointed. "We go that way. It's longer but less crowded."

When at last they reached a residential area, Bale stopped just around a bend near one of several nondescript doors. "This is my brother's place. He's not part of Mr. Harcourt's crew, so I'd appreciate it if you didn't mention him to anyone or say you came here," Bale said. He pressed the doorchime. "Stinky, it's me. Let me in?"

A few moments later, a voice replied, "That you, Tig? Hang on."

Bale frowned. He reached into a suit pocket, pulled out a small energy pistol, and checked the charge on it. "Trouble," he whispered.

"How can you tell?"

"He's never called me Tig in my life."

"Is that your first name?"

"Yeah, but he's my big brother, you know? He *always* calls me Smelly or Meatbag or Loser. You have brothers?"

"No."

"Then you wouldn't understand." Bale motioned for Fergus to pull himself back behind him as the door clicked and slid open. A man who looked much like Bale, only slightly older and thinner, peered out. "Tig? You have someone with you?" he asked.

"Just a friend," Bale said. He lifted the pistol up slightly from where he'd concealed it beneath his other arm, and the other man gave an almost imperceptible nod. *Yes.*

Bale backed up, planted his feet on the wall of the corridor opposite the door, and shot himself into the room with force. There was a shout of surprise, cut off mid-cry by the thud of two people colliding. Fergus peered around the corner to see Bale struggling midair with one man while another had his arm around Bale's brother's neck. Both attackers had blue stripes.

The man holding Bale's brother pulled out a small pistol. Bale's brother elbowed him sharply in the ribs, sending the man back into the wall. The shot went wide and left a small blackened circle above the doorway where Fergus floated.

"Asshole! Don't kill that one!" the man fighting with Bale shouted at his partner.

Fergus reached around the doorframe, grabbed a lamp from where it was magged to the wall, and slung it across the room at the attacker who had fired. It connected with the man's head, knocking him into a dazed somersault. The other attacker drew his own pistol. Bale grabbed his arm with both hands and flexed, sending them both into another spin. Fergus ducked as another wild shot went right over his head.

The two men were in a slow roll in the middle of the

room, fighting for control of the pistol. The attacker wrapped his legs around Bale's torso to give himself more leverage. At the same time, his free hand reached behind him and pulled something from a pocket on his suit. With a quick jerk of the wrist, he flipped it open to reveal a short serrated blade.

"Knife!" Fergus shouted. He grabbed a wallbar and pivoted around so he could push off and intercept. Bale tried to pull himself away, but the man tightened his grip with his legs and bent his pistol elbow, holding him just long enough to ram the knife up between Bale's ribs. Bale went limp, gasping, hands opening and closing in spasms.

The man let go of both knife and Bale. He was grinning as he placed the pistol muzzle against Bale's head.

"No!" Bale's brother shouted. He kicked out, sending both himself and the attacker in opposite directions. The attacker hit the wall and spun around. The smile was gone. Raising the pistol again, his gaze was intent on the two brothers in the center of the room.

Fergus killed the room lights. *One, two*, he counted to himself. Time for the moment of surprise, for Bale's brother to start pulling the both of them out of the line of fire. Time for the attacker to reach up and turn on full infrared on his goggles.

Three. He flipped the lights back on.

The attacker flung his arm up over his eyes as he waved the pistol, aimless and frantic, in a sweep in front of him. Bale's brother had shoved upward from the floor, pulling Bale toward the ceiling. Fergus ducked down low and kicked off the wall with everything he had, slamming into the attacker's midsection and sending him flying backward again. The man's head collided with a wall cabinet with a sharp crack, and he let go of his pistol and curled up, no longer moving under his own power.

His own momentum checked by the collision, Fergus grabbed a wallbar and snagged the pistol out of the air, then spun around, looking for the brothers. Small drops of blood curled around the room and over to the side wall, marking the path they'd taken. Bale was slumped to one side, pressed into a grippy chair.

"Is he . . .?"

"Not yet," Bale's brother said, one foot hooked under the chair, trying to apply pressure. "I need to get him to help. What's your business with my brother?"

"He was trying to get us off Mezzanine Rock," Fergus said. "He came here to borrow a suit so he wouldn't stand out as one of Harcourt's men. We knew we were being hunted."

"Yeah. They've been here for an hour, waiting for you. Toss me that energy pistol?"

Fergus turned it handle-out and gave it a gentle push across the room. Bale's brother plucked it out of the air and, briefly letting go of his brother, shot both of the attackers. Meeting Fergus's eyes, his expression was unapologetic. "They'd have killed us. Now there's two less fighters in Cernee to worry about, and even here it'll take a few days for Vinsic to replace them."

"They may be Gilger's men in stolen suits," Fergus said.

"Well, not that one. He's Vinsic's guy through and through." Bale's brother pointed at the dead man Fergus had kicked into the shelf.

"You sure?"

"Sure like the sun keeps shining. Vinsic broke up a mine strike on Kneewhack by having this guy and his friends shove the supes into vacuum one by one until the team gave in. I've owed him for years for that. Help me."

Fergus pushed off the wall. "What do you need me to do?"

"Put your hand over the wound and press as hard as you can."

"Got it." Fergus braced himself against the back of the chair, and when Bale's brother lifted up his hand, he slipped his own into place. "His suit's not self-sealing," he said, noticing it at last.

"No. Idiot's suit hasn't been working right for nearly a quarter now, but he won't spend money on himself, and he's too proud to ask his boss for a new one." Bale's brother was rummaging through a box of supplies. He came up with a small spray can of disinfecting emergi-skin and grunted. "This will have to do. On the count of three, lift your hand up so I can spray this straight in through the hole. One. Two. Three."

On three, Fergus pulled his hand away, releasing more blood into the room, and Bale's brother jammed the noz-zle through the tear and emptied the entire can onto the wound.

Tentatively he pulled the nozzle out and waited. One drop of blood pooled at the corner of the tear, but noth-ing more. "I've got to take him for help right away," Bale's brother said. "That knife wasn't big, but it was mean, and all that spray is gonna do is keep him from leaking on the outside, not the inside."

"I understand," Fergus said. "Where do we take him?"

"Sorry, not 'we.' You said it yourself: you're being hunted. You need to get off the Rock on your own, you understand? I can't help you, and if you wait here, some-one's going to come back looking for these two. I'm sorry, but you have to leave."

"It's okay," Fergus said. "I don't even know your name."

"Tobb."

"I'm Fergus. Take care of your brother; he saved my life."

"If you didn't save his in return, it was a damned good try," Tobb answered. He wrapped one arm up under his brother's armpit and across his chest, holding him gently but firmly. Bale was pale but breathing. "Security is go-ing to be full of questions. Is there anything you'd like me to tell them?"

Fergus glanced back at the two dead men. "It was two men, and one escaped with a hostage. You don't know any more than that."

"I certainly don't," Tobb said. "Someday, if we meet

under better circumstances, you can tell me if this was worth his life."

"By then maybe I'll know," Fergus said. Tobb slid the door open with his free hand, grabbed the corridor pull, and took off down the hall with his brother slung over his shoulder.

Fergus closed the door and contemplated the two bodies. Then, taking in a deep breath, he floated over to the taller one and began removing his exosuit.

He left Tobb's residence cautiously, keeping an eye out for anyone in the hall, but things were quiet. *Everyone is staying in, waiting for the trouble to die down,* he thought. That was good for moving undetected, but it meant that if he ran into one of the roving groups of armed men, there weren't going to be any crowds to hide in. Not that hiding would be easy anyway while pulling a corpse along behind him.

He tucked the body of the guy whose suit he'd stolen securely behind the safety gate to the old abandoned tunnel. A few days in the tunnels would be enough for the dead man to lead people to him, but until then, Fergus needed the time.

If Bale didn't make it . . .

Then what? he asked himself. *I'm just a thief.* He needed to get off Mezzanine Rock without anyone else trying to kill him, then hunker down somewhere safe long enough to figure out the handshake keys.

He checked his wrist, where two comms sat side by side. The dead man's had been biometrically keyed to its owner, but the reset was beneath a feeble lock Fergus could crack in his sleep before he was a teenager. He wished it would start talking, tell him what was going on out there, but one or both sides were still jamming the signals. Wherever Bale's safe house was on Boxhome, he had no way of finding it now. He needed time to work his way through the puzzle that *Venetia's Sword* had given him. Already he knew two answers and had a good guess at a third; there was always a pattern, so if he could get a fourth, the pieces should start falling into place. Then he'd just need to get close enough to the ship to broadcast the keys back to it, and this would all be over.

Bugrot probably wasn't safe to return to. Leakytown, though, was big enough to hide in and close enough to Gilger's territory to make a fast run from when he was ready. Forty-one hours left.

Bundled up inside his bursting-at-the-seams pack was the stolen blue-striped suit. He might not be able to infiltrate Gilger's crew, but if Gilger and Vinsic were working together, he might just get close enough to get his ship after all.

Chapter 10

◆──────◆

gren him. A moment later he turned and had a good ... so it think the theory should start falling into place ... hen he'd find ... ... the back to it, and the would-be ... Harper probably wasn't able to return to ... Was he enough to hide in and cross ...

Fergus backtracked through the abandoned tunnels, taking a short rest in the old emergency shelter. The ballroaches had already recolonized the hammock. If anyone else had been there since he and Bale left, there was no sign of it, but he didn't stick around any longer than necessary. It took him a few tries to find the path back into the cargo tunnels. Once there, he sat for some time in the small bypass, feeling for the vibrations of crates being loaded and timing how long it took them to go whizzing past. Once he had the pattern down, he moved.

Whoever had decided on the spacing between the cargo bypasses and maintenance niches liked to live dangerously, Fergus decided the third time he barely made it clear of the tunnel before a large crate flew past at crushing speed.

He reached an outlet into one of Mezzanine Rock's other cable terminals and was lurking just inside the gate waiting for the platform to empty when he felt the distinct rumble of another crate heading his way. Nowhere else to go, he pulled himself out of the cargo tunnel and into the middle of a small group of startled people.

"Sorry," he explained. "Lost a dare."

Before anyone could call security, he sealed his face shield, pushed past them across the platform, and cycled out through the envelope. The external platform was empty. Two lines connected here, but he had no idea which platform he was on, much less where they went.

Along the platform's edge, a lone flystick was locked to a rack, painted with purple glittery starbursts. Fergus took his kit out of his pack, cracked the lock on the flystick, and caught it as it popped loose. When he powered up the 'stick, the starbursts lit up and miniature holographic fireworks in glowing rainbow colors appeared all around him. He pushed off the platform and fired up the 'stick's engine, wanting nothing more at that moment than to be far away from that platform as quickly as possible.

The flystick was surprisingly well powered. He spiraled out and around Mezzanine Rock, trying to get his bearings, until he reached a platform sealed off with hullfoam. The view from there was familiar: a single distant hab, the thinning lights of the outer Halo beyond. *Blackcans.*

It gave him the point of orientation he needed. To the right of Blackcans was a tiny, indistinct blob that he was certain must be Leakytown. Thumbing the 'stick up to full, he cringed as it blew little puffy purple clouds of holo-glitter in his wake. *Please tell me there's an off switch,* he thought, cycling through the 'stick's menus in increasing desperation. He didn't find it before the glitter cut out; apparently the effect was triggered by acceleration.

I'm being punished for something, he decided.

Now that he was moving in a straight line toward Leakytown, mingling into a small flood of people fleeing the inner Halo on or along the lines, he had time to think about the handshake keys. "Ring Me!" was the tagline of the main character, Rocket, in a 40s 3-D interactive toon set on Mimas. It was also precollapse American Earth slang for requesting that someone contact you. If there were other obvious associations, he couldn't think of them. *Syrup of figs* was nineteenth-century Earth rhyming slang for "wigs"; it was a stretch, but there was a villain on some toonshow from when he was a kid named Mr. Wigs.

If the theme was toons, then *Moose* was obvious.

The comm he'd stolen off the dead man lit up, interrupting his train of thought. "Team Blue Five, this is

Blue Base. Check in," some unknown, unhappy voice spoke in his ear bud in a cloud of static. "You're late for contact."

Another voice responded. "This is Blue Four. We lost contact with Five and haven't been able to reestablish."

"Do you know the status of the shipment?" Blue Base said.

"Target Two is at a local med center. Rumor is Five acquired Target One, but we haven't been able to verify or locate. Golds watching the platforms say they spotted Target One leaving the Rock solo and sent a team to pursue."

Fergus glanced over his shoulder at the swarm of Halo refugees behind him. If the signal had gotten through the jam, that meant he wasn't far from a "Blue" transmitter/repeater.

"We don't want the Golds to take Target One," Blue Base said. "Check in with Blue Twelve; they are collabing with the Golds and may have more current info. Twelve is outside the circle, Blue Four. Repeat that you understand."

"Blue Twelve is outside the circle, Base. Got it. Will be back in touch in fifteen."

"Thanks, Four. Base out."

Silence again. *Outside the circle?* Did that mean Cernee's inner Halo or something else entirely? It seemed obvious he was Target One, but if so, why would Vinsic want him?

Glancing back again, he thought he caught a glimpse of gold. He could break from the pack and go to full burn, but once out of the crowd he'd be an obvious target.

"Base, this is Blue Four." His stolen comm came back to life, the signal clearer. "We have one man confirmed down from Blue Five, one missing. No sign of Target One. Blue Twelve reports the Golds left, quote, 'on a kill.' Should we pursue?"

"Negative. I've got Blue Three at the Leakytown platform waiting. If Target One is on the line, we'll get him first. In case he's not, keep working the Rock and try to locate the other half of Five."

"Will do, Base."

"Base out."

Fergus could speed up and get caught by the Blues or slow down and get killed by the Golds, but he couldn't see any way he could avoid them both. *Think, Fergus, think.* There was always a way out. Wasn't there?

Someone on a 'stick suddenly veered out of the crowd. Dreading the worst, Fergus looked back to see that a two-man had collided with a fast-moving four-man and become caught on it, a small cloud of debris spreading into space around them. People were in frantic disarray trying to avoid each other and the mess. It was a good distraction, the only one he might get. He pulled in just ahead of the thickest part of the chaos and then turned at a sharp angle away from the line, shut down his 'stick and suit lights, and went completely dark just as he moved out into empty space.

He was drifting away from the line at a good clip. Looking back, he couldn't see anyone following him, but there was no guarantee that someone else hadn't just done the same trick.

Ahead, the darkness of space was broken by a narrow band where the light of Cernee's white star leaked between the sunshields. He hunched over on the 'stick as he sailed across it, desperately hoping no one was looking his way. Once he was safely back in the shadows, he stared behind him to see if anyone else crossed the light. If they did, he didn't spot them.

Well, shit, he thought. *I got away?*

He had to change his trajectory to hit Leakytown on the far side; the hab was big enough that he doubted the Blues could have the entire thing covered. He reached down to thumb on the 'stick's engines, then froze, one gloved finger above the glitter-covered starter. If he hit that button, everyone within a thirty-degree arc was going to know exactly where he was.

He coasted, still moving fast, toward the edge of the Halo and open space beyond. His oxygen supply was good, his suit and the 'stick well charged. *Once I'm far enough out, the light show won't be as noticeable,* he thought. *Then if I turn around and come right back in, I should be okay.*

Leakytown passed by. To his left he could make out first Blackcans, then the Wheels where it protruded past the last of the sunshields. A small armada of ships surrounded it in a defensive line. Beyond it, like a wolf outside the sheep pen, the familiar shape of *Venetia's Sword* prowled past, a scattering of one-mans trailing in its wake. Fergus's heart ached to see the ship so near, so out of reach.

He had thirty-nine hours left to find a way to close that distance.

As he watched, a small torpedo shot from *Venetia's Sword* toward Harcourt's hangar where it hung off the Wheels. Covering fire from multiple directions caught it, and there was a brief flash as it was destroyed well away from its target.

The Wheels was defended and holding. He hoped Mari was safe and sound with the rest of her odd family, not trapped on the other side of the lines somewhere.

Unbidden, he thought of Dru, who had been about Mari's age when the Mars Colonial Authority dragged her off for being part of the Free Marsies, for committing acts against the government that he himself had participated in. He'd been even younger, knew nothing, could do nothing, but he still felt the guilt like a stone deep in his chest. *Never again.* The only life he was willing to risk, if he had any choice in the matter, was his own, and whatever bad end he inevitably met, he'd rather face it alone.

Speaking of bad ends, something Mauda had said struck him. Momentum had carried him past the nebulous borders of Cernee's outer Halo. There seemed to be nothing in front of him now except distant stars and emptiness, but he knew that wasn't quite true.

He needed quiet to think through the remaining keys, someplace where no one was going to look for him. He didn't have time to be picky about it, but even still . . .

Maybe it won't be there anymore, and I'll just turn around, he thought. But no, with his goggles on full zoom he could make out the dim shape against the stars, a medium-sized cylinder floating untethered, spinning slowly out beyond the thin edge of Cernee: the abandoned hab, Turndown.

Mauda had said it had been dark for more than a decade. He was certain spore ticks couldn't live that long. *Could they?* Fear crept into his thoughts on tiny black parasite legs, and he began to feel itchy, cruel pinpricks of his imagination.

He fired up the 'stick for a half second to adjust his trajectory. The void around him had just started to fill with scintillating gold smiley faces when he shut it down again. As soon as he was close enough, he reached out and grabbed onto the hab as it rotated past. He pulled himself along a bar that ran horizontally between solar panels until he reached the end of the cylinder and found Turndown's airlock.

Fergus took a deep breath and pressed the open button. Nothing happened for a long time. Then there was a faint grinding, and the outer lock opened.

The surface of Turndown was almost completely covered with solar panels; there should have been plenty of power unless they'd intentionally shut it down. *Wouldn't you?* he thought. *Die quickly of cold and asphyxiation, or slowly be eaten from the inside out by spore tick larvae?*

He climbed in, bringing his 'stick with him. Fear mounting, he tried to drop his shoulders and relax as the outer door closed and sealed. The inner door opened onto a dimly lit space, lights returning to life in tiny increments. He didn't know what he'd expected, but somehow he hadn't thought about actual *people* bodies. One floated, slumped over, on each side of the airlock door, suits on but face shields up, pistols in hand and trails of ice crystals encrusting their desiccated eyes and cheeks. On the other side of the room, several more hung near the far door like a macabre mobile; unsuited, their flesh was pocked, missing in ragged chunks. The two at the airlock must have been guarding the exit to make sure no one fled and carried the infestation with them to the rest of Cernee.

Pushing his way carefully across the room, Fergus ducked under and around the bodies and opened the far door. Turning his face away quickly, he fought to keep from throwing up. He closed his eyes, took deep, steadying breaths, and then made himself look again.

Families. Not anonymous gray corpses or casualties in battle, but small children in gaily colored dresses and overalls. One small girl, still in her mother's arms, legs consumed, throat slit for mercy.

Bad things happened in space, bad stuff just like this, all the time. He knew it, knew all about it in a detached, objective way, but he had never thought he'd come face-to-face with it quite like this. Here was death in all its ugliness, an entire community preserved for eternity as if the pain of these people's last moments were some grand, gruesome exhibit.

I shouldn't have come here, he thought, far too late.

Grimly, he turned the floating corpses in the airlock vestibule and gently propelled them through the door into the inner room, then did the same for the two watchers by the door. "Be with your loved ones," he said out loud, as if the words could matter to anyone but himself.

The chamber now free of the dead, he leaned against the door and wept, in fear and horror and loss, for the first time in a very long time.

Eventually he slept, then woke from terrible dreams of too many arms and hands dangling down around him, corpses crowding the ceiling trying to pull him up into their midst. He shook his head, trying to shake out the vision that felt like a physical weight inside his skull. He had never had cause to regret his bottomless pit of a memory as much as he did now. *Think about something else,* he told himself. *You'll revisit this place in your dreams enough as it is.*

He checked his suit display: four and a half hours of sleep, give or take. It wasn't enough, but it would have to do; he was not willing to slip down into that nightmare world again until he was well away from here. He needed distraction.

Taking out his pad, Fergus checked the keys again. *Moose, Syrup of figs, Ring Me, Tot, McFadden's Row, C'ga A¢, Pluto.*

McFadden's Row clicked. Another toon; another old Earth reference. That clinched it for him. He already had the first three, the fifth, and the last. *C'ga A¢* was a humanized transliteration of Celekai for *Help us,* famous words exchanged at humanity's First Contact, although he couldn't think of any toon associations with it. He set his pad to search his internal database for any animated productions made or set on Io Colony around the end of the twenty-second century.

That left *Tot,* a complete mystery. Fergus built a separate query for that. Then he closed his pad, let his eyes drift around the room, couldn't help but wonder what it had been like to die here, to know everyone you loved was going to die too, and horribly, for no reason at all.

Turndown's power reserves were slowly rebuilding, but air and heat stayed resolutely off. Once the airlock console had powered up enough to become responsive, it showed that they'd been intentionally disabled. Maybe that had been some small mercy at the end. He couldn't enable them from here, and he didn't want to; no matter what assurances his knowledge-base gave him about the maximum resilience of spore ticks to vacuum and the cold of space, he had zero interest in testing it.

The airlock vestibule had everything he needed in the short term except peace of mind. He powered up an outlet from the console and plugged in the flystick to recharge. Then he activated an air recharge station and second outlet. It took some doing to plug both into his suit without taking it off, but after some contortions he found himself floating cross-legged midair, loosely tangled in the cables.

Tot. How many thousands of cartoons over the centuries had featured small kids? It seemed way too broad a clue for the usual Shipmaker imagination, and as Fergus expected, his pad declared too many hits and asked for refinement. How could he refine it, though? There were no other clues. Unless *Tot* meant something else entirely.

A flash in his peripheral vision caught his eye, and he'd spent enough time thinking about spore ticks that he freaked, letting go of his pad and flailing against the cables, before he realized it was the comm unit on his suit flashing a tiny yellow light.

Incoming signal? he wondered. *No, it's the Boolean alert—*

"Hell!" Fergus swore. He unplugged himself from the wall and fish-swam across the room, putting the entire hab back into total shutdown. In moments he was floating in silence, everything pitch dark except that one insistent yellow light. Hardly breathing, he moved his hand off the wall panel and covered it up. *They can't see in here,* he told himself. *They can't see one tiny light through two meters of metal and insulation. You're being stupid and paranoid.* Still, he could not bring himself to move his hand away again.

Thirty-three and a half hours left. It was all he could do not to scream in frustration.

Gilger wouldn't dare blow up the cable, Mother Vahn had said. Gilger wouldn't dare risk a coup, Harcourt had said. The Asiig only fly by a couple of times a standard at most, everyone had said, and now here they were poking around Cernee for the *third* time since he had arrived barely more than a week ago.

It's like nobody here has any bloody fucking clue about anything, he thought. *Do I have any good information at all?*

Not that anyone had good information when it came to the Asiig. There were aliens, and then there were *aliens*. For all that humanity had moderately good relationships with dozens of other sentient species in the galaxy and understandings of peaceable distrust with even more, the Asiig were the only ones Fergus knew of that genuinely terrified the shit out of everyone equally. It was difficult to know what a species wanted when they returned your ambassadors to you turned inside out. Even the Bomo'ri condescended to terse exchanges—usually complaints—with humanity now and then, when they couldn't get someone else to do it for them.

Fergus pulled himself over to a small portal window to the outside and peered out at the universe as Turndown slowly rotated through it. Leakytown came into sight first, then Blackcans and the Wheels. What activity there had been, the flyby had put an end to it; everyone had scampered back into hiding when the alert had gone out like bugs back into the shadows.

Don't think about bugs.

The Wheels passed out of his narrow field of view, leaving him nothing but empty space to stare at. Eventually Leakytown appeared again, then the Wheels. Something seemed different, but nothing was obviously moving. He watched, face against the glass. On the next pass he spotted it: a small two-man, running dark, heading towards the Wheels obliquely from behind Leakytown.

Fergus checked his comm. Either he was out of range or the jam extended even this far. He had no way to warn anyone.

Or did he?

He threaded his way out of the vestibule, doing his best not to see anything in the dark that he'd have to add to his burgeoning stock of nightmare material. Surfaces parallel to the exterior were scattered with clumps of black dust, deposited there over the years by the hab's gentle rotation, and it was only when he dipped a boot down and accidentally stirred it that he realized it wasn't dust at all but pinhead-sized, newly hatched spore ticks. Deprived of living hosts, oxygen, and heat, they too had died here.

Fergus was painstakingly careful not to go anywhere near the walls or floor again.

He breathed a sigh of relief when he slid open the doors into the hab's central control room and found only a single body there, tucked in a far corner with a pistol still floating near her hand. *The one who shut the air and heat off,* he guessed.

As he'd hoped, the control room had a point-to-point comm system; they only worked if you had line of sight to someone else, but they were practically unjammable. It took him a long, desperate minute to find the auxiliary power lead. An emergency fail-safe: if your hab was dead, you'd want to be able to plug in a battery so you could call for help. He pulled the lead out and jacked it in carefully to the wrist comm he'd gotten off the dead Blue Fiver. There was more than enough power there to run such a simple system. Shielding the glow of the comm display with a cupped palm, he powered the P2P on.

He still had the rotation of the hab to contend with. Timing it, he found that he had about forty-two seconds of usable visibility on the Wheels on each pass with a two-minute-fourteen-second dead zone in between.

The Wheels were just beginning to appear along the bottom edge of his view. "Uh, hello," he said as soon as the P2P locked. "This is Fergus Ferguson. You've got a two-man creeping up on you from down-spinward on a deep arc, coming from Leakytown."

A few long seconds later, a tinny voice came back out of the comm. "Who the hell are you? Are you—"

The Wheels was out of sight again. Two minutes and fourteen seconds was a very long time.

"—ello? Hello? I lost him. I think—"

"I'm here. I only have a short window. Did you get my message about the two-man?"

"Yes, thanks." This time it was Harcourt himself. "We're on it. What's your status? Where are you?"

"We were ambushed on Mezzanine Rock. Bale was badly hurt; his brother has him. I'm safe somewhere else now."

"Where—" The Wheels slid out of view again.

When the connection returned, Harcourt was still on the line. "—dark. Fergus, if you can hear me, can you see the two-man from where you are? We can't pick it up."

He peered at the display, cursing the resolution. "Got it!" he shouted with just seconds left before losing the connection again. "About thirty degrees up from parallel with the line and outside by a good margin."

The connection went dead again before he finished speaking.

"—see it now. Go." *Go where?* Fergus thought, but Harcourt didn't seem to be speaking to him this time. There was a tiny flash from one of the spindles between the Wheels, and almost simultaneously the two-man powered up, changing trajectory wildly as it accelerated.

Not fast enough. There was a brief orange ball that collapsed instantly upon itself where the two-man had been.

"Ye—!" Fergus started to yell, then, where an instant ago there had been nothing but the afterimage of an explosion, there was now an enormous black shape, like a city-block-sized triangle made of darkness. "Fuck," he finished. His knees were weak, his heart pounding in his throat as if fighting to get out. If there had been gravity, he was sure he would have fallen down.

"Uh, Fergus?" Harcourt said, his voice deathly calm. "Wherever you are, keep your head down and don't move."

The Asiig were here.

Chapter 11

◆━◆

The alien ship was utterly motionless. Even though it did nothing, showed nothing, Fergus found it difficult to take his eyes off of it. The two-minute-fourteen-second window when he couldn't see it were an agony of uncertainty. On his wrist, the yellow light blinked at a frenetic pace. *No shit,* he thought. *Thanks.*

He should have been thinking about *Tot* and *C'ga Aȼ*. He should have been planning his incursion into Gilger's territory and subsequent escape. Instead he stared at the ship during each slow turn of his cold, grim hideaway and felt as if a dozen ghosts were staring over his shoulder, weighing whose fate would be worse.

A little more than an hour later, the ship twitched, inched forward just slightly, then was gone. *Well,* Fergus thought. *There's going to be a brisk business in new underwear on this side of the Halo after that.*

The P2P crackled to life again in the short remnants of window left. "Fergus? You still out there?"

"Still out here," he said, the words catching in his dry throat. "So what's this everyone keeps telling me about the Asiig only doing flybys a couple of times a standard?"

"You tell *me,* Fergus," Harcourt said. "They haven't come this close in fifty years. Everything was quiet until you—"

The signal was gone again, but the words that didn't transmit were hardly lost on him. *He can't really think this is my fault?*

When the P2P reconnected, Harcourt spoke again. "Everyone and everything started going weird the moment you arrived at Cernee," he said. "I don't . . . I'm not accusing you of anything, but is there something you haven't told us? Some reason everything went to hell as soon as you got here?"

"Nothing," he answered. "I have nothing to do with any of this."

Although . . .

They watch us all the time, Mari had said. What if instead of teen paranoia or old-lady delusion, that was the truth? If Mother Vahn had truly had some connection to the Asiig, then maybe it was her fault, not his.

Fergus opened his mouth to say as much, but the window was closed again. *If Harcourt knew there was a connection there, he wouldn't have asked if it was me,* he realized. By the time Turndown faced the Wheels again, he'd disconnected from the P2P and shut it down. The Vahns must have had reasons for not telling Harcourt, so he wasn't going to do it for them.

He made his way back through the rooms of the dead to the airlock chamber, powered the outlets back up, and plugged his suit and air tanks back in to finish recharging.

This was why he'd left home, why he had left Mars, why he never stayed too long at the Shipyard even though the Shipmakers were the closest thing he had to friends: complications.

He waited until the airlock was on the far side from the Wheels before he cycled himself through. With the hab between him and Cernee, he fired up the 'stick. This time a storm of tiny holographic clouds rained XOXOs all around him. Squinting, he found the tiny light-source projector on the 'stick's frame and, bracing himself, pressed his thumb against it until it snapped. The light show evaporated.

He was sure the universe would make him pay for that, but he needed to be gone from this place, away from its ghosts and back among the living.

"Down" was an arbitrary, planet-born concept, but down he went, letting the 'stick carry him low away from Turndown and the Wheels. He needed to focus, get his ship, and get out of this mad place with no more entanglements.

He docked at a small rock on the outskirts whose name he didn't know. He left the purple flystick there, secured to a public hitch post with a hastily purchased lock and a ten-cred Haudie South chip wedged up under the pedal in the hopes that it would make its way back to its owner and they'd be able to repair his vandalism. From an auto-vend he rented a new flystick devoid of any kind of sparkles or special effects. Fifteen minutes after landing, he was back out in the dark.

From there, he headed obliquely back up into the Halo. He kept his eyes open, looking for signs of Gilger's or Vinsic's people, but he found none. There were a few people about, some on 'sticks, some traveling the lines on spiders, but if he was being followed, he couldn't tell.

The rock he'd left was now little more than a potato-shaped lump behind him. *I wonder if it's named Tater-Rock,* he thought. Then: *TaterRock. Tater Tots. Captain Tater, toon from Ares Three, circa 2114.*

Gotcha! If that wasn't a classic bit of Shipmaker association, he didn't know what was.

Now it was down to *C'ga A⊄ Help Us.* Thirty-one hours left.

He was passing a small residential-only hab named Dented when the comm he'd taken off Vinsic's would-be kidnapper began to hum and whistle with traces of signal breaking through. "—Gold Nine and T . . . breached the interior of Blackcans . . . preparing to disable hab defenses. Heavy resistance."

"Any Blue teams on site, Blue Two?"

"Sixteen. They're outside the circle."

"Have them fall back. Blackcans is a Gold show. The—"

"—Base. Sorry. They—Shit. Blackcans has evacuated the entire hab."

"They abandoned it?"

"No. They opened it to vacuum. They blew out their own hab."

There was a pause. "Orders is for our teams to be fully suited in hostile territory."

"I . . . I'm not entirely confident our whole team was strictly following that instruction, Base."

"And the Golds?"

"I don't know, Base. Gold Leader Ten was the first to breach the interior, and he went immediately offline. There were reports of booby traps before we lost contact with the rest of his team."

"Order any of our people still alive to get out of the area. Regroup at Beggar's Boulder. This whole thing is shitting its own boots full. If . . ."

The last few words crackled over the link before the signal faded back into maddeningly unintelligible noise.

Blackcans was too far away to make out anything happening there, but as much as Fergus had wanted to personally cuss them out when he'd passed through with Mauda, he found himself sending silent good-luck wishes in their direction as he fell into the shadow heading up into one of Leakytown's docks.

Leakytown was made from a defunct Sfazili freighter, its own shuttles grafted onto the underside of its hull like large metal boils. One of the shuttles had a gaping hole cut in the side with a line running into it, forming the entrance to a platform.

A small crowd of people were clustered inside the dock, including several families with small children. No one seemed to be going anywhere. As Fergus passed the flystick kiosk, the attendant was loudly explaining that they were *all out* and that people should *go away*.

"And where do we go?" someone shouted.

"To hell, for all I care!" the attendant screamed back.

An argument broke out over whether hell was Gilger or the Governor and which of them would take over Leakytown first. Someone at the back of the crowd pushed off a wall, angling towards Fergus. Fergus shook his head *No* and kept going. Two or three more people launched themselves in his direction.

Shit. Was he about to get mugged for his 'stick? The last thing he wanted was to be trapped here with no way off. He grabbed a wallbar with his free hand as he passed it and swung himself quickly around the corner, kicked off from a wall, took another turn, then hid in a public bathroom.

He waited in the tiny pod-shaped stall until he was sure he hadn't been followed. When he left, he was careful to avoid corridors near the docks.

It didn't take long to find a small, vacant rent-a-room and stash his things, including his now-irreplaceable 'stick. Then he pushed his way down to the hab's central market through tight, badly lit, zigzagging corridors, desperate for information and something to eat.

Most of the market was closed, but he found a few booths still open and bought a tube of tepid soup. Hanging out on the netting as he sucked at it, he watched a small, harried man and his partner arguing about whether or not to wait the crisis out or shut down their stand and risk it being looted. They had a completely random mix of worthless goods: fake plants, a brand of Sfazili candy Fergus remembered spending days trying to get unstuck from his teeth, a giant mesh bag of tennis balls, gold and silver foil gift wrap, and what seemed to be sets of sexual accessories shaped like different alien species, distorted and arranged in a rainbow of Day-Glo-colored plastic.

Right, Fergus thought. *Too bad no one I'd like to think less of me has a birthday coming up.* He wondered if the merchants could even name any of the aliens so dubiously represented. There were a good number that lived on or passed through Crossroads with its active jump point, but he'd yet to see—or expected to see, honestly—any out here in the slowspace backwaters.

He tried to distract himself from the very bad soup by considering his obstacles. He had one more key to solve and an armed uprising exploding around him, making it hard to go anywhere. Then there were the sentry bobs and mines around Gilgerstone. Getting through them was a different problem altogether. At the same time, Gilger and *Venetia's Sword* were constantly on the move.

If he caused a big enough disturbance, Fergus might scare Gilger into returning to his home base. Setting off a whole lot of the sentry bobs and mines wasn't a bad way to do it, if only he knew how.

His stomach made a sound like someone trying to smother an apoplectic cat. He recapped the half-empty soup tube and, crossing the net, pushed it into a flash recycler.

The two junk merchants were now floating nose-to-nose, shouting, and Fergus wondered if they were going to start hitting each other. *That roll of foil would make a good blunt-force weapon, although it would be a shame to dent up something that shiny,* he thought.

He paused, halfway through the motion to push off back into the hall, and appraised the merchants' inventory with a new eye. *Well, huh,* he thought.

The merchants were too intent on their argument to notice him until he tapped one on the shoulder. "I want to buy some things," Fergus said. He pointed at their display of sex toys. "Do those vibrate?"

The men stared at him. "Uh, yes," one said. "There's six different sett—"

"Would they work in vacuum?"

This earned him blinking. "Yes, but we really can't recommend—"

"How much for all of them, the foil wrap, the candy, and the tennis balls?"

"What?"

Fergus held out a hand toward their display. "I don't want the plants," he said.

"I don't—" one man began. The other punched him on the shoulder, not gently, then named a figure in Cernee cred.

Fergus countered with a third as much. "And you help me get them back to my rent-a-room as part of the deal."

"Done," the second man said before the first one could speak. "You sure you don't want the plants?"

"I'm sure," Fergus said. They handed him an uninitiated cred chip, and after checking its integrity, he keyed it to his handpad and transferred the agreed amount onto it.

"Uh, what are you going to do —" the first man finally worked up the courage to ask.

His partner elbowed him sharply. "I'm sure it's none of our business, sir," he said. "Please do recommend us to your friends for all their . . . um."

Thirteen minutes later, it was all floating in a big cloud of junk in the center of his room. The merchants fled the moment they had offloaded their wares. Fergus didn't even have to argue with them about keeping the mesh bag. If he didn't get out of Cernee soon, he was going to get a reputation.

He slid the door closed, locked it, and broke out his tool kit.

The comms intermittently crackled to life while he worked, and each time he found himself listening intently. Most of it meant little to him beyond simple scorekeeping— Gilger's and Vinsic's people were forcing their way closer to Central. Authority was laying siege to Mezzanine Rock to reclaim it. Gilger's teams made up the majority of the front lines, along with those Blue teams that were "out of the circle." Mostly it was names and places Fergus had no context for, a melee of information he could make no sense of.

"Blue Base, this is Blue Two. We intercepted Blackcans casualty reports from Gold Nine and Ten to Gold Base. Sixty percent loss, primarily due to improper exosuit protocols."

Fergus looked up sharply. Sixty percent? *Oh aye,* he thought, *and I bet he's pissed about that.*

"Are all our people out of Blackcans?"

"Yes, Base."

"Good. Make it standing orders, both inside the circle and out, to stay the hell away from any ops on or near Blackcans. If Gilger's so set on cutting the Wheels out of the Halo that he'll abandon nearly a standard of careful planning, he can do it without us."

"Got it, Base."

Cut the Wheels out of the Halo?

"Blue Base, this is Blue Four." The next message started just as Fergus was plucking another tennis ball out of the interminable-feeling mass. "We've located the other half of Blue Five. Deceased, body hidden in an old tunnel bypass."

"Blue Four, did the deceased still have his suit and comm?"

"No suit, Base. Um . . ." There was a pause. "No, body is down to civvies. Gear gone."

"Don't say anything further. I am implementing Protocol Zero. You have sixty seconds. Base out." His stolen comm went silent.

Protocol Zero?

A blue light started flashing on the comm, increasing rapidly in frequency. Nervous, Fergus unclipped it from his suit and held it as the light grew more intense. It began beeping.

Sixty seconds? What would you do if you wanted to protect yourself from people stealing comms in a battle situation? Hastily he pushed across the room and deposited the stolen comm in the smartfridge. He had just slammed the door shut when there was a muffled bang. He ducked, throwing his hands up to protect his head. When he peeked again, the door to the smartfridge was bulging outward, wisps of smoke curling through the cracks.

Well, damn. Protocol Zero. There must have been some secure sequence that needed to be entered before time expired. There went his inside intel into what was happening.

He was about a third of the way through his new art project when there was a loud pounding on his door. It startled him badly enough that he let go of his tools, sending a humming, bright orange, Veirakan-shaped vibrator sailing across the room like an obscene torpedo. He floated, frozen mid-gesture, listening. Someone must have knocked by mistake.

Bang. Another knock, then a muffled, angry voice. "Fuck you, Fergus, let me the hell in!"

Mari?! He pushed to the wall, unlocked the door, and slid it open.

Mari tumbled in, breathing hard. "Took your damned time," she said.

"I wasn't expecting company," Fergus answered. "What the hell are you doing here? *How* are you here?"

"I followed you," she said. She unfastened her exosuit's air bottles and plugged them into his room's recharger. He could see the winking red lights on them from here.

"Followed me from *where*?"

"From Mezz Rock, asshole," she said. "If you're trying to be sneaky, leaving a trail of little smiley-faced holo-stars behind you isn't what I'd call mastery of the art."

Fergus put a hand to his forehead, closed his eyes, and took a deep breath. *Should've broken the projector sooner.* "If you followed me from the Rock—"

"I was trying to find you and Bale," she said. "Bale's alive, by the way, though barely. Nice of you to ask." She had finished with her bottles and finally seemed to be noticing the mess in the room. "Um . . . Fergus?"

He shook his head. "It's complicated," he said. Then he narrowed his eyes. "You couldn't have followed me."

"Why not?"

"Because you couldn't have. You bugged my suit back when I was at the farm, didn't you?"

"Well, we couldn't let you take off with Mauda and all our crates without having some way of finding you," she said. At his expression, she held up both hands. "It's an old sleeper channel, low power, cycling eff pattern. Nothing anyone else is going to pick up unless they're already looking for it. As it is, even knowing what I was tracking, I lost you between the Rock and here. Where the fuck did you *go*?"

"I was being chased, so I went the only place I could think of where no one would look for me: Turndown."

She stared at him, her face warring to find a single expression. At last she spoke, her voice quiet. "Was it? Safe, I mean?"

"Yes and no," he said. "I . . . Look, don't ever go there. It was bad."

"Yeah. Big surprise there." Mari looked away into the room, her gaze avoiding his for a while. "I guess that explains the unmatched P2P interval. Harcourt's got a few people here; they told me you'd been in touch with him."

"About Harcourt—"

She began to pluck loose scraps of foil from the air, wrapping them around one finger of her glove, making a little ball. "He told me he'd asked you if you had anything to do with the Asiig. You didn't tell him they're around because of us," she said.

"Even assuming that it's true—which I'm in no way convinced of—it's your business," he answered. "If you haven't shared it with him, you must have good reason. Either way, it's not my place to tell. *I* know it has nothing to do with me."

She looked up from her foil ball, met his eyes again. "Thank you," she said. "It's hard, growing up being told not to trust anyone."

"You saying you trust me?"

"Don't push it," she said. "Harcourt *is* family, you know? When you have as many aunts as I do, an uncle is a nice change. That must seem strange to someone coming from a normal family."

Fergus gave a short laugh. "There are all kinds of wonderful things people tell me exist or could exist in this universe—time travel, truly sentient machines, dragons on Venus, normal families—but I haven't seen any direct evidence of any of them. My Da and I both loved my Ma more than anything else, but in the end it only ever brought us madness. We took our separate ways out."

Mari nodded. "For a while I thought we were one family, the aunts and Harcourt and Arelyn and me. But I still never told Arelyn, though I wanted to a thousand times. And now after us playing and daydreaming everything Martian for most of our lives, she's actually gone off there for real without me. It hurts being left behind, you know?"

"You didn't want to go with her?"

"I did," she said. "More than anything. But I can't. Vahns don't leave the farm."

"Mars is far away, but it's not a one-way trip. Harcourt says he still has connections there. If he was willing to let Arelyn go, he could get you there and back again safely, even if just for a visit. I suspect he'd be happy to do it."

"I want to more than anything," she said. "But I can't, not ever, and the more Harcourt and Arelyn and now you talk about it, the harder that reality becomes. It's bad enough that I'm out here running loose in Cernee. Mother understood, but Mauda would implode if she knew. She doesn't know Arelyn is gone yet. When . . ."

She trailed off, her expression tightening. "What *I* need to understand," she said at last, "is what the hell you're doing in here. Really, I can't even guess." She pointed at the orange missile thumping forlornly along the distant wall.

"I'll show you," he said. He plucked a tennis ball out of the bag. Finding his knife, he opened the blade and carefully cut a slit through the ball halfway around, making a small notch at one end of the cut. Then he reached into the open box of adult toys and pulled out the next one, a lime-green E'zon, and snapped off the head. He extracted the vibration mechanism, careful to keep the switch intact. Then he squeezed the tennis ball to open the cut and slipped the vibrator in, pulling the switch out through the notch.

"I still don't—"

He held up a hand: *Wait.* Reaching over to one wall, he unstuck the big gooey mass of candy he'd wedged there, pulling out long, sticky strands that he wrapped around the tennis ball. Then he grabbed a roll of shiny foil, cut out a square, and wrapped it around the sticky ball. "See?" he said, holding it out to her.

She took it reluctantly, found the switch, and turned it on. The ball began to shake in her hand. "I still don't get it. What's it for?"

"Gilger uses both smart mines and sentry bobs," Fergus said. "I can make seventy-two of these, and when I turn them all on and throw them out on the edge of his territory, they'll set off any mines they hit. The sentry bobs will think there's some sort of attack. Every damn alarm Gilger has is going to go off."

"But they're just balls."

"But he won't know that until someone gets out there and catches one and takes it apart. Until then, he'll have to assume his home base is in danger. He'll pull his people back, and more importantly, he's going to come running home himself. In my ship."

"What about Vinsic?"

"Vinsic has his own game. I don't know what it is, but he's less than happy about Gilger's focus being elsewhere. Gilger attacked Blackcans because he wants to cut the Wheels off from the Halo, and Vinsic wants his people far away from that."

Her eyebrows went up. "How do you know all that?"

"I took a comm off one of Vinsic's men."

"Oh!" she said. "We can use that!"

"Not any more. It self-destructed." He pointed to the blackened, warped smartfridge. "Mauda said Blackcans are friends of yours?"

"Of a sort, yeah. We did business with them from the farm."

"Why is Vinsic so afraid of them?"

"They're close allies of the Shielders. Most of the energy that feeds Cernee is generated by the sunshields. If the Shielders decided to start unplugging things . . . I don't think they would, but they *could*, and that's enough, you know? Same reason Ili is protected by holding the oxygen farms. And us? We have foil-covered balls, apparently."

"*Vibrating* foil-covered balls," Fergus said.

"You're mad, you know." Mari looked around the room again, took a deep breath, then let it out almost regretfully. "What can I do to help?"

"Are you familiar with the Celekai phrase *C'ga A¢*?"

"What?"

Right. "Never mind."

"How much time do you have left?"

He stifled a yawn. "Twenty-five hours, give or take."

"And when was the last time you slept?"

"Turndown. I haven't really wanted to sleep since."

She rolled her eyes. "Show me again how to make these?"

"Why?"

"Because the only useful thing you can do for any of us is steal Gilger's ship, and if you doze off on your way there, you're going to get caught," she said. "So I'll make some of these while you sleep, and if you start having nightmares, I'll kick you till they stop."

"I don't—"

"Did I ask? No." Mari plucked his folded knife out of the air, took a tennis ball out of the sack, and stared at him until he gave in and showed her again.

———

He woke up five hours later, corpses and neon-colored organ replicas lurking in the periphery of his mind as he pulled his way back up into consciousness. His room stank like something large and unnatural had come in and died a terrible, gassy death. "What is that *smell*?" he asked, trying to untangle himself from the hammock.

Mari held out a takeout cup. "Lunch," she said.

"You've got to be kidding." Reluctantly he took the cup from her and peered inside.

"It tastes better if you don't look at it," she added, and handed him a small pair of blue plastic tongs. She plucked her own back out of the air where she'd let them go, pulled out a mass of brownish goo from her own cup, and stuffed it in her mouth.

Fergus dipped his tongs in, and closing his eyes, put some in his mouth. When he could speak again, he said, "I think this makes the fifth time someone has tried to kill me since I got to Cernee."

"Yeah, well, it's nutritious, I'm told. I got it just for you, too."

"What is it?"

"Some Celekai thing called something like *fooge-burm*. Don't ask me to spell it. You mentioned the Celekai, so I figured it was something you were into. There's an exotic-foods vending machine two levels away, and it was one of the few still working and stocked. And it came in a two-pack."

"Lucky us," Fergus said.

She snagged the empty carton the cups had come in out of the air. "'Best *Fooge-burm* in Human Space or Out!'," she read out loud. "It's even got a cute little cartoon character on the box, see?"

"I don't—" he started to say, then blinked. "There's what?" He snagged the box out of her hand and turned it around. A cartoonized alien in Celekai garb held out his hands over a stylized giant bowl of brown stringy goo. Over his head, it said, "Mr. Veekee says: Help me eat the delicious ⌈oo⌋g'B⊃rm!"

In a word balloon, the alien was saying, "*C'ga A⊄!*"

He grinned. "That's the last key. 'Mr. Veekee.' You solved it, Mari!" Then he took the cup out of her hands, pushed to the far wall, and stuffed both into the broken flash recycler.

"Hey, I wasn't done!"

"When someone who comes from the land of haggis and black pudding tells you something is inedible, you should trust them. We've got twenty hours left, which is enough time to finish up the last of these balls. Next meal is on me."

"You're damned right it is," she said. She picked out another ball and sliced it open. "How do you plan on deploying these?"

"There's a small untethered asteroid just outside Gilger's territory. I'm going to haul these there and send them toward his perimeter. Then I'm going to go as fast as I can around to the far side of Burnbottle. As everyone is reacting to the surprise attack from the asteroid, I'll sneak in and take the ship."

"Even with all the fighting going on, Gilger's got people on alert. You're not going to get far from that asteroid before they catch you."

"Well, that's why I said I'll go *fast*," Fergus said.

"I'll take them."

"Take what?"

"The balls. To the asteroid."

Just like Dru and me, he thought. They'd split up to do an end-run around a Martian Colonial Authority outpost, one the decoy, the other the courier. *We thought we were having fun.*

"No, you won't," he said as firmly as he could. "Look, I appreciate the offer, and I might not have gotten that last key if not for your attempt to poison me, but I'm not putting you in danger. I do this alone."

"First off, no one tells me what to do—not Mauda, not Harcourt, and certainly not you," she said. "Second, I know that asteroid, I know the old mine tunnels in it, and I can hide a lot better and a lot longer than you can. I've been spying on Gilger ever since I figured out how to get off the Wheels. So either you let me help you, or

I'm going to make my own attempt on Gilger. We both have a better chance if we work together, and you know it. Maybe our only chance. Do we have a deal?"

Say no, he told himself. *Find any reason you can to keep her out of this.*

But she was right—it was the best chance. And he wasn't going to be able to convince her otherwise. Dru wouldn't have let him talk her out of their plan either, and the hell he would have paid if he had even tried . . .

"Under protest, and only if you stay put deep in that asteroid until it's safe and then get the hell out of the area and back to the Wheels if you can, or somewhere else out of the way if you can't. You're not allowed to get yourself killed, not even slightly. That's my nonnegotiable condition. If you won't promise to keep yourself safe first and foremost, I'll stuff you in that smartfridge and lock you in till it's over," he said. "You got that?"

"I got it," she said, though her eyes flashed homicidal promises if he tried anything of the sort.

Fergus cracked the head off a neon yellow vibrator more violently than necessary and hauled out the little electronic guts. "Great. Gilger's waiting for us. Let's get this done."

She smiled and stuck the knife deep into another ball.

Chapter 12

◆——◆——◆

Mari retrieved her 'stick from Harcourt's local contact just as Leakytown declared a full lockdown. They had thirty minutes to get out or they were going to sit out the war—or be overrun by it—trapped here.

The public area was empty except for the booth with the unfortunate soup and a few furtive lingerers hanging on the wall nets. Black sheets had been tethered down across storefronts, some more carefully than others. Fergus snagged one that had drifted free and bundled it around the mesh bag of balls to keep it concealed. By the time he'd finished, more than one desperate person had begun moving to intercept them.

"We ought to get out of here," Fergus said.

Mari was already well ahead of him. "You're slow as dirt, Earthman," she called back.

It was awkward enough managing both the tennis balls and his 'stick while keeping a grip on the central bar, but with the added urgency, it became almost impossible. After a moment's consideration of the wide, deserted corridors, Fergus let go of the bar and fired up his 'stick.

"Hey!" Mari shouted as he roared past her.

This is really stupid, he thought as he had to put out a foot and push off a wall to take a turn without flattening himself. He was reaching down for the 'stick's kill switch when he heard Mari closing in behind him.

Screw that—I'm not losing my lead.

He careened around another corner, nearly clipping his head on a wall-mounted sign, then narrowly missing a startled man coming out of an adjoining corridor as he ducked under it. Mari's 'stick was higher quality, or she was a better flier—or both, most likely—and she had nearly caught up to him by the time he flew the last length into the platform. He flipped the braking thrust on the flystick as he raised his feet and hit the far wall, letting his knees bend with the impact before springing back out into the middle of the room.

Mari flew past, saw the wall just in time, and did a much less graceful version of the same maneuver. To be fair, Fergus had known before he entered the platform where the wall was going to be, but he still took a viscerally childish satisfaction in that brief look of panic as she'd flown past.

The rental kiosk that earlier had been surrounded by a frustrated mob was now a burned-out shell, with a security gate snapped down across the front of it.

When Mari had bounced back enough to reach him, he handed her the bag of tennis balls. "Hold this for a second," he said, "and keep an eye out?"

She took it, and he let go of his 'stick and began stripping off his exosuit. From his pack he unfolded the one he'd acquired from Vinsic's dead Blue and pulled it on with as much speed as care would allow. He would rather have changed in his room, but he couldn't risk being mistaken for an active fighter while still inside Leakytown. He unclipped his comm unit from his own suit, attached it to his stolen one, and folded his old suit carefully back into his pack.

"You ready?" Mari asked.

He nodded. "As much as I'll ever be."

"Three-one-five," she said, then sealed her face shield. As he switched his private link over to that channel, she pushed out through the platform envelope. Moments later when it rotated back, he followed.

Mari was tumbling away, twisting to get her 'stick under her with a graceful flair he assumed was meant to demonstrate that hitting the wall had been a singular lapse. Then, with the tennis balls dragging behind her, she disappeared out into the perpetual night. He took a deep breath and pushed off.

From Leakytown there was a line to a tiny, rusty residential hab named Humbug, which had locked all its outer doors and cut contact with the outside world as soon as hostilities had broken out. *Lying low and hoping they don't get run over,* Fergus thought, and couldn't blame them.

His plan had been to mingle with other stragglers, but with no one on or near the line, that wasn't an option. He got that itchy-back feeling of being too conspicuous immediately. When he was moving at top speed, he shut his 'stick down, going dark.

Somewhere out of sight, Mari was heading up on a long shot diagonally toward the fringes of the Halo, where she'd turn and make a beeline for the abandoned asteroid. He headed down, passing beneath Humbug. From there he made his way toward one of Cernee's many trash gyres floating in the dead space, caught up on fragments of old lines below Burnbottle and Gilgerstone.

Patrols of one-mans and two-mans roamed the space around the hab and rock just inside the perimeter of mines and sentry bobs. There was no sign of *Venetia's Sword.* Staying within the umbra of the sunshields, Fergus let himself drift far enough into the gyre to be camouflaged by it but not enough to get tangled in it. From here he had a perfect view of Gilger's territory spread out above. Much of the junk had come from Gilger himself; scores of stripped-out, skeletal ships dotted the debris field. He recognized some, including the burnt half shell of a Gaian scouter. There was no way that had been legal salvage.

A long-signal text from Mari popped up inside his shield. *In position,* it said. *You ready?*

Patrols were moving in the same pattern they had been during Fergus's earlier scouting mission, paying little attention to the junk pile below them. *Ready,* he sent back, and then he waited.

Ten minutes later a one-man broke out of the pattern, heading away from the perimeter. Almost immediately another peeled off and followed. It had started.

Fergus pointed his 'stick upward and gave one hard boost before shutting down again and letting go. He tucked his knees up against his chest and put his head down, letting momentum carry him like a cannonball. He was flying out of here on his ship, dammit. And if he didn't, it was probably because he wasn't getting out of here at all.

They're getting mad now, Mari sent. Both sets of patrols were in disarray, moving toward the far perimeter where sparks of light flared here and there like glitter: the mines exploding.

Stop watching and get under cover, he sent back.

Only a single one-man had stayed in position. Fergus was small and dark, coming from an unexpected direction. It wasn't the one-man he was worried about. If the tennis balls took out enough of the sentry bobs, the remainder should spread themselves out to cover the same ground and pull what remaining mines there were with them. Unless they didn't, in which case Fergus would never know if he'd aimed himself right at one until it was too late.

He sailed a hundred yards or so up past the starboard side of the one-man. His blood ran cold as a mine zipped past him so close he could have reached out and grabbed it on his way by.

You there yet? Mari asked.

He was coming up fast on the underbelly of Burnbottle. *Three seconds,* he replied.

Good, because we're about to have a lot more company.

Fergus twisted around in alarm, thinking she meant that someone had spotted one or both of them, and as a result his planned feet-first landing on Burnbottle turned into a shoulder crash and rebound that left him momentarily stunned.

He used the fine maneuvering jets in his suit to push himself back up to the hull of the hab, grumbling. Once he'd managed to snag a maintenance bar, he looked around more carefully. Burnbottle wasn't a spinner, so the hab itself was shielding him from view. He pulled himself around the curve of the hab to where he could just make out the abandoned asteroid without leaving the concealment of the hab's lee.

Most of the patrol was spinning around empty space like angry bees, trying to find the source of the attack. A few had converged on the asteroid, blanketing it with weaponsfire. Mari had said she knew the mining tunnels in the asteroid; he hoped to hell she hadn't been lying and that they were deep enough.

In the distance he could just make out an approaching ship. By the time it came close enough for him to make out the blue stripe along its side, he half wondered if it was the product of fervent wishing.

Venetia's Sword hovered in the midst of the frenzied one-mans for several long minutes, then suddenly broke away, nearly colliding with one of the smaller flyers as it hove to beside Gilgerstone. Whatever had spooked it, the ships blasting the asteroid stopped firing and pulled together to form a hasty defense line in an arc around the edge of the Halo.

Now what? Fergus wondered. Then he could make out the ships coming in in precise formation. *Mari, are you seeing this?*

I'm in the center of a rock, assvalve, she sent back. *I can't see my own fucking eyeballs.*

Stay there. The war just found us.

Took them long enough. And you're welcome, she replied.

It took a moment for that to percolate through. *Harcourt. You called him.*

Yes. You needed a distraction, he needed an opportunity. This works for everyone. Now go do your job.

Harcourt's ships were engaging Gilger's. From here,

Fergus couldn't tell who was winning, but he could see reinforcements coming in; four clusters of blue-striped people on 'sticks were heading for Burnbottle, each riding with a shrapnel cannon. More were trying to catch up from behind.

I'm going offline, he sent to Mari, then immediately shut down his comm, unjacked it from his suit, and tucked it into a zippered pocket on his pack. From that same pocket he took out the melted remains of his stolen comm, retrieved last-minute from the exploded smartfridge before they'd left Leakytown. He clipped it back in place as best he could.

He pulled himself along bars until he found a maintenance hatch. The far side let into a room barely larger than a closet, its one working light dim and flickering, with old tools and half-dissected equipment loosely shoved up against mag-bars on the walls. Hoping he wasn't committing suicide by stupidity, he pushed out of the maintenance closet and headed toward the crowd of blue-stripes gathered around the bottle rechargers. One spotted him and moved to intercept, talking inaudibly inside his shield. Fergus held up his wrist, pointing at the burnt-out comm.

With a visible sigh, the man flipped open his shield. "Protocol Zero? You had sixty seconds. What the fuck happened?"

"I was taking a crap," Fergus said, making as sheepish a face as he could manage and hoping he had the Cernee accent close enough.

"Brilliant," the man said. "Who the hell are you?"

"I'm Cheefer," he said. It was the name of his childhood dog, a short, fat, lopsided thing, blind in one eye and cursed with chronic gas, whom he'd loved like nothing else in life. A lesson he'd learned long ago was that if you were going to use a fake name, pick one that would still get your attention. "Blue Two sent me here to make myself useful."

The man appraised him. "And the rest of your team?"

"It's just me left," he said.

"And where's your 'stick, Cheefer?"

Fergus threw his hands up. "Some damned Gold took it when I landed. Said he was commandeering it. You know what that's about? I thought we were all on the same side!"

The man nodded his head slightly. *Good*, Fergus thought. *He's decided I'm not inside the circle, which means I'm not worth bothering to call in and double-check. Just another dumb grunt.*

"Damned Golds," one of the other men said. "Couldn't stick to a plan if it was fucking pasted to their faces."

"Okay, Cheefer," the leader said. "We're Blue Seven and Eight. Have you ever worked a shrapnel cannon?"

"Once," he said. *If you count having it fired at you*, he didn't add.

The man pointed at the other guy who'd spoken. "This is Derf, who used to be with Blue Eleven. His partner rewired his own comm so he could pipe music over it and didn't see the Protocol Zero signal."

"Blew his hand off at the wrist," Derf said. "In space."

Fergus winced. "Sorry," he said.

"Sometimes a man can be just smart enough to be really stupid," the leader said. "I don't expect you have that problem, Cheefer?"

"Not yet, sir," he said.

"Is your air full?"

"Full enough, sir," he said.

"Great. Derf here will take you with him. The cannon is self-propelling, so you just have to hang on. We're going to head up over Gilgerstone and try to take out as many Grays as we can. If you make it back, and if you can point out the Goldie who took your 'stick, we'll all help you get it back, okay?"

"Thank you, sir."

"Call me Blue Leader Eight, Cheefer. Any questions?"

"Uh . . . a comm?"

"I don't have any spares. You and Derf can use your

suit proximity channels, and he'll relay any orders from me to you. He's in charge. You set to go?"

"Set, Blue Leader Eight."

"Good. You and Derf are going to take the lead, seeing as how you both seem to be so lucky. Move."

Derf crooked a finger at Fergus. Fergus pushed off the wall toward him. "Channel one-one-one," Derf said. "Think you can remember that?"

Fuck you, Derf. "One-one-one. Got it." Fergus switched his suit over, then closed and sealed his face shield. "Can you hear me?"

"Loud and clear. Now don't talk unless I speak to you first," Derf said. He plucked his air bottle out of the recharger and slotted it into his suit behind his pack, then turned his back without a word, passing through the platform's envelope and out. Fergus followed. Once they were out, Derf pointed to where a cannon was tethered outside the platform. "Take the right side," he said.

"Okay," Fergus replied.

"Shut up," Derf said.

At least he wasn't going to be peppered with curious questions about where in Cernee he'd grown up, what had happened to the rest of his team, and so on. He'd just follow Derf's lead as long as it got him closer to *Venetia's Sword*, and then, like it or not, Derf was going to be partnerless again.

They left the platform, each riding one side of the bulbous cylinder of the cannon body. Fergus's side, where he held onto a thick welded bar with no safety tether, had no controls or instrumentation of any kind.

Behind them, the rest of the Blues pushed off the platform. Two more cannons and a half dozen men on 'sticks. Fergus felt uncomfortably surrounded. *Not that I understand* why *they're the enemy,* he thought. *I suppose I could always just ask.*

"Derf?"

"I told you not to talk to me, meatbag," Derf answered.

They floated along for a few long minutes while Fergus waited patiently. Finally Derf sighed audibly over the link. "Well? What is it?"

"I just figured maybe you had a better idea what's going on than me and could explain it, 'cause none of this makes sense."

Derf snorted. "Sense?! You're asking for a lot," he said. "Didn't your team leader explain it?"

"My team leader was so good at explaining things that I'm the only one not dead."

"Okay, I guess not," Derf said. "Look, we don't like the Goldies, and they don't like us, right? But Mr. Vinsic heard that the Governor was gonna hand over his seat to Harcourt, and then he was going to clean out the other houses that might make trouble for him, so here we are."

"Why help Gilger, though?"

"You gotta pick a side."

"Why not stick to our own?"

Derf laughed. "You really don't know shit, do you, Cheefer? Shut up, now. Time to fight."

They were heading up over Gilgerstone. Harcourt's formation was holding, forming a blockade between Gilger's territory and any easy way in and out of the Halo. A team of Golds was coming up and out of Gilgerstone itself, swarming past the trapped *Venetia's Sword* and toward the blockade.

"Blue Leader Eight says when we get in position we can fire at will," Derf said. "We've got one good shot with this thing, then we're gonna use it like a rocket and try to slam it into one of the big flyers. I've got EMP mines and a couple of can grenades. Whatcha you got on you?"

"Uh, one can grenade," he lied.

"Blue Leader wants us to open up a hole so Gilger can get his ship out and start doing some damage. We want the Grays to pull back and defend the Wheels again. Gold Leader's plan needs them to be there, not here."

Fergus glanced over his shoulder, wondering how easily he could ditch Derf and the cannon. Not easily; everyone was converging on the blockade. *Crap.*

"I'm shutting down the engines so we can set up to aim," Derf said. "I'll let you know when I'm about to fire."

"Okay."

The other two cannon teams were setting up to their left, roughly parallel to them. Loose men were scattered behind them, just far enough to be in no danger from their own side's projectiles.

Derf slowed the cannon and slowly rocked it back and forth, trying to line it up. "Should have it in about ten," Derf said. "Stop picking your nose and hold tight—there's a hell of a kickback."

Well, damn, Fergus thought. *I don't really want to shoot any of Harcourt's people.* He wrapped his arms tightly through his bar, thinking if he kicked off his suit's jets and timed it just as Derf pulled the trigger, he might knock off the aim just enough.

"I got lock. Firing in four, three—" Derf started to say, then, "—what the fuck?"

"What?"

"The Grays just dropped a ton of something into space."

"What is it?"

"How the fuck should I—Damn!" The cannon jolted as Derf fired up the engine into reverse without warning, pulling them back the way they'd come. Seconds later the space around them filled with tiny silver marbles. They swarmed around the cannon. A half dozen balls veered in Fergus's direction, then past and away.

"Grrrk," he heard over the comm channel.

"Derf?" he asked.

There was no answer.

He let go of his handle and pulled himself up over the top of the cannon. Derf was floating there, inert; five or six of the metal balls were embedded in the fabric of his exosuit. Carefully, Fergus let himself over to the cannon's left side and peered into Derf's face shield. Derf's eyes were open, seeing nothing.

"Damn," Fergus swore, backing away from the body. The main swarm of killer ball bearings had gone by, and the one or two that were still passing ignored them both. One cannon team was halfway back to Gilgerstone. Other than them, the edge of the Halo was littered with Gold and Blue bodies.

Why not me? Fergus wondered.

Harcourt knew he was out here. Mari must've given him the frequency of the bug in his suit—the suit he'd almost left behind at Leakytown to save on weight rather than stuffing it into his pack—and programmed the weapons to avoid him. He shuddered.

His cannon was still moving, coming up close on a Blue body. Letting go of the cannon as he passed, he grabbed the Blue's 'stick, firing it up and pointing it toward Gilgerstone. If anyone saw him, he hoped they'd assume he was just a panicked survivor fleeing the slaughter. And really, wasn't he?

Venetia's Sword lay dead ahead, surrounded by a small team of flyers. If he could just zip between them and grab onto the ship's hull, he'd only need a few moments to pass the handshake back . . .

He was so intent on the ship that he didn't see the one-man until it broadsided him, sending him hurtling off his 'stick.

Alarm lights flashed all over the display in the periphery of his face shield. The pain in his arm and side where the one-man had hit was blinding in intensity, crippling in shock. Tumbling, he could see the one-man coming back around. Two Golds on 'sticks were coming up alongside it, closing in. Even if he hadn't been hurt, there would've been no escape.

Reaching into his pack pocket, Fergus pulled out his original comm with its link back to Mari. He closed his fist around it, forcing the faltering grippers in the glove to crush it. Then he opened his palm and let the pieces float away in an arc around him. *You can get me,* he thought, *but you're not getting anyone else.*

The one-man stopped just ahead of him, and one of the Golds swung out a short pole. *Shock stick.* Fergus only got three-quarters of the way toward making a rude gesture before the man lunged the stick at him and everything went angrily and painfully black.

He was not as excited about waking up as he should have been, given his expectation that he wouldn't. At least this time he still appeared to have all his clothes, if not his stolen suit or pack. *Well, fuck,* he thought. *Now where am I?*

There was gravity—maybe 60 percent?—and a solid floor beneath him. He tried to push himself up, then fell back down as his arm collapsed under him. When he could think again, he sat up more carefully, keeping his right arm cradled against his chest.

He was in a small room, clean and utilitarian, devoid of anything except pale gray walls and a ventilation grille too small for anything bigger than a ballroach to slither through. He leaned against the wall, trying to breathe through the pain. The wall was vibrating just slightly. Perking up, he looked around more carefully. He was on a ship. And the only ship in Cernee big enough to have a room like this was . . .

"Gowan yerself," he said out loud. *Venetia's Sword.*

There was the sound of footsteps in the hall, and Fergus got to his feet as they paused outside the door. After a few moments the door slid open. Gilger stood in the doorway, a trio of Luceatans just behind him. "I know exactly who you are," Gilger said.

"Who I am?" Fergus asked, knowing how unconvincing it sounded.

Gilger's mouth twitched up on one side. "Let me introduce you to some friends of mine," he said, stepping into the room and to one side. The first Luceatan moved forward, his face a familiar mask of intensity, his sleeveless tunic a near match for Gilger's. *Graf.*

Graf's shoulder bore an angry pistol wound a few days old.

"You killed Katra," Fergus blurted out.

"Not technically," Graf answered as the other two Luceatans crowded into the room.

Shit, Fergus thought. *I'm in trouble.*

"I know you're Harcourt's hired assassin sent to kill me," Gilger said, stepping forward and looming over him. "And now you're mine."

"Hold him still," Graf said to his men. He pulled a thin sharp knife out of his boot.

Okay, make that in a lot of trouble, Fergus decided as the Luceatans reached for him.

Chapter 13

◆

His body returned to him one agonizing note at a time, as if his mind needed to acknowledge and assimilate each individual blaring arc of pain before the next could join the orchestra. Something hit his face, slamming his head to one side. "Open your eyes, damn you," a voice said. *Gilger.* So he hadn't hurt himself in some miraculous escape he couldn't remember. *Damn.*

Fergus tried to open his eyes, half out of determination to do it, half out of fear of being struck again, and finally managed. The blurry world swam in front of him.

He was upright in a chair. For all the pain, his body felt remote, like his brain was merely an audience to, rather than the conductor of, its screaming chorus. His bloodied hands were loosely bound to the chair's armrests, but it hardly mattered. No matter how furiously he demanded a shake, a twitch, even one miniscule tremor of a fingertip, his hands remained resolutely unreachable. Some sort of paralytic drug, he decided. At least he could breathe, although the ladder of pain up and down his chest meant he didn't dare try to do it with any enthusiasm.

"Mr. Anders," Gilger said, "is still with us because he's going to give us a hand with our Wheel problem."

Fergus tried to work his lips, get that simplest of F-words out between them, but he managed little more than numbly rolling spittle down his own chin. *Good job, Fergus. Dignified resistance, there.*

Gilger was walking away toward a large black backdrop. Startled, Fergus realized it was the forward screen of *Venetia's Sword.* He was on the bridge. The bridge! If only he weren't tied up, paralyzed, and full of broken bones and ruptured things.

He convinced his eyeballs to cooperate long enough to focus on the screen. *Venetia's Sword* must still have been parked beside Gilgerstone because he could see Harcourt's blockade arrayed in the distance, looking as much like solid a wall as it had before. Hope began to rise in him that despite the vicious beating and drugging, he hadn't been out very long. He tried to remember how much time he'd had left when he'd set out with Blue Eight, but his head hurt, and trying to count back to when he'd left Leakytown with Mari made his brain choke on mathematical bile.

Gilger sat in the captain's seat and swiveled around to look at Fergus. "You're lucky Graf didn't cut you up despite my orders. The only thing he hates more than damned soulless clones are Marsies, and I don't blame him for that one bit," he said. "The arrogance of you people amazes me, thinking you can go wherever you want and interfere with the social order and a man's business with impunity, as if you own the universe."

The defiance on Fergus's face must've shown, because Gilger leaned forward, fingers interlaced on one knee. "It's not like you made it hard to add up," he said. "Only a Marsie would have hair such a ridiculous shade of red."

Fergus blinked. *He thinks I'm from Mars because I have red hair?* Then: *My hair is red?* The nanites he'd used to color it black prior to the Governor's hearing should have lasted around forty-eight hours, just about the same window of time before the handshake expired.

His reflection on the shiny surface of the console beside him showed him an almost unrecognizably swollen and bruised face, his hair and beard red streaked with a few fading remnants of black.

Shit.

It hit him in that instant that, for the first time, he was going to lose.

"Well," Gilger said. "I guess we'd better get on with

this. Try to look pretty in the background for me, okay?"
He turned around. "Marrick, make the call."

His pilot ran his hands over his console, then nodded.
"All comm scramblers are off and the channel's open,
sir. Public local broadcast."

Gilger stood up, tugged on the collar of his tunic to
make sure it was straight, and then clasped his hands
behind his back like an elder statesman. "This is Arum
Gilger with an open message to Henry Harcourt. I have
something of yours that you may want back."

A long few minutes passed. Fergus flexed his lips,
breathing gently through them, trying to take back by
force at least his power of speech. His feet, somewhere
kilometers below, had begun to tingle and itch. *I wonder,* he thought, *if they took into account my size when
they dosed me with the paralytic?* Certainly no one had
been worried he'd regain control of his physical body, or
they'd have tied him down better. As it was, the ties
seemed more to keep him from falling out of his chair
than running away.

Not that he was running anywhere. *If that tingling
spreads,* he thought, *I can surprise the shit out of them
by suddenly flopping over.*

Gilger began shifting impatiently from foot to foot.
Finally he spoke up. "The channel *is* open, right, Marrick? I'd have expec—"

"Response incoming, sir," his pilot interrupted.

"Is there a visual?"

"Yes, sir."

"Then *display* it," Gilger growled.

The view switched from the blockade to the familiar
face of Harcourt, in his chair by the fireplace, leaning
nonchalantly on one armrest. "Gilger," he said. His eyes
briefly flitted to Fergus, but his expression didn't change.

"I have something of yours," Gilger said. "And I want
to know what it's worth to you to get back."

Harcourt shrugged. "Mr. Anders is no concern of
mine. His machine didn't even work."

"We both know that was a sham."

"Alas for the optimistic investor, not all new technologies pan out," Harcourt said. The nonchalance didn't crack, but Fergus knew better than to read anything into that; he would have played it the same way. There was too much on the line.

"The arrogance you have, to think you can introduce me to your assassin right in front of everyone, in public, as if you have nothing to fear from me." Gilger strode back to Fergus and grabbed him by the hair, yanking his face up toward the screen. "And yet here's your assassin right here. He failed."

"If he was my assassin," Harcourt said, "and he failed, what makes you think I'd want him back?"

"Oh, I don't expect you want *this* piece of trash," Gilger said. "I just wanted you to know that I broke him. And since you were thoughtful enough to send your fellow Martian trash after me, I thought I'd repay the compliment and send my own team to Mars for you. Or rather, for your brat."

Harcourt's expression didn't overtly change, but the careful ease was gone. "Arum . . ."

"Make your calls, Harcourt," Gilger interrupted, "but make them quickly. You've got one hour to get that blockade out of my way and three to stand down completely if you ever want to see her again. You never should have gotten in my way, much less left your red-sand shithole in the first place."

Gilger made a gesture across his throat, and Marrick cut the connection.

One hour wasn't enough time to get a message to Mars and back, even paying absolute premium jump-transfer packet rates. Harcourt would have to bounce the call through Crossroads to Haudernelle, then take the long six-step back to Jupiter, which was the nearest active-FTL transmitter to Mars. In the meantime he'd have to pull back and stand down until he heard back, giving Gilger time to cement every possible advantage.

That was the same calculation Cernee's security chief Katra had made back during that first ambush at Mezzanine Rock, Fergus realized, and the trap she'd spared the Governor from at the cost of her own life. Harcourt had no such easy way out.

Forty-two deeply boring and equally tense minutes later, the blockade began to spread out, backing off slowly. *Shit*, Fergus thought. He moved his lips, managed something halfway between a stuttering exhalation and an actual word. He couldn't imagine Gilger had much use for him now that he'd made his point.

Graf must have been thinking the same thing. He nodded his head toward Fergus. "Can I finish this?"

"He's not going anywhere," Gilger said. "Get us underway before that Marsie asshole finds a new way to make problems for us. Call up Scikan and Thord to deal with him. You get down to the cargo bay and make sure the shuttle is ready."

"Yes, sir," Graf said. He seemed disappointed, but left the bridge.

Gilger turned to the pilot. "Is Harcourt out of our way yet?"

"They're moving aside to give us a passage, sir."

"And Blackcans? Is it secured?"

"Enough, sir. There's some fighting in the halls, but it's limited to a few interior areas. Cable-cutter crew is in place and ready."

"Good. Have them stand by. Any rats jump hab from the Wheels or get in our way, cut them down. No one gets out."

Venetia's Sword began to move forward, sailing gracefully through the gap in the blockade. *Come on, legs—move a little. Let me do something here!* Fergus thought. Instead his head flopped forward, chin on his chest. *Great.*

The console in front of his chair was an assistant navigator station, locked down but live. He watched the lights flicker across it as *Venetia's Sword's* intelligence processed the pilot's actions and its own internal systems feedback stream. Little stutters in the lights corresponded to the minutest lags in their acceleration. It was the first indication of the damage that must have been done to its mindsystems when it was stolen from the Shipmakers.

Straining his eyes upward toward the screen, Fergus could see Harcourt's ships yielding as *Venetia's Sword* moved through.

"They're falling in behind us, sir," Marrick said.

"Let them. If they get too close, fire on them. Take us to where we have a full view of the Wheels and Blackcans."

"Almost there, sir. Three minutes. Vinsic's on the line."

Gilger glanced back at Fergus as if just remembering he was there. Then he shrugged as if it didn't matter. It probably didn't. "Put audio through to my earpiece," Gilger said.

Marrick nodded.

"Yes?" Gilger said, then, "No. No. Shortly. Well, it's a bad strategy. I'm not concerned about the Governor. No. *No*. If you're that worried about it, you go deal with it." There was a long pause. "I'll be at Mezz in a few hours and will evaluate the situation for myself. Yeah."

Gilger made a face, then punched a button on his chair arm and threw his headset down. "He thinks he can dictate to me?" he asked. "I don't care if he's dying; I'm doing this my way. If he doesn't like it, he can just die *faster*."

Vinsic was dying? Now that was interesting.

"We're there, sir," Marrick said. "Scikan and Thord are on their way up."

Ahead of them, Blackcans loomed large. Harcourt's people had backed away, forming a last defensive line between Blackcans and the Wheels. "Tell our cutting crews to go," Gilger said.

A moment later, Marrick looked up. "Blackcans is severed from the Halo."

Gilger touched his own comm. "Graf, launch the shuttle."

"With pleasure, sir," Graf's response came. "Shuttle is away."

A large four-man passed underneath *Venetia's Sword* on a trajectory toward Blackcans. Nothing got in its way. It pulled up to the end of the hab and set massive docking clamps against it.

"Shuttle's locked on, sir," Marrick said.

"How's our control?"

"Outside comm jamming is playing havoc with our teams, but the ship's P2P is talking to the shuttle and payload perfectly. Graf is monitoring from the bay."

"Well." Gilger stood up again, brushed imaginary lint from the front of his tunic, and began punching buttons on his arm console. Fergus could see the locked station in front of him responding.

"Initiating first burn," Gilger said.

The shuttle's engines lit up, far bigger than should have been in a ship of its size. Gilger's people must have stripped almost the entire interior to wedge engines that big inside. Blackcans, no longer tethered to the rest of the Halo, began to move, accelerating.

It's heading straight toward the Wheels, Fergus realized. *Shit.* The damage a collision could do . . .

"Setting sequence control to auto," Gilger said. In front of him, *Venetia's Sword*'s computer took over. "How are we doing?"

"So far, so good. There's still some instability in our systems, but nothing that's going to hurt us," Marrick said.

"You said you were going to fix it."

"Yeah, well, I haven't had time," Marrick said. It had the defensive ring of a repeat argument. "I'll fix it as soon as we're not busy using the ship."

In Fergus's peripheral vision, two thick-bodied men strode onto the bridge. *Scikan and Thord*, he thought. *I'd recognize those fists and boots anywhere.* In fact, he could probably match them up to bruises all over his body.

"Master Gilger?" one asked.

Gilger didn't take his eyes off the screen. "Took you long enough," he said. "Hang on. I don't want to miss this."

Blackcans was moving fast now. Harcourt's ships were trying to react, but they were hemmed in by Gilger's two-mans and had to fight their way out of the trap. Some of the Golds were concentrating fire on the Wheel Collective's dock, met by return fire from the Wheels itself.

Fergus thought of Mella, the little girl who was afraid of giraffes, and felt his heart breaking into pieces. *They're not going to get out in time,* Fergus realized. *Unless they can get their suits on fast enough—*

"Payload has been armed," Marrick announced.

"They're going to see this fireball as far away as Crossroads," Gilger said.

No! All that time trying to solve the stupid handshake keys only to be stuck here, tied to a chair, watching innocent people die with no power to do anything more than fall forward and bash himself against the console in undignified protest.

"Impact in ninety seconds," Marrick said.

Ninety seconds was a lifetime. Fergus stared down at the console in front of him. Using every muscle he could, he pushed forward until the upper half of his torso tumbled forward and his face smashed into the console. At the crash, one of the Luceatans looked over, chuckled, then returned his rapt gaze to the impending devastation on-screen.

Fergus had landed right atop the computer interface. He could see, through swollen eyes, the activation button. Carefully he stuck out his tongue—amazed to discover that was one part of his body that didn't hurt—and pushed it.

A small yellow light popped into life right under his eye.

How many seconds did he have left? *Speak, Fergus,*

he told himself. He moved his lips, trying to desperately summon a whisper: *"Venetia's Sword . . ."*

The console blinked at him. *Go, go! Go, you idiot!*

"Access security subsystem," he said, careful not to slur the words, his mouth parched with the effort. "Serial number gee-four-one-four-bee-queue-nine-nine-oh-oh-emm-five. Verbal handshake, ack."

Yellow lights lit up across the board.

"Fifty-five seconds. What the—?" Marrick was looking down at his console.

This is all I have, but it's everything, Fergus thought. *My memory: Moose, Syrup of figs, Ring Me, Tot, McFadden's Row, C'ga A¢, Pluto.*

He whispered into the console. "Squirrel. Mr. Wigs. Rocket. Captain Tater. Yellow Kid. Mr. Veekee." That left Pluto, a cartoon dog from the old Earth days, and a trap. He smiled. He knew the Shipmakers. "Planet."

The yellow lights went green. "Send halt signal to shuttle," he said. "Disarm payload. Shut down all consoles except this one and deny access to anyone but me."

Marrick gave an inarticulate shout as his console went dead, jumping out of his seat to see Fergus's face lying on the one live console. "It's him!" he shouted. "He's done something!"

Gilger whirled around, his face red with fury. "You two!" He pointed at the Luceatans. "Break his neck. *Now.*"

The two enforcers turned, and one wrapped his meaty hand around his other fist, cracking his knuckles. Fergus was still tied to the chair, unable to do much more than twitch in his own defense. But now he had the ship. "Disengage environmental safeties and reverse all shipboard gravity," he told *Venetia's Sword.* "Increase to two-hundred percent."

Marrick went airborne, his safety tether stopping him with a sharp jerk midway to the ceiling. Gilger, untethered, slammed into it headfirst, flopping over on his back like a fish gasping for air with his robes flapping wildly around him. The two Luceatans crashed into him a heartbeat later.

Fergus was tired. Too tired. It was all he could do to keep his face near the console as the gravity tried to pull him toward the ceiling like a favorite broken doll. "Shut down and disengage all remotely controlled systems and communications jammers. Sound interior alarms except on bridge," he told the ship, grateful his voice, at least, was growing stronger.

The muted *whoop, whoop* of the ship's alarms started up, loud enough even through the bridge's blast doors to make his teeth ache. "You fucking Marsie!" Gilger shouted. His nose was bleeding, dripping upward in a way Fergus would have found fascinatingly awful if he wasn't so close to the edge himself.

"I'm going to have to add a new tattoo for what I'm going to do to you," one of the Luceatans shouted.

"Fuck you," Fergus replied. "Good luck getting to me from up there."

On the screen ahead, he could see that Blackcans was still moving, albeit much more slowly; the shuttle engine hadn't had quite enough juice left to counter its forward momentum. Harcourt would have to stop it himself, but at least it wasn't going to explode now. *I probably ought to warn him,* Fergus thought. *That would be nice of me.*

He pulled himself together enough to record a message. "Blackcans rigged with bomb. Love, Mr. Anders," he said, then sent it on broadcast.

Marrick was pulling himself hand over hand down his safety cable toward his chair. "Release pilot alpha-position safety tether," Fergus told *Venetia's Sword*, and the pilot slammed into the ceiling beside Gilger, who was still struggling to get out from beneath the Luceatans.

Licking his top lip, Fergus whispered to the computer. "Override code delta," he told it. "Instruction set follows." The instructions were short, precise, dangerous. "Set complete. Initiate," he said at last. Then he closed his eyes, trying to ignore the shouting above him.

Gilger was screaming. "This is my ship! Where do you think you can go? Back home to *Mars*?!"

"Not from Mars," Fergus managed. "I'm from Scotland."

"And what fucking backwater planet is that?"

"It's planet I Win and You Lose," he said. To the ship, he added, "Voice response on. Narrate embedded instruction set."

Venetia's Sword spoke up, the voice tinny and full of skips, like an ancient LP left just a little too close to the fusion engines. "Relocating position to outside the Halo for maximum safe rad-ad-ad-adius. Shutting down shipwide life support. Self-destruct activated," it said. "Setting clock to minimum mandatory ten-minute window, per system regulations. Count begins. Six hund-undred—"

"Get out if you think you can, assholes," Fergus called up to the men plastered to the ceiling.

Then he stopped listening for a while.

Chapter 14

The bridge of *Venetia's Sword* was dark and cold when he woke up. He was alone, hanging upward in his chair, his hands white where the ties cut into them. The bridge doors had been forced open at the top using a zero-grav handhold bar that had been ripped from the ceiling.

At least that went right, he thought. "End debug mode. Set artificial gravity to zero." The sensation that he was being pulled apart eased.

"Terminating debug mode," the ship responded. "Self-destruct sequence simulation successful. Instruction code set delta fully ex-executed."

"What's our position?"

"We are point eight kilometers outside the Cernekan Halo at specified location."

"Status of life pods and life support?"

"All life pod-ods have ejected. Life support is terminated in all areas of ship except bridge and bridge antechamber due to blast d-d-door compromise. Air and heat have been at operating minimum, below threshold for biological survival, for approximately two hours."

"Any people other than myself still aboard?"

"No other people detec-tected."

Fergus could have cried in relief. "Us damaged two," he said. "It's time to go home."

Then he remembered the other thing: *I'm still tied to a chair.*

"Ship," he said, "does this chair release?"

"Detachment of bridge fixtures is not recommended by the safety p-p-protocols."

He had to see if he could fix that stutter on the long

jumps back to the Shipyard. Assuming he didn't die here still tied to this chair or when Gilger came back with reinforcements to retake the ship. Fergus had already met enough Luceatans to last a lifetime. "Override protocols and release my chair," he said.

"Releasing." There was a click, and he could just barely feel the chair shifting beneath him. He pushed off the floor with his bound feet, and the chair headed upward. Halfway to the ceiling, he said, "Ship? Gravity to 2 percent, reset to standard orientation."

He began to fall. So did the bar that had been torn free to wedge open the door. *Land in my lap,* he told it. *Come on!*

It hit his knee. "Auuurgh," he said, gritting his teeth. Straining at the ties, he scrabbled for the bar with his one good hand and managed to walk it up his leg far enough to wrap his fingers around it.

The broken ends were sharp. He wedged the bar into the tie on his other hand, trying to cut it against the chair's arm; he opened a long, ragged cut along the side of his wrist trying to get the angle right before he managed to worry the plastic tie into snapping. One bleeding hand free, he transferred the bar over and did his best to hold it steady as he cut the other tie, then the ones around his ankles.

"Ship, gravity zero," he said. Everything hurt so much, it was an effort to keep his voice steady. "Status of all ship mindsystems?"

"Higher mindsystem is shut down due to d-damage caused by hostile actions," the ship told him.

"Is it revivable?"

There was a long, worrisome pause before the ship responded. The cadence of its voice was different. "Mr. Ferguson?" it asked.

"You remember me?"

"You are a friend of my builders," it said. "Are you here to return me home?"

"I am," he said.

"Thank you," *Venetia's Sword* said. The voice flattened out. "Cannot sustain higher mindsystem interaction. It has taken damage. Returning it to an inactive state."

"That's okay. It's enough to know you're still in there," Fergus said. "Run full integrity verification on all systems, then calculate a course to the jump point near Crossroads Station. We're going home."

He put a foot gingerly against the console and pushed himself back through the damaged blast doors. The antechamber had a small bathroom for bridge crew. He pulled himself in and unclipped the suction tube from the wall. *Necessity trumps dignity,* he thought. If he turned the gravity back on, he wasn't sure he'd be able to stand.

From the swelling and discoloration, he was fairly certain one arm was fractured. The other was just thoroughly bruised. His hands were pins and needles as his circulation tried to make up for lost time. Adding to that, he had a couple of broken ribs, one tooth that seemed a lot less certain about its place in life, and a worrisome ache in his side that might be a kidney trying to break up with him.

He did appear to be pissing a fair amount of blood.

There was a small console in the bathroom. He unlocked it. "Are the systems checks finished?" he asked. The sooner he could leave this place, the better.

"Estimated time remaining: six mi-minutes," *Venetia's Sword* informed him.

Finished, he floated back out into the antechamber. It took several more minutes for the computer to bring atmosphere and heat back up to tolerable levels in the remainder of the ship. When the antechamber door status greenlit and he could pass through, he found garbage littering the corridor on the far side: mostly food wrappers and, inexplicably, a single boot. He floated through it all past the four discharged life pod bays. *Goodbye, Arum Gilger,* he thought. *I hope Harcourt finds you before any of your other enemies do. He deserves you the most. And I hope he shares whatever's left of you with Mari.*

The ship's health bay's door opened, and Fergus found himself face-to-face with his own belongings in a loose cloud around his empty pack. His own exosuit was there. The one he'd stolen from Vinsic's man was spread out, parts of it shredded. He didn't remember putting up a fight, but if he had, he felt a little better about losing.

Beside it all, tucked in a corner, was a med-chamber with a built-in scanner. If he had to, he could spend the trip back to the Shipyard at Pluto healing inside it.

"Systems check finished," *Venetia's Sword* announced. "No critical warnings. Thirteen intermed-med-mediate warnings. One system routine failed."

"Which system didn't self-check?"

"The water filtration subsystem."

Well, that probably wouldn't kill him. "Okay. Any of the intermediate warnings flagged as safety hazards?"

"There is an electrical anomaly in the cargo hold."

"What's the danger potential?"

"Eighty-eight percent chance that cargo hold environmental mo-onitoring controls have failed. Sixty-two percent chance of mechanical failure of cargo stacking system. Seven percent chance of failure of cargo control head resulting in fire."

Fire? Seven percent? Shit. Even if it was 0.1 percent, he'd need to check it. "Will engaging engines affect the risk assessment?"

"Normal and passive jump engines will not affect risk potential. Active jump will raise it by approximately fourteen percent."

"Okay," he said. With the star system's one active jump point farther in near Crossroads Station, he had time. "Initiate engines on course and monitor all systems for any changes in status. I'm going to go check out the electrical problem."

"Acknowledged," the ship said. "Engines initiated. Protocol minimum speed until Cernekan space is c-cleared."

Eighty-eight percent chance of the environmental monitoring systems being down, the ship had said. Did that mean he could unwittingly open a door to vacuum? To an inferno? To a bay filled with nothing but carbon monoxide? The idea of having to go down into the cargo hold and deal with what was probably a trivial maintenance problem made him unhappy; the knowledge that if he was smart, he'd put his exosuit on before he did it was enough to make him want to weep.

Pushing through the doorway, he retrieved his suit from where it gangled by the back wall and checked it over carefully. It seemed that Gilger's people hadn't done much more than pull it from his pack and power it on long enough to verify its genericness. Made on Mars, of course.

Putting it on was excruciating. Fergus added broken toes to the list of Luceatan gifts he'd been left with. Fuckers.

Once on, the snugness of the suit was surprisingly reassuring, except over his ribs. As the suit adjusted itself to him, he checked the oxygen and suit charge. Both were still nearly at full. *No excuses,* he told himself. *Let's do this. Then I can sleep until the only thing I've got left of Cernee is bad memories.*

There was a travel tube from the main interior of *Venetia's Sword* down to the cargo area. The shaft ended in a small platform and a set of blast doors, which opened easily to his touch.

He'd expected to feel the weight of the world lifting off his shoulders, his usual post-job got-away-again high, but instead his whole punching bag of a body felt like it had been stuffed with lead weights and despair. He wondered if Mari was still alive. Or Harcourt's daughter. It felt bad to be leaving like this without knowing everyone was going to be okay.

You're too hurt to help anyone even if you could, he thought. *Let it go. You aren't a hero, and they'll be better off without you getting in the way and dragging them into more trouble.*

Besides, he had a responsibility to the ship too.

Fergus checked the readings on his suit display. At least the air was good, if chilly; none of the lights worked. He pushed up his face shield, seeing his breath in swirling clouds around him. In the light from the doorway, he spied the suspect electronics panel and shoved off toward it.

Something fell at him in his peripheral vision. He was too startled to do much more than grope for the nearest handhold, but it hit him before he could turn himself around. Something sharp sliced into his back below his shoulder blade, and he cried out.

He managed a half turn, saw the glint of the blade raised again, and shoved himself upward on the bar with his one good arm. The knife stabbed into his leg, ripping downward until his boot reflexively kicked the hand away.

"Marsie bastard!" his attacker hissed at him.

Graf? Fergus looked down and saw the dark-suited man launch himself upward. He couldn't move away fast enough. Graf caught his damaged arm and yanked him painfully around, then placed the knife blade against his throat.

"Order the ship to stop," Graf said.

"Ship, stop and hold position," he said. He could feel the thrum of the ship's engines subside even as his own heart beat like mad in his chest.

"Ten minutes to get out of here, and you in complete control of the ship? There was no way we could have gotten to the escape pods if you hadn't wanted us to. So you made it just hard enough to scare everyone into a panic. Very smart."

"Didn't—" Fergus said, aware of the weight of the blade against his neck. "Didn't want you stopping to take the towels on your way out."

"So you're just a thief? No wonder Harcourt doesn't value your worthless life. Who sent you?"

"The Shipmakers of Pluto," he said. He saw no point in lying. "I came to retrieve the ship you stole. I have legal letters of marque."

"Oh, letters of *marque*," Graf said, sneering. "This is Cernee, not Earth, not Mars, and definitely not fucking Pluto. Release the ship back to my control, or I'll kill you right here and now."

"If you kill me, this ship is a paperweight in space."

"Marrick can get it working again."

"Yeah? Like he did such a great job last time? Sure. If you weren't in the middle of a war," Fergus retorted. He felt cold, felt a need to shake, but didn't dare with the blade so near. "Do you think everyone else is going to wait for you to get your shiny ship working again?"

"Like who? Harcourt?" Graf asked. "Arum sends the word, and his kid is dead. Harcourt isn't going to so much as shit without our permission."

"What about the Governor?"

"He can't stop us, not without Harcourt's help."

"And you're sure Vinsic is on your side?" Fergus asked. "Because from what I saw, it looked like he was playing you."

"We're playing *him*," Graf hissed. "And we'll win."

"Well, yeah, but only because he's dying anyway."

"How do you know that?"

Fergus managed a smile. "I know a lot about Vinsic. Maybe even more than you do. How do you think I got one of his suits?"

The blade wavered. *Gotcha*, Fergus thought.

"Arum has Vinsic under control," Graf said, pressing on the blade again. Fergus could feel it cut, shallow but long. "I could give you a one-man, enough to get you to Crossroads. Arum would agree to that. You could live."

A lie, Fergus knew. "And the Wheels?"

"Harcourt's an obstacle and an enemy, but the Vahns are a blight in the eyes of the One," Graf said. "You'd know if you'd met any."

"I did meet one," Fergus said. "On a cable car on my way into Cernee. A cable car you blew up out from under me."

Graf gave a half laugh. "It seems I missed an opportunity to save myself a lot of trouble," he said.

"Yeah," Fergus said. "Both of us."

"You know how many Vahns I've killed over the years?" Graf said. "I know they don't talk about ones who've left their pitiful little farm, but you know why they almost never come back? Because most of them never make it out of Cernee alive to start with. It's just a shame none of them except the old lady herself ever made it much of a challenge."

"You're evil," Fergus said.

"No. They're *clones, unnatural.* They have no souls. I am doing righteous work in my own redemption. The one-man: that's my offer. Take it or leave it. I want the ship back now." Graf gestured around the empty cargo bay with the point of his blade. "Or I can invite my friends back. Even Arum, who doesn't like getting his own hands dirty, would enjoy taking a stab at you. Do you like that idea better?"

"I hate it. I hate this job. I hate Cernee. I hate Arum Gilger. And I hate *you*," Fergus said. "Ship, override all safeties and evacuate the cargo hold. Immediately."

The knife punched into his stomach just as he locked down his face shield. The blast doors into the interior of the ship slammed closed behind them, and then there was a yawning gap where the far wall had been. Fergus's exosuit hissed, trying to seal the holes in his torso and leg, as he was pulled out into the dark in a shower of his own blood.

He caught the surprised O of Graf's mouth as the man, fumbling madly at his own open face shield, was pulled out into vacuum beside him.

The knife spun away, occasionally catching in the distant light.

I really screwed this one up, Fergus thought. He hoped his friends back at the Shipyard wouldn't be too disappointed in him.

His vision was becoming indistinct. The red lights on his display were hypnotic, beautiful, telling him the suit couldn't seal, couldn't save him. It didn't matter. He'd failed to bring home *Venetia's Sword*, but he'd effectively taken it from Gilger, and taken his right-hand man too. Some small victory for the Vahns, for Bale and Mari, and Katra, and who knew how many unknown others.

I failed, but at least there's some small justice, he thought. *Maybe the next person along will get it right.*

Then a yellow light joined the red ones, flashing rapidly. The Boolean alert.

He watched with bemused fatalism as a jet-black triangle of ship slid between him and the stars, and everything winked out.

Chapter 15

◀─◆─▶

Fergus opens his eyes. The shadow shapes of night-mares shift in and out of focus in dim blue light around him. There is a sound like water falling, so close it seems to tickle his ear, and he wonders if he is suspended in it, but he is neither cold nor hot, and he is fairly sure he's still breathing. Muffled sounds echo around him like the summer crickets of his childhood in the hills around Beinn Ime, deepened and amplified and made strange in this place. Thoughts of home—carefully never missed, not all these years—make him weep. Fresh tears pool around his face as he slips under again.

His father is rowing steadily away from shore, his leg in a thick, white cast bright with newness in the morning sun. Da has joked that it is from falling drunk off a barstool, but Fergus knows that's probably not far off the truth.

"What're ye doin', ye daft bugger?" he calls from the shoreline. "Ye forgot yer pole!"

His father waves and smiles, sets the oars in the boat, and pinches his nose tight as he tips over the back.

Someone grasps at his hand, sweaty and hard and shaking. "Help," a voice says, but he doesn't know how to use the word, how to make sense of it, and after a few moments the hand lets go.

Holding his mother's hand, dry and bony and cold. He is small. "See it, Ferg?" she says, pointing.

He sees it, half-buried in the mud and weeds, water lapping around it. Something white. He lets go of her and runs. Crouching down in his bare feet beside it, he pulls gently with his fingers. Tools break things, his mother has told him hundreds of times. He remembers and will not use them.

It's a small plate, only a tiny chip out of one edge, a wreath of leaves running along the rim and an elegant flower sketched in the center. He rinses it gently in the water, then stands and holds it up. This is treasure: a lost thing found.

"It's nearly whole," he asks. "Can we keep it for once?"

The crickets are loud.

His mother doesn't answer, but she takes the plate and tucks it gently into her basket, safe again. She will spend days cleaning it of dirt only she can see, over and over again, until at last she will set it out on the hillside with all the other things pulled from the water, her very own monument to a vanished place and time. She has tried to explain how she carefully places each item, but Fergus does not understand the logic of it, does not understand *why*. Instead he looks toward the sea, hoping to spot something else on his own, something that if he hides he can keep.

Mars. Ares Three. He's been here just shy of four months, crashing into walls, careening off ceilings, buoyed as much by the weaker gravity as he is by the sheer joy of being here, somewhere new, somewhere free. He even has friends, sort of, or at least a good start on them.

Dru is leaning half on his chair, half on his shoulder, her thick red mud-coated boots up on the café table. She's been filling him in on the latest MCA crackdown and atrocities, on sandstorm protocol, on Martian baseball— she's so eager to disabuse him of wrongheaded Earther ideas about the game that he doesn't have the heart to tell her he has no idea anyway. Her fandom is compelling, and in hindsight he will see all the other signs to which he is right now utterly oblivious.

"There's a game three nights frae noo," he ventures. He is almost completely broke, has been scrounging left-behinds in the café to feed himself while he tries to find something useful to do with himself to earn some cred. But almost broke is not completely broke. "I could gie us tix."

She gets quiet, sits up straight in her own chair. She's been getting better at understanding his accent, and he's gotten better at sounding Marsie, but for a moment he wonders if she missed what he said. "I can't," she says at last. "I have to go do a thing. I'll be out of dome for a few weeks."

"Is it mair fun than baseball?" he asks.

"It's dangerous," she says.

"Sae that's an aye?" he jokes.

She grins, though not for long. "What do you think of Mars?" she asks. The question sounds casual, feels anything but.

"It feels like home. Like I belong on Mars, like I was meant tae be here aw this time. Like I'm finally *alive*," he says. He laughs. "That sounds more mushy and sentimental than I mean it, but it's true."

She punches him gently on the shoulder. "Want to come meet some of my other friends?" she asks.

"Any friend ay yours is a friend ay mine," he says, and finishes his drink in one last big gulp as she grabs her bag off the back of the chair.

He is stretched, pulled from side to side, opened and closed. It is awkward and uncomfortable, but he does not mind. He remembers Graf's knife, and this is not so bad. It feels like his life is unspooling, golden threads extruding from his eyes and ears and wiggling away into the distance, but he does not mind that either. When he wakes, it will all come back inside.

_____

He is sprawled in a chair across from Harcourt, watching the blue-tinged flames of the gas fire, half-full bulb of scotch in hand. "You would have loved my mother," Harcourt says. "She was the epitome of the Red Sand grifter. The things she got away with . . . You'd hardly believe me if I told you."

Never mind that Harcourt has just told several of those stories, all riotously improbable, while they waited for Berol to bring dinner. "The woman could cheat space out of vacuum," he concludes. "She'd love your plan."

Fergus smiles. "At least that'd be one person," he says.

"And you?"

"What?"

"Your mother. Is she where you got your inventive streak?"

Fergus takes another sip of scotch, remembers that Marsie culture is matrilineal, remembers that everyone there eventually talks about their mothers. "I didn't really know her," he says, and that is, in a way, no lie at all.

_____

He has the key in his hand, is not sure what possessed him to take it, knows he has been thinking about this for years. *I should return it before anyone sees,* he thinks, and has half convinced himself to back out when his eyes catch the light glinting off his mother's collection. All the ragtag scraps and shards of a past that was never his own are lined up, enshrined on the bluffs above the shore. The collection appears haphazard, but the pattern is precise by whatever design lies in his mother's mind; once when he moved a piece ten centimeters to the left to see if she'd notice, she beat him with a broom handle so badly he'd had to sleep on his stomach for weeks until the cuts and welts healed. He'd been nine, he thinks. Maybe ten.

His gaze is drawn to the white circle of the plate he found when he was just a boy, helping his mother pull relics of the past from waters that had long since drowned them. He only has to raise his eyes a bit to see the blank patch of blue-green water, lifted in little lines of white by the wind, where not long ago his father had waved, and smiled, and disappeared.

The key is hot in his hand. He should put it back. He turns his back on the bluffs, on the carefully kept monument to lost people's broken things and broken hearts, and wonders if the bike will start.

———

He and Mari are floating in his room in Leakytown, surrounded by a swarm of foil-wrapped balls. Mari is cutting the next one open as he pulls a bright red alien from its box. Mari has been asking him about Mars, about what life is like there, how dirt feels, how the sky feels, if he'll ever go back there. Her wistful tone has made his answers more thoughtful.

She is quiet for a while. "Fergus," she says at last. "You ever miss someone so much it's like you're lost without them?"

"All the time," he says, breaking the plastic alien in half. "I just don't know who."

———

There are crickets, and a scream that doesn't last long. Neither belongs to him, so he drifts back to sleep again, into dreams of thunderstorms and the cold, steady Scotland rain.

———

Someone is shaking him, but he is not ready yet.

———

Mother Vahn is standing in front of him, smaller than he remembers in her bulky suit. He thinks this has not happened, that this is a dream, but he's not sure. When Mother speaks, she has Mari's voice. "What the hell is your problem?" she asks.

"*People* are my problem," he tells her. "I don't want to be a hero."

"Why not?"

"Because when I'm gone, I don't want to leave any trace I was ever here!" he shouts. "I don't want to leave behind people who will miss me, or need me, or who will pick up broken bits of my life to mourn over. I just want to be gone, like—" *Like water, closing over my head.* "Just gone."

"Gone is the coward's way out," she says, and she fades back into the darkness. Even the crickets seem muted, distant now.

———

She's got her bare feet up on the seat of her chair and her skinny arms wrapped around her knees, and she's looking at him as if he's some unexpected curiosity that has washed up on her shoreline. Hani, who'd promised to show him around, has already taken off, abandoning them both.

"Explain it again?" Fergus asks.

She sighs, puts her feet down, and leans forward. "Okay, maybe think of it like a maze. You know what a maze is, right? Good. So, you want to get from point A, the beginning of the maze, to point B at the opposite corner. Normally you have to walk the whole maze, back and forth, twisty-turny, except to you it all feels indistinguishable from walking in a straight line, and you can't see the maze or the walls or the turns at all. With me so far?"

"Aye," he says, though he's not sure he is.

"So, passive jump is like being in the same maze, except wherever you are, you can jump to any other spot in your line of sight. Can't go around bends, can't see the bends, and you still gotta go all the way through the maze, and it still *feels* like a straight line, but you're sorta hopping faster through it. Right?"

"Okay," he says, and he's definitely feeling lost now. "So then, active jump?"

"With active jump, even though you still can't see the walls, there are certain places where instead of following the maze, you can walk right through the wall and end up on the other side. Not instantly—walls can be pretty thick—but now you're not walking the maze or hopping through it but cutting across it. So you're breaking the maze rules. But it only works when you're at one of those magic crossing points. Space is like a big maze drawn on paper that's been crumpled up, and what makes those places where you can cross between points in space are big, complicated gravity wells that are adjacent to each other across folds. Well, they think. I dunno that they *know*. The Bomo'ri probably do, but they're so pissed at us stealing their tech in the first place, no way they're gonna tell us."

She meets his eyes and laughs. "You don't get it."

"No, I do a bit. I just need tae think about it fer longer."

"The point is, if you wanna go five kilometers but you have to walk it, it's effectively farther away than if you want to go fifty but can take a fast train, or five hundred if you can take a rocket. So if you wanna fly at sublight speeds from Jupiter to Pluto, it's gonna take you years and years, but you can jump from Jupiter to Haudernelle—"

"Haudernelle?"

"One of the big human colony worlds way out there somewhere," she says, waving her hands up at the ceiling. "Hundreds of light-years away. Way the hell on the other side of the maze if you're walking, but only a few walls away if you're not. So you can be there in a day or two."

"Have ye been there?"

She rolls her eyes. "No. Mars is the best place in the

universe. Why would anyone want to leave once they've been here?"

"I cannae imagine," he says, and in that moment he can't. Maybe, finally, his luck is turning.

"What did you say your name was?"

"Fergus."

She puts her feet up again and rests her cheek on her knees. "How did I forget that? I'm Dru. How long you known Hani?"

He laughs. "Four days. Ye come here aft?"

"Best coffee in the best city on the best planet in the universe," she says. "And since I explained space to you, you're buying. Then you can tell me where the hell you come from that they talk like you do."

He finds Theo in the control booth of one of the robotic fab bays, holographic schematics in front of him that he's idly moving his forefinger through as if he could touch the lines of purplish light. "You were looking for me?" Fergus asks.

Theo grunts. He is a large man in height and girth, much but not all of which is muscle, and he has a beard to rival any to ever grace the face of an Earthman. The beard is also, much to Fergus's surprise, the most brilliant color of neon blue.

Theo raises an eyebrow. "Kelsie keeps calling me Bluebeard," he says. "I did it to humor her, and I've decided I like it."

"It suits you," Fergus says, and he is surprised to find he means it sincerely.

"Noura said you were back for another visit, and I wanted to get your opinion on something before you vanish again."

"Oh?" Fergus asks. He can't imagine what for. The Shipmakers of Pluto are, hands down, the most weirdly brilliant people he knows, and he has always felt insignificant and dull by comparison.

Theo steps aside and holds out one broad hand to gesture at the windows beyond them. A ship is taking shape out in the bay, still just a half-formed skeletal frame surrounded by a swarm of robots. It is the perfect full-scale version of the holo-design in the room. "It needs something," Theo says. "Maybe not much, but something, and I can't figure out what. Here."

Theo taps the projector, and the schematics switch from purple line drawings to a fully realized model. The ship has a sleek, pointed shape and a large fin on the underside with the active jump engines. It's not like anything Fergus has seen the Shipmakers make before. "New style?" he asks.

"Yeah."

"You ask LaChelle? She's the professional designer."

"She's off on Titan," Theo says. "Maison suggested—and I hesitate to repeat it—'giant googly eyes.' Noura said it was perfectly fine as is."

"Ignatio?"

Theo chortles. "I'm not sure I even know what planet Ignatio is from, but I do know that what passes for aesthetics there is vastly different than in humanspace. You wanna have the weirdest three hours of your life? Ask em eir opinion of Picasso. Have a drink in hand first, though."

"I'm not any kind of artist, but . . ."

". . . but?"

"It's not the shape. I like the shape," Fergus says. "It looks like a ship that'll always keep you one step ahead of trouble. What about adding a bright blue stripe down the side, to break up the lines just a little bit? Blue for Theodoric Bluebeard."

"Maybe?" Theo's thick eyebrows go up as he considers. "Maybe! Thanks, Fergus."

"No problem. You decided what you're going to name this one yet?"

"Yeah. *Venetia's Sword*, I think. Noura's still working on the mindsystem, so we'll have to see how its personality fills out for a few days after initialization before we finalize anything."

"It's a good name," Fergus says. He's never sure how long he'll stay before the itch to move on becomes unbearable or when he'll be back here again, but he hopes he gets a chance to see it fly just once when it's finished.

Da is slumped in his armchair, staring at nothing, lost in memories, remembering lost dreams. Ma is somewhere out by the shore, hunting for relics alone now. She'd found the salvaged teacup he'd hidden from her and smashed it on the floor in a fit. They'd both cried, in separate rooms, for separate reasons, for days. Now she does not trust him, has abandoned him to his father.

"You." Da speaks, startling him. "Your one job was to make her love the both of us. What good are you?"

Even if he'd had an answer, it doesn't matter; the distant stare is back, and Da will not acknowledge him again until Ma returns, and then only with the back of his hand to show whose side he is on, who he is loyal to.

It is a warm enough evening that he can escape and sleep in the shed, where he won't be able to hear their silence.

Someone or something is shaking him. He wakes.

Chapter 16

◆━━◆━━◆

Fergus reached out and found fingers, then a hand on his shoulder. Opening his eyes, he stared uncomprehendingly at her face for a long time before he remembered about words. "Mari!" he said. It was quiet, wrongly quiet. "Where are the crickets?"

"The what?"

He blinked at her. "I don't know," he admitted. He tried to sit up, discovered he was in zero gravity, and went slow-tumbling ass-over-head around the small, unfamiliar space.

"How do you feel?" Mari asked.

"Fine," he said, catching the wallbar with two crooked fingers as he spun past and pulling himself over to it. He lifted up his shirt; the angry red marks from the shrapnel cannon and the flailing cable were gone, as were scars from a dozen different skirmishes over the years. Should he have expected something else?

"Where's my ship?" he asked at last.

"What?"

"*Venetia's Sword*. I had it. I was on board—"

Her eyebrows went up. "That's what you remember?"

His hand strayed back to his abdomen, fingers spread out across his skin, seeking. His shirt, he noticed, had holes in it. "There was something," he said. He frowned, trying to find the missing pieces half-buried in the mud of his memory. "Something happened."

An image of a knife flashed through his mind, there and gone again, but he remembered. "Graf stabbed me," he said, not entirely believing his own words. "He hid on the ship, disabled the environmental controls to keep from being detected. I flushed us both out into space."

"Yeah," Mari said. "I actually saw that part."

He looked at her, noticing the redness of her eyes. Had she been *crying*? "You saved me!" he said.

"No," she said. "If you can remember, you should."

"I can't." His head hurt. He stared around the long, narrow room. It was metal-walled, not rock, and curved slightly over its length. "Where are we?"

"Inside Sunshield One," she said. She was hanging back from him. Afraid? Angry? He didn't know, didn't understand.

He couldn't help himself, and grinned. "I'm so glad you're alive," he said.

She nodded warily. "It was close."

"Me too. Graf stabbed me a couple of times. And the Luceatans . . ." The words tumbled out in a rush. He remembered bits of the beating in the bay, the knife against his throat. "Everything's a jumble. I should be dead. How did you save me?"

"I said I didn't," she snapped. "*Think*, Fergus. *Remember*. It's important."

"I ejected us into space. I don't think Graf got his face shield closed in time. I'd been beaten. Broken ribs—two or three. Collarbone or shoulder, maybe both. One arm. And then Graf stabbed me in the back, and he ripped my leg open, and then he stabbed me in the stomach," Fergus said. He met Mari's eyes. "It hurt," he finished lamely, "but I didn't give him the ship back."

"Getting the ship was that important?"

"It wasn't just about the ship," he said.

"What was it about?"

It's about lost things, he thought. "It doesn't matter."

He broke his gaze away, looked around the room again. *Inside a sunshield?* There was a place he never expected to be.

"What happened after you ejected?" Mari asked.

"Nothing," he said somewhat angrily. "I woke up here."

"That's it?"

"Yes," he said, emphasizing the word. "Yes. I was in

space, and Graf was trying to get his shield down, and the knife was shining, and . . ." He trailed off.

"*And?*"

"Fuck you," he said. "There was a big black triangle, okay? It flew right past me."

"No it didn't, Fergus," she said. "It stopped. It took you and Graf. It only gave you back."

"I don't understand," he said. He floated there in silence for several long minutes, trying to absorb it all. He felt fine, looked fine. *Normal.*

"They kept you for two days."

"What?! No," he said. "I just—"

"Two days."

"Two days? What's happened? Where's the ship?"

"It's right where you left it," she said.

"No one's tried to take it?"

"No."

"But the war's over? Gilger's on the run, right? People have started cleaning up and fixing things? The Wheels is safe, Arelyn Harcourt is okay—"

Mari jerked her head back, staring at him sharply. "What?!"

The last of his strange detachment snapped and was gone. "She's not . . .?"

"What happened to Arelyn?!" Mari cried. She grabbed his shirt, shaking him.

"Gilger. He said he'd sent someone to Mars to grab Arelyn and if Harcourt didn't back off, he'd have her killed."

She punched his shoulder. "Why the fuck wasn't that the *first* thing you told me?!"

"I just woke up, and my head's been all full of crickets!" Fergus shouted back. "And you said it's been two days! What have you people been doing?!"

Mari buried her face in her hands for a few moments, then looked back up at him, no less steel in her eyes than before. "It took me most of that time just to get this far. All the comms were blocked, nothing was moving because of the Asiig, and Harcourt's people have all disengaged. I couldn't reach anyone who could help me. I guess now I know why. Shit," she said. *"Shit."*

"We can still fix this," Fergus said. Her flystick was tethered in one corner, plugged into a charging outlet. "We go get *Venetia's Sword*. We use it to pin down as many of Gilger's people as we can while the Governor moves in and demand Gilger release Harcourt's daughter in exchange for his own life."

"You really think it's all that easy?"

"No, but also kind of yes," he said. "Why can't it be?"

She grabbed his arm, not hard. "You need to see something," she said. She pulled him from the room, down a narrow hall, and into a small chamber with a hammock, her pack drifting beside it. On the far side of the room was a tiny portal, and she shoved him toward it.

He peered out. *Venetia's Sword* was a tiny beacon, bright and shining in the sunlight outside the Halo, right where he had left it. Above it and to each side it was dwarfed by three black triangles, unmoving, unfathomable. "I . . ." Fergus started, then realized he had no idea what to say.

"They've been there since they picked up you and Graf," Mari said. "There's a fourth making a slow circle around Cernee. No one's ever seen anything like this, and certainly never more than one ship at a time. No one knows what it means, but I think they're waiting for you to come back and get the ship."

"What? So they can kill me? No way."

"They had you for two days. Why not kill you then?"

"To play with me?"

"Play with you? Do you have any idea what they did to Graf?"

"You said they didn't let him go." *I remember screaming,* he thought.

"Yeah, well, that's not exactly true." Mari reached into a pocket, pulled out a small cube, and flicked it across the intervening space to him.

Fergus picked it out of the air, turned it around in his hand. It was reddish with white streaks, about a centimeter per side, and hard as stone. "What is it?" he asked. "Marble?"

"No. It's Graf."

He let go of it hastily. "What?"

"Started drifting into Cernee the day before they popped you out. I hear people are calling them meatcubes," Mari said. "They're impervious to any attempt to cut or break them, but if you put two next to each other that were, ah, adjacent in the original, they click together like magnets. You can pull them apart again."

"How do you know that's Graf?"

"There's a competition to see who can find and put together the biggest chunk of him. Someone has about a third of his head and got a retina ID match." She plucked the cube from the air and tucked it back in a pocket. "Word is Gilger has completely dumped his shitpack and he's taking his anger out on everyone and everything still in his reach, which thanks to the Asiig isn't much. Everyone's stuck where they are, terrified of being taken. If we can find you a suit—"

"Hold on! What happened to my suit?"

"The Asiig dumped you out in a big clear baggie," she said. "It disintegrated as soon as we got inside atmo in the sunshield."

A voice spoke up from behind them, startling them both. "The Vahn risked her life to reach you. It was foolish."

They spun around. A white-suited figure was floating in the doorway, its mirrored face shield a blank, intimidating wall. Fergus stared at the Shielder for a moment, then back at Mari.

"I was trying to get back to the Wheels—just like some idiot made me promise—by sneaking around the backside of the sunshields when the Asiig appeared out of nowhere and dropped you practically right in front of me," Mari said. "So I grabbed you and brought you here."

"Why not take us back to the Wheels?" Fergus asked Mari.

"For one thing, we only got here about three hours ago. I've been waiting for you to wake the fuck up. And anyway, you think you'd be welcome back at the Wheels? Or anywhere in Cernee? Everyone saw you get sucked up by the Asiig and probably saw you get squirted out again too. No one is going to trust you because no one knows what the Asiig have done to you."

"No one asked us if we minded," the Shielder interrupted.

"Well, *do* you?" Mari demanded.

"We cannot now know," the Shielder said. "It has been added to the Narrative, so it must be as it has been."

"What—" Fergus started to ask, but the Shielder shrugged, spun in the doorway, and was gone again. He looked to Mari. "What?"

She glared at him. "Just don't talk to them. They don't like it. That's why they almost never leave the sunshields. And unless you want to spend the rest of your miserable life here having enlightening conversations just like that one, you need to start thinking about how to get to your ship, because there's nowhere else you can go now."

"I'm the same as always." He held out his arms. "Look at me! It's just me!"

"When the Asiig change people, sometimes they add limbs, subtract limbs, change your skin to living stone, stuff like that. And sometimes they change things you can't see. When they took Mother, back when she was my age, they only had her for two days too. And look what happened to us."

"I don't—" Fergus stared at her, and she stared back with her defiant, green-brown eyes. *Not violet. Not like Mother Vahn's. Why hadn't that clicked before?* "Your eyes," he said. "They aren't the same as the other clones'. How is that possible?"

"We're not *clones*, you dumbass. That's what I'm trying to tell you. They changed Mother, but in ways you

can't see. We just replicate, one way or another. My birth
mother was Mother's eighth gene-identical granddaugh-
ter, and she ran away and met a man at Crossroads,
and . . . well. Here I am, anyway."

So Graf missed some after all, was Fergus's first thought.

Mari continued, "That's why we stay here. Whatever
the Asiig wanted Mother and her descendants to inject
into the human genome, we decided to keep it to ourselves instead. We assume we're dangerous. And if people knew, there'd be a lot more of them trying to kill us
than just Gilger."

"That's why you didn't dare go to Mars with Arelyn."

"Yeah. And now you're an alien experiment too, except unlike us, everyone knows it about you. You're a
freak."

"Fuck you," he said.

"Welcome to my world," she said. She dangled something out of one hand, let it float toward him. "The key
to my 'stick," she said. "Borrow a suit. Go get your ship."

"I can't," he said. He tilted his head to one side, let
the key sail past him. "I'm scared. I don't know what to
do. Does that make you happy?"

"No!" she shouted. "No, I'm not happy! Members of
my family have been killed, friends have been killed or
hurt, my best friend's been kidnapped in a war *you* helped
start, and you think it'll make me *happy* again to see some
poor, groveling dirtsider finally admit what everyone already knows, that he's useless?"

"Get out," he said, quietly.

"What?" Mari said.

"Go. Get out. Leave me *alone*," he said, pointing at
the door.

She pushed past him, grabbed her 'stick key, then did
a cannonball for the door. He knew he should apologize
but couldn't, could do nothing but stare at her as all the
anger and hurt he had ever felt sat like a lump in his
throat.

"Fine," she said. "You're on your own, then. Good

luck with that." She pushed her way out the door without looking back.

He pulled his knees up to his chest and floated, arms curled around himself, and tried to retreat back into his faded memories of sunlight, grass, water, open sky. Instead, all he had was himself, and failure, and the memory of crickets.

———

When he opened the door, he half expected Mari to be floating there, waiting with a caustic and well deserved *Took you long enough*. The hallway was empty.

Not having any better ideas, he picked a direction and went. The high-ceilinged corridors of the sunshield curved along its exterior lines, slowly narrowing as the giant concave disk thinned towards its edges. The walls were covered intermittently with light etchings, and he slowed down once or twice to look at them. Figures in a sort of endless metal-scratch tapestry.

"That's the Narrative," a voice said, and Fergus looked over to see another Shielder in the hall. Her face shield was open, and her face was painted in an intricate, abstracted floral design of dark reds and purples. "It is our record of everything that is, from when we built the very first shield to when others began to arrive to live in the protection of our shade, and someday it will show our very last day, if it does not happen too quickly."

"It's beautiful," Fergus said, not quite daring to touch the etchings, though he desperately wanted to. "Although I don't really understand it."

"Much the same could be said of history itself," she replied. "This is our way of seeing, of being observers without being a part of the observed. Both are imperfect and necessary arts, and depend on others not to drag us into their events. If you understand me?"

"Yeah, I think I do," he said. "I'm sorry we ended up here uninvited, but I don't think there was any other choice. History works that way too sometimes. Do you know where Mari is? Mari Vahn?"

"She's in the Sunpoint. Follow me." The Shielder floated off down the corridor, and he pulled himself along behind.

At last she stopped and gestured him forward toward a narrow tunnel with a heavy glass airlock. "In," she said.

He got in. "When the door seals, press the red button," she said. "At the other end, press the green."

"Okay," he said.

The Shielder slammed the hatch shut, leaving him alone in the dark and the faint glow of a red button. He pressed it.

It was like being sucked down the world's largest drinking straw. One moment he was floating, claustrophobic, in the tube, and the next he was being pulled down feet-first as if a giant had wrapped one hand around his boots and given an enormous jerk. "Whaaa—!" he started to yell when he suddenly hit thicker, stickier air and began to slow. *Slug field*, he realized, his heart pounding. *She could have warned me.*

Outside the tube was open space, stars, and a tiny silver ship with its three black triangle guards.

When Fergus's feet finally touched the far end of the tube, he was moving slowly enough for his knees to absorb the bounce without discomfort. He tapped the green button and exited as quickly as he could through the opening hatch into a small hab.

It was a circular room, quiescent monitors lining a long console bank in the center and a narrow band of windows running most of its circumference, suspended in space between Sunshields One and Two. A Shielder was working at a side console, and in the center, framed against Cernee itself, Mari sat in a grippy chair with her back to the room. There was a P2P unit in front of her, green light on top.

"—sorry she yelled at you," Mari was saying. "She's probably just worried."

Harcourt's voice rumbled low out of the speaker on the console, but Fergus couldn't quite hear what he said. When he fell silent, Mari added, "Well, it's still not your fault. I'd have found another way to escape the farm. It's just . . . I'm scared. I don't know what to do."

He tried to push off into the room and remembered too late that he was down to socks. Slipping on the floor, he sent himself tumbling head over heels through the empty space. The Shielder turned and watched him for half a minute before going back to his work.

"Gilger blew a rocket through Ficklecan," he heard Harcourt say, audible now. "There was an Authority squad stuck there when the Asiig showed up. They've been able to redistribute spare air to the residents who were suited up and survived the hull breach, but there are lots of dead. There was a crèche there for the children of gas miners away on the job, and the numbers . . . Everyone is a sitting target, and I'm sitting here unable to do a damned thing. Hell, part of me wants to fire up Gilger's shuttle and float the entire fucking Wheels to Crossroads, or Mars itself."

"Mauda would object."

"I'd rather she lived a long life never forgiving me for it than any of the alternatives."

"I suppose," Mari answered.

"You can't blame this on Ferguson, you know."

Fergus blinked, opened his mouth to speak up; it seemed unfair now that they didn't know he was there. Before he could, the Shielder turned again, opened his face shield to reveal a face painted with blue and purple swirls, and put a finger to his lips.

"Gilger and Vinsic must've been planning this for a long time," Harcourt was saying. "If anything, Fergus pushed them into moving sooner. Who knows how much more prepared Gilger might have been if he hadn't?"

"Maybe," Mari said. She didn't sound convinced.

"I never thought he'd go after Arelyn," Harcourt said. "If I did . . . damn, I hate what-ifs. If only Fergus—"

"If only Fergus what?"

"He knows Mars, maybe even better than I do. He wouldn't tell you this, but he was a fucking hero there. If anyone could've found Arelyn and brought her back . . . I mean, that's what he did: the impossible. But he's not on Mars, and who knows what monstrous things were done to him? It feels like he was my only chance, and now he's gone."

"But he—" Mari started to speak.

"Oh, your friend has just now this moment arrived!" the Shielder interrupted. He stepped forward, gently grabbed Fergus's arm, and propelled him toward a bar.

"Gotta go," Mari said, and disconnected the P2P.

"I'm sorry," Fergus said.

"Why are you even here? I thought you were going to go sulk in a corner for the rest of your short, crappy life," she snarled. She looked haggard and, much as he was loath to believe it, fragile. *This is her world crumbling,* he thought. *It doesn't matter that mine is too.*

"Was that Harcourt?" he asked. "Is he okay?"

"No, he's not fucking *okay*," she said.

"I'm sorry," he said again. "May I use the P2P?"

"Fine." She pushed herself up out of the grippy chair. He moved along the bar until he was close enough, grabbed the back of the seat, and pulled himself in. "Harcourt won't want to talk to you," she added.

Fergus knew that was meant to hurt him, to make her point that he wasn't welcome, but he understood where that anger came from and let it go.

"I wasn't going to call him," he said instead. It took him a long moment to find and center *Venetia's Sword* in the crosshairs. His hands itched as he lined up the scope. Magnified, the three alien ships seemed to be staring right at him. Chills ran through his hands and arms, tingling at the base of his skull as he flipped the P2P over to active. The green light came on. *Venetia's Sword* was receiving.

"Control, voice command, acknowledge," he said.

After an uncomfortable pause, the ship responded. "Channel authorized and-and open."

"Engage engines, three percent max, along P2P trajectory."

"Engaging," the ship said. A moment later, it added, "Failure. Forward propulsion has not occurred. Shutting engines d-down and running dia-dia-diagnostics."

"Ship, has there been any intrusion since I exited via the bay?"

"None has been detected."

"Run a full scan on the ships in your immediate proximity."

"There are no ships in my immediate proximity."

"There are three within a hundred meters of you."

"Unable to comply. There are no ships."

"Run an exterior environmental scan, full sensors."

"Failure. Sensors are unable to return data on ex-ex-exterior of the ship; there is no exterior environment." There was a pause, then tentatively, "Are you still coming to get me?"

"I am," Fergus said. "It might take me a while, though."

"Acknowledged," the ship said.

He leaned back and stared at the P2P, at a loss. "The ship can't move, and it can't detect anything outside of its own hull. It's so unreachable it might as well not even exist."

"We have already added it to the Narrative," the Shielder said, frowning. "So it must exist, then and now and next."

"What?" Fergus asked.

"Stars, you're an idiot," Mari said. She was angrily rubbing a tear from her cheek with a gloved fist. "Why can't history work like that? Until it's observed and recorded, it may or may not exist. So they draw the ship, and the ship becomes fixed, and the ship's past and future with it. It gets to keep its history forever, and because they've probably drawn your sorry ass—"

"We drew all of him," the Shielder said, offended.

"—we get stuck with you too. And you're no good for anything at all, are you? You *or* your stupid ship."

"I can't get the ship to come to me," Fergus said. "I'm stuck here too."

"Where do you feel your pull?" the Shielder asked. "That's how you become unstuck, by going where you are meant to be drawn, or where there are unfinished drawings of you that need completion."

My pull? Fergus thought. He felt split into a million pieces. Nothing had ever pulled him, nowhere, not since Mars. Mars, where he just might've been able to do some good if he were there instead of here. *Great hero,* he thought. *Always everyone's disappointment.*

Sitting on the surface of Mezz Rock, Harcourt had predicted that Mars would pull him back. *It's like Mars has crept into every conversation I've had here,* Fergus thought. *You'd think being a bazillion light-years and seven jump points away would be enough distance, especially without a ship.*

But if I had another . . . He stared up at the Shielder in some surprise. "Do you have long-range escape pods?"

"We do," the Shielder said. "Five. They were a gift from Mr. Harcourt in exchange for connecting the Wheel Collective to the power grid."

"Would one get as far as Crossroads?" he asked.

"Why Crossroads?" Mari asked.

"That's the nearest place to the system jump point, and I know people. From there, I can get us to Mars."

"Mars?" Mari asked. "And what do you mean, 'us'?"

"We can't do any good here. With Harcourt out of the battle, the Governor can't hold against both Gilger and Vinsic for long. The two of us . . . We wouldn't change that with anything we could do here. But if we can get Harcourt back in the fight—"

"How? He can't, or Gilger will kill Arelyn."

"That's what *we* can do. Don't you see? Everything

keeps pointing to Mars—Harcourt and Arelyn's history, Gilger's hatred, your fears. Maybe this *was* inevitable. I know Mars, and you know Arelyn. Together we could—"

"I can't leave here! You know that!"

"Even if I found Arelyn, why should she trust me? She's your best friend. You need to be there. And we have to go fast, because as soon as Gilger gets the upper hand, he won't need a hostage anymore."

Mari was silent for a full minute. "What if once I leave," she asked at last, "I don't want to come back?"

"What if? It's a big universe out there. When you get sick of it, Cernee will still be waiting for you," he said.

She turned to the Shielder. "Make him understand?"

The Shielder shrugged. "We have not yet drawn you staying or going, but if there were an easy way of depicting pointless arguing, we would have a whole wall of you two already. Follow me." He turned and pushed off for the door.

"Where are we going?" Fergus asked the Shielder.

"To the pod bay. It has been agreed upon that we should send you away from Cernee before further events follow you here to us." The Shielder turned at the transport tube, held his hand out to indicate they should go first. "We agree with the Earther; it is obvious you are both meant to go to Mars, although we will be satisfied with anywhere far, far away."

Chapter 17

◆━◆

Three tubes later, they emerged in front of a large pair of blast doors. The Shielder came in a few moments after them and keyed in a short code. The doors split apart, revealing a small bay. A row of white pods sat in a perfect line, shaped like little more than huge grains of rice. One on the end was open. Fergus stopped and stared, uncertainty crashing in, and a quick glance at Mari showed she wasn't feeling any more confident.

Hanging midair beside them, the Shielder was twitching his legs in a way that was distinctly reminiscent of someone tapping their feet. "You know your path. Why do you wait?"

Whatever Mari muttered under her breath, Fergus couldn't hear it. He entered the bay and peered into the open pod. It was a standard passive-jump pod with cryo and semicryo capabilities. Two long, thin beds partially separated by a thin wall of instrumentation and xglass filled most of the front third; the entire back was engine and powerstore.

Mari stared at Fergus from the other side of the pod. The Shielder made an inarticulate sound—half sigh, half growl—and turned to Fergus. "You understand the launch systems?" he asked.

"Yes."

"Good. Now leave." Without saying another word, the Shielder turned and floated out of the room.

"Well," Mari said as the echo of the blast doors closing behind the Shielder faded. "It's not a lot of space inside."

"The pod will low-stat us to conserve oxygen and resources, so we'll hardly notice."

"Oh." She frowned. "I've never been frozen."

"It's not full cryo, more like being in a really deep sleep. Which side do you want?" he asked.

"What the hell does it matter? Just get in."

Hand still on the edge, Fergus flipped himself over to gently land on one couch, grabbing the handholds inside to keep from bouncing back out. Stretching his legs into the pod's forward well, he found a toecatch and used that to keep himself steady as he pulled the retractable straps out from the sides and began to fasten himself down.

"Show-off," Mari said, pulling herself in with no less grace than he had.

"I thought you said Shielders didn't like to talk?" Fergus asked as he started powering on the pod systems.

"They don't want you talking to *them*," she said. "Although I'm starting to see two sides to that."

"Yeah," he said. "Do they all paint their faces?"

"All that I've met," she said. "And never the same twice. They've got strange ideas about obscuring their identities that's tied into this whole 'Narrative' thing, but I like it."

"Me too," he decided, "though I'm not convinced I like them yet. And I'm sure they don't like me, so we should get out of here before they decide to just space us instead. I'm closing the pod, then we'll launch, and assuming the pod and the sleep systems work correctly and there are no pirates or sudden rockstorms between here and there, we'll wake up coming into Crossroads."

He reached across his chest for the control panel, then pulled his hand back as it started tingling, itching.

"What?" Mari asked, noticing his hesitation.

"Nothing." His hand was fine, same as always. He reached forward again tentatively, felt nothing, pressed the canopy button. The pod closed smoothly over them and sealed.

A control arm extended from either side, meeting in the middle and forming a curved bar directly overhead.

The interior filled with a gentle, warm light. Energy levels were good, system checks were good—no reason to wait. He switched the tiny overhead display to the nav computer, set the coordinates, and triple-checked them.

"The bay has a rail-launcher system. It can be a rough start, but they're pretty foolproof. On the count of three?" Fergus asked.

"Just *do* it," Mari said. Her eyes were closed, and her hands were white-knuckled against the armrests.

He reached up, ignoring a resurgence of tingling in his hand, and initiated launch. The lights dimmed, and he could feel the grinding vibration of the launcher underneath the pod locking on. When the systems greenlit, he keyed the confirm, and automated systems took over.

The vibration grew, as did the sense of motion; Fergus knew they were dropping down through a chute and about to be crapped out into the universe at significant velocity, but the pod's interior dampers were good; Harcourt had done well by the Shielders. He found himself relaxing just a little. The screen in front of him flashed up stats as they soared free of the sunshield.

I'm finally really leaving Cernee, he thought. Instead of relief, there was a sharp pang in his gut, a reminder of unfinished business, unfulfilled promises.

The pod systems were still green. "We're out and on course," he said. "You ready for a nap?"

Mari's hands were still clenched, but she opened her eyes. "First tell me who Dru is."

Fergus froze. "How did you—"

"You said her name a lot before you woke up."

"Oh." Fergus struggled for an answer. "Dru was *you*, kind of," he said at last. "I was fifteen and new to Mars, she was nineteen and grew up there, and we were best friends. She wasn't afraid of anything. We went on dangerous, wild adventures together, playing rebels and heroes like it was a game until the danger caught up to us. To her. And I couldn't do a damned thing to save her."

"So you honor her memory by blaming yourself for

the fact that she made her own choices? Isn't that a bit self-centered?"

"You wouldn't get it," Fergus said.

"No? Aren't the two of us running off to Mars to play hero together, just like you two did then? Don't you *dare* think that gives you the right to feel responsible for me."

"Aren't I?"

"I'm here because of Arelyn, not you. I could've talked the Shielders into letting me stay. They know and trust me. It's you they wanted to get rid of," she said, though it sounded like she was trying to convince herself of that at least as much as him. "That makes me an equal partner. Whatever happens, I am not some damned do-over for your misplaced conscience, and you do not have my permission to believe I don't fully own my choices. Mother understood that, and so does Harcourt. Time you did too. You got that?"

"Yeah," he said.

"Great. Let's never talk about it again. Now put us the fuck to sleep before I change my mind."

"Right," Fergus said. He punched in the sleep sequence. Almost immediately he felt warm, tired, his vision blurring. "See you in Crossroads," he managed to say, but she was already out, so he closed his eyes too.

Coming back out of the haze, Fergus tried to count how many times he'd been low-statted over the years, but he couldn't manage to wrap his fuzzy brain around a solid number. One thing he was sure of was that he was developing resistance to the aerosol cocktail ubiquitous to the systems. Not only was he waking up faster—Mari was still out like a light—but rather than the elapsed time being so opaque it seemed like a jump from one instant to another, there were remnants of a slow dream state at the fringes of his memory.

That wouldn't be so bad if he hadn't spent most of it dreaming there was a black triangle trailing in their wake.

He checked their position. The pod had come out of jump about an hour outside of Crossroads and closed half the remaining distance in the time it had taken it to initiate wakeup and for him to drag himself up out of his stupor. Beside him, Mari's breathing and color were slowly returning to normal. She'd be awake in another ten or fifteen minutes.

The pod was close enough to the station to establish a comm link; Fergus popped a window open and sent a query to a "facilitator service" he'd worked with in the past. To his relief, the two-woman team was still in business—and not in jail or on the run—and took his call. When Mari finally began staring around her in disorientation, the meet was already set and the call over.

"What went wrong?" she said. "Why didn't we go to sleep?"

"We did," he answered. Now *that* was the sort of sleep he missed. "We'll be pulling into the Sunward Dock at Crossroads in about eight minutes, and if things go smoothly, we should be out of here again within three or four hours."

"Yeah? And how are we going to manage that?"

"Some friends are going to meet us," Fergus said. At her look, he smiled. "Don't worry. You'll like them."

"If you say so."

The docking signal came through right on time. He keyed the pod to follow it but kept a hand on the override. He knew this place too well. *Speaking of which . . .* "We should talk about Crossroads," he said. "Most of the people who live in Cernee are involved in legitimate work—growing lichen, asteroid, ice, and gas-giant mining, basic essentials trade. Crossroads isn't like that. If there's any honest trade here other than bartending, it's a sideline to most of what goes on. The population is always in flux, and everyone and everything is potentially dangerous."

"Even your friends?"

"Especially them," he said.

The station was visible now; much like Cernee, it was

a jumble of strung-together cans and dead ships, but un-like the loosely woven web of Cernee's lines, it was as if a giant galactic cat had pulled its strings apart, batted it around for a bit, tried to eat it, and barfed it out again. The Sunward Dock was a massive, blocky rustcube on the fringes, dangling off the end of a bent pipe, sur-rounded by a thick cloud of debris and trash.

Dammit, Fergus swore. Once in a while scavengers came out and dredged through the flotsam, looking for anything saleable, and inadvertently kept the approach clean. By the look of things, they were overdue. "I'm slowing down the pod to minimum," he said. "I'm also putting extra energy in the deflectors in the nose; if the lights dim, that's why."

Mari turned on her own screen. "What is all that stuff?" she asked. She jumped as the lower half of a body, desic-cated and frozen, passed up and over the pod. "No, forget I asked."

Something Fergus would've sworn was a can of beans bounced off the canopy right in front of the view cam-era, making both him and Mari reflexively duck. "This might be a bumpy landing," Fergus said as something else thudded along the underside of the pod.

The automated systems finally locked on and pulled them through the last of the debris and toward a small bay. A mechanical arm latched onto the pod and dragged it in.

The screens went dark. "Huh," Fergus said.

"Well? Are we in?"

"In, yes. We should have gotten atmosphere as soon as the bay closed. But the bay systems haven't connected to us to get a readout, and the docking systems have let go, so I've got nothing. No idea what's out there."

"Why aren't our screens working?"

"They are. It's just pitch dark. If the lights didn't come on, maybe the door didn't close, or maybe it's still vacuum inside. I wish I had my suit," he said. "Any suit. Even one three sizes too small."

"Do I have controls over here?" Mari asked.

"Yeah, full dual-pilot. Why?"

Mari scrolled through the interface for a moment, then hit a button. The pod groaned as if slapped by a massive hand, and the screen in front of Fergus flared white for an instant.

"What did you do?!"

She didn't answer. The screen flickered, then settled into a dim, orangish image of the inside of the bay. "Bay's closed," she said. "And there's atmo."

"Did you just blast one of the maneuvering jets? Are you off your head? That could've started a fire!" he shouted.

"Not if there wasn't air," she said. "And air means the door has sealed. Do you think the bay has fire suppression?"

"No," Fergus said through gritted teeth, working to unbuckle his harness as quickly as he could, "I don't imagine it has *working* fire suppression. Weren't you looking at this place as we flew in?"

Mari was freeing herself from her own pod couch. "Good point," she said.

He reached for the canopy control, his palm tingling again. Punching the button, he took a defiantly optimistic breath as the pod canopy unsealed.

Well, we're not already dead, he thought. *That's probably good.*

Hauling himself out of the pod, he vaulted into the bay space. On the walls a series of *Safety Is For You!* posters, Crossroads Security proclamations, and flyers from everyone from Humans First to the Singularity League burned and smoldered, sending little ashlets of flame out into the room around them. Fergus decided he was better off not knowing what flammable organic substance they'd been printed on this far from any place that had ever even imagined such a thing as a tree. Certainly the odor of the smoke was . . . earthy.

Unlike e-paper and anything else not nailed down

and guarded here, maybe the main utility of such paper was people's disinclination to want to steal it.

The burning flyers were not enough to damage anything else in the bay, much less threaten the pod; by the time he and Mari got to the exit, the last ember had given its ghost up to the room.

Mari turned up her handlight as Fergus tried to get the bay controls back online. "We need to get you a suit," she said.

"There won't be one here I can afford to buy that I can also afford to trust," he said. "Sellers in the central marketplace set prices based on how few holes they have in them."

"Great."

He gave up poking at the controls and hit the panel with the side of a fist. It flickered back to life at last. Scrolling through the settings, he enabled the bay security—such as it was—with an old aliased account of his, sufficiently disreputable for the identity to blend here.

"'Gord Gordon?'" Mari asked, reading over his shoulder.

"Yeah."

He *liked* his aliases, dammit. She just rolled her eyes.

The large docks were above them, a dozen clockwork octopus arms that, when working, connected up freighters and warships and pirate ships side by side. The rusty-walled, urine-scented corridors were deserted between their bay and the main dock floor. The security and customs post was also deserted. Mari frowned. "Is something going on?" she asked.

Fergus shrugged. "Always. In this instance, I expect that whoever is supposed to be on duty wasn't sober enough to drag himself here."

She shook her head. "This is definitely making me feel better about spending the rest of my life in Cernee."

They left the Sunward Dock and floated through the maze of tubes to a large hab-like structure that housed a single bar known as the Armpit. Although they'd passed almost no one on the way there, the bar itself was packed wall-to-wall, floor-to-ceiling. The lighting was dim, yellow-green, and strobing. A live band somewhere on the other side of the crush of humanity turned an unpleasantly claustrophobic mess into deafening chaos.

Mari said something, pulling at Fergus's arm, but he couldn't hear a word. He gestured toward the back of the room and began to push and shove his way through the crowd. Where there wasn't a convenient bar or post to use for leverage, Fergus planted a large hand against some random person and pushed off. No one seemed to mind—most were too intoxicated to notice—except for the few who'd come looking for an excuse to fight. He'd learned to spot them years ago, braced somewhere away from the bars and poles, drunken, dangerous smiles on their faces.

Along the back of the room there were small private booths, a fake candle on each table center providing just enough light to dimly make out the people in grippy chairs within. It took him a moment to find the one he wanted. He knocked politely, and a small-framed woman with deep black skin and neon green hair unlocked the door.

"Maha!" he said, and gave her an enthusiastic embrace.

"Fergus," the other woman in the booth spoke up. She leaned forward, her eyes glowing like silver-blue orbs in the candlelight, set deep in a fur-lined face.

"Qai," he said. "You've got your winter coat in."

The alien grinned, showing sharp teeth. "I spent a season back home on family business. It's come in nicely, but I'll regret it when it begins to shed. So much easier to keep short, even if I lose my stripes."

Mari was staring at her. "You're not human," she said, then shook her head. "I'm sorry, that's rude. Of course you're not human."

"So few people are," Maha said.

"I'm from Dzen Prime," Qai said. "Our home system

lies in a part of the galaxy that humans haven't reached, at least so far. I am likely the only Dzenni you'll ever meet, but I can say I've met many other species from all over, some known to humans and many not. Most are decent people, if always beset with their own unique quirks worth minding. Just like humans, really." She took a sip of her steaming drink and smiled.

"Are you drinking *tea*?" Mari asked.

"Yes. Our people quite like it. So very civilized of you to invent it for us."

Maha raised her own glass, which glowed red like lava and had a tiny paper umbrella in it. "Not me," she said.

"No, not you," Qai said. "I . . ." Her voice drifted off, and her eyes narrowed.

"What?" Fergus asked, glancing over his shoulder at the door, seeing nothing more alarming than usual.

"Neither of you smell right," she said. "If my eyes were closed, I'd swear neither of *you* were entirely human."

Beside him, Mari tensed.

"Qai, if that's your tactful way of telling me I need a shower . . ." Fergus said.

"Yet you are still also Fergus-scented, Fergus," Qai finished. "Very strange. It must be the air handlers in here interfering with my senses. Or you've been eating very odd things."

"Does Celekai food count?"

Qai laughed. "It could, and no, don't tell me why you'd do that. I prefer to imagine it as the penultimate challenge in some weird dare-based death duel."

"This being Crossroads, I think we can agree smells are an especially poor choice of conversation starter," Maha said. "Sit, you two. Fergus, you said you had something you needed to get to Mars of Sol System in fast time?"

"Yes. Us," he said.

"I don't run passenger space," Maha said.

"Shipping space is all we need. We come with our own pod."

She tilted her head toward her partner. "The *Gormless*?"

"Maybe." Qai raised a finger to her lips, chewed absently on the tip of an extended claw. "Or the *Doubtful Duchess*."

"*Gormless* would be faster."

"*Duchess* would be safer."

Fergus leaned in. "How much faster?"

Qai and Maha exchanged glances. "Three days for the *Gormless*, ten or eleven for the *Duchess*," Qai said.

"It's on a route through the Barrens," Maha added. "A couple of the bigger Enclaves are warring, so it's been a rough go lately. Ships get boarded, stuff gets taken."

Qai turned to Fergus and named a price, then added, "*Duchess* would cost you a third less."

Mari paled. "Fergus . . ." she said.

"*Gormless*, then," Fergus said. "Done." He reached across the table and shook hands with Maha and Qai in turn.

There was a violent crash as something slammed against the door of the booth, and all three of them were out of their seats in an instant. A short, curved blade appeared in Maha's hand, held down close to her thigh.

A man sprawled against the outside of the door left a red smear in his wake as he feebly pushed off and disappeared back into the crowd. In the distance, rising slightly higher than the rest, Fergus could see a dead-airspace squatter, cracking his knuckles and grinning.

Maha's knife disappeared, and Qai settled back into her seat, although the fur around her neck had bristled and Fergus could feel her long, sinuous tail twitching back and forth under the table.

"So," Fergus said. "Your usual account?"

"We've got a new drop on Haudernelle North," Qai said. "I'll give you the node and deposit access number."

Fergus spread out his empty hands, palms up. "I lost all my personal belongings recently," he said. "Including my pad."

Qai tapped two claws together. "Given what we're charging you for the lift, I'm sure we can throw a new pad into the deal. Was it at least a fair fight?"

Behind him there were three black triangles, waiting. "Not even close," he said.

"Ah. That's too bad," Maha said. "Drinks on us. You can tell us what you've been up to while we get your pod stowed, then it's down to the docks, and we'll get you on your way."

———

A little over an hour and a half later, Qai handed him a still-sealed handpad, *Property of Guratahan Sfazil Security Service* engraved on its back. As Fergus peeled off the foil and powered it on, he glanced up and caught his first good look at the giant packing crate Qai and Maha were sending them to Mars in. Their pod was already nestled securely in the center, tiedowns and expanded foam baffles holding it immobile.

"Seriously?" he asked. "Frozen cow fetuses?"

"Frozen *medical sample* cow fetuses," Maha corrected. "See? Contagion warnings. This is a genuine Moritau Ag Guild quarantine tag. People are terrified of this shit. No one is going to want to steal you."

It was hard to argue with that. Pulling up a secure bank node on Titan, Fergus routed the women's fee through it to the node they'd given him.

Qai glanced down at the pad in her hand. "Done," she said. "The *Gormless* should be ready to leave Crossroads space in about an hour. At the far end, we have crew on Ares Orbital Station Alpha to unbox you. Will you require your pod stored there?"

"No," Fergus said. "It's got some sort of odd static problem. Nothing serious, but it makes me nervous. Can you sell it for me?"

"I can. Set minimum or best price?"

"Best price."

"Minus the usual commission, I'll credit you back once it's sold," she said. "Unlikely, but if it doesn't sell, we split the disposal fee twenty-eighty, pain on your side. Done?"

"Done."

"Fergus, how are we going to get back home without the pod?" Mari asked.

"We'll have other options once we're on Mars. Besides, once we've got Arelyn, the three of us won't fit in it."

"Make sure you get some REM cycles along the way," Qai added. "You're not looking especially well."

Now that she said it, he wasn't feeling too great either. "Sorry," he said. "I'm just thirsty. It's nothing."

"If you say so," Maha said. "Crew will be here soon to load you up into the ship, and we're just waiting on departure clearance. Whoever answered at Airspace Control tried to tell me what kind of sandwich he wanted, so I'm going to go up to there and slap someone into cooperation. Qai will get you settled in." She waved and left.

Qai held out a hand to Mari to help her up into the crate. Mari hesitated just a moment, then took it. "Can I ask," she said, "about what it's like? You know, being an alien? Sorry if I'm being rude. I've never had a chance to talk to one before."

"You lot are the aliens, not I," Qai said. "Humans are a bit of a fad back on Dzen Prime. It's a cultural interest; your species has such wonderful contradictions that we find you a maddening puzzle."

"Thanks, I think," Mari said.

"Being a puzzle is good. It's certainly better than being boring!" Qai said. "That's almost a crime among my people. And speaking of boring, are you two ready for your long, dull slumber to Sol's Fourth World?"

"Ready," Fergus said.

They climbed into the pod and buckled in. After Fergus closed the canopy, they saw Qai wave on their screens, then darkness as the crate was sealed around them.

"I met an alien," Mari said. Her eyes were wide. "I mean, and not a scary one. We *talked*. She was just a person."

"What were you expecting?"

"I don't know. Not that. To me, aliens always meant something like the Asiig, kind of a vast, unknowable threat."

Dreamlike memories of giant, terrifying shapes moving in the dark popped into Fergus's mind, and he suppressed a shudder. "Well, see, the universe isn't all bad," he said. "You never know who you'll meet, or even become friends with."

"True," Mari said. "Even people who are trying to pretend they don't need friends at all."

Fergus didn't take the bait. He was in control, had resources and options and the ability to *move*. He could almost believe he was back to his usual self again.

He initiated the sleep systems. *Next stop, Mars.*

Chapter 18

◆—◆

"**N**o," Mari said.

"We have to—"

"*No.*" Mari was crouched down, heels tucked under her, arms wrapped tightly around her knees. In front of them, behind thick but nearly invisible glass, was the vast panorama of red-brown earth and yellow sky.

Fergus sighed, folded his legs, and sat down beside her. He waited for her to speak again. It took her a long time, but at last she rocked back and sat down. "So that's sky," she said, and then was quiet for another long stretch before speaking again. "Once when I was a kid, Mother Vahn took a couple of us to Central, where they have this thing called a swimming pool. You know what that is? I never understood why she took us there, because it terrified the hell out of me and my sisters. Sky is just like underwater, you know? How can we breathe without it crushing us? How does it not fall? Or just dissipate into space? Don't say gravity, because right now that just sounds stupid."

"Earth's sky is blue," Fergus said quietly. "So's the water. I grew up right at the edge of both, wondering which would finally take me. I picked sky. Sometimes if I stand still too long, it feels like being crushed by the whole universe."

"So moving helps?"

"No," he said. "But it's a good distraction. We'll wait until you're ready—"

"Fuck that," she interrupted. "If everyone always waited till they felt ready, we'd all still be fish living on trees."

He couldn't help it and started to laugh. He sprawled over on his back on the composite floor, staring up at the underside of the Ares Five dome, tears streaming down his face. Other people moving through the concourse on their way to and from the shuttle bay up to Alpha Station gave them a wide berth.

"What?!" Mari said, glaring peevishly at him.

"Do you know what a fish is?"

". . . Yes." Less certain, more defiant.

What did it really matter? She wasn't staring at the sky anymore. "Tell me what you know about Mars."

"It's a big rock," she said.

"So, quick history lesson. When people left Earth, first they built some science stations on Earth's lone moon, then they came and built some here. It used to take a lot longer to get places, so they couldn't just come and go and had to have longer-term settlements. Colonists built the first three domes, then there was a big pandemic on Earth, and the oceans were dying, and things were collapsing left and right. Nobody cared about Mars anymore. The colonists had come from a bunch of different nations on Earth, and over the years those who survived and stuck it out drifted into a hybrid, independent Mars-centric culture. Then about sixty ago, people on Earth realized Mars had resources they needed, so as soon as they got their shit together again at home, they came to get their colonies back, and they brought guns. The war officially lasted eighteen years—that's when Earth installed the Mars Colonial Authority as the governing body—but it's never really ended."

"That last bit I knew," Mari said. "Arelyn talked about it a lot. I guess that's why they left."

"Yeah. So the MCA answers to a coalition of governments and super-corporations on Earth. And on the other side there's the Free Mars movement. Some of them work openly through diplomatic channels to try to resolve conflicts between the MCA and the citizens of Mars. And some are hiding out in the sands, armed and able to defend themselves. That brings us to Ares Five." He slapped the floor with his hand.

"Because this is where Gilger called?"

"Yeah. Olympus Mons University, where Arelyn was studying, is an annex of Ares One. Qai's contact at the Alpha Station comm sat was kind enough to give us the call logs. My guess is that Gilger sent people over to One to collect Arelyn, and then they brought her back here and are holding her somewhere. And because of the politics, it's likely she's somewhere inside the city."

"Wouldn't the detached settlements be easier to hide in?"

"Yes, but they're full of Free Marsies. Because fewer women went into space in the early colonizations, Marsie culture developed as matrifocal and family-oriented; they wouldn't like the idea of anyone holding the daughter of a fellow Marsie hostage, even one who doesn't live here anymore. But inside the city ... A lot of people here are first-gens from Earth, and a fascist authority like the MCA is just another familiar piece of Earth-home to them. And because the MCA cares more about stomping down Free Marsies than actual criminals, Ares Five is not a bad place to run a shady business."

"But the city is huge."

On a Cernee scale, it certainly was. Unlike Cernee, Fergus knew his way around. "I have a plan," he said. "You ready?"

Mari's eyes darted back to the window. "We're not going to have to go outside, are we?"

"Not if I can help it," he said. "First I want to show you something." He got to his feet, happy for the feel of true gravity again, and held out his hand. She took it and pulled herself up.

They mingled back into the crowd and stopped in front of a long, narrow black electronic board that stood on poles in the center of concourse. A constant stream of symbols scrolled from one end to the other. "This is called a Pierreboard," Fergus explained. "It's a relic from the early colony days when people moved around a lot and there wasn't a global comm network. Essentially it's a message board for letting people know who is in town."

Mari watched the board. "How does it work?"

"People have their own symbol called a tag," Fergus said, "and when they arrive, they add their tag to the ticker. When they leave, they remove it." He tapped the screen as a symbol moved past, a green teardrop with a fox silhouette in it. An infobubble popped up. "See? This person is a human from the Gaian Ecosphere who goes by the name ArcxFlyer, arrived four days ago."

"Why does it say 'limited'?"

"The three options are open, which means anyone can leave a message for you—very bad idea; closed, which means no messages at all, in which case why bother; or limited, which means someone can leave a message only if they have a tag associated with this one. ArcxFlyer doesn't want to talk to strangers but is looking for their friends. Pretty standard." Fergus closed the infobubble. "The MCA hates this, because the Pierreboards aren't wired to anything outside of themselves. Each city has exactly one active board, and it's a blackbox. Its internal data is deeply encrypted in a rolling changeover scheme, and the tags are, with a few exceptions, anonymous."

"So why don't they just take them down?"

"Oh, they've tried. The locals get very upset, including a lot who otherwise don't mind the MCA. It's a part of Mars heritage. So they track the boards closely and probably know who a fair number of the tags belong to, but the Free Marsies and others change up their tags all the time or insert bogus ones. Often the tags themselves *are* the message."

Mari was regarding the board thoughtfully. "How is this useful to us?"

Fergus took out the handpad Maha and Qai had given him and held it up to the comm eye on the side of the Pierreboard. "Easy. We add a tag."

There was a faint beep, and a new icon appeared on

the control window. It was a complex symbol in gold on a red background. Fergus set messaging to closed, verified it, and disconnected. "The board will randomly insert our tag into the stream sometime in the next six hours," he said. "Another protection to keep the MCA from just staking out the board and matching each person who uses it to whatever new icon appears."

"Red and gold are Gilger's colors," Mari said.

"Yep. And that symbol is the Luceatan glyph for 'boss.'"

"Wait . . . Did you just put a symbol on the board announcing that *Gilger* was here?"

"Yes."

"But he's in Cernee. Surely they know that."

"Oh, certainly."

"Then . . . why?"

"Think of it from their point of view. They're holding the daughter of a dangerous man hostage in hostile territory. They used to have regular communication with their boss, but all of a sudden: nothing."

"Why nothing?"

"Because Gilger no longer has a ship with its own high-powered comm system, the few interstellar-capable settlement comms are effectively unreachable because of local jamming in the system, and he can't take a small ship far enough out of the Halo to bounce something off Crossroads because—"

"—because of the Asiig!"

"Right. Those ships are buying us time in several ways, whether they mean to or not. It's likely that no one here has any idea what's happening back there. If Gilger trusted them to do this job and not turn around and blackmail him in turn, that means his people here are loyal and not very imaginative. So probably they are very anxious right now for someone to tell them what to do."

"And?"

"What would you think if you spotted a tag that could only mean your boss was here on Mars when you know he can't be? What would you do?"

"I wouldn't believe it, but I wouldn't know what to think. I'd try to call back to Cernee, I expect."

"That's exactly what I'm counting on," Fergus said.

Mari frowned, stealing another glance toward the wide window. "So what, we hang out here around the board and wait for someone to come by and visibly panic?"

"There are cameras that pick up and broadcast the tag stream on half the channels in the city, so we don't have to wait here. Also, we have time before our tag goes up, and we have some errands to do first."

Fergus put the handpad away, then led Mari through the concourse, with its faux marble floors made of fused Martian sand and colored glass, to a small but prominent desk along the perimeter. A woman with dark hair and piercingly blue eyes looked up and broke into a grin. "Scottie!" she called.

"Alena," Fergus said. "It's been a long time."

She put her chin in hand and her elbow on the counter. "Two years at least! Since you never come to see me just for fun, what can I do for you?"

"A favor," he said. He pulled an anonymous credit chip out of his pocket, bought at a machine moments earlier, and laid it down lightly on the counter.

Alena raised her eyebrows. "And what's the favor?" she asked, not moving to take it.

"Someone is going to want to fast-bounce a call to Cernee in the next day or so."

"Cernee?"

"Cernekan. A settlement out near the Gap, in the Ohean System, off the Crossroads point. This person will be anxious, with a thick accent, paying for the fastest drop."

"Ah," she said. "Yeah. He's been here a few times."

"Today?"

"No, not for several days."

"Okay." Fergus rubbed his chin. "We didn't miss him, then."

"And if he comes back? I can't drop calls. I'd lose my job."

"I'd be happy if you could send it on the slow channel, though. By mistake."

"That happens sometimes," she said. "By mistake, of course." She put her palm on the credit chip and slid it toward herself, where it disappeared behind the counter.

"A hundred marks, Atlantic States Coalition backed," Fergus said.

She smiled. "Slow as slow can be," she said. "Good seeing you again, Scottie."

"And you." He smiled, tapped Mari gently on the arm, and they walked away.

Once they were past the booth, Mari chuckled.

"What?" Fergus asked.

"Nothing," she said. "It's just weird, knowing there are all these random people out here in the universe who actually like you."

"Ha ha," he said. "Let's go find me a new exosuit. There is no way I'm getting into any more crates or pods without one."

Ares Five was old familiar territory, and he moved with confidence through the halls and shops. Once they were away from the last of the windows, he could see Mari visibly relaxing. It made him, conversely, more tense. Maybe there was a chance they could find Harcourt's daughter, but were the odds any better than those of him getting them both killed chasing her down? Mari might be insistent that he wasn't responsible for her choices, and he'd be smart enough not to say he was out loud, but that didn't mean he could just stop feeling as if he were.

They reached the shop just as his conscience started into the guilt and doubt in earnest.

"'RedZoots'?" Mari asked, looking up at the sign.

"Trust me," he said. He strode straight to the back of the store, where a young man was watching a holonovel behind the counter. He was thin, short, his face and head completely shaven except for a thin golden ring of hair on the crown of his skull. *Zero-gen*, Fergus thought. *There's no way that's ever a Martian fashion.*

Mari arrived at Fergus's side just as the clerk deigned to look up. "Oooh," he said, eyeing Mari up and down. "Shouldn't be hard to improve on *that*."

"Actually, I'm the one in need of a new suit," Fergus said.

The man's eyes traveled over to him doubtfully. "Yes," he said at last, "I imagine you might."

"I thought you said you *liked* this place," Mari said.

"I did," Fergus answered. He leaned over the counter, doing his best to loom. "What happened to Red Bart?"

The clerk backed up a half step, to Fergus's satisfaction. "The MCA came looking for him, and he ran off. Turns out Red Bart was, to no one's surprise, a Red."

"Maybe we should go somewhere else," Mari said.

"No, this will still do," Fergus said, annoyed. "What have you got in the SuitSmythe B-series?"

"Not much," the clerk said. "Their C-series is coming out in a few months, so we're waiting on the release. But I can recommend the SpaceMart Alpha-Three—"

"I'd rather stick with SuitSmythe," Fergus said.

"I do still have some B-series inventory," the clerk said reluctantly. "I'd have to check it against your size. If you'd care to step in the sizing booth . . .?"

The clerk pointed at a small door, and Fergus stepped inside, letting the door close and latch. There was barely enough room to stand, and it took him a moment to turn around and orient himself in the center of the floor, where a pair of footprints had been thoughtfully stenciled as a guide.

The lights dimmed, and blue scan lines moved up and across his body from three directions. He'd done this so many times before, he knew the procedure cold. "Three, two, one, done," he muttered under his breath, and exactly as he said "done," the lights came back up. He put his hand out to unlock the door. The moment his fingers touched the latch, there was the sharp sting of static, and the lights in the booth went out completely.

What the hell? Fumbling around in the dark, he got

the door open and stepped back out onto the sales floor. "Uh, there's something wrong with your booth," he said.

"Lights in the whole store flickered," Mari said.

"This has never happened before," the clerk said, glaring at Fergus. "Are you wearing some sort of electronic kill switch device? Did you touch something?"

"Do I look like I'm wearing anything?" Fergus said, holding his arms out wide. "And what is there to touch? The bloody door latch, and that was it!"

"Well." The clerk went over, peered into the measuring booth, then shook his head. "The measurements were logged before the failure," he said. "I'll see what I can do for a suit, and while it's fabbing, I'll call tech support."

He turned his console around to face Fergus. "If I may recommend optional features—" Fergus reached for the buttons, but the clerk held up a hand. "Why don't you let me?"

Fergus curtly listed his needs while Mari's face shifted between amused and anxious. Finished, the clerk set to work on the config for the fab in the back of the shop, and Fergus sank into a chair near the sizing booth. Mari sat down next to him. She looked tired.

"You okay?" he asked.

"Yeah," she said. "I was going to ask you the same."

"I'm thirsty again. When we're done here, we should get some food and find a room." He put his handpad away. "Here comes Red Bart's inadequate replacement."

He stood up to meet the clerk, who was rolling a fab case out of the back room. "This is a B-forty-four base— my last one—with the options you specified," the clerk said. He had recovered his customer-service composure. "Given the problems with the booth, for which I apologize, we ought to make sure it fits properly."

"Good idea," Fergus said. "Uh, and thanks."

The clerk cracked open the case and extricated the new exosuit from it, checking the material carefully as he did so. At last he held it up. "The forty-four has the sleek-style integrated control panel along the forearm," he said, waving a hand along it. "Much less bulky than the thirty-ex models."

"My last was a twenty-eight."

"Ah, well, then I think you'll be pleased with this," the clerk said. He powered it on, showing a sequence of green lights along the forearm. "Would you care to try it on?"

Fergus reached out for it, and just as his fingers touched the fabric, a big spark leapt between his hand and the suit. "Ahhh!" he shouted, letting go even as the clerk jumped back and dropped it.

The brand new suit fell to the floor, a wisp of smoke coming up from the dead display of the control panel. The clerk stared at him.

"Whoa," Mari said.

"What the hell?" Fergus said.

"I'm calling security," the clerk said, and he backed up to his counter, reaching around the far side.

"It wasn't me!" Fergus protested, but Mari grabbed his arm.

"We've got to go," she said. "Now."

"But . . ."

"*Now.*" She pulled him out of the store, stumbling around the corner. "You know this place. Where do we hide?"

"Hide?" He was confused, dizzy, *thirsty*. "I didn't do anything! It was that clerk and his crazy store!"

"Sure, and who is security going to believe?" she asked.

Fergus was fairly sure Ares Five security would have more than one officer who'd remember him. "Right," he said. "Follow me."

They sprinted out of the mall area, up a few escalators, down another, and into a crowded open-concourse market. He walked at a fast clip—not so fast as to catch anyone's attention, but enough to make good time through the maze of stalls and booths. His mouth felt parched, and his stomach was cramping, a dull ache somewhere just north of his kidneys, and he stumbled, shoulder tagging a doorway painfully.

Mari caught him. "What's wrong with you?" she asked.

"I don't know," he said. "I don't feel good, not since that booth and then the suit zapped me."

They left the far side of the market and headed into the public bunkspace. Fergus found the first bunk flagged as available, transferred over enough credit for a day, then pulled open the door and half fell inside the tiny, closet-sized room. Mari followed him, closing and locking the door.

He made it to the small sink and poured water into his hands, drinking it down greedily, not caring about the meter ticking up charges. Beard dripping, he finally shut off the spigot and pulled a bunk down from where it was folded up against the wall. He collapsed onto it, barely able to keep his eyes open.

"You don't look good," Mari said.

"I'll be fine," he answered. "I just need to close my eyes for a minute or two." He did just that, lying there, feeling his body start to relax, unclench itself. The pain in his gut eased.

"Fergus, what's going on?"

"I don't know," he said. He made himself sit up. "Why don't you stay here, get some rest? I'll go get us some food."

"I don't think it's a good idea to go out."

"I'll be careful," he said. "Trust me."

She looked like she was going to argue, but at last she nodded. "What do I do if you don't come back?" she asked.

"I'll be back."

Before she could argue, he left.

What's your plan here? he asked himself. He knew he should stay in the rent-a-bunk, lay low until he heard from Alena, not leave Mari alone in a strange city on a strange planet while he went out and pushed his idiot luck for no good reason.

The sort of idiot luck that had left him drifting in space, mangled, broken, and bleeding out and two days later had returned him miraculously to full health. Had he genuinely believed there weren't strings attached?

Fergus did what he did by assuming everyone and everything around him were variables that just needed understanding, maybe a little manipulation, to get them all lined up where he needed them to be. And he was good at it because he knew, at his core, that he was the constant in the equation. The only thing he could count on was himself.

He took an elevator up and over several levels, then wandered the public sector until he found what he wanted. It was a small booth with a frosted glass door marked with a red caduceus. He stood in front of it for a long minute. *This is stupid,* he thought. *There's nothing wrong with me. It's just a coincidence, some weird side effect of the pod sleeper systems.*

If it's nothing, Fergus, he told himself, *why not go in and prove it?*

Before he could talk himself out of it, he opened the door and stepped inside, trying not to touch anything he didn't absolutely have to.

"Welcome to Dr. Diagnosis!" a friendly, comfortably artificial voice piped up. "Please indicate your species. For human, say, 'Human.' For Vei—"

"Human," he said.

"Thank you. Please listen to the following diagnostic selections. To give a bodily fluid specimen, say, 'Sample' and wait until a receptacle is provided. To have a blood specimen taken, say, 'Blood.' For a general internal scan, say, 'Scan.' For a colonosc—"

"Scan," he said.

"Please transfer thirty credits local or say, 'Indigent.'"

He transferred over the thirty credits without hesitation. Fresh off Earth and not even sixteen years old, he remembered thinking 'indigent' sounded like 'free.' It had taken weeks to shake the stink of the complimentary parasite bath the booth had given him before letting him go again.

"Thank you for your payment. Please stand still. Scan will commence in ten seconds," the voice informed him. His hands began itching again. The booth lit up, changing color from blue to red to yellow—he wasn't sure if that was necessary or if it was just to make the patient feel like something was happening—and then returned to its normal state.

"You have an unknown abdominal anomaly," the booth reported. On the screen, an animated hypodermic needle with big googly eyes appeared holding a pointer, and it tapped at a grayish blob among other grayish blobs on the scan. Lines radiated from it. "This is the location of the primary anomaly. It is approximately 4.5 cm by 3 cm by 2.5 cm. Please submit to further analysis."

An arm extended from the wall with a circular cuff in it.

"What's that?" he asked.

"Please submit to further analysis," the booth repeated. "The cuff will draw a small blood sample in a painless and routine procedure."

"Uh, no, thanks," he said. He moved carefully around the cuff to push on the booth door, but it wouldn't open. He pressed the emergency release, and still nothing happened.

"I'm sorry, but your condition requires precautionary isolation. Please remain calm while medical professionals are summoned," the booth said.

"I do not consent," he said.

"Consent is not required for type-five anomalies of probable nonhuman origin," it said. "Please remain calm."

Calm? Fergus thought. *I am* not *having a good day with booths.* He pushed the door again, then kicked it, then rammed his shoulder into it. It didn't budge.

"This booth is now dispensing an aerosol agent to help you remain calm," the booth said. There was a hiss, and a minty scent filled the air.

Bloody hell. Fergus held his breath and punched at the screen near the door. He raised his hands again, felt that familiar tingle, couldn't fight it down. As he hit the panel, there was another bright arc of electricity, and the booth went dead at the same time as there was a click and the door swung open.

He stumbled out, took a deep breath of fresh air, and then noticed people staring in his direction. There were sirens somewhere down the hall, and glancing back, he saw a flashing red light atop the booth he'd just busted free from.

Feeling sick, Fergus ran.

Chapter 19

H e took the steps down to the next level two at a time, his stomach in knots, his body parched, and his head spinning. Down here, away from the windows and views, the Martian city became more like the bright, busy honeycomb he knew and loved. Despite his fear, his heart rate slowed with his footsteps, and he merged into one of the currents of people flowing through the wide halls at an almost calm pace.

It'll be okay, he told himself. He'd get back to the rent-a-bunk, lay low there until they heard from Alena, then with luck he and Mari could track down Arelyn and get out. He just needed to avoid any more complications.

There's something alien inside me, he thought. *How will that ever not be complicated?*

The little paranoid voice in his brain, emboldened and shrieking, was convinced that everyone who glanced his way knew him for what he was: something *wrong*.

There was one more flight down to a food court. At this time of day it would be crowded, so he should be safe enough to get some water, catch his breath, try to pull his shit back together. Then he could grab some quick takeout and get back to Mari. And then ... He didn't want to think any further ahead, wasn't sure he could bear the future at all right now.

If he even had one.

"Food court it is, then," he mumbled, and he headed down the stairs toward that promise of brief sanctuary, trying to keep his pace casual, not draw attention. Turning a corner midflight, he stopped short just in time to avoid knocking over someone hurrying up from the other direction.

It was the clerk with the dumb hair from RedZoots. "You!" the man exclaimed, then grabbed at the arm of the person who was with him—a person who was wearing a blue MCA uniform, Fergus recognized belatedly. "That's him! This is him! The Marsie terrorist who fried my shop!"

"Never even been near the place. You must have me confused for someone else," Fergus said. The MCA officer's expression was one of bored forbearance, as if he were just counting down the seconds until he could reassure the citizen he'd get right on his complaint and get away. Fergus gave him a sympathetic smile—*Crazy locals, right?*—as he stepped to one side, yielding the way, and he saw the officer's expression shift from boredom to relief to realization.

"Hey," the MCA officer said, and he turned on the stairs, his hand moving toward his weapon, though he didn't draw it. "Hang on a second, sir."

"I'm afraid I'm kind of in a hurry," Fergus said. He could see that was the wrong answer as soon as the words were out of his mouth, and he hastily added, ". . . but I'm happy to help, of course."

The officer was now facing him directly, sideways on the staircase with the clerk twitching in anticipation beside him, wearing a smug grin. In the center of the officer's chest was the small, shiny button circle of a scene recorder.

Scene recorders kept a rolling cache of two minutes before uploading to central memory, theoretically to give officers discretion when dealing with personal or confidential matters and informants but typically treated as a free window for beating the crap out of someone while retaining plausible deniability. How long since Fergus had come around the corner? No more than thirty seconds.

The officer clearly didn't miss his glance at the camera. "I'll need you to accompany me to the zone station until we can clear a few things up," he said, and his hand tightened on his pistol. Gone was the *sir*.

"I—" Fergus started to say, but what was there to say after that? How could he get out of this? Even if he ran away, he was in the officer's image cache. If he went down to the station, they were going to connect the dots to the Dr. Diagnosis booth, and he was going to end up on a dissection table in an Alliance lab somewhere.

"He's going to run away!" the clerk shouted, and he lunged forward, grabbing Fergus's arm with both hands. Fergus lost his balance, started to fall, and took a half step down to try to save himself, which brought them both crashing into the officer.

The officer shoved them off and hauled his pistol clumsily out of its holster just as Fergus felt the dreaded tingling well up inside him like angry bees spilling out of a hive deep in his gut, and without thinking he reached out and ripped the button camera off the officer's chest as sparks leapt off his hands and arms.

The RedZoots clerk shrieked and let go, falling upward on the stairs. Fergus shoved the stunned officer, who dropped his weapon even as he fell atop the clerk, and in that brief moment of freedom, Fergus leapt down the stairs and away as fast as he could, panic wrapping itself around his heart and squeezing like he hadn't felt since that day he tried to reach his father in the sea.

The button camera in his fist burned like a coal, and he let the melted, obliterated bit of plastic fall somewhere behind him as he fled.

Alarms blared. In his wild panic, Fergus thought it was the flyby alarm at first, that the Asiig had come for him again. But no, he recognized the three-trill pattern from his days on the fringes of the Free Mars movement; it was a zone lockdown.

He reached the food court, and tried to worm his way as quickly as he could into and through the suddenly tense crowd. People began to murmur, and the tables thinned out, anger and anxiety the two clearest notes in the changing swell of noise.

Unwilling to be carried along with the tide of people

back out into the wider public spaces, Fergus found a small alcove behind a row of food stalls and huddled in its darkest corner. He imagined crickets in the hall, in his head, and he put his hands over his ears. The thirst was unbearable.

When his pulse had finally stopped hammering in his throat, he peered miserably out from his shadows and watched as shop owners finished with their last few customers. An older, weary-looking woman pulled down a gate over the counter of her stand, Wrap-a-Tap-Tapas. "Another drill?" she complained.

"I don't know," the next man over said, wiping down the counter in front of his own food stall. "Someone said it was a runaway infected with a dangerous alien parasite. Who the hell knows? Probably a training thing."

"A friend up in the skydome said a squad of MCA soldiers is coming in, armed up, with sniffers," Tapas Lady said. "Probably just clearing the decks so they can track down some poor Marsie who pissed them off and cut 'em down without witnesses."

"You're too sympathetic to them," the other man said.

"It was their damned planet. You should be more sympathetic," Tapas Lady said. She locked her gate. "Still, it doesn't matter, drill or whatever. Day's shot either way. See you when the lockdown's over."

Both walked away, parting near the stairwells. After a while, the area lights, sensing no activity, dimmed to conserve power.

The Dr. Diagnosis booth had been a potentially lethal error, another stupid move born out of Fergus's own unthinking arrogance. If the MCA was bringing in sniffers, there was no way he could hide for long. If only he hadn't dragged Mari along. She was resourceful, though, smart, a survivor. He had gotten her this far; she'd find Arelyn and get home again. They'd be okay. *Right?*

You're so full of shit, he told himself. *She has no cred, no idea how Mars works, how anything outside of Cernee works.*

He didn't know anyone he could call in Ares Five who could help him now. Alena was in this zone, but she'd hand him over; she couldn't afford not to. His shit was entirely his own.

If they were going to hunt him down, he was going to make it as difficult as possible for them. He inched along the wall until he could see a maintenance closet across the way. Time was worth more than stealth. He bolted across the concourse, bringing the lights back to glaring life, and looked around for anything he could grab as he passed the shuttered stalls. There was a gelato stand just past the tapas booth where someone had left a half-full bottle of water. He grabbed it and a handful of spoons, scattering more on the floor, and kept running.

The maintenance door was miraculously unlocked.

Racing into the darkened space, he tripped over an inert dustbot and sent himself crashing the remaining distance. He rolled over and found what he'd desperately hoped would be here: a rusted, greasy hatch in the floor leading down into the city's underground. He could hide for a little while among the pipes and tunnels and machinery that kept the city above alive, and maybe even escape the zone before he was found.

He drank the water down in big, noisy gulps, then dropped the bottle into the closet's industrial-size flash recycler. Marginally less ill, he hauled the hatch open. A line of rungs set into a sandcrete tunnel led down. The underground was vast, complex, and dark, but not infinite; the nearest MCA base was at Ares Four, outside Schiaparelli Crater, so he couldn't waste what head start that gave him. He knew the underground well, but without a suit, he was ultimately trapped.

An awful thought occurred to him: what if they found Mari? The RedZoots clerk had surely described them both, and who knew how many people had seen them together? Worse, there was nothing he could do. He was useless to her, playing for time because it was the only thing he had left, and not much of it at that.

Every city had its invisible people crouching in the dark places, either dreaming of a life above or hiding from one. Fergus had once spent weeks down here, living among them while stalking a dealer of stolen art. Now, though, everyone he came near would be a potential MCA target or informant.

Closing his eyes, he leaned against a giant, humming brick of a machine and pictured the tunnels and crawlways and spots where people gathered, trying to recall the gaps and empty spaces.

There was only one place he could think of to hide. He turned back, retraced his steps for a hundred meters or so, then took a different way. The only uninhabited corners down here were the dangerous ones. *Sixth inning, semifinals against the Titan Tigers,* he thought. He'd had tickets to the sold-out Marsball game, a self-reward for catching the art thief, and was sitting in Section E when an atmospheric transformer below Section B blew and nearly suffocated half the people at that end of the ballpark. The explosion had done major structural damage beneath the park, and it had stayed that way while a circus of finger-pointing, rhetoric, and legal action slowly played out between the city, the machinery contractor, and the operations subcontractor. In the meantime, they'd just locked the area off and forgotten about it.

It didn't take Fergus long to find a gate installed between two support columns, sporting a mechanical lock easily picked with a snapped-off piece of stolen polyplastic cutlery. He closed the gate behind him, locking it again from the inside. That would buy him a few more minutes, maybe.

The last few working lights were just inside the gate, shining feebly onto a thickened patchwork of steam burns and moisture-fed mold. He was loath to touch the walls to help find his way. *I wish I had Mother Vahn's glowing lichen goo,* he thought, but that was a lifetime away now.

How badly, though, did he need that light? Was this thing the Asiig had done to him something he had any control over, or would it just be one unpredictable disaster after another until someone put him out of his misery for good? The Vahns secluded themselves to protect the rest of humanity from whatever "gift" they'd been given. How much weaker was he that, only a few days later, he was already yielding to temptation?

He held out one hand, palm up, and concentrated. He didn't know which frightened him more: the thought that it wouldn't work, or that it might. In answer, a tiny spark leapt from fingertip to palm, the white-blue arc enough to destroy what little acclimation to the dark his eyes had built up. It was also enough to light up his surroundings in a single brief flash of sharp relief.

Don't think about how this moment changes you forever.

"Okay. That way, I think," he mumbled to himself, trying to change the subject on his own thoughts. Sharp pinprick spots danced at the periphery of his vision as he cupped his hand, held it outward, and did it again.

A dark stain at the edge of the shadows proved to be a puddle of water. The air was humid here and growing warmer as steam leaked from somewhere ahead; it would make body-heat-seekers useless, scent-chasers not much better. He was careful to stay out of the puddle, not wanting to track sludge into a trail. He was so thirsty he could cry, thirsty enough to wonder if the puddle, which had glinted oily and iridescent in his brief light flash, would kill him faster or slower than the MCA soldiers. He moved on quickly.

Hopping over another flooded section of corridor, he tripped over something unseen on the far side. A cable snaked across the corridor only a half meter past the edges of the water. He made more light, illuminating the melted and blackened cable casing, and felt a sympathetic tingling in his hands. Live, then. And very, very hot.

Using the toe of his shoe, careful to touch only the

section of the cable still bearing insulation, he nudged it into the pool. Steam began to boil off the water's surface almost immediately. That would give him more cover.

In the depths of the damaged area, he found what he was looking for: a niche tucked between dead, half-slagged machinery. It was barely big enough to squeeze into, with a sharp bend between the opening and the slightly wider dead end. No one would find him here without coming in, and there was enough room for him to sit, lean against the bulkplate behind him, and rest.

Concentrating, he let just enough of a flash leak out between his fingers to be bearable in the confined space. *Don't get too used to the spark, Fergus,* he told himself. *You don't know what else it's doing to you.*

He checked the corridor again, listening intently for any sounds beyond the hiss and drip and hum. *And when they do come?* he wondered, retreating back into his hideaway. *What then?*

He imagined he could hear crickets again in the distant, distressed whine of the machinery around him. Crickets chirping and chirping, insistent, like . . .

. . . like the chime on his handpad. He pulled it out and stared stupidly at it. *Scottie: your man was just by,* the pop-up read, Alena's stylized "A" watermark behind it, accompanied by a photo of a very skittish-looking Luceatan man.

Couldn't stop by before *I went to the stupid medical booth, could you?*

Shutting the handpad down, he barely resisted throwing it away into the darkness.

It wasn't long before he began to hear the sounds of boots. Crouching in the sweltering shadows, his tattered and filthy Firebowl shirt plastered across his body, he considered what an absolutely dumb way his life was about to end: half-drowned in the steamy air, armed with nothing but spoons.

"These seekers are fucking useless down here with all this steam," someone said, not far away at all.

As the squad passed, their lights flicked up and across the walls and floor, barely touching the edges of his niche. "Somewhere in this vicinity, sir," someone else said, and he heard the familiar buzz of guns powering up as the lights faded. He thought that the voice now came from past his hiding place, around the next turn down the corridor.

Go! he told himself. He inched his way out of the niche and crept along the wall back toward the gate, away from the soldiers.

It was impossible to see, and he didn't dare make light. Concentrating on remembering the path here, he stepped lightly along it, turn by turn, unerringly back the way he had come. He only forgot one last small puddle, stepping in it with a faint, low splash. A voice called out from around the corner ahead, sounding young and scared. "Sir? Is that you?"

Of course they'd left someone guarding the gate.

Fergus froze midstep, trying to decide what he should do, and heard the buzz of the soldier's gun. He flattened himself against the wall around the corner and stood as still as he could, hardly daring to breathe. Listening intently, he heard a cautious bootfall. *Damn, damn, damn.* He was trapped. How long until the rest of the squad turned around?

The tiny green light on the side of an energy rifle caught his eye as it emerged from around the corner. Hardly believing he dared, he reached out a hand and found the arm gripping the gun, and before the soldier could shout or pull away, Fergus put as much energy as he could into one good spark.

The soldier jerked and fell to his knees, and Fergus grabbed for the gun. This close, he could see the soldier's wide, dazed eyes, see the status lights inside his helmet flickering back on already. *Fast-rebooting suit. Military grade.*

And then it clicked: it was a suit that could both conceal him and tolerate his newly acquired physical problem, at least for a while. Maybe there was a way to escape after all.

He grabbed the soldier's wrist, zapped his comm unit, then pointed the gun at him. "Give me your suit, please," he said, keeping his voice low. "And remember, I asked nicely."

The exosuit fit, although it wasn't until he'd pulled it fully on that he realized the soldier he'd taken it from—hardly more than a skinny, scared kid once he'd peeled himself out of the suit and handed it over—had wet himself when Fergus had zapped him. The internal environmental systems would eventually clean it, but that didn't make him feel any less gross.

He left the kid inside the gate with instructions not to make noise or else. He shifted the suit into stealth combat mode, shutting down all external signaling; the last thing he needed was a live homing beacon wedged up his ass as he tried to evade the rest of the unit. The gun he ditched in the deepest shadow he could find. As he expected, seconds after he'd disappeared from sight, the kid started screaming his head off. *Could've at least given me a five-minute head start to make up for pissing in the suit,* Fergus thought crossly.

Even after years away, he wagered he knew these tunnels better than the MCA ever could. He detoured the long way around the fringes of the ballpark's underside, not taking the closer exits, not taking the shortest path to any of the others. He knew a way out of the city, out into the sands, but he couldn't think of any way to get to the rent-a-bunk and get Mari without being spotted. And surely by now the MCA knew he had one of their suits.

He took a deep breath, tried to shake off the panic and shame still coiled around his mind. Moving around a building-sized brick of machinery that whined and clicked with atonal regularity, he glanced back over his shoulder for the millionth time and collided with some-one on the far side of the block.

Reaching out in surprise, he caught the man before he fell over, steadying him. It was an older man with the multilayered thinness that went along with a life spent in the underground. "I'm sorry!" Fergus said.

The man pulled back, yanking his arm out of Fergus's loose grasp and backing up, a mix of fear and anger on his face. Out of the shadows, another man stepped forward and bent down to pick up a length of pipe from the ground.

It was Fergus's turn to step back. He put his hands up, showing that he wasn't armed. "It was an accident," he said.

"And now you're going to have one yourself, MCA scum," the man with the pipe said.

Fergus blinked at him as what the man was saying sank in. "Oh," he said. "Oh! I'm not MCA! I stole the suit!"

The man with the pipe stopped moving but did not lower it. "Riiight," he said at last, although he didn't advance. "And that's why you're all alone down here without your buddies?"

"If it makes you feel any better, when they catch up with me, they'll definitely kill me."

"So maybe we should help them, then," Pipe Man said. "Why not?"

"Because Marsies look out for each other?" Fergus said.

Pipe Man laughed. "You're no Marsie."

Fergus gritted his teeth. *Damn Harcourt,* he thought again, *digging up my past and setting it loose to haunt me.* "I was here during the '49 Riots. I was here when they capped and gassed Ares Seven," he said, hating himself for it. And then, worst of all, "I was in the group hiding out in the dunes of Nereidum Montes that took back Sentinel."

"Now I know you're a liar," Pipe Man said. "Only five good Reds came back out of those hills."

"Four good Martians," Fergus said. "Tophe, Kaice, Dru, and Abhi. And one sad bugger from Scotland."

"Yes," the older man spoke up. "I knew Tophe and Kaice. If you knew them, you knew Kaice's nickname."

And I still do, Fergus thought. "Yes. Kaypop."

"Let me see your hair."

Fergus obliged, pulling back the suit hood. "Shit," the man said. "You *are* the guy who stole Sentinel!"

"I'm the guy who stole it *back*."

"What in the name of Ares are you doing down here in this fucking basement wearing an MCA suit?!" Pipe Man said.

"Running away from the MCA in it," Fergus said.

Pipe Man looked around. "Which way did you come from?"

"From under the ballpark. I went around past the reservoir tanks and the sewage plant before heading this way."

"I know the area," the old man said. "I had tickets to that damned game. And we were *ahead*. Always wondered if it was sabotage to get the games moved back to Titan turf—"

Pipe Man shook his head. "Not this again!"

"You were really at Nereidum Montes?" the old man asked.

"I was. It was bitterly cold, and the parts that weren't terrifying were boring as hell," Fergus said.

"That I bet." The old man held out a hand, and Fergus carefully shook it. "I'm Sunset Alvarez," he said. "You here on a mission?"

"I was, but . . . it's gone all wrong," Fergus said. "I got separated from my partner, and I don't know how to get to her."

"She's down in the tunnels?"

"No, she's up in a rent-a-bunk, and I don't know if the

MCA knows about her yet. She's not from here, and isn't a part of any of this. I don't have any way to warn her."

"I could get word to her. Least I could do. You're a hero."

"I'm really not," Fergus said. "It was stupid luck and that's it."

"If it weren't for stupid luck, wouldn't be no one alive on Mars in the first place," Alvarez said. "Tell me the secret of how you got Sentinel away from an entire squad of elite MCA troops, and I'll go warn your friend."

"A dumb trick," Fergus said. "We intercepted a ground runner, and I took his uniform. Then I hiked out to their secret encampment, which we'd been watching for days, and told them the Reds were coming and they were under orders to destroy Sentinel before they got there—something they knew no Martian would dare say about such an important historical relic. So they set up the charges and hunkered deep down in their bunker, and by the time they figured out the charges weren't going off, Kaice and Dru had it up the dunes and over. Abhi and Tophe laid down covering fire as the MCA troops tried to come out, and I got away in the chaos and rejoined them for the trip back."

"What order was the runner actually carrying?"

"The same one. They'd arrested some of our people domeside and found out we were out there. That's what made it so plausible—didn't have to forge a thing."

"And dangerous! If Sentinel had been—"

"They couldn't anyway. I got into their storage depot the night before and I'd disabled the charges." *And nearly lost three toes to frostbite getting back,* he didn't add. It had taken him two years to be able to afford med-tech good enough to have the toes regrown. And that was still two years sooner than the Free Marsies the MCA had rounded up at random afterward were released: never charged, but silent, scared, scarred, and permanently broken. *Dru.*

Sunset shook his head. "Well, it worked, right? History is history."

"So, can I ask you something?" Fergus asked, desperate to change the subject. "What are *you* doing down here in the underground?"

"Came here as a kid with my mother and three sisters," Alvarez said. "We were fleeing the Texas Republican Army crackdown right before they declared war on Arizona. Arrived only days ahead of the Blue Invasion, and I lost everyone except one sister in the dome collapse. We were evacuated here to Five, and I've failed to become a well adjusted, repatriated colonial citizen ever since."

"I'm sorry to hear that," Fergus said. The Blue Occupation was established fact before he'd even been born, but it was still-living history for many people on Mars. "I need to get moving before the MCA catches up."

"Which way you heading?"

"Trying to get topside along the northwest arc," Fergus said. "There's a maintenance garage there. If I can steal a buggy, I can get clear."

"If I'm going up to find your partner, we're heading the same direction." Alvarez turned to his friend. "You coming?"

Pipe Man shook his head. "I'm staying here. MCA doesn't get a free pass to walk around in my underground." The two men clasped hands briefly.

"This way. I know the fastest route," Alvarez said, and he led Fergus between a narrow row of pipes into another section of tunnel.

"Thanks," Fergus said. "I—"

He was interrupted by his handpad chiming; he'd half forgotten he was carrying it. He opened the window to a close-up of a very angry Luceatan. *Back again. This time placed calls to Luceatos, Crossroads,* and *Cernekan. Yelled at me. Bad breath. You owe me a drink,* the note read.

"Your mission?" Alvarez asked.

"Yeah," Fergus said, "until the MCA got in my way."

"Another Sentinel job?"

They're all Sentinel jobs, he thought, *ever since some crazy-stupid Earther kid with a need to prove himself thought that if he could steal a motorcycle, he could steal anything and convinced other people to trust him.*

"Pretty much, yeah," he said.

This got a raised eyebrow. "Something important, then?"

"Someone, yes. Kidnapped daughter of a Marsie friend."

Alvarez gave a curt nod. "So, your partner. How do I find her?"

"She's in the rent-a-bunks near the shuttle terminal. Number 4415. There's a chance the bunk is being watched or even that they've taken her in. I just don't know."

Alvarez led him down into another set of subtunnels, kicked open a door, then back up another access ladder. "She won't know or trust me."

"Right," Fergus said. "Do you know if there's any-place up on the restaurant levels that would have Celekai food?"

"Ugh! Have you *tried* that stuff?!" Alvarez made gagging sounds. "One place, I think. Caters to the historical buffs. You know we get reenactors? And I don't mean actual Veirakan Celekai, I mean people who put on goofy masks with assholes in the middle of their foreheads as if it gives some sort of meaning to their lives."

"I didn't," Fergus said. "But it's a weird universe out there."

"That it is. So what's the food for?"

"You can say you're just a delivery guy if anyone tries to stop you. And my friend will know you were really sent by me," he said. "If they've called off the lockdown—"

"There's a lockdown up there? You *did* piss them off," Alvarez said, brightening. "Good for you. People don't like lockdowns; it reminds them they're living under occupation. Some low-rank'll be apologizing by morning for overstepping drill protocols. What do you want me to tell your friend? You want me to bring her to you?"

And that, really, was the question. When Fergus had said they should come here, he didn't know, didn't understand that he'd been changed. With the MCA after him, was there any chance of them finding Arelyn? Did having Mari here improve the odds more than it risked her life? If he'd been honest with her about what was happening to him, maybe things wouldn't have gone this wrong, but there wasn't anything he could do about that now.

"No, it's not safe," Fergus said at last. Maybe this time he could actually save someone, and it helped that she wasn't there to object. "If you can get her to a woman named Alena at the Offworld Cable Office, have her contact a ship named the *Gormless*; they'll send someone for my friend Mari. Whatever it costs, I'll cover. And Alvarez—"

"Yeah?"

"My friend won't want to leave. She doesn't understand how dangerous things are. You have to convince her to go."

Alvarez climbed off the ladder and kicked open another door. "This is where we part ways," he said. "Down this hallway is your buggy garage. If I can get to your friend, I'll do what I can to help her. Do you want me to contact you after?"

"Just let me know she's safe and on her way home, if you can," Fergus said. He held out his handpad, and after some maneuvering, Alvarez produced a battered old-model pad from his pocket and synced contacts. "Thanks for everything, Sunset."

"Yeah. I hope you find a way to win another one for Mars," Alvarez said. He thumped Fergus on the shoulder, turned around, and disappeared back toward the underground.

Fergus stared after him for a while, awash in his own cowardice. *Win one? Right,* he thought. *I've already lost, and I'm kidding myself if I don't think I've failed every-*

body, and that I'm doing anything more right now than running away again.

Long after Alvarez's bootsteps had faded, Fergus leaned the side of his head against the door, his ear against the cold metal. He couldn't hear a thing. Peeling back a suit glove, he raised a fist and knocked as loudly as he could. After a pause, he did it again. No answer. Pulling the door open a few centimeters, he peered around it. The bay was empty.

He stepped inside and closed the door behind him. Ahead was the docking lock, a dust-pocked window looking out over Mars, and as Alvarez had promised, a surface buggy. Rummaging through the tool drawers, he found what he needed, climbed under the buggy, and began dismantling the tracking beacon.

Chapter 20

◆━━◆━━◆

Fergus slid out from underneath the buggy. The engines, drive train, and life support had all checked out fine, so if the buggy had any unfinished maintenance, it was either something he didn't care about or something he would deal with if and when he needed to.

Alvarez had not called.

He will, he told himself as he climbed in through the buggy's airlock and took the driver's seat in the front cabin. The old fear resurfaced, that memory of trying to get word about the fate of his friends after the Sentinel job kicked off months of violent suppression from the MCA, long silence punctuated by occasional rumors of torture, and then eventual terrible proof.

How many times had other people paid the price as he got away free? If he'd never gone to Cernee, Mari never would have left its safety. Not that it was particularly safe anymore, although that was probably at least partially his fault too.

He drove the buggy into the adjacent garage bay, waited for the door behind him to seal, then watched as the outer door ground its way open to the orange-yellow vista beyond. Dust made a thick haze on the horizon. If anyone could smuggle him out of the area without alerting the MCA, it was the Free Marsies. He still had connections to the west in Ares Three, over near Elysium Mons, and there were enough independent townships scattered here and there in between that he could stop to resupply fairly safely.

He reached down to put the buggy in gear, and his handpad buzzed. *Please be Alvarez,* he thought, picking it up off the seat beside him. He needed at least the small comfort of knowing that Mari was safely on her way off Mars.

It was a message, not a live call. "Take buggy to NE city gate. Wait there. 20 min.—Sunset"

Fergus stared at it. He didn't want any more complications. He reached for the pad, not sure what his intention was, when a spark arced out of his fingertip. The screen flashed and went black, smoke curling out of the casing seam. The message was gone, as well as any means to reply.

"Oh, fuck you!" he shouted up at the sky as loudly as he could, willing his words to fly the vast distance and smash themselves across the noses of those arrogant alien triangles who had done this to him. He either went to meet Alvarez and fell back into this whole mess, or he went somewhere else and was free from everything except his conscience, and his own unbearable uselessness.

Swearing under his breath, he put the buggy in gear and drove out of the bay into the swirling sand.

Fergus parked the buggy among the other municipal vehicles clustered near the surface road south to Ares Six. The goggles of his stolen MCA exosuit had better magnification than anything he'd ever owned. From this distance he could see the observation deck of the Welcome Center and the roped-off area outside it where people new to Mars's gravity—or gravity at all—could get used to the feel of it by hopping around in the sand. He would have saved himself a lot of headaches if he'd done that when he'd first arrived, rather than learning the hard way through one ceiling collision after another.

There was a group of people already out, most waving their arms as if to fly like birds, a few crouching down as if being squashed by an unseen hand. Once past a certain age, the spaceborn were rarely ever truly comfortable on planets.

It had been eighteen minutes since Alvarez's message.

As that group trickled back inside, another emerged. Even at this distance, Fergus instantly recognized Mari. She was hunched over, ducking from the sky above. Moments later he picked out the two MCA ops in civilian exosuits who were discreetly following her. There was no sign of Alvarez. *Dammit, Sunset,* he thought, even as his heart soared to see her still free. *You were supposed to get her safely offworld, not bring her to me.*

Orientation outings were usually fifteen minutes at a stretch; that's how long he had to figure out how to separate Mari from the pack without the ops seeing. He climbed over the seat into the back, knocking over an empty can of resin used to seal windows, and inventoried what was there. More resin cans. A giant extending squeegee. Bottled potable water, which he immediately popped open and guzzled down until he felt almost sick. A stash of cheap readymeals. For no obvious reason, or at least any that he cared to know, a pair of men's underwear was beneath it all; he used the squeegee handle to shove that farther back in the buggy. In the emergency locker he found another exosuit.

A spare was never unwelcome; he plugged the suit into a power block to charge and left it draped over an equipment chest as he climbed back up front. He still had no idea how to get to Mari.

He glanced out the window just in time to see one of the newbies go careening over the ropes and out over the dunes, their arms flailing frantically. Two instructors and one of the MCA ops took off after them while the other op lingered on the fringes of the crowd, watching Mari. She stood with the others, and at last the second op's attention drifted to the rescue.

Mari turned her head, scanning the line of buggies, and when she was looking his way, Fergus flashed the lights. After that, it was like watching a brilliant stop-motion piece reenacted on sand. Mari slid slowly toward the edge of the crowd, but every time the op glanced over, she was standing still.

The remaining instructor apparently decided the fly-away student was more excitement than the others needed and started herding the group back toward the door. In moments there was a good-sized group of people between Mari and the op. She merged in among those closest to the door, then slid behind the emergency storage locker beside the entrance and disappeared. At the back of the crowd, the MCA op was starting to shove his way forward; one gravity-clueless newbie he pushed went flying and knocked over three others. The op found himself face-to-face with the instructor, and even from this distance, Fergus could tell the undercover op was getting a blistering chewing-out.

Most of the students had reentered the building by the time the op finally pulled out his badge and shoved it in the instructor's face. The instructor stepped out of his way, but as the op passed, the instructor's foot snuck out. The op reentered the city on a near-horizontal trajectory. "Another small victory for Mars," Fergus murmured under his breath.

He backed the buggy up behind the others so it was out of view of the Welcome Center and waited. Two minutes later, Mari was pulling herself into the seat beside him, looking tired and worried and also very pleased with herself.

"That was well done," he said. "But if that newbie hadn't gone flying off, I'm not sure I had any good plans to get you away."

"That newb? Sunset's friend Inga. She's a second-gen Marser, but as far as the poor instructor knows, she only speaks in something called *Swedish*?"

"That's brilliant. But . . . why are you here? Why aren't you on your way home?" That last came out more plaintive than he'd wanted.

"Because the MCA is quietly emptying all of the underground looking for you. I thought you were just going to go get dinner, not start a citywide manhunt."

"Me too," he said.

"What happened?"

"There was an incident. It was my own stupid fault."

If Mari saw the easy opening, she didn't take it. "Stirring up the MCA has done us a favor, if that makes you feel better," she said. "The Luceatans bolted in a supply truck towards something called 'the Warrens' about forty-five minutes ago. I have to hand it to you and your luck, Fergus. You wander into the underground and manage to come back out having accidentally befriended a man with an entire network of eyes around the city. I don't know how you do it."

"Me neither."

"So, we going after them?"

"I don't want to be responsible for anything bad happening to you," he said.

"Didn't we already have that conversation? Besides, you said it yourself—it's going to take both of us to get Arelyn back safe. We're a team. Equals, equally responsible for ourselves and only ourselves. I'm not a kid, I'm not the friend you lost, and I'm sure as shit not your *follower*. You got that?"

"Got it," he said.

"Are we going?"

"Yeah." He put the buggy in gear. "We're going."

They trundled along the perimeter of the city at the same slow pace a window washer looking for sand damage would move. "What are the Warrens?" Mari asked.

"It's an old apartment site that was built for the construction crew while the Ares Five dome was being raised. It's just outside the city, officially abandoned, but a lot of skunk-heads, smugglers, and people too crazy or violent to be tolerated by the rest of the underground lurk there."

"Sounds wonderful."

"Yeah. But listen: it means Arelyn must be alive."

"How so?"

"The Luceatans could have just cut their losses and taken a shuttle out. If they've retreated to the Warrens, they're still trying to figure out what to do."

"And the plan? Do you have one?"

"Window washers drive around the city all the time. It'll be almost full night by the time we get to the side near the Warrens, so we'll park and make a quick run over the sands as soon as it's fully dark."

In the silence after he finished talking, his stomach growled loudly enough to elicit a wry chuckle from Mari. "Didn't think to eat before kicking off a manhunt for yourself?" she asked.

"No."

She sighed. "I'm hungry enough I almost wish I still had that Celekai stuff you sent Sunset with."

"There are readymeals in the back," he said. "Take one out of the box and twist the pack side to side. Takes about five minutes to heat itself up. At least it's designed for humans to eat. Desperate humans, maybe, but humans nonetheless."

"You want one too?"

"I'll make one once we're parked," he said. "Those cartons are so flimsy it's impossible to eat while driving without burning the hell out of your crotch."

Mari climbed back over the seat, and he heard the familiar clang of cans. Over the popping sounds of a readymeal initializing, she said, "I like that it gets dark out for a while each day. It's not so bad inside the buggy, but it'll be a relief not seeing the whole sky at once, looming overhead like that."

"It's a clear night," Fergus said. "We should even see stars."

"Really?"

"Yeah."

She came back up front, careful not to spill the steaming meal. Putting her boots up on the buggy's dash, she balanced it carefully on her knees and pulled the wrap from it. "Nice suit," she said as she waited for it to cool. "You didn't go back to that RedZoots place, I hope?"

"Oh, hell no," Fergus said. "I'm at least a little bit smarter than that. I stole it."

"Oh? Who from?"

"You know that entire squad of MCA goons that was searching the city top to bottom looking for me? That's who from."

She laughed. "You are good at pissing people off."

"It's my greatest talent."

He thought about telling her about the Dr. Diagnosis, then changed his mind. "Look," he said. "I should've insisted that the Shielders let you stay behind. You've been in danger you shouldn't have been in, both here and back at Cernee, and a lot of it is because of me. Some of that wasn't in my control, but some of it was. And whether or not I'm responsible or allowed to feel that way anyway, I'm sorry."

"You should be," she said.

He took a deep breath, bracing himself to tell her about the electricity, the *thing* in his gut, when she spoke again.

"If we're being honest, I'm not regretting that I came here," she said. "It's been . . . eye-opening. When I first started sneaking off the farm, Cernee seemed so big, you know? But before long it became tiny, a trap, like I was a bug in a bottle. It's good to get away from home and look back at it from a new perspective. Changes how you see yourself too, you know?"

He mulled that over. "You're right. Except I try to never look back."

"We're a lot closer to your home than mine."

"Only in terms of distance."

Mari nodded. Maybe she understood, at that.

"We're almost to the Warrens," he said, pointing. "You see it ahead?"

She leaned forward, peering out through the front glass, clearly more comfortable now that the sky had settled down into the bluish remnants of sunset. Ahead of them, the Warrens was a large, irregular pile of blocks poking up out of the sand, just a few hundred meters away from the dome wall. "I see it," she said. "No lights?"

"No. Ares Five cut power hoping the squatters would either go find some other city to haunt or just politely die where they were."

"So how do they live? Is there air?"

"The Warrens are kind of a heavily condensed version of Cernee without any of the charm. They've got both wind and solar gens on the top to bring power down, but the systems are old and unreliable. In some spots there are pockets of stale air that'll just drop you dead."

"Great. I can't wait for the tour."

"It's going to be dangerous. Especially with me in an MCA suit; I might as well have a target on my back," Fergus said. "We need to be careful and quick. If we find Arelyn and you have a chance to get out, get out. Don't worry about me."

Mari snorted.

It was nearly night by the time they parked the buggy. From there the Warrens looked like a rocky outcropping against the last remnants of the day. Already Fergus could make out a few of the brighter stars above them, and one he knew wasn't a star at all fading out toward the horizon.

The small corridor that had once connected the two structures looked like a bomb had been dropped on it; blackened and twisted wreckage jutted out of the sand like the ribs of some terrible worm, finally slain at the door to civilization.

"If they hate the Warrens that much, why not level them?" Mari asked.

"It's like cockroaches—or ballroaches, I guess. If you take away their hidey-hole, they'll just scurry into the next nearest," Fergus said.

"Ah. Yeah," she said. She climbed over the seat again, poked her head back in a few moments later. "If you're worried about the MCA suit, why not wear this other one?"

Because I'll short it out and then probably die in it, he didn't say. "It's too small for me. Did it check out?"

"All green."

"See if you can find a bag or something to carry it in. It's a good bet Arelyn doesn't have a suit," Fergus said. "Mars is nothing but prisons if you can't go outside."

Fergus had shut down all the buggy's lights long before they'd come within sight of the Warrens, and other than the dim reddish glow of the buggy's windowless interior, they were comfortably dark. He dialed up the zoom on his goggles, switching over to infrared, and watched the decaying apartment block for any signs of life or movement. Wedged into one of the many irregular corners of the block's perimeter was the tall, wide door of a vehicle entry bay. A faint tracery of tire tracks and footsteps thickened and converged at it and the small airlock beside it. *That's our way in,* Fergus thought.

"Anything back there you think we could use as a weapon?" he asked.

She climbed carefully back over the seat and handed him a hot food tray. "Not unless that's your underwear back there," she said.

"Not mine."

"Nothing else obviously offensive, then. Eat quick."

He'd forgotten both how awful readymeals were and how good being hungry made them taste anyway. Mari fidgeted while he gulped down the last few bites and tossed the empty tray over the back. They sealed their suits, and then he climbed to the rear airlock and cycled himself out first. If someone was going to jump them, he'd rather it was him. No one did.

A few minutes later Mari joined him. It felt like walking into a canyon, with the high wall of the city slowly curving up and away from them up on their left and the Warrens closing in on their right. They crossed the rubble of the corridor, then moved along it, hugging the wall toward the vehicle bay. For the same reason as before, Fergus went through the airlock first. It was dark on the far side, a small corridor with a door at the far end and another to the side facing the vehicle bay. As his suit readjusted to the interior atmosphere, he could hear faint sounds through the door. "Hang on for a minute," he told Mari over the comm. "There might be someone in the bay."

He pressed very gently on the door, opening it far enough to peer in. The vehicle bay was unlit, but there was a supply buggy inside with its rear hatch open and bright light inside. The sounds and the movement of shadows against the far interior wall suggested someone working inside.

Fergus felt it coming like a quick warning blast of jitters. There was a bright spark between his hand and the door handle. Both hands tingled inside his gloves as his suit rebooted.

Great, he thought. It was hard not to panic during those long six seconds before his air started circulating again. No one had come out of the truck, at least.

"—gus?" Mari's voice came over the comm as soon as they were back online a moment later.

"You okay, Mari?"

"I'm fine. You went off-comm," she said. "I'm in the airlock now. What happened?"

"My suit rebooted," he said.

"You stole a glitchy suit?" She laughed, although there wasn't much mirth in it.

"Yeah, just my luck. Stay back until I give the word."

He pushed the door open the rest of the way, stepped into the bay, and quietly closed the door behind him. Then he crept up to the side of the truck and, taking a deep breath, risked a quick glance around the back. A fist shot out and knocked him to the floor.

A man jumped down from the back of the supply buggy and put a heavy boot down on Fergus's chest before he could get up. A bright light shone down at him, blinding him.

"Angus?" the man said, incredulous, leaning down to stare into his face shield.

I know that voice, Fergus thought. "Red Bart?"

"Shit! Angus!" Red Bart said.

The light switched off and was replaced by the red circle of a pistol's targeting light. Fergus reached up and slapped Bart on the side of the neck, dumping as much juice as he could muster into the contact.

The pistol discharged, going wide, and left a blackened, smoking mark on the floor a hand's width from Fergus's left ear.

His suit started another reboot as he rolled out of the way. Red Bart crumpled to the floor beside him as he scrambled to his feet and kicked Red Bart's pistol under the supply buggy.

Adrenaline and post-shock jitters left Fergus unsteady. Leaning against the buggy, he patted his pockets and found, to his relief, a small stash of MCA handbinders. Fumbling out a pair, he looped one end around Bart's hand, the other around his opposite ankle, and activated them.

When he could speak, he pinged Mari. "Mari?"

"You're alive? Your channel was open, and I heard a shot, then nothing."

"Suit rebooted again," he said.

"It's not the suit that's glitchy, is it? Same with the pod," she said. "This is something with you. Something new since . . ." Her words trailed off.

"Yes," he said. The word hurt to say out loud. "I was going to tell you, but it's hard to talk about, and now's not the time. Where are you?"

"I'm in the corridor past the airlock. I thought you'd been taken down and wanted to get out of the area before they came looking for others."

"Good thinking," he said. "I've got someone here we can ask questions when he wakes up."

"Do what you have to. I'm going to keep going."

"Mari—"

"Tunnels and me are old friends, Fergus. Don't go all auntie on me. I'll check back in ten."

The connection dropped into standby. *Well, hell*, Fergus thought.

Everything was quiet except his own breathing. Leaning over, he took Red Bart's comm off his free wrist and put it on below his own with no small amount of deja vu. He picked up the man's limp hand and activated the fingerprint scanner, unlocked the comm, and set it to receive only.

"—shit," someone was saying in a thick Luceatan accent. "Whole place is a maze. Which way now?"

"Up," another voice said.

"I say we just leave her to the scummers. Graf will make the boss understand, and if he doesn't, he can take it out on Lerd for letting her get away in the first place."

"We can't risk her escaping alive, and you know it. Gotta find or make a body, the sooner the better. Checking another crapper cubbyhole, so shut up now."

The channel went quiet.

"Mari?" Fergus called on his own comm.

"What?" She sounded annoyed and out of breath.

"When you and Arelyn were kids, who won at hide-and-seek?"

"About even," Mari said. "Why?"

"Because the good news is that Arelyn is alive, and she got away from the Luceatans," Fergus said. "The bad news is, they aren't looking to get her back alive anymore. Now it's a race to see which of us finds her first."

Chapter 21

F ergus kicked Red Bart, not as hard as he might have but not gently either. The man groaned, grudgingly opened one eye, and tried to unbend himself. The binders held. His eyes found Fergus. "Angus," he said.

"Bart. I went by your shop yesterday to buy a suit. I was disappointed you weren't there."

"Oh, so you met Nimer? Little fucking weasel," Red Bart said. "I hope you kicked his ass at least as good as you just did mine."

"Well, we didn't part friends," Fergus said. "You and I did, or so I thought."

"Nimer worked for me for less than a month, then called the MCA and claimed I was a Free Marsie. They kept me in lockup for three weeks, probably hoping I'd lead them to my 'connections.' Couldn't get a fucking job because between the MCA and Nimer, everyone was convinced I was too hot to touch. I was born in fucking *Cleveland*, Angus. I need to eat and breathe. What was I supposed to do?"

"So you hired on with criminals? What do you want, a sympathy card?"

Red Bart looked miserable. "I didn't have any other choice! Shit. This was supposed to be a one-day gig moving stuff."

"Where's the camp, Bart? Where are they keeping the woman? How many are there?"

"Ah! *You're* the Mars assassin they got word of right before Poppa Graf stopped answering their calls," Red Bart said.

"Graf's dead," Fergus said.

"I always wondered what kind of work you did. Figured it was something sly, but didn't take you for the killer type. The way they talked about Graf, I'd've thought him invincible. You killed him?"

"Wasn't me. How many Luceatans are there, Bart?"

"Four, all vicious bastards with barely two brain cells between them," Red Bart said. "You wanna know their names, ages, heights, favorite stupid filthy joke? Just ask."

"I'm in a hurry, Bart."

Red Bart banged his head gently against the floor. "Camp is in the old mess hall. The girl got away when a bunch of scavengers from the upper floors came down and tried to unplug and cart off our oxygen generator. There were six Luceatans until that fight. They're working their way up through the Warrens from the bottom looking for her. Sent me here to load up the truck again, get it ready to go. I was going to leave without them when you came along."

"Sorry, Bart."

"Yeah, well. I shouldn't have tried to shoot you, but I panicked. I can help you."

"I can't trust you."

"You don't have to. Take my comm—" He tried to lift his wrist, saw it was now bare. "Ah, you already did. Smart. You gotta know, though, they're going to kill the girl when they find her. Probably me too. No loose ends. They just want off Mars. I don't want to die here, Angus."

"Me neither," Fergus said, "but I can't promise you anything." He patted down the pockets of his suit, found what he was looking for in the same one where the binders had been: perp tranqs. He pulled one out, no bigger than a crayon, and jabbed Bart with it. The man grunted, then fell slack.

Fergus flipped his comm back on. "Mari, you still okay?"

"So far," she said. "No luck yet."

"Listen, there are four Luceatans working their way up from ground level. Be careful. I'm going to climb up to the top floor and start searching down. Shout if you need help or if you find her first."

"Okay," Mari said. "Thanks, Fergus."

"No problem."

He glanced down at Red Bart. *Not a lot of choices, are there?* he reminded himself. Careful to shut the door behind him, he started searching for a way up.

Stairs, Fergus thought, *should be outlawed on all civilized worlds. Or at least they should not be the sole means of vertical travel in any structure over five stories tall.*

He finally reached a landing with no more flights up but a small, wide airlock instead. A half flight down was the regular door into the maze of cubes that was the zenith of the Warrens. He was at the roof. There were scuff marks in the dirt, recently made, around the airlock door. *It couldn't have been Arelyn,* he thought. *Or could it?*

He tried to peer through the airlock's tiny glass porthole, but it was thickly fogged with dark grime on the other side. He pressed the button, and there was the long grinding noise of the outer door closing and sealing. After an interminable wait, the inner door creaked, shuddered, and drew open. The floor of the airlock was covered with blackened, burnt garbage and the remains of an air canister that had had the valve pried off. By the marks on the walls, the airlock must have been nearly full to the top with burning trash.

But why? he wondered.

Then, "Ah!" he said. "Clever!"

Cycled out, the burning garbage would have been pulled out of the airlock by the pressure difference, creating a brief, bright flare atop the building. Someone had tried to send a signal, probably not knowing that the whole of Ares Five could watch the Warrens burn to the ground and not shed a tear.

Fergus picked up the air canister. His gloves registered it as still warm. Dropping it, he practically leapt down the stairs to the landing below in his excitement. How far could she have gotten if the canister hadn't even gone fully cold?

The first two rooms were empty. The third held a body that looked desiccated enough to predate Mars colonization itself. The fourth was shut, and the door radiated a small amount of heat in infrared. He put a hand against the door, pressing very lightly, and it gave. Taking a deep breath, he tried not to smile—he'd found her! Pushing the door open, he half ran into the small room.

Six men, barely less wasted than the corpse one room over, turned from where they were huddled over a small stovebox to stare at him. The heads-up display in his face shield processed the odors in the room and ran a list in green letters down his peripheral vision, but he already knew from the box, the men, and their expressions: they were making skunk.

"MCA!" one of them shouted, his face an almost comical mask of surprise. "Wain, protect the stuff!"

The skunkers staggered to their feet.

Oh, shit, Fergus thought. He backed up, slammed the door shut, and ran. At the stairwell, he jumped down to the landing below, grateful for the low gravity. At that floor, he opened the hall door, closed it behind him, and threw the emergency bar. It wouldn't stop six normal men, much less popped-up skunkheads, but he hoped it would slow them down enough for him to find a place to hide.

He went two-thirds of the way down the hall before picking a room. The door was bent in at an angle and covered in scorch marks; in places it had melted into the door frame. He grabbed it and tried to pull, but it wouldn't move. *Perfect.*

Fergus got down on his belly and pulled himself through the gap at the bottom of the bent door. The room was dark, filled with broken and burnt furniture and an overturned portable air-blast shower at the back that was ideal cover.

Down the hall he could hear the crashing of metal on metal. He hoped the emergency bar would hold a little longer.

A table was propped upright against the shower. As soon as he put his hands on it, the table flew at him, flattening him to the floor beneath it. Someone came out of the shower, jumping onto the table and knocking the breath out of him. She was the spitting image of Harcourt except younger and much angrier, and she had a portable oxygen tank in one hand and a large length of pipe in the other.

"Arelyn?" he tried to say, but he still hadn't caught his wind yet and couldn't manage more than a pathetic gasp.

"Asshole," Arelyn said, and hit him.

Pain woke him up, as it so often did. His head, of course, but also his chest and ribs. Woozily, he managed to open his eyes, then wished he hadn't. He was in the hall now, four of the skunkheads hunkered together nearby fighting over the things they'd raided from his pockets. Whatever they'd done to him, it hadn't been bad enough to break anything. Yet.

Skunk made people dangerous but also distracted and paranoid. Fergus inched his hand across the floor until he found a small chunk of debris. Closing his fist around it, he waited until the argument seemed to be reaching a crescendo, then tossed it down to the far end of the hall and feigned unconsciousness.

The skunkers panicked at the clatter. "He's got a partner!" one shouted.

"Of course he does, you idiot," another answered. "They always do. We took down one, we can take the other."

One by one they stepped over him, banded together in some semblance of bravery. As soon as they were far enough down the hall, Fergus scrambled to his feet and ran the other way for all he was worth.

He threw himself through the stairwell door, slammed it shut, and dropped the emergency bar back into place. Dizziness nearly overwhelmed him, and he teetered for a few moments against the stair rail. "Mari?" he called on the comm, but there was only silence, not even the echo of empty signal. Putting a hand to the side of his head, he found the comm relay there was smashed. *Smart kid,* he thought. *Good aim too.*

It made things more complicated, though.

If he could get down to the ground level, maybe he could steal a relay out of something in the supply truck or from Bart's suit. Then he could let Mari know where he'd seen Arelyn and, more importantly, warn her about the gang of skunkheads coming down from the top floor.

Of course, on his way down he'd be heading right toward the rising Luceatan search party. He'd worry about that when he had to; he had enough other things to deal with right now. Such as: he hadn't heard the emergency door up above. Either the skunkheads had given up without even trying, or—

Or there's another way down, he thought as a shape leapt at him out of the shadows on the next landing. He managed to dodge but crashed shoulder-first into the railing and stumbled, trying to catch himself as he staggered, off-balance, down the next set of stairs.

He landed heavily, threw one hand out, and grabbed the railing as three skunkers gathered above, ready to jump. Twisting, he threw himself down the next flight. *Thank you, Mars gravity,* he thought, *for not killing me quite as much as some other planets might have.*

One of the skunkers leapt out, arms spread, through the gap between flights. The man didn't even scream as he missed Fergus and fell the remaining stories, arms and legs bouncing off railings and walls on the way down.

Fergus looked away before the body reached the murky bottom. The wet thump echoed up the stairwell.

It didn't seem to discourage the other two. Fergus ran down the next flight, trying to stay at least a staircase ahead of his pursuers. At the next turn, something crashed into the wall where his head had been a moment before, and he glanced back long enough to discover that one of his pursuers had thrown his oxygen bottle at him. Two more flights down, that man fell to his knees, hands scrabbling at the metal landing. Fergus didn't wait, didn't need to see anyone else die, even people who were trying to kill him.

Dead air pocket. Maybe I'll make it after all, he thought.

Four more skunkers appeared on the landing below him. He leapt, tucking his knees up, and hit the clustered skunkers like a cannonball. He fell onto a pile of people and tried not to care who or what he stepped on as he pulled himself away from their grabbing hands.

Three more floors to go. He hoisted himself up onto the rail and slid down the next flight before the first of the skunkers had disentangled himself from the pile. Surprise had given him a good lead, but the reinforcements weren't exhausted or beaten, and they had a lot of drugs in their systems convincing them they were superhuman.

Second floor. Fergus dodged a thrown rock and a pipe. At the landing he spun as a skunker jumped at him, trying the same maneuver he'd just successfully used on them. The man missed, hit the floor hard, crumpled.

First floor. He went wide around the roughly manshaped mess on the floor, trying to see as little of it as possible. Throwing open the door, he slammed it behind him, dropped the emergency bar, and ran down the long corridor back toward the bay with the supply truck and Red Bart.

No Luceatans anywhere. He hoped they'd run into a skunker horde themselves; if ever there were two groups of people who deserved each other . . .

He just wanted to find Mari again.

Coming into the bay, his suit's pressure alarms began to go off; someone had opened the door to the outside and not closed it again. The supply truck was gone. Red Bart lay where Fergus had left him. He'd managed to close his suit up but was gasping for breath, eyes wild. Leaning close, Fergus saw his oxygen was down to less than five percent, and his spare suit tank was gone.

Shit. How long did he have before the skunkers got through the last door? Did he have so little time that he'd willingly leave a man to die?

There goes my new reputation as a fearsome assassin, Fergus thought. Reaching down, he undid the handbinders, and Bart groaned as he was finally able to unbend himself from the unkind position Fergus had left him in. "Any spare tanks we can reach quickly?"

Red Bart pointed.

Fergus ran across the room to a small charging niche he'd missed before. A single tank was hooked in. It was only at forty percent, but that was better than nothing. He brought it back to Bart, who jacked it into his suit and took several deep, gulping breaths.

"Thank you," Bart gasped out.

"Don't thank me yet. I've got about a half dozen very angry skunkheads coming down behind me. Where did the truck go?"

"Luceatans," Bart said. "Left me . . . die. Not long."

"Yeah, well," Fergus said. "Did they have two women with them? Or one? One mean-looking one with a pipe?"

Bart shook his head *no*, tried to say something, and instead fell into a lengthy coughing fit.

Did the Luceatans give up and leave, or were there two new bodies he just hadn't found yet? He went to the door, staring out into the night sands of Mars. One lens of his goggles didn't want to focus anymore, but with the other he could make out two figures stumbling across the surface about halfway to the window-washing buggy. One still carried a pipe.

The spare suit had come in useful after all.

Fergus's heart soared. For the first time in longer than he could remember, he didn't feel haunted.

"They got away," he said, turning to Bart. "You think you can walk out of here?"

"Give . . . minute," Bart said, between coughs.

He could hear pounding now on the corridor door. "How about twenty seconds?" he asked.

"I. Take it."

"Good."

Fergus checked his seals again, then peered out to see how Arelyn and Mari were doing. They were running now. Behind them, the supply truck was racing toward them at full speed. *They're going to run them down,* he realized with horror. Mari and Arelyn were out on bare sand with no cover, nowhere to hide.

The two women split up. Mari headed off at an angle, probably hoping to draw the truck away. It remained resolutely after the taller Arelyn.

"Not gonna make it," Bart said, stumbling over to where Fergus stood.

"No, they're not," Fergus agreed, and his eyes met Bart's for just a moment before he ran as hard as he could out onto the surface of Mars.

His lungs pounded in his chest, his ribs ached, his body was full of angry bees. The bees spread through his chest and down his arms, his fingers burning and crackling with their fury as if they were consuming him from the inside out.

At last he fell to his knees, stretched out both his hands toward the speeding supply truck as if pleading for it to stop, and poured himself out through his fingertips. White light arced across the intervening space, a single sharp curling bolt of lightning.

It enveloped the truck for just a fraction of an instant. Then the truck seemed to twist and turn, rolling over on one side. From the interior he could see the bright blossom of flame.

Oh hey, Fergus thought. *I hit something important.*

His suit tried desperately to reboot.

He fell onto his hands, then laid his face down against the sand, wishing he could feel the cold, wishing there were an oasis here he could drink from until the awful fire in his gut was quenched.

He could see, in a blur, Mari and Arelyn converging on the window washing buggy. Minutes later it started up and drove away at top speed. *Go!* he thought. *Go Mari! Yeah!*

Maybe, just maybe, he could finally forgive himself a little bit for Dru.

Turning his head, he spotted Bart edging his way along the side wall of the Warrens, away from the maintenance bay and toward the cover of another corner. In the wide doorway, the gang of skunkers had gathered. At last, one began walking across the sand toward him. A second, then a third joined in behind him.

No big black triangles here, come to save him from certain death a second time.

It doesn't matter, Fergus decided. *I still win. I just need to stop winning quite so badly.*

Chapter 22

———◆———

Bits of things were clearer than others. He remembered them grabbing his boot and dragging him back into the Warrens. When he struggled, they'd hit him, so after a few feeble attempts to fight them off, he gave up; he didn't have the strength to get away. *Tell yourself that, Fergus,* he thought. *Pretend it's not because there's just nowhere to get away to and you're more okay with this being the end than you should be.*

One of the skunkers closed the bay door, and the five men gathered around him, all talking at once. He didn't think any of them realized others were speaking or that no one was listening. He met the eyes of one—surprisingly young, for all that the man's face sported the wrinkles and heavy staining of a long-term skunk addict—and found an emptiness in those eyes that hurt to see. He felt, for an instant, as much pity for them as for himself.

During that brief connection, the man blinked, his grimace showing eroded and blackened teeth, and kicked him. It wasn't a hard blow, but the action caught the attention of the others, and they all began kicking at him, head and stomach and back, wherever they could get a boot in. They shouted, some of it about the MCA, frustrations with the injustices of the world, ex-lovers, disloyal friends, being sold bad skunk. Most of it was unintelligible.

Fergus put his arms over his head and curled into a ball as kick after kick added up in relentless numbers to something devastating and unbearable and infinite. Retreating into himself, at some point he noticed that the kicks had stopped, and he heard screaming, but he didn't care.

"Fergus."

One clear, familiar voice.

"Snap out of it, Fergus!"

He heard it, spent an eon rolling it around in his head, trying to figure out where to put it, what to make of it. Was there something he should do? He didn't trust the voice, thought it must be his imagination, some desperate distraction.

"Fergus, we can't help you until you wake the fuck up."

He opened his eyes.

He was still curled up on the bay floor. His face shield was cracked, blood running down the inside, blood in his eye. The world was bright, flickering like a strobe light. He knew that if he tried to reconnect with his body it would hurt too much, so he just stayed there, peering at the outside world through one tiny crack in the door of his self.

There were feet that were not kicking him. Someone was kneeling just out of arm's reach. A face, bent over to look at him, was filled with concern. *Yep, that's really Mari,* he thought. *Shit.*

"You got *away*," he said, a universe's worth of aggravation in that last word. "Go away again before they come back."

"Fergus." Mari glared at him. "Are you listening to me?"

"Dangerous. Got to get—"

"Are you listening to me?"

He tried to find where to hide her voice, somewhere he couldn't see or hear it, and gave it up as futile. "Yes," he answered, resenting it.

"You need to stop zapping."

"What?"

"Stop. *Zapping.*"

He could feel it now, a bristling cocoon around him. It leapt across his skin, through his suit, dancing in the air. He didn't want to let it go, didn't want everything to go quiet and violent again, but Mari had said he should. He relaxed. There were a few more flickers, and then the room sank into a monotone dark.

"Now stay that way," Mari said. Someone was lifting him, then carrying him. They put him in a buggy, pulled off melted bits of suit, threw a portable air pod over his mouth and nose.

Eventually he focused, found Red Bart beside him. "I think that makes us even," the man said.

Fergus nodded. That seemed fair.

Mari sat down next to Bart. "I thought you'd been killed when your comm went dead again," she said. "Arelyn almost knocked me over coming down the stairs, and we ran for it."

"That was good," he said.

"Then you came running out of the Warrens like a damned fool. If I'd let you die saving us, I might have started feeling conflicted about my very solid and satisfying dislike for you," she said. "So we—Are you falling asleep on me, Fergus? *Don't do that.* You need to stay awake."

"You should get away," he said. He closed his eyes. "Thanks for coming back, but you should get away. Not safe here. Go. I'll be fine."

"Fergus . . .!"

He lost the rest of what she had to say as he curled back up on the floor of his mind, in the dark.

At least this time he couldn't hear crickets.

"Yeah, he's coming around again," another voice said.

Fergus cracked open one eye, abandoning the comfortable darkness in his surprise to find a familiar face, chin scar and all. "Bale!" he said.

Bale was sitting next to him on the bunk, looking much better than when last Fergus had seen him. Fergus tried to sit up, but a strong hand held him down. "Don't get up," Bale said. "You took a good beating, and you were so dehydrated you were starting to look like some kind of turd fossil."

They weren't in the bay at the Warrens, nor in a buggy. The walls were clean, plain, nondescript, lined with jump-safety bunks. "Where . . .?" he asked.

"The *Oleaja.* Private jump ship. We just left the Mars Orbital," Bale said. "Mari and Arelyn are up talking to the pilot, so I'm here babysitting your sorry ass."

"Why are you here?"

"I said, babysitting—"

"No, *here.* Mars."

"Mr. Harcourt shipped me here, not that I remember any of it," Bale said. "I needed surgery, and with the fighting he wasn't sure Medusa would be safe. And he thought it wouldn't hurt to have another person here he could trust to keep an eye on Arelyn. Only by the time I got sprung from the med center, she was already gone. I was about to start taking Ares One apart millimeter by violent millimeter when Mari and Arelyn sent a call out for help. Then we came back for you. Your friend Bart led us to you."

"You should have left me. It would have been simpler."

"No argument there. You're a complicating guy," Bale said. "More than that, you're like a black hole. None of us seem able to escape you once you've pulled us into your orbit."

"Sorry. It's not intentional. I never wanted to put any of you in danger."

"And that's why we came back for you," Bale said.

He heard a door open and craned his neck to look. Arelyn Harcourt. "Sorry about hitting you," she said. "The Luceatans bribed some MCA grunts to let them in and out of the University dome, so I just figured you were one of them."

"Suit was stolen," he said.

"Yep, well, not like you painted GOOD GUY in giant neon letters on it, did you? No way I could have known."

"No," he said. "Good hit on the relay, by the way."

"Thanks. Good hit on the supply buggy."

"Thanks."

"Well," she said. "I guess now we just need to decide what to do with you."

"It's okay to leave me here," he said. "I can find my way to safety on my own."

Bale snickered. "I'd like to see that."

Arelyn took a handpad out of her jacket, turned it on, and held it up where he could see it. "Or we could just hand you over to the Alliance and collect the reward," she said. "Fifty thousand cred, Alliance backed."

"Fifty—?!" Fergus blinked. "That's a terrible picture of me."

"Probably, but it's still pretty identifiable." She held it next to Fergus's head. "What do you think, guys? Do we have the dangerous alien infiltrator or what? Same beady eyes."

"Same dirty beard," Bale said. "I'm betting that's where the aliens are hiding."

"Ha ha," Fergus answered. "I can see why you people all get along. Just get the cred up-front and get out, okay? The MCA is notorious for suddenly deciding you're collaborators instead of helpful citizens if it'll save them a buck."

Arelyn turned off the handpad and thumped it down on his chest. He winced, stifling a groan. "Mari did warn us that you were an idiot," she said.

"She did," Bale said.

"I did," Mari said, coming through the door Arelyn had left open. "What idiotic thing is he saying now? Oh wait, let me guess: *just leave me on Mars, waaah waaah.*"

"More or less."

"I did not *waaah*," Fergus protested.

"So here's the deal," Mari said. "We've got six jumps

back to Crossroads. Four of them are Earth Alliance worlds, and as you've probably noticed, you're in shit shape to be a wanted man on the run right now. You can barely sit up on your own, much less play bug-in-the-walls with the MCA after you. That leaves Coralla or Zanzjan Minor."

"For what?"

"For dropping you off," Mari said. "You're done."

"What?" he said again.

"The cable car. Mezz Rock. Graf. The Asiig. You could have turned your back on all of us a dozen times, but you didn't. I saw the skunkers drag you back into the Warrens, and I figured we'd finally managed to get you killed, and yet here you are. All of us here owe you our lives. When your luck does finally run out, we don't want to be the cause of it," Mari said. "So you're done."

"We have contacts on Coralla," Bale said. "They can help you get back on your feet again."

Coralla! Fergus thought. He'd dreamt more than once about living out the rest of his life on a Corallan beach, but as a retirement, not a refuge.

Should it matter?

"Coralla will do," he said at last. "But what about you? What's happening in Cernee?" He tried to count it out, but he'd lost too much time to be sure. Seven days since they'd left? Eight? A lifetime, a blink.

"Not that I should tell you, but I got a message from our contact on Crossroads right before we lifted," Bale said. "The Asiig are still camped out with Gilger's ship off the spinward perimeter. The ship circling Cernee disappeared shortly after you and Mari left for Crossroads. Inside Cernee, nothing big enough to be visible is moving independently, although our contact has seen weaponsfire deep inside the Halo. Parts of Cernee are dark."

"The Wheels?" Mari asked.

"Still lit and spinning. Other than that?" Bale shrugged. "We don't know. But if people can't move or are restricted to movement on the lines, being cut off is an advantage for now."

"And communications?"

"I sent a message back telling our guy to launch a talker," Bale said. "It's like a tiny missile, except it broadcasts an encrypted message on a very narrow, high-powered band. If we can get it far enough into Cernee before someone shoots it down, we might be able to get a message through to Mr. Harcourt that everyone is safe on Coralla."

"Everyone?" Arelyn asked.

"Yes. All of you are getting dropped off," Bale said. "You're going to wait there until the situation in Cernee is resolved one way or another. This is nobody's fight except mine."

"You don't mean—" Mari started.

"Yep, *all* of you. And it's not open to discussion." Bale stood. "We've got four hours until we hit the Jupiter jump point, so I suggest you all bunk down until then. The pilot has graciously invited us to make use of the ship's kitchenette for the duration of the trip, by which I assume she's telling the rest of you to stay the hell off the bridge."

Arelyn crossed her arms across her chest. "No offense— I get that he saved us, and I don't want to seem ungrateful— but Ferguson isn't one of us. We got him away from Mars; why can't we just let him go his own way at Jupiter?"

"Because we're not stopping anywhere we don't have to, and we're not dropping anyone somewhere they'll be unsafe," Bale said. "Until we part ways, we're all going to get along and be nice. Got it?"

"But he's not even human anymore!" Arelyn protested.

"Ari . . ." Mari started.

"What? You all know it. The Asiig got to him. He's their *thing*."

Mari pointed at Arelyn. "You. Kitchenette."

"I don't—" Arelyn started.

"Kitchenette, *now*," Mari growled. She half chased Arelyn from the cabin.

Bale watched them go, then looked at Fergus. "No way I'm getting anywhere near that," he said. "I'll be in the cockpit, away from you crazy people."

"Nice to see you again too," Fergus said, and he closed his eyes. He wondered if once he was standing on the beaches of Coralla for real, he would finally have outrun his need to run away.

He breathed easier when they hit the jump point at Jupiter and left the Sol system behind. It took him several tries to get himself out of his bunk, and he had more than a little regret for having done so once he was up. The kitchenette was a tiny room with a small table and enough grippy chairs for four. It would have been the perfect number if not for the fact that Mari and Arelyn were unwilling to be in the same room at the same time.

Bale had an ornate, hexagon-shaped deck of cards, and lacking any other options to pass the time, taught them an obtuse and suspiciously cheatable game called Venusian Monkeypoker. After his fifth losing hand in a row, Fergus got up stiffly and paced, checking cupboards for something other than the ubiquitous packages of rock-hard grain biscuits that seemed to fill every shelf. They had enough rations for the trip, but only just, and boredom had driven everyone into foraging. As such, the biscuits were a cruel disappointment; so far, no one had managed to swallow more than a bite.

Fergus found a single teabag and sniffed it. Deciding it wasn't entirely dead yet, he made himself a hot-water bulb to soak it in as he watched Bale and Mari finish the hand.

"Ha!" Mari shouted, slapping down two queens and a rocket. "Venus Minor! Hand over, round to me!"

"Not so fast," Bale said. "I counter with my bag of moon rocks, and then I play the Monkey King." He set down the gold-foiled card, and Mari groaned and threw down what was left of her cards.

Arelyn came in as Bale started gathering up the cards again. She looked around the room, didn't meet Mari's eyes. "The pilot says we'll be dropping out of jump at Haudernelle to refuel in about two hours."

Bale looked back and forth between the two women. "Okay," he said, "I guess I have to ask. What the hell is going on between you two?"

"You think you know people," Arelyn said. "You think you can trust them—"

"Yeah, trust them to be your *friend*," Mari retorted.

Arelyn turned and stomped out of the room again.

Bale scowled at Fergus. "Is this your fault?" he asked.

"It's mine," Mari said. "Whose deal?"

"Yours," Bale said. "Fergus, sit your ass down. Watching you wince all over the room is distracting."

"Har har," Fergus said. His tea had managed a feeble tint, so he scooped the bag out and tossed it in the flash recycler before he sat.

"When we get to Crossr—" Mari started to say.

"Nope. Not happening," Bale said. He put the deck in the center of the table. "Shut up and play, both of you."

Mari cut the deck. Then she put one finger atop a single loose card at the side of the table and slid it over to Bale. "You get the Copper Cup for being an asshole."

Two more days of this, Fergus thought in despair.

"Coralla has famously beautiful beaches," he said, speaking quietly, as Bale dealt the hand. "Pure white sand as far as the eye can see, water so perfectly warm you can hardly feel it, a sky so blue you can't even tell where it ends and the water begins. And the food . . . I have heard such things about the food it could make you cry for want of it. It's supposed to be one of the most peaceful places in the known universe."

"You saying this for my benefit?" Mari asked, eyebrows arched high.

"No, entirely for my own," Fergus said. "Now, can whoever has the damned Nickel Rat start the bloody hand?"

The pilot came back to the kitchenette, a large bulb of aromatic soup in her hands. She was short, dark, middle-aged, and modded with black-market neurojacks in an arc along the right side of her skull. Bale had called her Fox, but Fergus knew that didn't mean much: Tanduouan pilots were notoriously superstitious about giving out their real names. "We're at the fuel exchange," she said. "Mr. Bale, if you want to check in with your contact at Crossroads, now's your chance. I want to be in the queue for the jump to Tanduou in twenty-five minutes."

Bale set his cards down and got up from the table.

"Uh," Mari said, looking at her. "Where'd you get the soup?"

"Last one," she said. "Help yourself to the biscuits, though." She left, Bale following.

Arelyn came in, took Bale's seat, and turned it facing backwards before she sat on it, her arms across the back. Mari stood, clearly intent on leaving, but Arelyn shook her head and pointed firmly down. "Sit," she said.

Fergus stood to leave. "You stay too," Arelyn said.

"This is between you and Mari—" he began, but she glared at him until he sat back down.

"I think what hurts me the most," Arelyn said, her eyes completely on Mari, "is not so much that you kept this secret from me for as long as you did—that you didn't trust me—but that this Earther jackass comes along, and within a *week* you've told him. And I don't get that."

"I—" Fergus started to say.

"Shut up," Mari and Arelyn said simultaneously.

"You have no idea what it's like," Mari said. "Growing up with all my sisters and aunts telling me that if anyone ever found out what I was, it would get us all killed. That if you knew, you wouldn't be my friend anymore. It's like having a part of you that's cracked and broken and ugly and always having to keep that part out of sight because if people see it, they'll just put you out with the garbage."

"You know I wouldn't—" Arelyn started.

"Do I?" Mari countered. "By the time I thought I did, it was already too late to tell you without you reacting just the way you are *right now*."

"But you told him?!" Arelyn waved wildly at Fergus. "A complete stranger?"

"Because I didn't have anything to lose," Mari said. "More than that, because I knew he was broken too."

Fergus remembered that plate he had pulled from the Inland Sea as a child, and the tiny chip out of the edge, and imagined it still sitting there on the hillside where his mother had placed it, facing the setting sun and waiting to be lost again. *I suppose I am,* he thought.

"So you just told him like it was nothing," Arelyn said.

"It's *never* nothing," Mari growled through gritted teeth. "It's everything, because the only thing I was ever afraid of losing was *you*."

"But you wouldn't have lost me!"

"No? I did when you went off to Mars."

"You could have come with me! I asked, but you said no."

"You could have asked why!"

"You could have at least told me something was wrong! We could have found a way to fix it!"

"Fix it?!" Mari shouted. "How do you fix what you *are*?"

"There are doctors—"

"I'd endanger my whole family!"

"There are doctors so far away they've never heard of Cernee, or the Asiig, or any of it!"

"I can't take that risk. I am what I am, Arelyn," Mari

said. "If you can't be friends with me without 'fixing' me first, then we aren't friends."

"I just want what's best for you." Arelyn looked at Fergus for the first time. "You explain it to her," she said.

"Well," he said, wishing desperately that he were anywhere else. "Arelyn is probably right that there are doctors far enough from Cernee for you to be safely anonymous. There's no guarantee they'd be able to do anything for you or that if they could, the change would be one you'd want. And Mari is right that being her friend can't be conditional on her changing who she is for you."

Arelyn stood up, flinging the chair back. "And here I felt bad for hitting you with that pipe," she said, and she stormed out.

The sudden silence in the kitchenette was almost painful.

"Great food?" Mari said eventually.

"So I'm told."

"How big's the sky?"

"Don't think about it," he said. "Try a biscuit."

The *Oleaja* was, to Fergus's surprise, not only atmosphere-capable, but had the proper permits to land directly on Coralla. The pilot took them in without delay and set down on the shuttleport tarmac. "Rintennan Island," she announced over the ship's comms as they gathered at the open cargo bay door. "Don't forget to check under your bunks for your personal belongings as you get off my ship."

Fergus snorted. "All I have is the clothes on my back."

"I heard that," the pilot answered. "You can also keep the towel you were walking around in when your clothes were in the wash. The ship surveillance footage will cost you extra."

Bale coughed. "I have something for you," he said. He picked up a cargo bag, held it out.

Fergus took it and undid the flap. Nestled inside was his MCA suit. He held it up, scrutinizing the military-grade smartfabric, unable to find a single blemish. "How the hell did you manage to fix this?" he asked at last, astonished.

Bale smiled. "I didn't."

"Then how—"

Bale cracked his knuckles, one set after the other. "The highly skilled application of the element of surprise," he said.

Mari snorted. "Somewhere there's a very tall, very pissed off, very freshly scented MCA soldier trying to explain how he got stuck in the Mars Orbital laundry processing chute."

"I swapped out the screen on the pad you left in the buggy, so that's in there too," Bale said. "It's not much, but, well. Didn't have time to buy you goodbye flowers."

"You going to be okay?" Fergus asked.

Bale frowned. "I don't know," he said. "We can't reach our Crossroads contact. We've got six hours in dock till the next launch window, and then one way or another we've got to go. I don't know what's waiting for us or how I'm going to get back to Cernee under the nose of the Asiig, but hey, if you can pull off the impossible, maybe I can too. Especially if I'm not worrying about the rest of you lot."

Fergus held out a hand, and Bale shook it. "Good luck," he said.

"Try to stay out of trouble for once, okay?" Bale said. He turned to Mari and Arelyn. "You two. If all goes well, I'll be back for you soon."

"Thanks, Bale," Arelyn said, while Mari stood with her arms crossed, lips pressed tightly together, scowling.

Fergus stepped out of the cargo bay into the shuttleport, giving them a few minutes alone whether they wanted it or not. It wasn't about him anymore. Standing at the threshold of the gates, he felt unbalanced, wavering on a point, like he could teeter and fall into this new world or back into his old one.

The guard at the gate had his back turned, was talking

to someone over his comm. "Yeah, long gone now," he was saying. "Too fast for anyone up at the orbital to get a good look at it. Yeah. Like a big black triangle, they said."

Fall forward, Fergus told himself. *Fall away from all of this as fast as you can.* He hurried past the guard, away from the *Ọlẹaja,* out into the warm air and sunlight and clear skies of Coralla. He stopped on the edge of the boardwalk and stood there, trying to feel real again.

After a few minutes, the other two emerged behind him, and the security guard pulled the gates closed. Mari put her hands up over her eyes and hunched over in the bright sun, groaning. "I hate this place already," she said.

"It's almost sunset," Arelyn said. "You'll live. Dad's got a contact on the other side of the island who says there's a decent hotel a short walk down the beach from here. You and I can get a room for the night, and then he'll meet us in the morning."

"And Fergus?" Mari asked.

Arelyn threw a dangerous glance in his direction. "What about him?" she said.

"It's okay," Fergus interrupted. "I'll find my own way from here. You two were friends before I came along, and even though I didn't cause this fight, I don't think you'll figure out how to be friends again until I'm gone. So I'm going." He picked up his duffel, turned his back on them, and walked down the boardwalk toward the gentle sloping sands beyond.

"Fergus . . ." Mari called after him, but he kept walking.

The boardwalk curved toward the beach, then finally disappeared beneath it. The pure white sand was tinged a faint pink now as the sun slid toward the far horizon. There were people and umbrellas scattered like strange weeds here and there, and the beginnings of a bonfire near the waterline. The ocean went on forever, the water dark, the waves mesmerizing.

At last Fergus dared to turn and look behind him, up

toward the shuttleport. There was no one standing there any longer, no one waiting for him, no one watching him. *That,* he thought, *is for the best.*

He dropped the duffel and sat down in the sand, digging his fingers into it as if to burrow in. It was still warm from the sun, and it ran through his fingers like liquid silk.

I'm alive, he thought. More than that, his friends were still alive, and without him around, maybe they'd stay that way.

The sun finally kissed the horizon, a giant orange globe of fire. The bonfire was now a roaring beacon, and he could hear the mingled chaos of music and laughter from the people gathered around it. The pale half circle of one of Coralla's moons was just visible in the deepening dark high above. He let out a long breath, feeling as if he were exhaling air that had been trapped in his lungs since the day he left Earth. Most peaceful place in the galaxy? He believed it with all his heart. This was the place people ran away to, to find—or lose—themselves forever.

I could stay right here for the rest of my life, he thought. *I'm free. I can be nobody, nothing, without disappointing anyone else ever again.* He was tipping over the boat, ready to sink, no one standing on the shore to watch him go. Everything he'd ever been had been scoured clean.

He was ready to drown.

Except.

There was one thing, one promise, one last indelible piece of who he was that refused to yield. Letting the last of the sand slip from his hands, he stood up, brushed off his legs, and picked up his duffel. He stepped back up onto the boardwalk.

"What're ye doin', ye daft bugger?" he asked out loud. Then he turned back toward the shuttleport and its bright lights and began to walk. He could imagine the waves of the ocean behind him reaching out, trying to close over him and pull him down for good. He was sick of being pulled from one place to another, one job to another, like a bit of flotsam. It was time to *push*.

"I am Fergus Ferguson, and I find lost things," he answered himself. "I'm going to bring *Venetia's Sword* home because I said I would, and if I have to go through Gilger and the Asiig to do it, so be it."

Chapter 23

◆—◆

He had a handpad, an MCA exosuit, a T-shirt that looked like it had come out the back side of a black hole, a small amount of credit left to his name, and not much else. He needed to get back to Cernee, and there was only one ship he was sure was heading that way. Assuming he could get back onto it—as laissez-faire-bordering-on-absentee as Coralla's work culture was, he was certain that if shuttleport security asked Bale if he should be let in, Bale was going to say no. Shout it, probably.

Improvise, Fergus.

There was a small village just past the port, 90 percent of which was stores dedicated to souvenirs, sunscreen, and a wide range of intoxicants. He found an app kiosk, jacked in his handpad, and bought the only useful thing he could think of: the aptly-named Dot Is Down. It was designed for people in nonplanetary environments where gravity could appear, disappear, or change direction without warning.

As he had expected, the shuttleport gates were closed. The guard from earlier was gone, replaced by a bored-looking night-shifter perched on a tall stool. Fergus closed the distance with as much purpose as he could put into his gait, trying to recreate the mental feel of the fancy bizsuit he still owed Harcourt for.

It worked well enough that the guard got down off his stool and stood. Before the man could speak, Fergus pointed at him and scowled. "First, if anyone asks," he said, "I was never here."

". . . What?"

Fergus held up his pad with its Guratahan Sfazil Security Service logo bright on its case. "I'm Agent Cheefer, and this is an undercover operation," he said. "I've been tracking a dangerous fugitive across half the galaxy, and I need to get into that berth before that ship launches."

The guard stared at him. "You don't look like an agent."

Fergus scowled. "If I showed up in a bright red jumpsuit with 'AGENT' scrawled across the back, I wouldn't be undercover, would I?"

"Um, no," the guard said. "Why this ship?"

Fergus held out the pad with its bright red, blinking dot in the center of the display. "See?" he said, tilting it toward the doors and slightly down. The red dot moved to the leading edge of the pad, blinking faster. *Yep, gravity is still down,* Fergus thought. *Let's hope this guy hasn't spent much time off-planet.*

"Oh. Well, okay." The guard stepped back and keyed open the gates.

Thank you, thank you, thank you, Fergus thought.

As he stepped forward, the guard put a hand on his shoulder, stopping him. "Before you go in," he said. "Your fugitive. You can tell me. It's the woman, right?"

"What?"

The guard nodded, a smug smile on his face. "I knew that story about forgetting her dance shoes was total buggo."

Nonplussed, Fergus hurried through the gates and onto the tarmac of the shuttleport. The *Oleaja* sat serenely in the center like a giant gray origami bird in a nest of cables. Standing under a wing with his back to the gates, Bale was shouting at someone, punctuating his words with expansive gestures.

There was only one person Fergus could think of who could make Bale that mad, other than himself. Sure enough, Mari peered around Bale and threw her own hands up. "Oh, *fucking* great!" she shouted.

Bale turned, whatever he was saying frozen on his

lips. Behind Fergus, the guard called from the doorway. "Do you need me to call some backup for you, Agent Cheefer?"

"What the hell is going on?" Mari demanded.

Fergus raised his pad to show off the GS Security Service logo. "You know why I'm here. Either we can go on board and talk this over quietly, or I can have a squad here and we can talk it over on the way to a detention facility."

Bale was staring at him. "Are you serious?" Mari asked.

"He's undercover!" the guard helpfully called out from the gate.

"We aren't even on Guratahan Sfazil," Mari said. "Isn't this out of your *jurisdiction*?"

Bale rounded on Mari. "This is your fault!"

"Yesssss!" the guard shouted, pumping his fist. "I knew it!"

"Are we going inside?" Fergus asked.

Bale turned to the guard. "If you let any more people into my *private* shuttleport berth—I don't care who they are—I will come back out here and shoot you!" he hollered.

The guard hurried outside and closed the gate.

"Where the hell is Arelyn?" Bale asked.

"Back at the hotel," Mari said. "I told her I was going out for fresh air."

"You just *abandoned* her?"

"It was my turn," Mari snapped.

"And when she comes looking for you?"

"I was hoping not to wait around until then."

Fergus suddenly sidestepped around Bale and through the open cargo bay door onto the ship. Bale raced after him, and Mari slipped in behind. Bale turned, waving his hands in frustration. "Get back out!" he yelled.

"I just want to go home," she said. She stabbed a hand toward Fergus. "You got what you wanted and a full out. Why the hell are you here?"

"Because I promised a ship I'd bring it home," he said.

The pilot's voice came over the comms. "We've got clearance to go, and I'm disengaging the resupply lines," she said. "You have a problem down there, you solve it in the next thirty seconds."

"That's it—no more talking. Both of you get off my ship," Bale said.

Fergus held out his hands and jumped a spark from one palm to the other. "You going to throw me out?"

Bale turned to Mari, though whether it was for help or sympathy wasn't clear. "I bite," Mari said.

Bale gave a wordless snarl. "You," he said, pointing to Mari. "If anything happens to you, I'm telling your family you stowed away without me knowing. And you!" He turned to Fergus. "If anything bad happens to you, I'm going to tell everyone I killed you myself. I'll probably get a medal."

"I'm sealing the ship," the pilot announced. "Say your goodbyes to the nice warm sandy beaches and fresh air. I strongly advise you all to be strapped down in your bunks in three minutes or less."

"Yeah," Mari said. "You two stay here and argue. I don't need any more bruises." She grabbed the ladder up onto the main deck of the *Oleaja* as the bay door swung up and shut. The sealing bolts locked like muffled gunshots.

"Move fast," Bale growled.

———

By the time the all clear sounded that they were safely in the jump conduit, Fergus was the only one still awake. He unstrapped himself and got up, grateful for the solitude. He still felt insubstantial, tenuous. Wandering back down to the cargo bay, he stared for a while at the escape pods, then returned to the kitchenette. He tried soaking a packet of biscuits in water to see if they'd turn into a more palatable mush.

The pilot came in, watched him for a few minutes, then laughed. "Those biscuits came with the ship," she said. "A whole lot of people far more desperate than you haven't found a way to make them edible either, but it's always fun to see what people try." She walked over to the cabinets and, with her back to him, did something he couldn't see; when she turned around, the cabinets looked the same as before, but she had two bulbs of insta-coffee in her hands.

She handed him one. He shook it, waiting for it to heat itself up, as she did the same. "So, you're still with us," she said.

"Yeah," he admitted. "Through to the bitter end."

She nodded. "Mr. Bale's contact at Crossroads is still offline," she said. "We've got one last jump at the Zanz-jan Minor orbital. If we don't get word by then, we aren't going to."

"I have contacts at Crossroads that I can try to reach from there," Fergus said.

"We'll only be in normal space in the Zjan system for half an hour before we jump for Crossroads," she said. "I've already locked and verified the jump window for our mass rating. You could send from there, but we wouldn't get a reply until we're already out the far side."

The Crossroads jump point was in the wake of a dead and heavily pocked ice planet named Dadekan that once upon a time had been the third-closest object to Cernee's star. Planets one and two had been chewed to crumbs by rockcrappers during the early days of system settlement. Thanks to the substantial speed differences, it was a short trip via active jump into the system at Crossroads, but a much longer one in passive, past a trio of gas giants out to the orbit of Cernee. Having some idea of what—and more particularly, who—might be waiting for them at Cernee was critical.

"If we don't hear from Bale's contact at the orbital, I'll send mine a message," Fergus said. "It's better than nothing."

"As you like," the pilot said.

"If nothing else, it'll give me something to think about

as I'm losing yet another hand of Venusian Monkey-poker," Fergus said. "I can't help but think everyone knows some secret rules I don't."

"Of course there are secret rules. It depends on what cards you hold," she said. "That's why it's so hard to know who's winning until they've won. Misleading the other players is key. If you make them spend most of the game trying to guess your strategy, at some point they'll hand you just what you need because they think you don't want it."

"Huh," he said.

"I grew up in the undercity of Tanduou. There, if you're not gaming the system, you aren't playing at all," she said. Tanduou was a moon of Guratahan Sfazil, one of the larger and more prosperous human worlds. Both places were renowned for their markets and merchants, and Tanduou in particular for not letting laws get in the way of good trade. Fergus had gotten his confuddler there, among many other probably illegal and inadvisable things, and he could not imagine surviving a childhood in that place. Coming from his background, that was saying a lot.

"Thanks," he said.

"Cheers." She tapped her coffee bulb against his and went back to the bridge. He sat down at the table by himself and sipped at the coffee, thinking about Venusian Monkeypoker and Cernee.

"Sixty seconds until we're out of jump," the pilot called over the ship comms.

Fergus had been staring at the underside of the bunk above him and trying to put all the pieces of information he had so far into some rational order. There were holes, strategies he couldn't see. And always there were the Asiig, waiting, wanting something from him.

The shift to realspace, when it came, was so smooth he almost missed it, a change of pitch in the engine sound that lasted too few seconds to count. *The pilot is good.*

"Normal space," the pilot announced. "Comms coming back online." There was a brief silence, then a new rumble as the pilot shut down the jump engines and diverted power over to the normals. Gravity faltered for a second, then kicked in hard as the ship accelerated. "So hey, I just scared the crap out of a ship lurking in Dek's shadow," the pilot added.

Fergus's handpad chimed. He picked it up and stared at the short, sharp message from Maha and Qai. "Uh. We have a prob—"

"Hold on." The ship pitched sharply and decelerated, banking. Proximity alarms went off as something shot past them, and then the ship was accelerating hard, pressing them all down into the bunk foam. "We've got a second bogey on our tail. Looks like they knew we were coming," the pilot said.

"We have a hefty bounty on us," Fergus said. "Three hundred and fifty thousand, South Haudie-backed. Dead or alive."

"Damn!" the pilot said. "That's a new personal record. We have a third raider on our tail, and I'm catching echoes of more ships out there. Crossroads is too hot. I'm circling back around to the jump point and getting us out of here. Anyone who doesn't have a suit on, get into one now. If I talk to you again, it's because I saved your lives. If not, well, no refunds." The line went silent.

Fergus began unbuckling the tethers holding him to his bunk. "What are you *doing*?" Mari hissed. "You've already got your suit on."

"Much as I enjoy your company, I'm going to Cernee," Fergus said.

"How are you going to do that? Jump out and fly?"

He got the last buckle off, sat up, and threw his tether clip up onto the safety bar that ran the length of the bunk area. "Escape pod," he said.

Bale began undoing his own straps. "I'm going too."

"It's safer if I go by myself," Fergus protested. He reached the droptube down to the pods on the ship's underside as Bale managed to get free of his bunk.

"Sure," Bale said. "You've been doing very well for yourself every time I've had to rescue you. Now hang on and wait for me."

"Oh, there is *no way* you two are leaving me," Mari said.

There was a crash, and the ship rocked sharply to one side. His hand still on the droptube bar, Fergus went briefly horizontal midair as the internal gravity burped. He hit the floor with both feet and hopped down the droptube to the cargo bay. Bale was right behind him, Mari practically crashing into them both at the bottom of the tube.

"Last chance," Fergus said.

Bale hit the bay comm up to the bridge. "We're bailing," he said. "Get home safe, and say hello to the missus for me."

"Will do. Count to twenty, then go. You'll have brief cover in Dek's shadow," the pilot answered. The *Oleaja* banked sharply again. "And tell that boss of yours he owes me another one. Out."

Fergus cycled open the circular hatch, counting to himself. *Six, seven.* Grabbing the upper edge of the pod frame, he lifted himself up and slid inside feetfirst. "We need to run dark," he said. "I'll be on channel five-one-five."

"And where the hell are we going, exactly?" Bale asked.

"You can't guess?"

"No, Mr. I-Should-Have-Left-You-On-Coralla."

"Attic," Fergus answered. "Or as close as the pod can get me to it, anyway."

Not waiting to hear what the others did—hoping, really, that they'd change their minds—he closed the hatch. As soon as the launch systems greenlit, he counted *nineteen, twenty* and punched the button. Instantly, 95 percent of the contents of his body tried to stuff itself into his head as the pod shot him feetfirst out into space.

He pulled up the viewer just in time to see the tiny

flash of light that was the *Oleaja* as it hit the jump conduit and vanished. He couldn't see the other pods, which was the point of running dark, but it left him feeling cold and alone. Almost alone. There were at least three black triangles out there waiting, and he knew that once he played out the rest of the hand he'd been dealt, it would come down to him and them and his ship. He shivered, dreading that future, and unbearably impatient for it.

When he reached the first hab on the edge of the Cernee Halo, Fergus ejected himself out of the pod into space. The suit jets were more than enough to keep him moving at decent speed toward the tiny, dark can.

"Fergus," Mari's voice came over the comm. "Where are you?"

"About thirty meters from the surface of Flatcan," he said. "Be there in another half minute or so. Where are you?"

"Behind you, ejecting now."

"And Bale?"

"I undershot and hit Bogstone," Bale answered. His signal was weak, crackling with interference. "Losing signal, but working my way back to you. Assuming this place doesn't explode on me, which would be my luck since meeting you."

"What? Explode?"

"Waste processing facility. Doesn't like not being minded," Mari said.

"Ah." Fergus made a short blast with his jets, then grabbed onto the hab. A sliver of light passing between the sunshields lit it up like a small moon.

Caught in that same narrow slit of intense light, he could see the Stacks. Or rather, what was left of them. Fergus tore his gaze away from the ruined habs and could now see someone on approach fifteen degrees or so below. He waved; after a moment, the figure waved back. Mari. She was heading for the hab's terminus.

"Someone killed the Stacks," he said when he caught up with her.

Mari turned to look and was quiet for a while. "A lot of Authority personnel bunked there. And their families, of course. I wonder if they got out," she said at last.

Fergus zoomed his goggles out as far as they would go and scanned the inner Halo. "There's a lot of debris. Must've been one hell of an explosion. I don't see any bodies, at least outside of it."

"Can you see the Wheels?"

It took him a few minutes to orient himself, but he found it. "Still lit," he said. "Hard to see much more from this far away, but it looks whole."

Mari let out her breath. "Okay," she said, the word heavy with both worry and relief. "So, what are we doing, exactly? Why Attic? Why not go straight for your ship?"

"Remember what you said about how they're waiting for me to come back for it? I think you were right. But if they just wanted me to take the ship and go, they wouldn't have dumped me back out into space again to start with. So they want something from me. And they're watching me."

"You think so?"

He didn't say, *They came to Coralla.* There wasn't room in his own head yet to process that info. "Notice how the Asiig ships happen to be pointing right in our direction?"

"My zoom's not that good. You're the one with the military suit, not me."

"Well, take my word for it. They were also pointing right at us when we were in the sunshield nearest the Wheels, which is way the hell over *there*," Fergus said, waving.

"Oh."

"Whatever started at that cable car, I think they want me to finish it. I got some good advice recently—"

"About the Asiig?"

"About Venusian Monkeypoker. Think about what everyone here has shown us about their hands. We know what Gilger wants, and every move he's made has been consistent with that: power, control of Cernee, the destruction of his rivals. We know what the Governor wants: stability, security, to retain control. And we know what Harcourt wants and why he's folded. So which player's moves don't make sense?" Fergus asked.

"Vinsic," Mari said. "But he's dying, you said. People don't do rational things when their stars are going dim."

"Vinsic may not be a moral man, but he's always been methodical, organized, and careful. By all accounts he detests Gilger. But then he secretly allies with him and starts a war, all while keeping an inner team operating on separate orders. Why?"

"Whatever the reason, people have died, a lot of them civilians and children," Mari said, gesturing toward the devastated Stacks. "If he's just playing a game, that's *cold*."

"Yeah, but he's a cold guy," Fergus said. "He killed a lot of innocent people consolidating his own power in the early days before the Governor got things stable. So I'm going to go ask him what he's up to, and I'll even ask nicely the first time. Maybe he'll be more willing to cooperate because everything's gone to shit already anyway, or maybe he'll do it just to spite Gilger for ruining it all. I'm just hoping to get enough info to figure out how to end this before more people die."

"And if he won't help?"

"I don't know. But I don't know anywhere better to start. I'm open to ideas, if you've got any."

"Nope," she said. "Let's do it."

Fergus peered out, saw movement in the dark. "Bale, is that you out there?"

There was an answering burst of crackle. "If that's you, wave," Fergus said, and the figure gave him the middle finger. "Good enough. Time to go get some answers."

Chapter 24

To their good fortune, Flatcan's lone terminus connecting it to Beancan and the rest of the Halo had a small but fully charged stash of flysticks and a modicum of emergency power, so they took a break to recharge their air. Fergus went to the tiny window beside the lock and stared out at Cernee while they waited.

"What do you see?" Mari asked him.

"Not much movement," Fergus said. "But I saw something pass between the sunshields. I think the fourth Asiig ship is back and circling."

"Great," Mari said.

Bale hung by the terminus console, trying to get some sort of signal from the rest of Cernee. "No luck," he announced at last. "Not even a new episode of *One Star, Bright and Distant*. That's serious."

"If we weren't at war, there'd be rioting," Mari said as she pulled her aircan and backup from the recharger.

They picked out 'sticks, hit the edge of the platform, and threw themselves into space, heading deeper into Vinsic's territory.

Beancan was a large, three-line hab, connected through a few detours straight to Central. "Go down and dark," Bale said, and pointed; two small groups of men were huddled along the platform in the dark, wearing gold-striped suits. Fergus and Mari shut down their 'sticks moments after Bale, and they glided under and past the stationary hab. Once they were well clear, they powered up again.

"Time to turn in-Halo," Bale said. "Keep an eye out for trouble, all of you."

Fergus could see something ahead in the dark, floating. "Uh . . ." he said. "What's that?"

As he got closer, he saw that it was an arm, still suit-clad, neatly severed and floating in a small cloud of red ice pellets. More body parts lay past it, enough to be more than one victim. *Enough to be more than a few,* he thought. "Bale," he said, coming to a complete stop, feeling sick to his stomach. "Bodies."

Bale and Mari came up beside him. "Shit," Bale said. "Filament. Stuff's practically invisible and will slice you to shreds before you even know you're in it."

"These weren't fighters," Mari said. "I see a GoRound city mark. These were families, probably just trying to escape."

"Is there a way through it?" Fergus asked.

"Pure, stupid luck, and a lot of it," Bale said. "For all we know, we're already in the middle of it."

"Right," Fergus said. "Is filament tethered somehow or a free-floating tangle? How big?"

"Could be, could be, and there's no way to know."

"How expensive is it?" Fergus asked Bale.

"Very. Why?"

"Do you have a pistol?"

"Yes, I—"

"Hand it over."

"I don't—"

"Hand it *over*," Fergus growled.

Bale slapped the pistol into his hand. "As long as you give it back," he said.

"Sure," Fergus said. He pulled out the energy clip, pressed the pistol against the stock of his flystick, and switched on the pistol's magnetic grip. He wrapped his hand around the energy clip and put enough zap into it to send it into a cascading overload. His suit rebooted, and he had to slap the clip back in blind.

"—the hell are you doing?!" He caught the very end of Bale's anger as his comm came back up. Slipping his feet off his 'stick, he pointed it straight ahead at the filament trap and thumbed the throttle on so hard it jammed upright.

His 'stick rocketed forward, thrusting him backwards as it left his open hands. Streaking across space, at first it was unimpeded, but then it swerved suddenly as if it had struck something invisible, continued forward at an angle, and then stuck, hanging motionless at full power.

Seconds later, the overloaded pistol exploded. Tiny wires, visibly glowing with the heat from the explosion, split and spread away. "Go that way," Fergus said, pointing. "And if you would, please take me with you."

Mari fired up her 'stick and grabbed Fergus by his pack as she fell in behind Bale. Via infrared, he could see the fading streamers of cooling filament, undulating streaks around the hole the exploding 'stick had blown. By the time they had passed through, the filament had gone back to the temperature of space, invisible again.

"What if the trap had been thicker?" Mari asked. "We could have gotten halfway through and then been cut apart."

"Bale said it was expensive, so I guessed that they went for height and width over depth."

"And if you'd been wrong? What then?"

"Then we would've been back to stupid luck," Fergus said.

"What's our plan now?" Bale asked. "We're down a 'stick."

"Maybe we can find another at Pitch?" Fergus said. "We have to pass it to get to Attic anyhow."

"Pitch is one step in from DockRock Four, which was in Authority hands when this all started," Bale said. "There could be fighting."

"Unless you want to carry me—"

"I'm just saying!" Bale shouted in exasperation. "Before you ask, no, I didn't have a better way through the filament, but being down a 'stick is a problem, and we're lucky we've had it this easy so far. If the Asiig weren't prowling right outside, we'd be neck deep in all-out war."

"I'd almost prefer that," Mari said. "I don't like this quiet. I feel conspicuous."

"It won't last long. We're not the only ones moving off the lines, if those poor people back there are any indication. As soon as word spreads that you can be out without getting nabbed by the Asiig, fighting is going to pick up again," Fergus said. "So what do we know about Pitch?"

"Solidly Vinsic's," Bale said. "Some mine workers, a number of people who work at the Dock, some who work on shuttle runs between there and Crossroads. Peaceful under normal circumstances, but who knows? I don't suppose either of you is armed?"

Mari snorted. "Not in any conventional way," Fergus said.

"Great. Let's just hope we can find a flystick and move on quickly," Bale said.

Pitch's outer terminus, where the line from DockRock Four came in, was still lit, and the emergency doors weren't sealed. If that was a good sign or a bad one Fergus wasn't entirely sure, but they approached it with caution.

There was nothing they could use outside the envelope, so Fergus volunteered to cycle through first and see what was what. When he pointed out that he should be the one to go because he'd blown up their only weapon, Bale grudgingly agreed to let him.

He cycled himself through and found himself in the inner terminal that was almost, but not quite, empty. Two men in Vinsic's blues had a third in a civilian suit pressed up against the wall, one holding him steady as a second punched him in the gut. A fourth man lay on the floor, not moving. They were intent enough on their victim that they didn't even hear the envelope rotating Fergus into the room.

One of the two Blues pulled out a pistol. "Should I put him down now?" he asked his partner.

Fergus coughed. "Yes, you should put him down," he said loudly. *Good, start something unarmed, ye idiot*, he thought. Over the suit channel he shared with Mari and Bale he added, "Fight."

At least he had managed to startle them both. They

dropped the man, who even in the low gravity of Pitch's mild spin sank to the floor. One of the men, his suit battered and poorly repaired, was wearing a Blue Eight patch. They both rounded on him.

"Who the hell are you?" one asked.

"The only survivor of Blue Eight, as it happens," Fergus said. "You stole suits off the dead, huh? Must be some of Gilger's trash trying to move up in the world."

The one with the Eight patch rushed him, which was what he'd been hoping for, because it prevented his partner from getting a shot off.

Behind him he could hear the envelope cycling again.

His attacker drove his shoulder into Fergus's chest, feeling more like an iron battering ram than just human flesh. *Damn those Warrens skunkers*, he thought, gritting his teeth and resenting all his previous injuries. Despite the pain, he wrapped his arms around the attacker in a tight hug, then let the electricity flood through his hands. The man jerked once and went limp.

"Sorry about this, but I need you a bit longer," he said, keeping the man's unconscious body in front of him as he moved toward the other Blue.

The partner was aiming his pistol at them. "What did you do to him?!" he demanded.

"Aw, he's just having a wee nap," Fergus said. "Don't wake him up, now."

"I have reinforcements coming," the Blue said.

"So do I," Fergus replied as the envelope turned and a fire extinguisher sailed through the growing opening. The Blue barely ducked in time, and Fergus took the opportunity to throw the body he was holding at him; both fell in a heap, and Mari dashed forward and snagged the dropped pistol before the guard could recover.

The imposter Blue raised his hands.

Fergus winced as he crouched down beside the man they'd been beating. He was middle-aged, his face heavily lined and pocked like most lifetime miners. The man was conscious. "My nephew?" he asked.

Bale was kneeling next to the other body and shook his head. "I'm sorry," he said.

"He was only fourteen," the man said quietly, then went limp again on the floor. "They just *shot* him. Like it was nothing."

"What the hell?" Mari asked, keeping her sights steady on the two men on the floor. "Why shoot their own people?"

"They're Gilger's men, not Vinsic's," Fergus said. "Looks like Gilger and Vinsic aren't friends anymore."

The beaten man nodded. "Came in dressed in blues and killed Yefa, who was stationed here. Around a dozen, and they're sweeping through the hab knocking doors down looking for Vinsic loyalists. I was just trying to get my nephew out; my brother is Blue Two, so I didn't think he'd be *safe*." The last word was deeply bitter.

Mari looked at Bale. "But still . . . why shoot a kid?"

"It's *war*," the still-conscious attacker on the floor protested. "That's what happens in war."

"Yeah? These people thought you were on their side," Mari said. She stomped up to him, her magboots slapping on the platform floor, and shot him, then his partner. "So war it is."

She stared at the two bodies, her face shifting from fury to confusion to horror, and then she started shaking. Bale gently took the pistol out of her hand.

"Don't you dare tell me something dumb like I'll get used to it," she snarled.

"Nope," Bale said. "Think about it later when you can afford to, when we're not in danger. For right now, just put it all somewhere else in your head and don't even let yourself peek at it. When you want to talk, I'll be there."

Mari bit her lower lip, her hands curling into fists, her face deathly pale. "All these years dreaming about killing Gilger, face-to-face, just like that . . . At least I know Gilger's fucking *name*. I don't even know who these two are. Were."

"Murderers," the uncle said, "and they weren't done yet."

Mari nodded, never taking her eyes off the bodies.

"Where were you going to go?" Fergus asked the uncle.

"Beancan," he said.

"You can't go that way. There's filament," Mari said.

"No reason to go now anyway," the uncle said. "Where are you people heading to?"

"Attic," Fergus answered.

"You're not one of us," the uncle said. Eyeing Bale's suit, he said, "Wheels and Mezz Rock? Mr. Harcourt's crew?"

"Sort of," Fergus said.

"We're trying to help end this thing," Bale said, "or at least make trouble for Gilger, if nothing else. We just stopped to find an extra 'stick because we lost one."

The uncle managed to get to his feet, wincing. "No 'sticks left here. But I'll tell you what: I figure whatever Mr. Vinsic is doing, he's either forgotten about the rest of us or he can't help us anymore. I'll give you my Attic doorpass if you let me have both pistols you just took off those two."

"What are you going to do with them?"

"Free Pitch," the man answered.

"I want one of their comms," Fergus said.

"And I get the other," the uncle said. "Deal?"

"Deal," Fergus said. He glanced at Bale, who looked down at the pistol in his hand, sighed, and handed it over butt-first.

The uncle unfastened a pocket, took out an ID chip, and handed it to Fergus. "No guarantee they haven't changed the security systems over there, of course."

"Understood," Fergus said. He bent down and took the wrist comm off one of the dead men, then stripped off the corpse's glove to fingerprint activate it. The uncle watched him, then did the same with the other man.

"These guys were bragging about taking over the

Rollers, so I wouldn't make any stops there. I don't know about Dout," the uncle said. "Be careful."

He held out his hand, and Fergus shook it. "I'm sorry again, and good luck," Fergus told him, then headed back to the envelope with Mari and Bale. As they cycled out, he saw the uncle sit down next to his nephew's body, lean his forehead on the kid's chest, and start to weep.

On the platform, Bale slung Fergus over his shoulder, and they launched. Mari stayed at their side but wasn't speaking, and Fergus decided it was best to let her be for now. "I'm going to patch the Goldies' comm into our shared suit channel on receive only," he said. "Maybe we can find out what we're heading into."

"Trouble," Bale said. "We're heading into trouble. And we still don't have any weapons. *And* I'm still carrying your sorry ass."

"Yeah, well, don't drop me for saying so, but I think I already see that trouble you mentioned," Fergus said.

They were running roughly parallel to the line from Pitch to Dout, but to their left off another line were the three cylindrical habs tethered together called the Rollers. People in suits crawled all over the surface of them, exchanging pistol fire. Bodies—some moving faintly, most not moving at all—drifted in space around the habs.

"Those must be Vinsic loyals," Bale said, and pointed. While the floating casualties were a mix of both blue-striped and civilian suits, there were a few Blues fighting on the side of the civilians, who had tied blue strips of cloth around their upper arms to distinguish themselves from the attackers. "I hope they're winning."

"Too late for Roller Three either way," Mari said quietly. Fergus could now see the gaping hole rotating into view, spewing a slow-motion cloud of burnt and broken debris. Not all the bodies trailing in its orbit were wearing suits.

The comm he'd stolen, which had been mostly echoing jammer static, burst into coherence. "—traveling off

the lines!" a voice called in a distinct Luceatan accent.
"Eal, get your partner and intercept them before they
can contact anybody!"

"But the Asiig—" someone protested.

"You see any Asiig? Me neither. Now go! Or I will
add the marks for cowardice and disobedience to your
corpses myself."

"Uh-oh," Bale said as a shrapnel cannon rose up from
behind the remains of Roller Three and turned in their
direction. "Here comes Eal. It's going to take them a few
minutes to get up to speed, but when they do, they'll be
faster than us. There's nothing between us and Dout to
use as shelter, and we don't know if Dout is in hostile
hands or not."

"Hell, we don't even know if *both* sides are hostile,"
Mari said.

"Maybe you should go ahead—" Fergus started to
say. She flipped him a finger over her shoulder. He took
a deep breath and persisted. "Your 'stick is a faster
model anyhow, and there's only one of you riding it. At
the very least, if the fake Blues haven't gotten as far as
Dout yet, you could warn them."

"It's a civilian hab," Bale said. "If they don't know
about the imposters, they could be caught completely
unprepared."

"And leave you two behind?" Mari asked.

"I think I have a plan," Fergus said. "You go ahead in
case it doesn't work. You know how my plans go."

"Do I get a say in this?" Bale asked.

"You wanna ask Eal his opinion too when he gets
here?" Fergus answered.

Bale grumbled loudly over the suit link.

"Fine, I'll go warn them," Mari said. "But don't fucking die on me, or take off without me, or anything that
might make me at all pissed at you. Agreed?"

"I'll do my best?" Fergus said.

Mari opened up the acceleration on her 'stick, making a beeline for Dout.

As soon as she was out of range of their suits, Bale spoke up. "You don't have a plan, do you?" he said.

"That was it. Get Mari out of range of the cannon, maybe save some lives. Sorry."

"Don't apologize. It was the right thing to do," Bale said. "But I still don't want to die out here with you clinging to my back. Now hang on tight, because I'm about to make us harder to get a lock on."

Bale jerked the 'stick's throttle to one side and took a sharp dive, then straightened briefly before shooting back upward, sharply braking, then speeding up again. Eal tried to keep the shrapnel cannon aimed at their awkward, irregular sine wave, but despite its better speed, its maneuverability was crap, and it swung around wildly enough to blow most of its momentum.

Ahead, Fergus saw Mari reach the platform and immediately accost a blue-stripe waiting outside. Fergus had to assume it was a genuine Blue, since Mari didn't seem to be tearing his limbs off. He glanced back at the cannon, which was now falling behind, and saw one of the two riders—Eal or Not Eal—raise something large and cylindrical up over the cannon body. "I don't know what that is," Fergus said. "Bale?"

Bale zagged in a new direction before glancing over. "Fuck! EMP wave gun!" he shouted.

"Can we dodge?"

"At this range it's got a fifteen-meter diameter cone. Only if we're lucky and they're really shit shots," Bale said, throwing the 'stick forward, braking again, then rocketing straight up. "Gonna try anyway. If we—"

The suit comm cut as a bizarre tingling sensation, almost like a cold wind, started to wrap itself around Fergus. The electricity deep in his gut responded instantly, and it was as if he were pushing a static blast out from his entire body in a wave. The two competing fields intersected, intertwined, and collapsed into nothing.

Fergus's suit rebooted.

"Bale!" he shouted as Bale stiffened upright. "You okay?"

"Yeah, I think," Bale said. "My suit rebooted. I've got a lot of yellow lights, but nothing too critical. 'Stick display is shot, but engines are still responding. I think they must've just grazed us, or we'd be well on our way to corpsicles right now."

"Let's get out of here before they fire again," Fergus said, not at all sure he should tell Bale what had just happened.

"Those things take six and a half minutes to recharge, and they stopped chasing us to fire it," Bale added. "I think we're gonna make it."

As they neared Dout, a small team of blue-striped men on 'sticks launched outward in a fast-moving, incoherent swarm. They went right past Bale and Fergus and fired on the cannon from multiple directions the moment they were in range of it. Whatever or whomever they hit, the cannon didn't fire back before it was overtaken.

"That helps," Bale said.

"Looks like Dout has 'sticks too," Fergus said. "And maybe we can get some water while we're here."

"You better not zap anything while you're touching me," Bale warned. "And here comes Mari."

A familiar slight figure in a civilian suit was heading in their direction from the Pitch line platform even as the raiding party began hauling the shrapnel cannon back toward the hab. Two bodies were left floating behind them.

"Keep going," Mari said as soon as she was close enough for their suit comm signal to overcome the background jamming static. "They appreciate the warning, but they say they'll shoot anyone who approaches—friend or foe—on sight. They don't seem to care where we go as long as we leave, and quickly."

"Some gratitude there," Bale muttered.

"Their gratitude is that they didn't take us out with the cannon crew. I don't know about you, but I'm willing to call that even."

"Me too," Fergus said. "Can we get out of here before they change their minds? I feel like I have a great big target on my back."

"I *do* have a great big target on my back," Bale said. "It's called you."

"You two!" Mari snarled. "Cut the fucking chatter, and let's get this over with."

She took off ahead of them, and Bale and Fergus followed. Fergus opened a private channel just to Bale. "Do you think she's going to be okay?" he asked.

"I think she's not going to be okay until all of this is done and behind her, and only then will we maybe know," Bale said. "It's gonna take time, and sometimes you never put stuff behind you, you know?"

Fergus knew that only too well. "Yeah," he said.

"Anyway, that's what friends are for: distracting you from your bad headspace. You must have people for that?"

"I would if I'd ever talk to anyone about it," Fergus said.

"You should get the fuck over that," Bale said. "My professional advice. Now look alive—Attic dead ahead, and we've got company."

Over Bale's shoulder, Fergus could see the large rock that was Attic, Vinsic's home base. Much of it was obscured by a cloud of personal flyers in Vinsic's blue stripes, and the intervening space between it and a smaller rock tethered close by was filled with mining equipment and repair robots working methodically in total oblivion to the war raging around them.

As Bale and Fergus approached, a robot reached one arm out to snag a body that had drifted into its path and added it to the trash gyre that had collected past the small rock. Despite his iron control over all mining in Cernee, Vinsic had stayed hands-on in the working details of his business. It explained why some people were so loyal to him, and made his apparent sudden collaboration with Gilger even less believable.

At least we're about to get a chance to ask, Fergus thought. *Maybe.*

There were a lot of people in blue-striped suits gathered around the main platform, all watching them head in. The few that had their weapons drawn kept them lowered by their sides; that was as close to a gesture of welcome as they were likely to get.

"They could've already shot us by now if they were going to," Bale said, echoing Fergus's thoughts. "That's something."

"Something? Yeah. A trap," Mari said. "Dead guy in the watch station."

The watch station was a floating sphere tethered not far from Attic that functioned both as a guard post and a remote doorman. Dark blotches marred the curved expanse of xglass that ran the circumference of the top half but didn't hide the floating body slowly spinning in circles inside as they passed it.

"If we turn away now, they'll shoot us down for sure," Bale said. "Only way through is forward."

The suits gathered along the platform parted as they landed and set their magboots. One man stepped forward. The public comms were still filled with a low static, but they could hear him. "Come in," he said, and he gestured for them to follow as he stepped into the envelope.

"That's Parat, one of Vinsic's," Bale said over their private channel. "Small-time muscle, even smaller brains."

There were more suited people inside, including a woman in blue stripes with her face shield up who grinned at them as they entered. It was not a friendly expression.

"That's Doani, definitely Gilger's," Mari said.

"She's not a Luceatan," Fergus noted.

"She's part of his original crew. They were locals, mostly Tamassi's former people who figured they'd hang on and see if their fortunes improved," Bale said. "Dunno if they did, but once the Luceatans moved in, it didn't matter. No one was going to dare to leave knowing they'd always have to be looking over their shoulder for Graf."

"Now they also have to check their pockets for him," Mari said, and Fergus involuntarily snorted inside his suit and nearly tripped. Their escort glared at him.

Attic wasn't all that dissimilar to Mezzanine Rock, if not as large. The walls were a mixture of fabbed panels and original cutaway rock, the corridors wide, well lit, and clean. They passed a few other people, all blue-striped, all standing to one side as they went by, none of them speaking.

"I don't like this," Bale said, and neither of them made the effort to disagree.

Parat led them straight into the heart of Attic and into a medium-sized room that was well decorated without losing the utilitarian feel of the rest of the rock. There was carpeting—the worse for the wear, lately— several large armchairs on each side, and a table with a mostly empty bottle and dirty glasses. There were also five more blue-stripes, standing just inside the door. A large desk with a high-backed chair stood near the far end, and in it, leaning his chin on one hand as he watched them enter, was a bone-thin man in blue.

He was faintly shaking, the tremors almost unnoticeable, and Fergus wondered how much an effort of will that took.

"Visitors," Vinsic said, and the word was almost a curse. "Your timing is terrible, but I'm curious what sort of imbeciles would come *here* in a war." He waved them toward chairs on one side of the room.

Fergus, Mari, and Bale exchanged glances. Mari flipped up her face shield, threw back her hood, and slouched into a chair. "Might as well," she said. "I'm tired."

"Ah, a Vahn," Vinsic said. "I've never met any of you other than your 'Mother.' I didn't think any of you poked your noses out of your little hiding place behind Daddy Harcourt."

Mari's eyes narrowed.

Fergus pushed back his own face shield and hood. The air was cold and smelled faintly of old oil and dust. "I wouldn't underestimate the Vahns," he said.

"You," Vinsic said, and then he laughed. "Of course! I shouldn't be surprised you're here now. It's only fitting. Sit, be comfortable, and I'll tell you a story. That's why you came here, right?"

Fergus warily took the chair next to Mari's, and then Bale sat a few moments later. Parat stood by himself now, his expression sour.

"I'm getting old," Vinsic said, "but I'd expected longer. Except—"

"Except you're dying," Fergus interrupted.

Vinsic's expression sharpened. "Yes," he said. "Imminently, as it happens."

"We were hoping you could tell us—" Fergus started to say.

"Shut the hell up," Vinsic said. "This is my house, and I do the speaking until I'm dead or I say otherwise. I'm not normally a talkative guy, but Parat here is tediously stupid."

Parat glared, and Fergus noticed he was rolling something small and cylindrical around in his hand.

"The war is going very badly for the Governor, especially without Harcourt on his side," Vinsic said. "Even with Gilger going off the lines and doing his own stupid shit, he's almost won this. See for yourself."

Vinsic tapped the desk, and a live holo-display of Cernee lit up; it was much like the one the Vahns had, except this one was riddled with red and the deep maroon of dead habs. What little pockets remained free outside the embattled Central itself were surrounded by an ocean of red. "You see?"

Bale slumped in his chair. "That's bad," he said.

"Very bad," Vinsic said. "Say it."

"Very bad," Bale said.

"Effectively, you've already lost. It's important that you see the inevitability of that, staring you right in the face, right here, right now." Vinsic turned the display off. "As you know, Gilger and I have an alliance."

"I've seen," Fergus said. "I spent a little time inside the circle, even."

"Oh? That will simplify things," Vinsic said. "You see, Gilger doesn't want my organization sprouting a new head once the current one—me—has died. He knows that's one of the biggest threats still facing him in Cernee. So over the last half standard he's been bribing away as many of my people as he could, and he sent them back here to betray their friends and make sure my legacy dies with me. Parat here is my designated executioner. Isn't that right, Parat?"

Parat was staring, taken aback. "Uh . . ."

Vinsic chuckled. "I'll take that as a yes. He didn't think I knew, the idiot. You see, there are a large number of explosives, and Parat is holding the trigger. He's just waiting for word from Gilger to kill me, then get out and set them off, destroying Attic. Only word hasn't come yet from Gilger even though it should have, which is why Parat is fidgeting and sweating now. He doesn't entirely understand the situation and hadn't realized that fact until *just this moment*."

"Fuck you, and see you in hell," Parat said. He activated his device, then threw it to the floor and put his hands over his head as if that could save him.

Nothing happened.

The others in the room had not reacted, other than to quietly pull out their pistols. Parat hadn't noticed. His eyes were on Vinsic. "What the fuck? The explosives didn't work!"

"They worked perfectly fine," Vinsic said. "Only Gilger didn't buy off everyone he thought he bought off, and the explosives were never planted *here* after all."

"What? Where?" Parat asked.

Vinsic leaned forward and grinned. "Gilgerstone," he said. "Also Burnbottle, where most of his ships dock to recrew and refuel. They were going to go on his fancy new ship, but these dishonest gentlemen inconveniently went and stole it from him, so I've had to improvise."

"Why?" Parat asked.

"Because Gilger isn't one of us, and he doesn't *care* about Cernee except as a stepping stone to more power," Vinsic said. "Eventually he'd destroy everything just to show he could. And I wasn't going to leave Cernee, everything I've built and everyone I love, in *his* hands."

Parat turned and bolted for the doors, and one of the Blues in the room shot him down. The Blue turned to Vinsic. "Send word?"

"Yes, thanks, Blue One. Tell the Circle it's time," Vinsic said. "Defend our habs and vital infrastructure. Shoot Golds on sight, no advance warning necessary."

"Was Gilger . . . home?" Fergus asked after the Blue leader left.

Vinsic sighed. "I haven't been able to get good intel on his exact location for days. For a double-crossing Basellan bastard, he was always paranoid about getting the same back, and he's never fully trusted any locals. Even so, I believe I've just fucked up his plans one last time and given your lot a small fighting chance again. Don't underestimate him. Gilger will do anything, kill anyone and everyone, to keep from losing."

Vinsic stood up, swaying and shaking violently, and Fergus was shocked by how much thinner he was than he'd been just a few weeks earlier at the cable car hearing. "Asshole couldn't just let me kick off in my own time in comfort; he made me come back here to finish it. It's too chilly in these old rocks. Damned meds keep me mostly pain-free, but they make me so fucking *cold*. I might as well be a corpse already." He gestured to the remaining Blues. "See them out, and make sure none of

Gilger's trash gets in their way. The tall one took out Graf for us, so we owe them one last running head start."

He walked over, almost falling, and carefully picked up Parat's pistol where it had fallen next to his body. "I hope she's satisfied," he said. "When she asks, tell her I died peacefully on my own terms. Good luck with the rest of the war. You'll need it."

Vinsic put the pistol against his own head and fired.

Chapter 25

There were many more bodies on the way back out of Attic, but no one got in their way. They made it to the platform, stepped over the sprawled bodies of Doani and several others, and cycled themselves out as quickly as they could.

Bale unhooked his 'stick from where he'd tucked it into the charger outside, looked at Fergus, and heaved a full-body dramatic sigh. "I know, I know, still down a 'stick," Fergus said. "You wanna go back in and ask?"

"Hell, no," Bale said as Fergus grabbed hold and he launched. "I wish I'd asked to use the P2P when we first got there, though. Mr. Harcourt still doesn't know Arelyn is safe, and I don't think we can get back to anywhere friendly, much less the Wheels, from here. My air is also starting to get low. You have any ideas?"

"Medusa," Mari said as Fergus was opening his mouth to say the same.

"What? Are you hurt?" Bale asked, speeding up to pull alongside her.

"No," she said.

"Mari's right," Fergus added. "Ili's the only one left. And it's reachable."

"You saw the map, Bale," Mari said. "You see anywhere else left untouched by this war so far?"

"That's because Ms. Ili has carefully stayed out of this fight, just as she always does. And she runs the only major medical center and Cernee's oxygen farm. Like the sunshields, she's too dangerous to target. Even Gilger isn't that dumb."

"Vinsic said, 'When she asks.' You know anyone else 'she' could be?" Mari said.

"Cernee is more than 40 percent women," Bale said. "That seems like a lot of possibilities."

"Yeah? And who gave him the meds? And would've let him stay and die somewhere warm? Vinsic said he didn't want to hand everyone he loved over to Gilger—you ever heard of Vinsic being a romantic guy?"

Bale grumbled. "No. Maybe," he said. "We had intel that he was spending a fair bit of time in Medusa, but we just assumed—"

"—that he was sick?" Fergus said. "And he was. But maybe that wasn't his only reason. And anyway, now Ili is the only one who can hurt Gilger. Harcourt's still out, the Governor is losing, and Vinsic's dead. Either she's already involved and no one knows it yet, or she's going to be whether she likes it or not. If she was pulling Vinsic's strings all along . . ."

"Then Vinsic wanted it that way," Bale said. "So, okay, let's say we go to Medusa. Then what? Wait for Gilger to come after us there?"

"Can you think of a better place for a last stand?" Mari asked.

"Ms. Ili isn't going to want us there. If word gets out, you know Gilger won't be able to resist coming after a Vahn *and* his Martian assassin."

"Yeah, well, I wasn't planning on ringing the doorbell and asking nicely if we can come in," Fergus said. "Even if she's not involved, Medusa has to be overrun with casualties right now. Which, incidentally, is our way in. One of us gets to be a casualty. I vote me."

"Not that I'm disagreeing, but why you?" Bale asked.

"I can pass as injured better than either of you, mostly because I still am," Fergus said.

"You'll need to look injured more than that," Bale said. "They'll just slap a narcpatch on you and tell you to stop whining and go home. No offense, but this *is* a war zone."

"You could break both his legs," Mari suggested.

"Or I could have something so uniquely wrong that

I'm not just in desperate need of help, I'm *interesting*," Fergus said. "Like, say I've somehow become electrified."

"You want to reveal that right out front?" Mari asked.

"If I have to. You got a better idea?"

"No," she said.

Bale shook his head. "Right. At least it explains why you don't have your own 'stick, you being a near-corpse and all. But if it turns out Vinsic blew up Gilger and the war is over and I'm carrying you around for nothing, I'm going to make you personally carry me everywhere for a week."

"That seems fair," Fergus said.

Medusa was a large spinning ring station, second in size only to Central. It was almost a straight run from Attic to where it sat at the outer edge of the Halo, and as soon as they were clear of the workings that surrounded Attic, Fergus could see it ahead. Dwarfing it from behind, three large tethered ice rocks were slowly being carved down into water. Hundreds of long, beaded strings of greenish cylinders hung out into space from Medusa's spindle, glowing in the sunlight outside the last of the sun-shields: the oxyfarms. The rest of Medusa was surrounded by a swarm of one- and two-mans, small shuttles, and other vehicles, all waiting for their chances to land at the platform that functioned as a staging and triage area. A number of silver-and-green two-mans were stationed as sentries along the incoming routes.

Bale, Fergus, and Mari bypassed the queue and landed on the main platform. Two suited attendants in red stepped out, both armed, and Fergus tensed up. His fingers were tingling.

"Stop wiggling," Mari said over their private channel. "You're supposed to be mostly dead."

Around them there were other people in line or piled up against one wall. Fergus turned his face away. "What's the problem?" one of the assistants asked over the public channel.

"Some new weapon," Bale said. "He's hurt bad. Maybe dying."

"Bring him in and set him down."

As soon as they'd passed through the rotating envelope, Bale dumped Fergus like a sack of potatoes on a rolling flat. One of the attendants stepped forward and ran a quick scan over him. "This man doesn't seem that hurt," he said. "You're wasting our time and that of everyone else waiting their turn ahead of you."

As he spoke, he reached down to touch Fergus's suit where one of the MCA patches had been removed. "Don't touch him!" Mari shouted.

As soon as the hand lightly brushed his suit, Fergus zapped him just a tiny bit. The attendant pulled his hand back in surprise.

"Some new weapon of Gilger's," Bale said. "He's all electrified."

"Trick suit," the other attendant said as the first stood there, shaken.

He pushed Mari aside and used the butt of his energy pistol to lift Fergus's face shield. "See?" he said, and reached out with a finger to touch Fergus's bare nose. When his fingertip was a centimeter or so away, Fergus zapped him too, more strongly than the last guy.

The man jumped back with a startled oath, wrapping his free hand around the hurt one. *I'm getting better at this,* Fergus thought.

"You're one of Mother Vahn's, aren't you?" the first attendant asked Mari.

"Yes," Mari said. "I got separated from the farm when the line to the Wheels was cut."

"And you?" he asked Bale. "Mezz Rock? You work for a color?"

"I was with her," Bale said, evading the last question. "We were making our way past Snaps looking for somewhere safe to lie low when we saw this guy and several other civilians get shot by a squad of Goldies."

"It was horrible," Mari added. "He was the only survivor."

"And you went all way out of your way to bring him here?"

"We didn't have anywhere else to go," Bale said. "We couldn't get home because there's some kind of molecular razor wire past Beancan."

"Someone's strung out filament?!" the attendant exclaimed.

"There were body parts," Mari said.

"Right," the attendant said. "We'll see what can be done about *that*. I'll take him in for tests. You two can leave."

"Can we wait?"

"Why? Do you know this man?"

"His name's Angus, and he's very fond of lichen," Mari said, and her lip curled up as if she were trying not to cry. "I just need to know he's going to be okay."

"Fine. You can wait out in a waiting room," the attendant said. "If you can fit."

"But—" the other attendant started to complain, still holding his zapped hand.

"The Vahns aren't trouble-makers, Lenof, and if Gilger has something new, we need to know about it. Show them to lounge five, then call security and tell them there's a report of filament. They can get word out to Doublecan and Shadefill via P2P, and they can spread the warning from there. I'll roll this guy in for a better look."

The attendant started the flat rolling, then walked beside it, looking down at Fergus. "How do you feel?" he asked.

"Hurt," Fergus said. "Like I'm filled with bees. Thirsty. So thirsty." None of that was a lie.

"Well, we're going to take care of you as best we can," the attendant said. "You just close your eyes and rest."

Fergus was tired enough not to argue. The smooth rolling of the flat was lulling him toward sleep, and his thoughts drifted off into circular and increasingly irrelevant arguments.

". . . bringing something in," the attendant was saying, and Fergus pulled himself out of the murk enough to realize he wasn't talking to him, but on a comm. "Maybe a new weapon. Taking him to bay nineteen. Yeah, see you there."

Ah, Fergus thought, lying peacefully still but no longer feeling sleepy. *This plan might actually work. Right up until they get a real scanner on me and find all the alien squidware in my gut, anyway.*

They reached the end of a line of injured queued to move through security. His attendant parked him, then hailed the woman in front of him. "What's the word?" he asked.

"A lot of dead and dying in Gilgerstone and Burnbottle, but none of them are the outworlders, just locals. No one's found Gilger himself yet," she answered.

"That can't be good."

"No," she said. "I expect he's holed up somewhere no one can reach him and furious enough to kill every man, woman, and child left in Cernee with his own bare hands, if he could."

"Oh, that's comforting!" Fergus's attendant said.

"You ever met the man?"

"No."

"Yeah, I did once. 'Comforting' is not a word I'd use to describe him, and he was in a good mood when I met him. We better hope he's a burnt corpse drifting in the rubble after all. My turn."

She rolled her patient ahead, and Fergus's attendant nudged his flat into the space she'd vacated. Around him he could hear moans, crying, and the ragged, uneven breathing of the injured and dying, and he felt like a shit for taking the place of someone who genuinely needed to be here. He liked to hope the deception was for a greater cause, but so far everything had been a lot of effort and danger for very little in the way of answers, and none of them helpful.

Their turn came. His attendant keyed them through a thick blast door and handed him off to a pair of green-and-gray-uniformed medics. "Patient cleared for triage, section one, bay nineteen," he said, and the lead medic looked surprised but nodded. "In and out of lucidity. Don't touch him."

"Contagious?"

The attendant shrugged. "Ask Lenof in a few days."

The medics parked Fergus's flat in one of the several small rooms. One shined a light in his eyes. "I'm Medic Zofia," she said. "Do you know what happened to you?"

The other two attendants were each holding one of the flat's side rails, which looked potentially conductive. He moaned and flailed a hand onto one rail. As soon as his fingers connected, he sent enough juice into it to knock both attendants to the floor. He met Medic Zofia's surprised gaze.

"Sorry," he said, and reached up and zapped her. He only barely managed to catch her as she fell. It was getting easier and easier to use the Asiig's "gift," and he was grateful that he was too damned busy and in the middle of things to think too deeply about that.

He collected the medics' access cards. Swiping one to unlock the comm console, he pressed the button for the routing desk. "Uh, this is Assistant Medic Peyn," he said. *That figures.* "Can someone send Attendant Lenof back to collect the two who came in with the patient in bay nineteen? They're in lounge five. We have pressing questions."

"Will do, Peyn," came a response. Fergus let go of the comm button and looked around the room. It had the console, a bank of cabinets full of supplies on one wall, and a tall closet. He opened the closet and smiled.

He'd already changed out of his suit and into a clean medic tunic and pants by the time the door chimed. Lenof entered with Mari and Bale behind him and was several steps into the room before he realized he wasn't looking at a medic he knew.

"Uh," Lenof said, taking a half step backward and bumping up against Bale behind him. "I—"

Fergus put his palm on Lenof's chest, zapping him. Bale left him slumped against the wall beside the medics.

Rummaging through the cabinets again, Fergus found clean bottled water and drank one down without pausing for breath. "Damn, that makes me thirsty," he said.

He also found a small roll of sleep patches. Peeling four off with care, he stuck them onto the medics and Lenof, then put the remainder in the pocket of his borrowed tunic.

"What's the plan now?" Mari asked.

"Keycards," he said, holding them up. "Spare uniforms in the cabinet. I'm afraid we're going to have to ditch our suits, but we can hide them here."

Mari snatched one of the cards out of his hand as Bale pulled uniforms out of the cabinet, and they changed as quickly as they could. "Nothing better happen to my suit," she told Fergus, folding it carefully and tucking it away in the cabinet, "or I'm going to punt your creepy pale head so hard they'll be patching the hull where it exited."

"Now what?" Bale asked.

Fergus swiped his access card from the triage room into the inner halls, and almost immediately an alarm sounded.

"*Excellent* plan," Mari said.

"That's a full-station defense alert," Bale said. "Medusa must be under attack. Looks like Gilger *is* dumber than I thought after all. We need to go now." He pushed the inner door open, and Fergus and Mari tumbled through after him.

The hall wasn't crowded, but there were people hurrying up and down its curved length, some with patients, some with empty flats stained a deep, terrible red. "What we want is Section Five," Bale said, keeping his voice low. "Came here once with Mr. Harcourt to see Ms. Ili, so I have some memories of the place. Several security layers to get through."

"Let's hope everyone is distracted," Fergus said as he swiped his stolen senior medic ID at the next corridor heading deeper into the station. A security squad, heavily armed, nearly ran them down passing the other way.

Behind the squad, another man in a medic tunic was hurrying along. As he got closer, his eyes narrowed. "Who are you people?" he demanded.

"Medic Peyn," Fergus said, holding out a stolen card. When the medic reached for it, Fergus grabbed his hand and zapped him. Mari had already walked forward to the next set of doors. "Retinal scan," she said, snapping her fingers. "We need him."

Together Bale and Fergus held the man upright, prying open one eyelid in front of the scanner as Mari swiped his card. The lock light turned green, and the door slid smoothly open.

"Hey!" someone shouted behind them, and both Fergus and Bale dropped the medic as they whirled around. A guard had rounded the corner and was drawing his weapon. Mari grabbed the back of Fergus's collar and yanked him through the doorway as Bale threw himself after them. A shot rang out, then another as the doors slid shut again.

"Run, idiots," Mari said, and turning around, immediately ran into the chest of another guard.

"What the hell?" the guard said, reaching out to grab Mari's shoulder. "Who the hell are you people?"

"We're from Section Two," Fergus said. "The station is under attack! There are medics down. They need help!"

The guard pushed past them, drawing his weapon as Mari, Fergus, and Bale sidled deeper into the corridor. There was pounding on the door as the guard yanked his mouthpiece down and started talking rapidly into it.

"Go," Fergus said, and they fled. Another guard came

running the other way, and before he could stop and question them, Fergus pointed back the way they'd come and shouted, "Help him! We're under attack!"

The man ran past without stopping.

"It won't take long—" Mari started to warn.

"I know, I know," Fergus said. "Bale, where next?"

"I'm looking," he snarled, moving ahead of them. "We need an elevator into the hub—*there*!"

They crowded around the door, trying every access card they had to no avail. Behind them they heard shouting and weaponsfire. There was too much of it to be just Medusans. "We don't have time for this," Fergus said; he put his hand against the plate and fried it. He and Bale pried the door open, and Mari slipped between them and held it from the other side as they took turns pulling through before it slammed closed.

The inside of the elevator car was dim red, emergency lighting the only thing on. "Now what?" Bale said.

Fergus peered at the control panel, then up and around the car. "I think they shut down the elevator to try to hold us in here."

"It's working."

"Yeah." Fergus stood there thinking as muffled sounds of fighting echoed through the elevator tube.

"You really think that's Gilger?" Mari asked.

"Who else would attack Medusa?" Bale said. "If he decided Ili was behind Vinsic's betrayal, you know he'd be all over this place in an instant. I didn't think we'd be safe here for long, but I didn't think we'd get caught in a fucking elevator on the way in."

"Maybe they'll still let us ask Ili a question or two before we all get executed," Mari said. "I'm sure that would make this entire adventure feel worthwhile."

Fergus got down on his hands and knees, feeling around on the floor. His fingers found the small ridge first, followed it to a corner, then around in a square. "Stand back against the wall?"

"What?" Bale asked, but he moved back.

Fergus punched the emergency release, and a small square panel slid open at the very bottom of the car. Bracing himself on either side, he lowered himself through. "You guys coming?"

"That's a long way to fall," Mari said.

"Gravity neutralizers in the tube," Fergus said. "Keeps the cars from turning into missiles in a spin crisis. You just have to push off and float your way down."

"And what happens when you hit the far end?"

"There'll be a slug field to slow down the car."

"What if that's also powered down?"

"Emergency lighting is on, so the other safeties should be too."

"And if not?"

"Then I'll cushion your fall with my broken body," Fergus said. He let himself through the rest of the way, hanging from his fingers, then gently let go with one hand. Doing a slow somersault, he managed to hunch up and brace his feet against the underside of the car, then sprang into the tube.

He moved faster than he'd expected; the neutralizers must not have been at 100 percent. *Please have a slug field,* he thought as the end of the elevator tunnel zoomed toward him.

Suddenly it was as if he'd dived into invisible gelatin. *Invisible gelatin with no air,* he realized. It seemed to take forever for his outstretched fingers to touch the emergency release for the doors at the bottom of the shaft, which dumped him out into the corridor like he was being ejected from a treacle cannon.

Unprepared for the transition to full gravity, he mashed his face into the floor, then rolled over, gasping for breath. It was some moments before he realized there were two boots in front of him, leading up to legs. From there he focused on the pistol pointed at his head. Coughing, he blinked up at the guard. "Hi," he said.

Bale came tumbling out of the open doors, landing heavily on top of Fergus. "Neither of you move!" the guard shouted.

"You didn't say there wasn't air in there," Bale complained, chest heaving as he lay down next to him.

"I didn't know," Fergus said.

"*Hey!*" The guard shouted. "No talking! Don't move. I've got backup coming."

"Hey, Bale, what did you do with the bomb?" Fergus asked. "You didn't drop it in the tube, did you?"

"I didn't—" Bale started to say.

The guard glanced up at the doors, and Fergus reached out, grabbed the end of the pistol, and yanked hard. The guard tumbled forward just as Mari barreled out of the shaft and crashed into him with both feet.

Fergus hauled himself out of the people pile, found the roll of sleep patches in his pocket, and stuck one squarely in the middle of the dazed guard's forehead.

New alarms began blaring, red lights flashing at intervals, and there was the sound of boots coming from around the tight curve of the hallway. "Move, you two!" Bale shouted.

The three ran, pelting down a long, empty stretch of corridor. Ahead Fergus spotted a wide pair of what appeared to be genuine oak doors. "Uh . . ." he said.

"That's it!" Bale said. "Ms. Ili's personal office."

Together they took hold of the doors and pulled, but they didn't budge. Behind the three of them, the shouting and sounds of boots were getting closer. "Guys . . ." Mari said. "Fergus?"

"It's not an electronic lock," he said. He patted his pockets again, found a handpad stylus, and snapped off the tip. He knelt and wiggled the sharp edge into the lock.

"Fergus!" Mari said again from behind him, more urgently.

"Shush!" he shouted, trying to hear the tumblers and nothing else as he felt his way around with the makeshift pick.

Just as the lock clicked, someone grabbed the back of his stolen tunic and hauled him backward. He fell on his ass, staring up at the face shield of a heavily armed man in an Authority uniform.

A second soldier had his arm around Bale's neck, and a third his pistol pointed right at Mari.

"Um . . ." Fergus said.

The soldier holding Bale flipped up his face mask. "Bale?"

"Gurne?!" Bale asked. "What are you doing in yellow?!"

The man with the grip on Fergus's collar let go and opened his own face shield. Fergus blinked, staring into the face of the Governor himself.

"*You,*" the Governor said, and he made a sound of deep exasperation. "Our very own ghost, haunting us each in turn. I should have known."

Chapter 26

"**G**urne, kick the door in," the Governor said.

"I already picked—" Fergus started to say, but Gurne let go of Bale, raised his boot, and sent the left door crashing open.

"Put your hands up and go in first," the Governor said.

"They're not any less likely to shoot us than you," Mari protested.

"Yes, but still, they won't have shot *us*," the Governor said.

"Really sorry," Gurne said. "In you go."

Fergus stood slowly and put his hands up. Together he, Mari, and Bale were pushed through the door into the room beyond. Behind the wide oak desk in a high-backed chair sat Ms. Ili, her hand on the top of a large console screen. Also in the room were four men in Ili's gray and green and two in Vinsic's blue, all with weapons raised and pointed in their direction.

"*You,*" Ili said, eyebrows arched high in surprise.

"Everyone keeps saying that," Fergus complained. "What have I ever done to you people?"

"You can put your hands down," Ili said. "Whatever trouble you've come to cause, I don't expect it'll make a difference, and it makes me tired to look at you."

"Uh, we can't," Mari said. She jacked a thumb over her shoulder back at the door.

"That would be because of us," the Governor said, stepping into the room, carefully keeping Fergus in front of him.

"Lord Governor," Ili said. "*You* I was expecting."

"Where's Vinsic?" the Governor demanded.

"He's not here," Ili said.

"He's dead," Bale added.

Ili and the Governor both stared at him. "We came here from Attic," Fergus explained. "Vinsic . . . well, he told us as we were leaving to tell you he died peacefully."

"Then you don't know for sure that he's dead?" the Governor asked.

Mari shuddered. "No, he's definitely dead."

"'Died peacefully' is typical Vinsic bullshit," Ili said. "He shot himself, didn't he? After he blew up Gilgerstone?"

Fergus nodded.

"I need to ask you to surrender, Ms. Ili," the Governor said. "At least until we sort out the roots of this conspiracy. If we live long enough to do so."

"Is it your intention to kill me or my people?" Ili asked.

"Not unless you force me," the Governor said. "But I need this war to end, whatever it takes. I came here hoping Vinsic had answers, some information that might give me a way to stop this bloodshed. I never would have expected you to be part of this."

Ili gave a slight nod, as if both acknowledging and dismissing his disappointment, and walked forward to stand in front of Fergus. She was as tall as he was, and she looked him over like she was assessing a plague victim with an eye toward spacing him for the safety of others. "And why are *you* here?" she asked.

"It was the only logical place left to go," Fergus said. "Vinsic didn't do all this just for some last-minute fun; he did it for someone. For Cernee itself. And even more, for *you.*"

"I didn't ask him to," Ili said.

"Nevertheless, here we are," the Governor said.

Ili snapped her fingers. Her men lowered and holstered their pistols, followed by Vinsic's. "Call security. Tell them Medusa is fully cooperating with Authority on my orders. No one else needs to get hurt, and we have better things to do than *make* more wounded," she told her people. Then she looked at Vinsic's men. "I'm not sure what orders Vinsic gave you or what his intentions were after he died, but he's gone now. You have no obligation to either of us except as your own needs and consciences dictate. You can stay and fight with us or find your own way out of here."

The two Blues exchanged glances, and it was clear they'd already discussed this. "We want to go back out and try to protect our people," one said, a woman barely older than Mari but built like she'd grown up in the mines. "Gilger's main jammer went down when Gilgerstone did, and we're hearing that the Golds are in disarray. Now's our best chance to reclaim our habs before they regroup."

"Fair enough, Saffa. Do try not to get killed," Ili said.

"Any word of Gilger himself?" the Governor asked.

"No, and no one's seen any of the Luceatans," the woman—Saffa—said.

Fergus unclipped the comm from his wrist and held it out to the two Blues. "This was a Gold comm," he said. "I don't know if they're even still sending, but it hasn't squawked once since we arrived at Attic. It might help."

Saffa took it. "Thanks," she said. She and her partner both bowed to Ms. Ili. "If we hear any rumor of where Gilger is hiding out, we'll send word immediately."

They left. Once they were gone, the Governor turned back to Ili. "Okay. It's time for an explanation."

"Everyone is aware that this was not a new ambition of Gilger's, yes? He knew he couldn't take control without unseating at least one of the other powers first, and he had been trying to bribe people away from all our houses to find out who was weak."

The Governor gave a short bark of a laugh. "Graf even approached Katra, though he was smart enough not to make his intent explicit, or she'd have gutted him right on the spot and strung his intestines throughout the Halo as a warning. In hindsight I wish she had anyway."

"Vinsic was also informed of the attempts. He had already learned he was dying and knew that Gilger's predations would only become more bold. So at his request, I let one of my people who Gilger had been courting let slip that Vinsic was dying, and she sold Gilger a copy of the report for a healthy sum of cred," Ili said. "I let her keep it. She also told Gilger that Vinsic had been talking about how afraid he was that Harcourt would join forces with the Governor and quash all independent habs. That was, of course, a lie, but one that Gilger found easy to swallow. At Vinsic's request, I provided a neutral space for their first meeting. That was about half a standard ago."

"So you've known all along," the Governor said.

"Only in a limited way," she said. "Vinsic kept most of the details from me, telling me only what he felt I needed to know except when he wished to consult me on what the right action would be. He had an alliance with Gilger and a plan to turn the tables as soon as Gilger had irrevocably shown his hand. Vinsic believed that casualties and damage were inevitable but that this way they could be minimized. He called it 'a controlled burn.'"

"So what happened?" the Governor said.

"Gilger is Gilger," Ili said.

The Governor strode around Fergus and dropped himself into an empty chair, setting his pistol down on the table. "Gilger has never been stable," he said.

"But he's always been predictable, at least in his goals, and usually unimaginative in their pursuit," Ili said. "None of his crew would dare step out of line against his orders for fear of Graf. And Graf was under control except when it came to the Vahns."

"We noticed that," Mari said bitterly.

"Vinsic didn't know about the cable car attack in advance. He suspected Graf set it up and Gilger either didn't know or had decided there was now more value than harm in letting him go forward with it. The Luceatans were getting impatient for the talking to end and the glory-seeking to begin. Afterward, Vinsic tried to get Gilger back on track, but then this Earther came along with his ridiculous LARD machine, stole his spaceship, got Graf turned into meatcubes, and just generally complicated everything. Gilger went completely off the rails, and Vinsic couldn't nudge him back into line for the take-down. Vinsic was not a good man, and he used whatever means he deemed necessary to protect his interests over the years, but in the end he wanted Cernee to survive."

"More than that, he wanted *you* to survive," Fergus said.

Was that a blush? Ili shook her head. "I made him promise me that he would make decisions for all of Cernee, to protect it as he wished I'd allow him protect me. He said . . . no, that's none of your business. As I said, he was not a good man, and he was stubborn and set in his ways and as impervious to reason as they come, but he was a better man in his last days than some men ever manage to be."

"And now what?" Bale asked.

"Now we wait for Gilger to make the next move," the Governor said. "He certainly will. He has to."

"Maybe he'll just . . . run away?" Mari asked.

"He can't, and not just because of the Asiig. Because of *you*, Mr. Ferguson," Ili said. "How much do you know about Luceatos?"

"It's a Basellan sinner colony, semi-independent; they look for redemption for their sins through death in a righteous cause," Fergus said.

"Right. Gilger is Basellan aristo, and class is *everything* to those people. I don't know why he's out here or how he got Graf under this thumb, but Graf brought half of Luceatos with him," Ili said. The Governor was nodding in agreement. "The Luceatans' loyalty to Graf, and thus by extension to Gilger, was unbreakable. But with Graf gone, Gilger's having trouble managing them. They expect glory, and he needs to give it to them to keep them from abandoning or turning on him."

"What does that have to do with me?" Fergus asked.

"Luceatans are deeply superstitious," the Governor said. "The ones who had been aboard *Venetia's Sword* saw both you and Graf taken up by the Asiig and saw you both returned as you were. Since then, word has spread. You terrify the Luceatans, Mr. Ferguson. They want to get away from here so badly it is nearly mutinous. Gilger *needs* you dead, spectacularly and soon, to reassert his own authority. No one's been able to find you for a week and a half, and trust me, even with current movement difficulties, people have been hunting you."

"We went to go free Arelyn Harcourt," Fergus said.

"But we haven't been able to make contact with Mr. Harcourt to tell him she's safe because of the comm jamming," Bale added.

Gurne spoke up. "Mr. Harcourt sent us to back the Governor because he couldn't risk being seen fighting Gilger directly. We launched a repeater out past the Halo on the way in case we had to get back in touch in an emergency. If you have a P2P—"

Ili pointed at one of her men. "You. Show them to the comm center immediately. And make mention that we have a Vahn here, as I imagine someone is worried about her."

Bale left with Ili's man and one of the Governor's.

"So . . . what now?" Fergus asked. "When I last saw a map, things looked very bad."

"That they are," the Governor said. "With Gilgerstone and Burnbottle gone and Gilger himself holed up in hiding somewhere planning his next move—and it'll be soon, I guarantee you—some of the crew he left behind have become desperate. They know that if Authority retakes control, they're going to get spaced as traitors. Some are digging in where they are, using civilians as shields and hoping to hold onto that territory when all is done. Some are grouping together and trying to coordinate attacks following Gilger's old strategy. The Blues have mostly turned on them, but some are sticking with the Golds or have abandoned allegiance altogether. In short, it's a huge fucking mess out there."

"I mean . . . what do *we* do now?" Fergus said.

"We wait," Ili answered. "Gilger will be here soon

enough. It's the last place left, and all the arrows are pointing right to us."

"Central—" Fergus started to say, but the Governor shook his head.

"It was about to fall when we set out here to grab Vinsic, thinking he would give us leverage," he said. "I don't know whose hands it's in right now, but it was being overrun by active fighting behind us. I lost good people buying us time to get here."

"Central was where Gilger was aiming his arrow, though," Fergus said. "You could read it in all the maps."

"Metaphorical arrow, yes," Ili said. "I'm speaking of real arrows. Three of them. Black. Triangular. Pointing here because of *you*."

Chills ran up Fergus's spine, and he felt like all the hairs on the back of his neck were standing straight out. *Right, the Asiig*, he thought. *The solar system's living compasses that always point due me.* "If I leave—"

"Where would you go?" Ili said. "And do what?"

Fergus opened his mouth, wanting an answer to fall out, but none did.

"I thought so," Ili said. "As much as I wouldn't be especially opposed to letting Gilger resolve the problem of *you*, Mr. Ferguson, if I thought it would end this nonsense, it would strengthen his command over the Luceatans immeasurably. He would be unstoppable, at least in the short term. And we don't have a long one."

The Governor sighed, and rubbed at his face. "No, we don't," he said. "Time is running out. As soon as Gilger—"

The lights in the office flickered, then plunged them briefly into darkness. When they came back on, they were dim and unsteady. "What the hell *now*?" Ili said, pulling her console over. "Some sort of power glitch?"

The Governor's wrist comm beeped, and he took his eyes off Ili to read it. "Son of a worm-infested, garbage-trolling—" he started to say.

"—bile-filled sack of shit!" Ili finished, and the room was utterly silent as they stared at each other.

"Power problems reported in Central and every other hab we're still in contact with," the Governor said. "Someone's messing with the lines. And the only place you can mess with all of them at once is—"

"—the sunshields," Fergus said. "Bloody hell. Has anyone heard from the Shielders lately?"

"No," the Governor said. "Not that they were in the habit of talking to anyone, anyway. If Gilger has control of one or more of the sunshields or Suncage, he can kill us all. The sunshields power ninety percent of Cernee. Heat, light, oxygen, food storage, waste processing, defense. A few habs, cut lose, might make it for a while off their own emergency power sources—Medusa is one, Central another, and of course the Wheels—but without power, stabilizers go too, everything starts drifting, and it's not long before things start crashing into each other. People will panic. Everyone is going to head for the few safe places left, and not everyone is going to fit, and there will be a lot more deaths. And we can't evacuate Cernee."

"Why not?"

"Because while your alien friends may not have minded you coming and going, they've picked up everyone else who's crossed the perimeter set by their circling ship. We're locked in. We've lost."

"The power isn't off yet," Ili said. "That means he still wants something from us."

"Or he wants everyone to know he's the one killing us before he pulls the plug," Mari said.

"Or that," the Governor agreed drily.

Ili's console pinged, and she shifted her attention from glaring at Fergus as if he were personally to blame for everything. "Incoming P2P message, bounced through the emergency repeater on Central. I'm afraid you'll have to acknowledge it, Governor, as the repeater encrypts everything with Authority keys."

The Governor joined her behind the desk, tapped in a long sequence, then laid his hand flat on her palm scanner. Then Ili hit another key, and the large screen on the side wall came to life with a familiar, unwelcome face.

"I've set it to incoming only right now," Ili said. "Anyone who doesn't want to be in the picture, stand at the back of the room and shut your mouths. That definitely includes you." She pointed at Fergus.

He stepped back into the corner she'd indicated and folded his hands in front of him. Mari joined him, leaning against the wall, her face a mask of pure exhaustion and despair.

Ili cleared her throat, then tapped once more at her console before leaning back in her chair. The Governor stood behind her. "Arum Gilger," she said. "So nice of you to call."

"I'll cut to the chase," Gilger said. "You know I am well positioned to destroy Cernee at will, yes?"

"Yes," Ili said. "You have made that evident. Since you haven't done it, I assume you want something."

"I want the Governor, plus Vinsic, Harcourt, and his asshole Martian assassin delivered to me. And then I want your unconditional surrender of all your operations to my people. You have three hours."

"Vinsic is no longer among the living."

"You lie," Gilger said.

"His body is in Attic," Ili said. "I'd say you could ask your man Parat to verify that, but I expect you'll find his body—probably with a very surprised expression—not far from Vinsic's own. You'll have to find another source for confirmation."

"Harcourt isn't here either," the Governor added. "Also, we don't have Harcourt's assassin in our custody. The man is dangerous and elusive."

"That's not my problem," Gilger said. "I know he's there somewhere. Find him and surrender yourselves. I'm leaving the main cable line from Central through Suncage open for you. All three of you better be here—alive or dead—by then, or the price will be higher than you can imagine. But I'll give you a taste now. Consider it my memorial to Vinsic."

Gilger disconnected the line.

"'Taste'?" Ili said. "I don't like that."

"Me either," the Governor said. "I—"

Alarms blared, saturating the air around them. Everyone in the room put their hands over their ears, wincing, as Ili grabbed for her console. Her lips pursed together in grim disapproval as she shut off the alarm.

"We just lost Sunshield Six," she said. "BurntHead's been obliterated in the explosion. Rock Two, Boxhome, and Cubetown are heavily damaged. The lines that fed that sector are down."

"More than two hundred people lived in BurntHead," the Governor said. He was pale.

One of Ili's gray-and-green assistants came into the room. "Ms. Ili! We're going to have another wave of incoming wounded." His voice was trembling. "It's more than we can handle. What should we do?"

"Don't waste time on those who can't be helped. Work your way down from there, do the best you can, and remember that the only number to count is the people we save. It could get a lot worse than this," she said. "Tell everyone to remember to breathe, while we still can."

The assistant left at a half run.

"I don't think we have a lot of choices here," the Governor said. "Gilger will trash Cernee to get what he wants now, or he will later to keep it. Anything that buys our people time also buys them a chance."

"As soon as he has Harcourt, he'll tear apart the Wheels and kill my whole family," Mari said.

"I know," the Governor answered. "I'm open to better ideas, if anyone's got any."

Mari punched Fergus on the shoulder. "You. This is your area of expertise: hopeless situations. Figure out how to get us out of this without any more people dying."

The Governor regarded Fergus. "She has a point. I don't know how you do it, but you've bounced from one narrow escape to the next like some sort of hyped-up mutant ballroach. By all logic, you should be dead several times over. So can you find us a way to save Cernee, or what's left of it?"

"You have two hours and forty-six minutes," Ili said. "Closer to an hour and a half, if you subtract the time it'll take to get to the sunshields from here."

"Come on, Fergus," Mari said. "I trust you. You've got to be able to come up with something."

Fergus slumped in an empty chair. "Something, probably. Something good? Who the hell knows?" He sighed. "I need water. And I haven't eaten in close to a day. And I need some time to think."

"Time is not something we have a lot of," the Governor said.

"Twenty minutes. If I can't come up with an idea before then, I'm not going to. I also need a tactical map."

Ili gestured to one of her men in house grays. "Derrit, see everyone else out and find them something to eat, and then bring Mr. Ferguson some food and water."

"Yes, ma'am," Derrit said. "If the rest of you will follow me . . . ?"

"I'll stay here," Mari said.

"No, you'll go," Ili said firmly. "I'd like to have a word with Mr. Ferguson in private."

It was a mark of how tired Mari was that she didn't argue.

After everyone else had left the room, Ili turned and regarded Fergus again. He resisted squirming under her scalpel-sharp gaze. "Thank you for not killing any of my medics," she said.

Uncomfortably, he nodded. "I don't want to kill anybody."

"Yes, I gather all the deaths in your wake have been *accidental*," she said.

"I didn't start this mess," Fergus said, stung. "Vinsic did. Out of love, it seems?"

"And Gilger took him up on it out of hate. What motivates you? Greed? Fear? Don't answer; I don't need to know. I see no real chance that any of us will survive long enough for it to matter," she said. "But tell me: how many people have died because of your plans, because they trusted you? Do you hold yourself accountable for them? Does it weigh on you?"

"Every single minute of every day," Fergus answered.

"Good." She punched a few keys on the console, and a 3-D map of Cernee resolved itself in the air over her desk. It was nearly all red, now. "Your tactical map. Good luck," she said, and she left.

Fergus sat in Ili's chair, the holo-map of Cernee in front of him, and mulled over everything he'd seen and done since stepping onto that cable car to Mezzanine Rock. Derrit brought him water and a small packet of cookies, eyeing him suspiciously but saying nothing. Fifteen minutes later, when Derrit returned to refill the dry pitcher, Fergus cleared his throat. "Could you please tell Ms. Ili that I need to talk to everyone together?"

Derrit nodded and left.

A few minutes later, Ili and the Governor returned. "The others are on their way," Ili said. "We also have an open connection to the Wheel Collective fed up here from the P2P room now, so we can include Mr. Harcourt in our decisions."

"Good," Fergus said. "Do we know exactly where Gilger is?"

"There are—were—seven sunshields. We expect Gilger has made camp in the central one; it's the superior strategic position, and Gilger knows we can't risk damaging it," the Governor said. "It's also where the cable line goes, via Suncage, which is how he expects us to deliver ourselves into his hands."

As Mari and Bale walked in, Fergus cleared this throat.

"All of you know that my plans tend to be ridiculous and go wildly wrong and weird in unanticipated ways, right?"

"Mari was kind enough to entertain us with the story of your sex toy tennis balls, so I think we have the gist," Ili said. "Do you have a plan or not?"

"I do," Fergus said. "No one is going to like it."

"I never expected we would. Tell us what you've got."

"Is the connection to the Wheels live?"

Ili sat on the corner of her desk and pushed a button, then swiveled her screen around to face the room. "It is now."

Mr. Harcourt was sitting in his chair, fireplace behind him, as he leaned forward toward the screen. "Bale told me about Mars and what you did for my daughter," he said. "I owe you an apology for my earlier suspicions and a debt I can never repay, Mr. Ferguson. Whatever you need from me, even if it's my life, is yours for the asking."

"I need you to make a stop on your way here without being seen," Fergus said.

"I can do that," Harcourt said.

"You may not feel so charitable after I tell you what I need," Fergus said. "And it'll have to be fast; I don't get the sense that Gilger has any flexibility in his deadline. I need other things too, but they can probably be found much closer. Ms. Ili, you don't have any artists on your staff, do you? We need one."

"An *artist*? Probably," Ili said. "Is that all?"

"Uh, no."

Ili sighed. "Shall we start a list?"

Harcourt was still twenty minutes out from Medusa. Fergus poured the last of the water into his bulb and drank it down, waiting in a silence punctuated by the occasional casualty update. Shadefill had started to tear itself apart from damage sustained by debris and the loose BurntHead cable, and the Governor was on Ili's console trying to coordinate help evacuating the survivors with the few people he had left who weren't already tied up elsewhere.

"I can either fight a war or try to save people, not both. There's no way to win anything without losing everything," the Governor said. His face was tight, angry, anguished. "And if this keeps up, I don't know where we're going to find room to put anyone we *do* manage to save. If other habs go, we're going to have to choose between a number of very bad options."

Ili stuck her head out of her office door. "Derrit!" she shouted.

"Yes, ma'am?" he asked from his desk.

"Has Second Medic Rena been found?"

"She's been in surgery, ma'am. We're too short-handed—"

"I am keenly aware. Still, I require her here by the time Mr. Harcourt arrives and absolutely not one second beyond. She should bring her paint kit, whatever she has."

"But . . . ma'am, if I may ask—"

"No, you may not. Thank you, Derrit."

"Yes, ma'am."

Ili slammed the door shut again.

Ten minutes later, Derrit stuck his head in the door. "I have Second Medic Rena," he said. "Docking control is trying to clear a path for Mr. Harcourt's two-man. It's crowded out there."

"Thank you, Derrit. Please send the medic in."

Derrit held the door wide. Second Medic Rena was a short, round, exhausted-looking woman. In one hand she clutched a small case. "Ma'am?" she asked, her glance darting around the room at the strange collection of people there.

"Ah, Medic Rena. About time you showed up," Ili said, and the woman started to shake.

She's scared out of her wits, Fergus realized. "I'm

sorry," he said. "We need your help. It's going to sound crazy, but it's important. Do you have paints that will hold up on skin?"

"Um . . . for a while," she said. "I'm painting *on* someone?"

"Yes," Fergus said. "Me."

"And me," the Governor said. The woman blanched even further. "Also Mr. Harcourt."

"If I go alone . . ." Fergus said.

"We agreed. Your plan stands a much better chance of success with more of us in it," the Governor said. "And if your plan fails, we'll have met Gilger's demand, and maybe some of Cernee will be spared."

"I—" Fergus started.

"I appreciate that you were willing to take this risk on your own," the Governor said, "but this is our home. None of us are willing to sit by if we can do something."

"Mr. Harcourt has docked and should be here in ten minutes," Derrit interrupted. "And your runners have returned. Um, where do you want them to bring—"

"Here, Derrit, bring it all here," Ili said. "And something strong to drink, as I have a feeling we're all in need of that. And save one for yourself as well."

"Oh, I have already taken the liberty, ma'am," Derrit said, and closed the door before he could see the expression on Ili's face.

"I hope this works," Fergus said.

The Governor nodded. "We've got nothing else, and he's certainly not going to see it coming."

Harcourt walked in and gave Bale a tired pat on the shoulder. "I'm here," he said. "Let's do this."

"You two, strip for Medic Rena. Then talk," Ili said.

"I'm in too," Mari said.

"What?" Harcourt said as Fergus looked up sharply.

"I'm not missing Gilger's fall. I owe him."

Bale put a hand to his forehead. "I'm an idiot," he said. "A big, stupid idiot. Count me in too, but if anyone tells my brother I volunteered for this, I'll come haunt the shit out of you from the afterlife."

"I don't want—" Fergus started.

"It's our choice," Mari said. "We've been through this with you since the beginning, and you can't keep us out now. Besides, Gilger will almost certainly kill you first, so you won't have to be faced with actual guilt at our subsequent deaths."

"Oh, well, that's *fine*, then," Fergus said.

Ili opened the door, reached out, and pulled in a startled assistant. She pried a nearly empty bottle of Saturn Screech from his hands. "You," she said to Derrit, "go make sure our guests have a clear exit. We'll need a six-man—"

"They're all out helping with the evacuations, ma'am," Derrit squeaked.

"Then find *something* that six people can fit in that flies. I need it ready in ten minutes or less, or we're going to strap a rocket to your head and use you as a human scooter."

"Yes, ma'am!" Derrit backed out the door, tripping on the threshold, and caught his balance as he turned and ran.

"A little fear is good," Ili said, setting the bottle down on the table with a loud thump.

"Well, I've got plenty extra, if anyone needs more," Bale added, starting to take off his shirt.

Chapter 27

Derrit commandeered an ambulance just after it had off-loaded a dozen burnt, bleeding, and crushed people from Shadefill. Ili and a shell-shocked Second Medic helped them load up the back. "For all our sakes, good luck," Ili said, then closed the doors firmly between them.

The Governor climbed up to the front and took the seat beside the pilot. "To Central," he said, "by the most expedient path you can find."

"Yes, sir," the pilot said.

The back of the ambulance had no view-portals, and Fergus was relieved not to have to see any more of the devastation. He'd grown up with the aftermath of history erasing entire peoples and places, and he didn't want to be reminded of what was poised to happen here. *I'm doing what I can to stop it*, he told himself, ignoring the voice that told him it was a last futile, crazy gesture.

The ambulance pilot turned to them as they docked at Central. "Whatever you all are up to, good luck," he said. "I'll keep my comm on in case you need a fast escape."

"I don't think we're likely to get one," the Governor said, "but thank you."

"It's been my honor, Lord Governor, sir."

"Where you from, Pilot?" the Governor asked.

"Rattletrap, sir. Lost my parents and two brothers."

"I'm so sorry."

"Don't be sorry. Be our revenge, sir," the pilot said.

"We'll do what we can," Harcourt said. "Can't promise more than that."

"Can't ask for more than that. Heading into the spinward three dock now. Hang on, there's some damage. From here your people are holding the path clear to the cable platform."

The pilot brought the ambulance in without the least discernable bump, then helped them offload onto the dock, where four exhausted Authority officers met them to escort them through the heavily damaged station. As soon as they were clear, the ambulance lifted off again and headed back toward Medusa and the waiting wounded.

The Governor had called ahead, and a cable car stood ready and empty, waiting for them at the main terminal. They moved their stuff over, and once the cable car was sealed, the five of them began the long journey down the line heading straight for Suncage and the center shield. The four officers watched them go, and their expressions ran the same range from hope to despair that Fergus felt warring for control of his own heart.

He let his gaze drift over the collection of people on the bench opposite him, half expecting to see the ghost of Mother Vahn among them, grinning her old lady grin. "Trouble on the line," he said.

"What?" Mari asked, perking up out of her own thoughts.

"Nothing. Just remembering. I promised someone I'd give Gilger a boot up the backside, and if this works, I think she'd have been satisfied."

Mari gave a sad half smile. "I miss her," she said.

"Yeah," Fergus replied. "She seemed like one hell of a person."

He drifted out of his seat, accustomed now to the pitch and yaw of the cable car, to stare out the front window. Suncage was a tiny glint against the massive dark backdrop of the central sunshield, outlined with the brilliant white fire of Cernee's distant star.

"We've got about fifteen minutes until we pass through Suncage," Harcourt said. "Everyone ready for this? Fergus?"

Fergus nodded, as much truth as lie. He took off his

threadbare Firebowl shirt and shed his pants. Underneath he wore a tight pair of black shorts. Then he took out a tube of lichen goo, popped the cap, and started drawing glowing spirals and runes on his arms. When those were done, he began working his way down his torso, then his legs. The others watched, fascinated despite themselves. When he was done, he stood up and handed the tube off to Mari, who filled in his back.

"You know this is going to make you really easy to shoot in the dark," she said.

"Explain what these mean again?" Bale said.

"They're sin marks. Luceatans permanently ink themselves with special symbols to remember each sin they've committed that they must atone for through righteous or glorious acts. I've just declared myself a sinner of every blasphemous, horrific, obscure, and disgusting sin I could think of, and on top of them all"—Fergus tapped the ornate circular glyph on his forehead—"the Bringer of Armageddon. In short, I have made myself Sahte, the Faither Devil."

He lifted his arms, turning them back and forth, satisfied with the glowing lines. "It's not woad, but I think my ancestors would still approve."

Harcourt was looking at him strangely, and when Fergus caught his eyes, he shook his head. "I'm sorry," he said. "It's the Asiig thing. It shouldn't matter, not after everything you've done for us. It's just . . ."

"Yeah, I understand. Wasn't anything I had a choice in, but we do our best with the hand we're dealt, right?" Fergus said. If only he felt that nonchalant about it. He picked up the jug of water he'd brought along and took another long swig, trying to get ahead of the thirst he knew was coming. "Remember, I go in first. If they shoot me dead, figure out your own plan B. If not, come in behind me, and be careful. With any luck, the Luceatans will let me clear a path through them right to Gilger."

"You know not to accidentally lick the goo, right?" Mari asked.

"Yeah. Mother Vahn was pretty clear about how terrible it would be."

"Speaking of terrible, don't forget your *thing*," Bale said, pointing. There was a long tube, capped tightly, leaning against the seats. No one sat near it.

"As if I could," Fergus said. He picked it up and looped the carry strap over his head and down under the opposite arm, making sure the tube sat across his back where he could easily reach and grab it. It felt itchy against his bare skin, and a chill crawled up his spine.

"We're almost at Suncage," the Governor said. "Time for you to go dark."

Fergus wrapped a blanket around himself and over his head to hide the glowing runes as Bale killed all the lights inside the car.

Suncage was a thick, cylindrical, hollow structure the cable passed through, the inner surface lined with controls and monitors for the settlement power grid, protected from stray space debris. Their car bumped and shook, lights flickering, as it crossed each exchange between the cable and the power station, until at last they emerged out the far end. The central sunshield filled their entire field of view. It was a massive concave structure, thick struts and structural beams making it look like an enormous rectangular kite. The tiny cable station was embedded in its center.

"We've got company," Harcourt said. Fergus turned and could just make out three shapes putting spiders on the line from Suncage, jumping in behind them. His heartbeat quickened. No retreat now, not that there ever had been.

The cable car slid into a docking terminus in the sunshield's station, magnetic grapplers taking hold of the underside and guiding it to one of several airlocks inside. The car hit with a small bump, and then there was a grinding vibration as the two airlocks locked together. After a few tense seconds, it greenlit on their side, and the door unlocked.

"Here we go," Fergus said. "If this doesn't work, it's been a pleasure. And I almost mean that without sarcasm."

"We feel exactly the same about you," Mari said.

Fergus went through first. When the outer door had cycled closed, he reached up and carefully shorted out the light inside the lock. Shedding his blanket, he could see the green glow from his paint reflecting dully on the walls around him and nodded in satisfaction. If anyone survived this misadventure, at least they'd be able to say he had made one hell of a try.

The inner door opened, and he stepped out of the dark, a glowing apparition. A half dozen Luceatans stood ranged in a semicircle around the lock, each with a pistol raised. As he walked out, the pistols wavered. "Sahte," one whispered.

"*SAHTE!*" Fergus bellowed.

One Luceatan dropped his weapon and slid behind a fellow man, touching his chest above his heart with four fingers together, a sign of protection. Fergus raised his hands and let the electricity flow from his fingertips, enveloping the two men. They screamed and collapsed to the floor, no longer a threat. "Sahte," Fergus said again, and his voice carried through the bay, echoing off walls. Another Luceatan turned and ran. Three down. *Be the devil*, Fergus told himself.

He strode forward, raising his arms as if summoning rain, and coated himself in a bristling aura of energy, arcs of electricity leaping from one point on his bare skin to another, connecting knee and shin, elbow and wrist, shoulder to chest. One of the Luceatans fired, the shot going wild, and Fergus brought the man down with a blinding bolt. His steps brought him up beside another man, who sank to his knees, still trying to raise his pistol, spittle on his lips and his hands shaking.

Fergus had read enough Luceatan myth-texts to play this part. "Sahte is walking among His ken," he said, putting his hand on the man's head and wreathing it in the same leaping light that surrounded him. The pistol fell from the man's hand as he went limp. "One by one, collecting them for Hell, as He has already collected His son Borr Graf."

The last Luceatan dropped his weapon and ran.

Behind him he heard the airlock door slide shut and begin its next cycle, bringing the others. Time for him to clear the way forward. Past this bay was a long, wide corridor leading to a large auditorium with a heavily tinted xglass window where visitors could look out at the inner solar system through the shield itself. Everything else should be storage rooms and mechanical facilities and small quarters, if the map the Governor had provided him remained accurate. Fergus's best guess was that Gilger would be waiting in the auditorium.

There were no signs of Shielders or any Shielder bodies. He hoped that meant they'd escaped Gilger's invasion and were holed up somewhere safe until this was over.

He pushed open both of the double doors at the end of the bay, stepping through with a confidence he didn't feel. Movement on either side flickered in his peripheral vision, and without having to think about it, he reached out and zapped both Luceatans hiding there. A third hiding in a side doorway ahead gave himself away with a short cry of fear.

Before he could run, Fergus reached out and caught him, wrapping one hand around the man's shoulder and practically throwing him around to face him. "Sahte is walking now, knocking down false men who do not honor His name."

The man was shaking. "I renounce sin! Leave me free!"

"Evil does not renounce *you*," Fergus retorted. "Go, warn your false master that Sahte is coming!" The man got shakily to his feet and ran straight down the corridor toward the auditorium. *Good guess*, Fergus thought. *So far, so good.*

As soon as the man disappeared through the far door, two dozen armed Luceatans poured out, the ones in front bracing to take aim. Fergus slapped a hand on the wall and sent sparks flying down it along the plating, and all those touching the wall shouted in pain and pushed away, knocking into others.

"Sahte is here!" Fergus shouted.

"He's a fake!" one shouted back. "It's the Mars assassin, you idiots. Go!"

Not all seemed convinced, but some started haltingly forward. Fergus let the lightning crawl across his bare chest, tracing the sin marks there, and a few more hesitated. He sent another blast of electricity down the corridor, feeling it tapering off sooner than he wanted. Deep inside, the angry bees felt quiet, small. *Dammit*, Fergus thought. *Now is not the time to run low on juice.*

Running forward, he shouted as loudly as he could, a wordless cry of rage, startling the Luceatans. He reached out and grabbed one, slamming his head into his knee, then took hold of another by the neck and swung him into a wall. He fought his way into the midst of them, once again that skinny kid who'd started too many late-night bar fights in New Glasgow trying to prove something he couldn't even name. The memory of how badly he'd lost most of those fights did not dim his momentum.

One Luceatan who had already fallen grabbed onto his leg, trying to hold him as the rest still standing closed in, swinging fists at his head and chest.

There was the sound of a shot, and a Luceatan on Fergus's arm let go, falling to the floor. Fergus glanced over his shoulder to see Harcourt, pistol still raised, in the bay door. The Luceatans around him saw as well and scrambled for their dropped weapons, not sure which threat was the most immediate.

"Sahte!" Fergus shouted again, flailing his fists and kicking his feet, making sure to nail the one who'd called him a fake hard in the groin. He was running on adrenaline now, almost enjoying himself as he broke through the last of the Luceatans and flung himself through the doors into the auditorium.

It was a wider space than he'd imagined, and there were easily three dozen more Luceatans inside, all heavily sin-marked, surrounding a man in red and gold who stood, hands folded across his chest, calmly waiting in front of the podium like a lecturer awaiting tardy students.

Arum Gilger.

Gilger snapped his fingers, and the Luceatans began to slowly, nervously close around him. "I am Sahte!" Fergus shouted. Some stopped in their tracks, but not all.

"Yeor, now, please," Gilger said. A broad-shouldered Luceatan stepped out of the ranks holding a fat-barreled pistol pointed at the floor.

Fergus mustered some electricity, letting it dance on his fingertips as more Luceatans stopped in their tracks. Yeor smiled, squinted, and fired.

Something hit Fergus's leg, exploded inside his skin, and he screamed and fell to the floor. A long, thin metal spike was sunk into his lower leg, and through tear-filling eyes he could see the barbed point protruding from the gory mess of what was left of his calf. "Auhhh," he groaned, trying to push the excruciating pain away somewhere and failing.

Desperate, he tried to summon what last juice he had, intent on blasting Yeor or Gilger or both, and raised his face to see a thin cable running from the spike back to Yeor, who had wrapped the other end around a sharpened metal bar. Another Luceatan lifted a hammer, and they pounded the bar into a hole in the metal floor plate.

"Well, *Sahte*," Gilger said. "How does it feel to be grounded?"

"F . . . Fuck," Fergus said.

Gilger stepped down from the podium and walked toward him with all the swagger Fergus had tried to fake while walking up the corridor. "The rest of you, take a lesson from this: If you're going to fear a man, look at this pathetic bastard on the floor and ask yourself if you picked the right one."

Not all the Luceatans looked chastened by this. Gilger stopped in front of Fergus, staying carefully just beyond arm's reach. Fergus felt a vague glimmer of satisfaction deep in the well of his own agony.

"Well, that's one demand met," Gilger said. "Bring in the others."

Two Luceatans opened the doors, and Harcourt, the Governor, Mari, and Bale stood there, disarmed, another dozen Luceatans behind them. Mari paled when she saw Fergus on the floor in a pool of blood. "Fergus?" she asked, voice carrying in the hall.

"Fergus," Gilger said. "What a ridiculous name for a ridiculous man." He faced his Luceatans again. "This man didn't kill Graf. The Asiig did. They made this man their creature, but *I* brought him down. Graf's soul is with us in this victory, in this place right now!"

"Not just his soul," the Governor said, his voice calm. His hand slipped out of his robe and held out a small collection of cubes. "I have his ear."

Gilger's expression transformed in an instant from triumph to white-hot anger. He walked forward and slapped the Governor's hand, sending the collection of cubes to the floor. They broke apart and scattered into the recesses and shadows of the room. "How *dare* you?" He spat. "He was my *brother*."

"Ah, I get it now!" Harcourt said. "That mysterious connection none of us could figure out. So which one of you was the bastard? Him, obviously. Oh, and lemme guess: half Marsie too?"

Gilger's face twisted, and he punched Harcourt hard in the stomach, then brought his fist down on Harcourt's head when the man doubled over, knocking him to the floor. "It is *not your business*," he said. "I would not be so smug if I were you! We were going to rule together, him at my side, as we should have back on Baselle. And I will rule here, or I will leave this place and all the tiny,

meaningless, inadequate people in it a burnt and deso-
late tribute to his memory."

He turned on Bale and Mari. "And speaking of the
inadequate, who the fuck are you two? A flunky and a
Vahn?"

Mari had knelt beside Harcourt, but she stared up at
Gilger with more hatred and fury than Fergus had ever
seen in one person. "I came to look a murderer in the
eyes," she said.

Bale coughed. "I came along because I figured these
idiots would need help getting home again after they'd
finished with you," he said.

Such bravado, Fergus thought. *I love these people,
but I wish they'd shut up.*

Gilger apparently felt the same way. "Really?" he
said. "Finished with me? I suppose your alien puppet
bleeding to death on the floor will leap to his feet with
one last deadly trick? I don't think so. What do any of
you have except brave words? Do you know what I have?
I have your entire little shit settlement here in the palm
of my hand, and that palm can just as easily be a *fist*."

"None of the people you killed ever did anything to
you," Mari said.

"They didn't do anything *for* me, either," Gilger said.
"And that dumb asshole Vinsic stabbed me in the back
and blew up my damned *home*. I hate all of you, every
single one of you, and I am no longer interested in sympathy or subtlety to get what I want. Which sunshield
should I destroy next? The one right next to your pre-
cious Wheels? Or Seven, all the way across Cernee near
Medusa, which would take out your medics and your
oxygen production in one blow? Pick one."

"I'd rather not," Mari said.

"Then should I pick?" Gilger said. "Would you like
that better? Yeor, call the team in Sunshield One. Have
them prep and back out, then wait for my signal. If the
fucking Shielders won't come out and surrender, they
can die wherever they're hiding."

Everyone was looking at Gilger and his prisoners, ignoring the fallen man on the floor.

Fergus straightened his arms, pushing himself up against the floor, trying to get his one good leg back under him while ignoring the sticky puddle beneath the other. As soon as he was steady, he reached behind his shoulder and grabbed the tube that was there, letting himself fall the rest of the way over into a sitting position.

"I'd rather you didn't, either," he said, and although his voice wasn't as loud as he'd hoped, he was pleased that it didn't shake. Gilger turned and saw him, saw the tube, and snapped his fingers again. Instantly three dozen pistols were pointing his way.

"What's in the tube?" Gilger asked, taking a step toward him. "A weapon? A copy of your will? Do you think you can get it out before every man in this room fries you into a blackened smear on the floor? Or is this just a ploy for a faster death?"

"Or a slower one," Fergus said. He held up the tube. "Want to see which?"

"Don't you even *think*—" Gilger said, but before he could even finish his sentence, Fergus had slapped the bottom of the tube, and the tiny rigged mechanism embedded there blew the entire contents out in a cloud of black dust that settled over Gilger and his people behind him.

"You're going to kill me with dust?" Gilger asked, brushing at his clothes. He started to laugh, but then his hand paused, frozen, as he stared at it.

The Luceatan beside Gilger shrieked, slapping at his clothes. "Something bit me!" he shouted.

Gilger began furiously shaking his tunic, jumping away from the others quickly. "What the fuck?" he said. "You didn't—Ouch!" He began scrabbling at his neck, trying desperately to dislodge whatever was there.

Fergus dropped the tube, fell back onto his elbows. "Spore ticks," he said. "Now we all die. Everyone in this room. If you run away, you take death everywhere you go: to your people here in Cernee or back to Luceatos, to your families, your children. *Now* which pathetic bastard do you fear?"

The Luceatans around them began to shrink back as one, and as they did, one cried out and grabbed his shoulder. "It bit me!" he shouted, and without hesitation he raised his pistol, put it against the side of his head, and blew his own brains out.

The ranks broke, panicking, running from the tumbling corpse of the dead man toward the doors.

Something bit Fergus, and he winced and looked down to see the black shape scuttling away, leaving a red welt already growing in its wake. "Pissed you right off, didn't I?" he said.

"You!" Gilger roared. "You'll die too!"

"Yeah, but I was going to anyway, right?" Fergus said. He pointed at the harpoon impaling his leg. "Faster than you."

"And your friends? You've condemned them!"

"Assassins don't have *friends*," Fergus scoffed. "There are people we can use, and people who get in our way, and no one else."

Mari shrieked and began to tear at her suit. Her shoulder where it met her neck was a bloodied red-and-purple mess. "Aaahh!" she cried. "Help me! Someone help me!"

Bale and Harcourt were both pulling at their own clothing, showing similar patches of spore tick blight. "Kill me," Harcourt begged Gilger, falling to his knees. "It's what you wanted, so do it! Don't make me die this way."

Gilger's eyes were wide, and he was breathing hard. "No," he said. "You can die this way, but not me. All of you can die and rot, but I will not die here with you!"

He turned, stumbling up the auditorium steps toward the rear door, slapping at his leg and stumbling as he was bitten again. "Yeor! Where the fuck are you? We need to get to an escape pod!"

Yeor stepped out of the shadows by the door. He was

pale and sweating, several red welts on his face and neck. "I'm sorry," he said, "but there's no going back to Luceatos. I won't let you kill my friends, my ken." He raised his pistol, and as the astonished Gilger opened his mouth to shout, Yeor shot him.

Gilger fell, tumbling down the stairs to land face-up and unmoving not far from Fergus.

Yeor raised his weapon again. "For mercy," he said, pointing it at Fergus.

"Uh, you know, I'm actually okay with the long, lingering death," Fergus said. "With my leg and all. I appreciate the kindness, but honest, I'm good here."

"Me too," Harcourt said, raising his face up from the floor where he'd been writhing in a mindless stupor moments before.

"What in Hell?" the Luceatan said. "Some *trick*? I—"

He was hit from behind by the door crashing open and several of the Luceatans who had fled tumbling back into the room, screaming. Yeor turned and was shot by someone beyond the door. He dropped his pistol and crumpled.

A half dozen people in white suits pushed through the door, firing with startling efficiency. A few minutes later, Fergus and his friends were the only remaining living people in the room besides the Shielders. "Which one of you assholes," the lead Shielder said, her suit carefully closed and sealed, "brought the fucking *spore tick* plague into our home?"

"It's a fake," Fergus said.

She walked up to where Fergus was lying on the floor bleeding and held out her palm. In the center of the white glove sat a perfectly still, tiny black shape. "This is a spore tick," she said. "It is most certainly real."

"Yeah, but it's *dead*," Fergus said. "They're all dead. Years dead."

"These men have fresh stings!"

"Ballroaches. I mixed them in with the dead spore ticks. They're almost the same size, move too fast to get a close look at, and bite the shit out of everything and everyone when they're agitated."

"Your friends all exhibit the sores of infestation," she said.

Harcourt lifted a finger, wet it on his tongue, and ran it across the sore on his exposed abdomen. The sore smeared and came off on his finger. "Paint," he said.

Now the Shielder opened her face shield and stared at them all one by one. Her eyes, in a field of blue-and-gold paint, were wide in astonishment. "This was a *hoax*?" she said. "None of you are dying?"

"I am," Fergus said, pointing at his leg. He was feeling light-headed, afraid he was about to pass out, and thought it worth pointing out. "Shot with a harpoon gun, as it turns out. Just stand there and let me die here, okay, and yeah, you're welcome for saving the rest of your sun-shields, by the way. Don't forget to put that in your Narrative."

The Shielder rolled her eyes. "This is why we don't like talking to you people," she said. "You're all fucking crazy. And if I find out you're back because someone drew you here, I'm going to shove them out an airlock." She signaled, and the rest of her people moved into the room and began checking the bodies to make sure all of them were dead. "Other than this man, does anyone else need medical assistance?" she asked.

"Find us some sort of anti-itch cream," Mari said, scratching furiously, "and I'll be indebted to you for the rest of my life."

Chapter 28

◆—◆—◆

"**Y**ou can stay here," Harcourt said. "As long as you want."

Fergus leaned forward, tapping the end of his cane on the floor, trying to get a feel for it. His leg ached—sometimes the pain came in burning waves that left him speechless—but Ili had assured him it was healing nicely and he'd heal faster if he stopped complaining about it. It wasn't, all in all, the worst advice he'd ever been given.

The Wheels and Blackcans had been temporarily reconnected while they waited for a permanent cable. Disconnected habs that were still habitable but lacked any self-generation capability were being prioritized. Power was being rationed carefully, but with fewer habs—some had been obliterated, some damaged enough to render them unsafe—it was sufficient for the short term. A new sunshield would take years to finish, but the Shielders had assured everyone they would take care of it and would everyone please *go away*. The beginnings of normality were starting to peek out through the chaos.

"I have some things I need to do," Fergus said.

"They're still waiting for you," Mari said. "I think you're their last unfinished business here, at least for now."

The Asiig had given back a handful of the people they'd picked up crossing the Halo during the war, mostly frightened families who did not—or would not—speak about what had happened to them. Whatever changes might have been made were not obvious, not yet. Right now they were in Ili's care, and Mauda was quietly consulting.

"Yeah," Fergus said. "I think it's time."

He slowly stood, leaning heavily on the cane, and tested his leg on the ground. He could step as long as he didn't put too much weight on it. He was looking forward to being back out in space with no gravity to pull down on him. "I've spent most of my life finding things," he said. "Never thought to go look for myself. And now I'm someone else entirely. I need some time to get my head around that."

"If you can't get into the ship, come back here, and we'll figure something out," Harcourt said. "I'm sure we can find some task to occupy your prodigious need to get into trouble."

"Bogstone erupted," Arelyn added from where she stood behind Harcourt's chair. She and Mari seemed to be talking again; the friendship wasn't yet back to where it had been and still might never be, but at least it was improving. "They'll be looking for cleanup crew. Might be just your thing, being neck-deep in shit you're possibly responsible for."

Fergus laughed, not taking her bait. "I'll pass, thanks. Besides, the Shipmakers are waiting on me too, and they're probably very worried by now."

"If they know you, they're probably worried all the time anyway," Mari said.

"A new suit is waiting for you at the platform," Harcourt added. "Top anti-EMP military tech there is. And there's a 'stick waiting for you, fully charged. I bought it for you special. It took me some effort to find just the right one."

"Thanks," Fergus said. "And I mean it."

Harcourt smiled. "It's the least I could do."

Fergus walked carefully toward the door. Bale stood there waiting. "I'll give you a hand," he said. "Suits are no fun to put on when you're hurt."

"Thanks," Fergus said again. He waved to the gathered people in the room and followed Bale toward the dock. "Going to be a while, if ever, before Arelyn forgives me for existing. Speaking of grudges, how's your brother doing?"

Bale shrugged. "Pissed that I survived only to throw myself right back into danger."

"And how's Ms. Ili handling Vinsic being gone?"

"Same as Ms. Ili takes everything, I expect. In other words, who knows? She's not thrilled that the Governor and Mr. Harcourt are working so closely together—something about power vacuums and trust issues—but she'll get over it when things settle down without trouble."

Stuck in Medusa for the first week after the confrontation in the central sunshield under the very intentional care of a less-than-fond-of-him Medic Zofia, Fergus's access to news had been sparse. What was obvious, then and now, was that nearly everyone in Cernee who could had pitched in to save those parts of Cernee that needed it and that lines of political power seemed irrelevant, or at least less relevant than saving lives. It made Fergus proud of this place, even if it was not his own.

"Can I ask . . ." Bale said. "Did you really think that trick with the ballroaches was going to work?"

"Not a shot in hell," Fergus said, "but it was the only thing I could think of. I was hoping I'd get lucky."

"Okay," Bale said, digesting that. "I hope you stay lucky," he said at last, "and that we see you again."

Fergus nodded. At the platform, Bale held up a suit. It was plain black, but on the back, between the shoulder blades, were the concentric green, blue, and red circles and spokes of the Wheels city-mark. It was, he knew, both an apology and an offer. Fergus smiled as Bale helped him struggle into the suit. Once on and sealed, it fit perfectly.

Bale handed him a small pack. "Three bottles of water," he said, "since you get thirsty. And Mauda kindly sent you a care package of lichen cakes. In the event you ever find yourself tempted to eat them, Mr. Harcourt generously also included a bottle of the cheapest Crossroads grain-alk we could find. That'll kill your taste buds for a week. Oh, and he says to remind you that you still owe him for the business suit."

Fergus nodded. *I hate having to say goodbye,* he thought. *It's always so much easier to sneak away.* "Well, I'm going," he said. "If I don't see you again, please thank everyone for me one more time."

"Sure."

He closed and sealed his face shield, then turned and cycled through the airlock and out onto the platform.

There was a lone flystick waiting for him in the center of the platform, covered in purple, glittery starbursts. He started laughing and couldn't stop until his suit's monitoring systems started registering alarm. Taking hold of the 'stick, he fired it up, and the air around him filled with holographic, rainbow-colored ballroaches. Strapping his cane over his back, he launched into the stars in a cloud of smiling and waving cartoon bugs.

"Fergus?" Mari's voice came over his comm.

"Yes, Mari?"

"Thanks."

"For what?"

"I spent my whole life thinking I didn't count as a real person, that everything I am is a lie, and that maybe— just a little—Gilger and Graf were right to hate us. It wasn't until I left Cernee that I realized being a person had nothing to do with being human. Maybe someday Arelyn will see that too."

"I think she's already starting to," he said. "Give her time."

"Yeah," Mari said. "You too, Fergus. Whatever happens, remember you're still you, not someone else's idea of you."

"Right," he said. "That's good, because a lot of people think I'm an asshole."

Mari laughed. "Not everyone, but give them time."

"I'll do my best," he said.

There was silence on the line for a while, and then she spoke up again. "Those two guys I shot . . ."

"It was war, Mari."

"Yeah," she said. "I've been at war my whole life. I don't want to be anymore. How do you do that?"

"One day at a time," Fergus said. "And if that's too much, one hour at a time. Trust your instincts, your friends, and definitely any strange little old grandmothers you meet on cable cars. They never stop looking out for you, even when they're not around."

"You think so?"

"Yeah, I do."

"And what about you?"

Fergus laughed. "I think I'm learning that I've always been running away from the wrong things, and it's time I went back and fixed some stuff. Might take me a while to get it all sorted, though."

"Yeah, well, if you do . . ."

"If I do?"

"Next time I am definitely gonna stab you with the pitchfork and keep your socks. You were way too much trouble."

He laughed. "I'll miss you too," he said.

She disconnected.

Turning as soon as he was clear of the Wheels, he headed out to where *Venetia's Sword* waited patiently for him. A single Asiig ship remained, dark and ominous and unmoving above the ship it dwarfed. *This is crazy*, he thought, but then, when had his life ever not been?

He slowed, tense for the slightest sign of movement, but the ship just sat there as if sleeping as he flew beneath it and up to *Venetia's Sword* itself. A faint, almost iridescent sheen surrounded it, like it had been caught in a soap bubble and frozen there. He coasted closer, constantly glancing up and around him for signs of movement, until he could reach out and touch the bubble with one gloved hand. It felt springy, yielding slightly to his touch, but it did not pop and vanish as he'd hoped.

If they wanted me to get in, he thought, *they should have given me a key.*

Maybe they had.

He reached out again, put the palm of his glove against the strange field, and let electricity seep through, increasing the strength until in an instant the bubble that had been there was suddenly not. The suit blinked at him and rebooted.

When it came back up—four seconds, an impressive recovery speed—he kicked the 'stick forward, reached *Venetia's Sword*'s airlock, and with a last look around him at the still-unmoving ship, pressed the external comm. "Control, voice command, acknowledge," he said.

"Restate authentication," *Venetia's Sword* responded.

He gave the code again, and the outer door slid smoothly open. Pulling himself and the 'stick in, he closed it, waited for the lock to fill with atmo, and exited into the interior of the ship.

It all seemed exactly as he'd left it. Garbage was still strewn in the hallways from the ship's misuse by Gilger's crew, dispersed more widely by several gravity shifts that had been his own doing. The remnants of the ties that had held him prisoner still dangled from the arms of a chair lying on its side at the back of the bridge, patches of dried blood on the floor and console beside it. He walked around that chair to the pilot's station instead, glad to have that harsh reminder of his last visit out of sight behind him.

"You returned," *Venetia's Sword* spoke. He could see the flicker on the console of the ship's higher mindsystem waking up and trying desperately to stabilize itself.

"I did," Fergus said. "Are you ready to go home?"

"Yes."

After a few more flickers, the light went out.

"Gravity to thirty-eight percent, Mars standard," he said. He felt the weight drain off him.

In front of him, the viewer was on, and he could see the point of the Asiig ship directly above. He wondered where the others had gone. Would they follow him when he left, follow him the rest of his life? It hadn't occurred to him until that moment that they might. How would the Shipmakers feel if he brought back aliens with their ship?

They better be happy they're getting it back at all, he thought, *or I'm going to punch somebody.*

He took the pilot seat, reattached and clipped himself onto the safety tether, and reached to power up the panel when he froze. Sitting there on the top of the helm controls was a motorcycle key.

Startled, he spun his chair around and stood up.

A man stood in the bridge doorway, about his own height, arms folded across his chest as he leaned against one of the blast doors. His suit was thin and strange, and there was something odd about his face that Fergus couldn't quite pin down. "Well," the man said, his accent equally unfamiliar. "You came back."

"I did," Fergus said. He picked up the key and slipped it into a pocket, instantly comforted to have it there. "You're human."

"Oh, don't start this conversation off like that," the man said. "I haven't been human in a very long time. How about you?"

"More human now, I think," Fergus said.

The man chuckled. "Whatever helps you sleep," he said.

"How did you get on board?"

The man sighed. "Not in a way you'd understand even if I tried to explain it very slowly," he said. He stepped forward and to one side, and something moved behind him.

Fergus lost his balance and nearly fell.

The alien was as tall as the doorway, walking on six legs that seemed too skinny, too jointed, to hold up the thick plated shell above it. *Like someone crossed an ar-*

madillo with a daddy longlegs, Fergus thought, *except a hell of a lot scarier.*

Below the shell, a rounded body hung on multiple stalks, its front dominated by a cluster of what Fergus could only assume were eyes, all different sizes and shapes and all, like the body, a gleaming black. It made a sound like crickets, and the man straightened. "It says you have damaged your leg," the man said.

"Yeah. It'll heal. Were they really watching Mother Vahn all this time?"

More crickets, and the man said, "They watch."

"Not a very clear answer."

"You don't think?" the man said.

The Asiig spoke again, and the man chittered back at it for a moment before sighing. "This is an imperfect translation, but just answer as best you can. What word is now in your heart?"

Fergus blinked. Without thinking, he said, "Gratitude. I—"

"No, don't explain, you'll only ruin it," the man said.

"Fine," Fergus said. "So tell me this: why me?"

"Your proximity to the Primary Vahn when we lost her and your unlikely survival that returned you to them in her place were too fortuitous events to ignore. The Asiig listen intently to the signs of the Universe, always."

"Why?"

"Why? To understand it," the man said. "You are a piece of the dialogue the Asiig are having with the Universe, whether you hear it or not, whether you understand it or not. Whether you want to be or not."

Fergus stared at them, trying to make sense of that information. The Asiig stared back, its eyes blinking like camera lenses, closing from all sides at once down to a point. Then it turned, moving smoothly despite its bulk, and began to leave.

"Wait!" Fergus shouted. "What, that's *it*?"

"That's what it wanted," the man said.

"Is this all a *joke*?"

The alien stopped, was silent for a moment, then chirped briefly at the man. "It says that's a somewhat profound question," the man translated. "It will consider it."

"But . . . what about me? Will you fix me?"

"We could only fix you if we'd broken you," the man said. "I don't think we see that the same way you do."

"Then what am I now? What am I supposed to *do*?"

The Asiig chirped again, then left the bridge.

Fergus stared at the man, desperation making him tremble. "What did it say?"

"Ah," the man said. "Sometimes they're hard to understand, you know. Shades of syntax and all that."

"Tell me," Fergus said, almost begging.

"It said, 'Be interesting.' Now, is that a command? Or a prediction? I can't tell you." The man shrugged. "Not really my problem. Don't know yet if we'll meet again. Good luck."

He turned and followed the alien out.

Fergus stood there, wanting to cry, wanting to laugh. All he'd been through, and *that* was the answer he got?

Venetia's Sword's helm beeped at him, and he turned to see the black triangle looming above slide forward and vanish back into the dark.

Fergus stared at the empty space for a very long time. It was his aching leg that brought him back to himself, and he sat, taking several deep breaths, before reaching for the helm again. "All systems check?" he asked. His voice trembled.

"All systems functioning," *Venetia's Sword* answered.

"How big is the universe?"

"Calculating a current estimation will take me—"

"Never mind; big enough. Set a course for Crossroads, and run a full integrity check on the jump engines as we get underway."

"Commencing," the ship said.

Fergus leaned back in his chair. A few jumps, a few days, and he'd have the ship back to its makers, who could fix it and make it right again. This job would, at long last, be done. He will have met his last obligation.

Still not quite the last, he realized. *I have a motorcycle to get out of storage and take back to its owner, if I can.* He'd have to avoid Mars for a while, probably; the MCA had a long memory when it came to people who'd gotten away from them, and if they were peeved enough, they might even have passed on a fugitive description to the Alliance. The Alliance, for its part, couldn't care less about Marsie problems unless he got right in their faces. Which he'd have to try to avoid if he was going to get back to Earth.

Earth.

He was starting to get the glimmer of an idea for how to get through EarthPort security without raising any flags, but beyond the cold logistics, the thought of actually being there—his feet standing on Earth with its oceans and mountains and memories—left him lost. He didn't even know where to start, much less if he was ready. Was he just one more long-lost broken thing, coming home?

And what after?

He could take another finding job. He could go back to the Shipyard, see *Venetia's Sword* made right again, hang out with Theo and the others until they kicked his useless ass out. He could go back to Coralla and live on the beach, maybe study with a Tea Master. He could help Cernee rebuild, work for Harcourt, or maybe open Cernee's first curry shop. Bugrot hadn't seemed bad. Or he could do something else entirely, something that he hadn't even thought of yet, something different and new.

Whatever he did, he was certain things weren't over with the Asiig.

Be interesting, he thought, and he tapped the helm sequence to go.

Acknowledgments

Over the years I've become that sort of person that often reads acknowledgements in books, but I've never had the opportunity to write them before, so naturally this is an occasion for much AAAAAAAH PANIC FLAIL. (This is something that authors do a lot of, and never let them tell you otherwise.) I wouldn't have the chance to write this if it hadn't been for the incredible support, patience, wisdom, and occasional justified dope-slap from a lot of people, all of whom I am extraordinarily grateful for in ways this brief acknowledgement can't come close to adequately expressing.

My agent, Joshua Bilmes, has been a steadfast guide from our earliest conversations, and this book would not be here without his patient efforts. Thanks also go to Katie Hoffman, my editor at DAW, for her enthusiasm and for loving my book enough to bring it the rest of the way into the light of day, and to all the other wonderful folks at DAW who have worked on it and helped this anxious n00b through the process without strangling me.

I wouldn't have gotten this far without my first writing group, the Rosleyians, nor the instructors, staff, and my fellow alumni of the Viable Paradise Writer's Workshop. Special thanks need to go to Laura Mixon-Gould, without whose support and timely words of wisdom I would have thrown in the towel entirely, and to Macallister Stone and my many friends at AbsoluteWrite who made me feel like I belonged somewhere again. Much of my writing gets done in the evenings while I'm logged into the AbsoluteWrite IRC chat channel, and while it would be going too far to say they've kept me sane, certainly they've kept me excellent company. A shout-out is also due to those editors (Sheila, Neil, Trevor, and Andy, among others) who believed in my short fiction work and whose encouragement still keeps me reaching to do better. Taking up writing has introduced me to an entire, diverse community of thinkers and creators and amazingly talented, weird, funny, clever, good-hearted people, all over the world and right here in my tiny happy valley in western Massachusetts, that I cannot imagine life without. There are no riches in this world more shiny than friendship.

And I wouldn't be on this writing journey at all if not for my early teachers who got me hooked on reading science fiction and fantasy, my friend Kelly Fenlason who dragged me off to my first real SF convention (Boskone, the year with the orange t-shirt . . .) as a teenager, and all my friends from the UMass Science Fiction Society, many of whom are still hanging out with me all these years later. Particular thanks are owed to Jonathan Turner and Robin Holly, who provided invaluable feedback when I sorely needed it, and the rest of the weekend gaming crew.

Likewise, none of this would be possible without the support of friends near and far (*waves to the September Moms*) and the understanding and forbearance of my family, including my children who no longer blink when I wander around the house muttering about blowing up shit in space, my big floofy dog who gets dragged on long walks whenever I get stuck (and loves it like it's a brand new adventure every single time), and most of all my extraordinarily talented oldest daughter Tarian who knows just when to bring me tea and does her best to make me eat more vegetables, though she is never gonna sell me on kale. Love you all, every day. Sorry I forgot to do the laundry again.

And last, but so not and never least, all my thanks and love to my best friend Laurie Vadeboncoeur, who dared me to write something all those years ago, and forgot to tell me I could stop. For her sins, she gets to beta-read all my work, and she hasn't changed her phone number yet so I must still be doing okay.

Thank you for reading. Peace (-:

—Suzanne
NOVEMBER, 2018

Available May 2020 from DAW,
the thrilling sequel to *Finder*
by Suzanne Palmer

DRIVING THE DEEP

Read on for a special excerpt.

In the center of the spindle tube between two sections of the Shipyard, tumbling with the casual grace of zero gravity, there was a giant, magenta, inflatable hamster. Fergus Ferguson reached out to a wallbar to slow himself before he collided with it; the last unattended animal he'd run across had been a four-meter-long robotic snake that had chased him through three sections of hab before he managed to lock himself in a closet. The footage—perspective of the snake, naturally—was looping on all Shipyard vid monitors for a week.

"Maison?" he called.

There was no answer, no sound of snickering from beyond the next set of blast doors.

Wary, he moved closer, inspecting it from arm's length. There was no faint, resonating buzz in his gut to indicate something electrified, no detail that stood out to suggest it was anything other than the obvious. Fergus backed away, skirted along the smooth gray-blue wall until he was well past it, then shoved off through the doorway with only a few paranoid glances behind him.

The hamster didn't explode, didn't call out to him, and best of all, didn't follow.

In the two months or so that he'd been back there, Fergus had explored far more of the Shipyard than he ever had before, but still figured he'd seen less than twenty percent of it. Most of the remaining spaces weren't easily accessible and, even if they had been, too dangerous for casual, solo adventuring. The army of bots doing the heavy work of building spaceships vastly outnumbered the tiny handful of people doing the thinking and inventing and goofing off, and it was best not to get in their way.

From the spindle that ran the length of the orbital station, he dropped into a connecting corridor that led to one of the habitable rings, and as he floated down, he admired, for the thousandth time, the edge-on view through the thick portals of Pluto's surface below.

The planet—hundreds of years later, there was still active resistance to its demotion to microplanet—was a beautiful tapestry of browns and blacks and tans spun together like a rich, poorly stirred hot chocolate, even down to the tiny hint of foam at its polar cap. There were only a few lights visible from there, nav beacons and communications boosters and automated science stations, none of them designed for occupation. Pluto and its partner rock, Charon, were positioned in precisely the sweet spot, in terms of privacy, of being far enough out that, if you were going to go this far, odds were good you'd just keep going until you found brighter skies again around some other star, and never even notice it as you passed it by.

Between spindle and ring, the artificial gravity kicked in, and he walked rather than floated into the main lounge. Noura and Kelsie were both there, hunched over a holo display with data scrolling rapidly past underneath an undulating set of blue lines drawn in air.

"Hey, Ferg," Kelsie said, glancing up from the console. The roundness of her face was accentuated by her close-cropped blond hair and nearly consumed by the omnipresent wide grin that was the essence of Kelsie to the core. Noura was her opposite, with long, tight springs of black hair that, when not painstakingly tied down in tiny braids, spread out in a glorious halo around her olive-tone face, as it was now. Her expression was somber, her brow furrowed in puzzlement.

"You two know anything about the giant hamster floating in corridor nine?" Fergus asked.

"Did you touch it?" Kelsie asked.

"No."

"Then no, I know nothing about it. You'd have to ask Maison."

Noura waved her hand through the screen, and both pattern and dataset changed. "You have a message," she said without looking up.

"Me?"

"Yes, you."

"Who from?"

"Do you really think we'd violate your privacy by watching your personal messages?" Kelsie asked.

"Yes," Fergus said.

"Then it's from your friend Mari," Noura said. "We like her."

Fergus headed over to Ignatio's console, brushed green fur off the chair, and sat. His leg ached dully from the transition into grav, but he was grateful he still had a leg at all. For a while, it wasn't clear he would.

"Tomboy?" he asked.

The steady green iris above the console stared at him. "Good morning, Fergus," the smooth, ungendered, artificial voice of the station intelligence said. "Have the others already informed you that you have a message?"

"Yes, thanks," he said. "Could you play it for me?"

"I would be happy to," Tomboy said.

Mari's face appeared on the screen. She looked different. Not older, he thought, but less unsettled. Not the same surly nineteen-year-old he'd been dragged through a war with. "Hey, Fergus," she said. "Calling with the news, as you asked. We've finally permanently reconnected the Wheel Collective and Blackcans to Cernee's halo, and we're using what salvage we can pull from the destroyed habs to repair the others. No sudden decompressions anywhere in more than a week, so I think we're making progress."

Cernee was a deep-space settlement made of strung-together junk that barely held its air under the best of circumstances; the war there had pushed survival to the very brink.

"The good news is that the Governor thinks we can repair the sunshield that got bombed," Mari continued.

"The bad news, of course, is we can't afford to, not for a while. But for now, the shell seems stable, so eventually we'll get there. Oh, and the Shielders gave me something for you." She turned away from the camera, rummaging through something out of sight.

"This is the best part," Kelsie said from over the display.

"Shhhhh," Noura said. "I'm concentrating."

Mari sat up again, and held a large square of velopaper in front of her. On it was a drawing of a figure in a suit, small lightning bolts coming out of his fingers, near one edge of the paper. On the far side was a shape clearly meant to be a sunshield, although Fergus conceded it was possibly also a giant space banana. Between them was a large quantity of stars.

"They tell me to tell you that they've drawn you staying far away from Cernee, and of course as you know, once something has been added to their Narrative, it must be so," Mari said. "I think they're still mad at you."

Fergus thought that likely and couldn't say one way or the other if he deserved it.

"Aaaanyway, the Shielder who gave me this? I showed him how if I folded it just right, I could hide all the stars and put you right next to the sunshield," she said, demonstrating. "He actually screamed and ran away."

She set down the paper out of sight. "We could use someone with your problem-solving skills, if you ever do come back. Mr. Harcourt and the Governor and Ms. Ili seem to be working together for now, but the cracks are showing. The miners and other people who worked under Vinsic but weren't part of the coup attempt have banded together and seem to have nominated Tobb—Bale's brother?—as spokesperson. He's doing okay with it, though Bale has had to keep him and Harcourt from hitting each other a couple of times. Everyone is still on edge, whether they'll admit it or not. You probably won't believe me, but sometimes it's really nice to be back home in the peace and quiet of the family farm."

"What do they grow that far from their star?" Noura asked.

"Genmod lichen," Fergus answered. "Now hush."

"Uh, that's really about it," Mari continued. "The usual people say hello. If you're not still at the Shipyard, I guess they'll forward this on or save it for when you get back. If you're still there, call back and let me know why the hell you're procrastinating and getting on everyone's nerves instead of doing what you need to do. You know what I'm talking about."

The message ended. Fergus stared at the screen until Tomboy spoke up. "Would you like me to play it again?"

"No, thank you," Fergus said, and got out of his chair. Both Noura and Kelsie were watching him, leaning back in their seats and looking unsatisfied.

He went over to the kitchen alcove, made three bulbs of coffee, and set down two of them in front of the women before taking an empty seat. "What are you two looking at?" he asked.

"Either we've stumbled across a whole new phenomenon in physics, or we've got bad data from a sensor calibration problem on *Falconer*," Kelsie said. "So, yeah, trying to figure out how the sensor went *whumpf*. Here, look. Running this in super slo-mo."

She waved her hand through the console again, and a curved field appeared above it, a smooth grid of lines widening out. Just before the field popped, there was the briefest flash of something. Kelsie backed it up, and Fergus could now make out a tiny break in the lines of the grid. "Looks like a pothole," he said.

"Lasts about a thousandth of a second. A few dropped data packets, is all. Can't reproduce it."

"Except you can, but only running the exact same sequence along the exact same trajectory," Noura said, "which is what makes it odd."

"You ask Ignatio? Jumpspace physics is eir expertise," Fergus said.

"Ignatio was not helpful," Noura said.

"Ignatio wiggled all eir limbs at us and said it was nothing and went off to the kitchen to play with food," Kelsie said. She sighed and shut the display down. "I've been messing with the sensor array, but this really isn't my area. *Falconer*'s sensors are running Effie's latest firmware, which tested out fine in the sim lab, so if I can't find the issue, I'll pull them. When she gets back, we'll rebuild. I just wish I knew what went wrong. I'm an engines-and-hardware person, not a coder."

Kelsie swiped her hand through the display, clearing it, then brought up the firmware logics and the array schematics. "Still, I might as well get to it," she said. "I wouldn't want anyone to call *me* out on procrastinating!"

Noura leaned back on the couch and regarded Fergus. "About that," she said. "Your friend Mari is right: you *are* procrastinating. Though she's not correct about getting on our nerves—we enjoy your company, all of us; there are so few people we can bounce ideas off of."

"When you seven get going on engineering and computer intelligence stuff? I'm lost within a minute," Fergus said.

"Which is about fifty-three seconds better than everyone else," Noura said. "That's not the point. You brought us back *Venetia's Sword* from the man who stole her, at great personal risk and no small amount of injury, and we're deeply grateful. The ship is too. But you're not here just hanging out for our company; you're here because you don't want to go do the next thing. You don't want to go back to Earth."

"No, I don't," Fergus said. "I ran away from home when I was fifteen for good cause. I have no reason to ever go back."

"Except one," Noura said.

"Yeah." Fergus reached into a pocket in his shorts, pulled out an old key, set it beside the display. "One."

"It's been . . . seventeen years? Eighteen? You don't think your cousin has forgiven you for stealing his motorcycle, given the circumstances?"

"I don't know," Fergus said. "I haven't forgiven myself."

"So, go do it, and then you can."

Fergus laughed. "As if it's that easy! Last time I was in-system, I managed to make myself a wanted man on Mars, and who knows how far that's spread? And even if I can get to Earth without someone catching me, it has been *nineteen* years. I don't know where my cousin even is!"

"Fergus, you find things all over the galaxy for a living," Noura said, her dark eyebrows knitted together. "Surely, you don't think those are good reasons for not going. Unless your cousin is dead or gone off-planet himself, he'll be in the node listings. You land and fetch the motorcycle out of storage. It's been sitting a long time, but Kelsie can give you detailed instructions and a botkit for maintenance. Then you locate your cousin, meet up with him and give it back, buy him a drink and say you're sorry, catch up on old times . . ."

"I don't want to catch up on old times," Fergus said. "They were all horrible. That's why I ran away."

"Well, then, do this and you're free. You don't ever have to go back to Earth again."

A rail-thin, shirtless, hairless man wearing thick, opaque red goggles strolled into the lounge. "I think you should just stay," the newcomer said, his accent a perfect meld of Earth West Indies and Lunar Colony immersion-net-five. "Never look back."

"Maison," Fergus said. He and Kelsie were the youngest and newest of the Shipmakers of Pluto, originally founded by Noura's mother and Theo's uncle, both long since passed. "Is that your hamster in section nine?"

"Did you touch it?" Maison asked.

"No."

"Then I'm sure I know nothing about it. Hey, I have a project you could help me with, Double-Eff, my man."

"Yeah?" Fergus said. "Remember the last time you said you needed my help testing a new exosuit insulator, and you filled my suit with spraycheese? While I was wearing it? It took me weeks to get that smell out, and it gave me a *rash*."

Maison beamed. "I found it informative."

"I'm sure. No, thanks."

Maison parked himself on the arm of the sofa near Noura. "What's on the agenda for today?" he asked.

"Reviewing *Falconer*'s sensor code," Kelsie said without looking up.

"The rest of us are all still waiting on schematics from you for the new ice-driver prototype," Noura said. "Need I remind you, we have paying customers waiting—Enfi Maub has given us a substantial deposit—and having a good reputation for reliable products delivered in a timely manner is necessary to fund the fun, experimental projects?"

"Yes, yes," Maison said. "I'm working on it. Up here." He tapped his forehead.

"Great," Noura said. "Meanwhile, I've been overseeing the repairs to *Venetia's Sword*'s mindsystems and working on the next-gen model *Whiro* with Tomboy. LaChelle has cloistered herself in the design VR and won't show anyone what she's got so far except to say she's going for a 'dangerous' look. Theo can't start prepping the fab units until either she's done or you are, so he's off in the garden wheel, communing with his bonsai, and until we start constructing *something*, Kelsie has nothing to try to break, so she's sitting here overthinking a sensor firmware bug. I gather your primary agenda, despite all of us waiting on you, continues to be pranking Fergus?"

"Mostly," Maison said. "It's a delicate art."

"Where's Effie?" Fergus asked.

"Pluto's atmosphere is precipitating right now. Effie took a rover down to the surface to watch," Noura said.

"Ignatio go with her?"

"No, ey're still in the kitchen, trying to turn an egg perfectly inside out. Don't ask me. It's an alien thing."

"Anything I can do to help? I mean, except for the

egg," Fergus asked. "Ignatio is on eir own with that one.
But the rest of you . . ."

Maison raised a hand. "Yes!" he said. "I—"

"Not you either, Maison."

Kelsie laughed. "Go do your Earth thing, Earthman.
Get it over with. You'll come back to Pluto feeling like
you weigh a twelfth as much, I guarantee it. And maybe
by then, we'll have *Whiro* online and you can help me
test-drive it."

"But I still haven't figured out how to get down to Earth
without risking Alliance orbital security," Fergus said.

"The Alliance never even ID'd you on Mars, unless
you've been up to no good elsewhere and haven't told
us," Kelsie said.

"No," Fergus said. "Not that I've been caught at, as
far as I know. But I can't be *sure.*"

"That's how we know you don't want to go. If you did,
you'd have a dozen crazy schemes by now even if you
knew the Alliance was looking for you," Kelsie said.
"So, how about we solve this one for you? We have a
droneship cleared to pick up a half-ton of maple from a
sustainable forestry provider in the Atlantic States Coalition, because LaChelle wants it for *Whiro*'s interior.
We have environmental controls in the cargo bay to
keep the wood from getting damaged in transit, so you'd
be able to ride it down. Not a comfortable trip, but Alliance oversight wanes drastically once you're inside
Earth's gravity well. As soon as you're dirtside, you
think you can do a run around local authorities enough
to get yourself from eastern North America to Scotland
without getting caught?"

"I don't—"

"If it was for a job, could you do it? Be honest."

"Yeah," Fergus admitted.

"Well, you're on a job," Noura said. "Your client is
you. What you're finding is peace with your family, whatever that means."

"And it's about time," Kelsie said. She suddenly laughed, clapping her hands together. "Oh, look how sad Maison looks at the idea he might lose you!"

"Am not *sad*," Maison said. His face was a scowl. "I have other things to do."

"Like ice-driver schematics," Noura said.

Fergus looked back over at Kelsie and Noura. *Everyone is right*, he thought. *I'm procrastinating.*

"This cargo droneship . . ." he started to ask.

"About five hours 'til I launch it. Knowing you, you need about ten minutes to pack, so that gives you some time to kill," Kelsie said. She reached under the table and pulled out a too-familiar deck of hexagonal cards. "Ever played Venusian Monkeypoker?"

"I'm in! I'm in!" Maison shouted, vaulting over and into a chair.

Fergus groaned. "Not me," he said. Only three months before, he'd spent several days trapped on a very small ship with too many angry people and one lone Monkeypoker deck between them, and it was still too soon to even look at those cards again.

Noura got up from the couch. "Come on, Fergus," she said. "We can go down to the kitchen and, if Ignatio hasn't coated every single surface with egg already, you can help me with lunch and tell me about what you might want to do after Earth. For real, not this Corallan Tea Master thing you keep bringing up as a dodge."

"Maybe it's not a dodge," he said.

"Of course it is," she answered, following him to the door. "Even you would have difficulty getting into trouble there, and you and I both know you just couldn't abide that for more than an hour."

"Hey! I made it almost five hours, the one time I was there," he protested.

Noura laughed. "Five whole hours? Well, that certainly proves me wrong," she said. "One of these years, I'd love to scan and map your neural networks, just to see what sort of ship mindsystem I could build out of that."

"Now, that would just be cruel to a poor ship," he said, and headed for the kitchen, desperately hoping Ignatio had committed something spectacularly messy with the eggs and they could talk about that—or really, anything else—instead.

The droneship, nestled in the shuttle dock between several larger ships, was about one-third storage, one-third engine, and one-third control systems, which left, Fergus figured, exactly zero-thirds room for an inconveniently tall Scot.

"This is *Constance*," Noura said, patting the blocky silver hull with affection. "Passive jump only, of course, because she's uncrewed, but she's pretty fast otherwise. She's a class-two intelligence, so she won't be much company on the ride in, but I've programmed her with a pleasant recital voice and the entire works of Rumi, Ghalib, and Bashō."

"Tell me you're not expecting me to ride loose in the cargo compartment—they'll detect my freshly battered corpse on every single waypoint scan between here and Earth."

"I modified *Constance*'s maneuvering parameters, so she won't pull too many hard gees on you," Kelsie said. "Which is too bad; she's really nimble for such a basic model."

"Not entirely basic anymore," Maison said. He walked to the back of the cargo bay and swung open an instrument panel. Inside was a person-sized padded compartment. "It locks from the inside and can only be overridden by *Constance*. Scan-proof, full safety straps, field-buffered against acceleration. Integrated console and bio facilities. And when you're in transit, you can bop around the cargo bay all you want, stretch your legs."

"People-smuggling doesn't seem like one of your usual businesses," Fergus said.

Maison shrugged. "It's not, but Effie's been on a big

stealth-tech kick and said it was almost impossible to build the perfect, scan-proof hiding place in a ship this size, so I took it as a challenge. It beats 97% of military-grade scanners, and the other 3% too if the operators aren't paranoid, hyper-thorough bastards."

"I'm going to be mostly stuck in that tiny space for three days?" Fergus said.

Noura crossed her arms in front of her chest. "What's your other plan for getting to Earth, then?"

Fergus let his shoulders slump. "Fine," he said. "Can it low-stat me?"

"Not really, but it does have sleep aid functions," Noura said. "And we packed you plenty of food and water in the tool cupboard. Are you ready? You've got fifteen minutes until launch."

Fergus nudged his pack with his foot. "I've got everything I need right here. Just need to put my exosuit on and then I'm set."

"The pod is fully programmed for comfort," Maison said. "You could ride this baby naked all the way to Earth without a single goosebump."

"As much as flying seven billion kilometers or so stuffed naked into a cupboard has always been a fantasy of mine, I'll pass," Fergus said. He unfolded his suit and stepped into it, pulling it up and over his shoulders before sealing it and putting his boots back on. The suit was top-of-the-line military-grade with some black-market enhancements and had been a gift when he'd left Cernee, and it was virtually irreplaceable.

Noura noticed the small circular patch on the back, below his neck, as he was pulling the hood up. "What's this?" she asked.

"It's called a city-mark," Fergus said. "Harcourt and Mari gave it to me. It means I can call Cernee's Wheel Collective *home* if I want."

"That's sweet," Kelsie said. "You're getting better at this making-friends thing, you know."

Maison mimed wiping tears from his cheeks with double fists. "Our boy is growing up!" he said.

Noura embraced Fergus. "Ignore him," she said. "Be careful, and try not to spend the entire trip worrying. Either it will go smoothly and the worry will have been pointless, or something will go terribly wrong and you'll handle it as you always do. I've known you for over ten years now, and I know you've got this."

Kelsie whacked him on the shoulder. "You're gonna be fine," she said, grinning. "We'll be here waiting for you when you're done, with drinks to celebrate. Oh, hang on!"

She pulled a small packet from her coveralls and handed it to him. "Bot maintenance kit, for the motorcycle engine. It's been sitting a long time, but this should take care of the worst of it. Instructions inside."

"Thanks," Fergus said. "I hadn't thought of that."

"That's why I'm the engine person and you're not," she said.

"Hey, bring us back some real ice cream, Double-Eff, if you can," Maison said. He dropped a flattened disk in Fergus's hand. "Encrypted comm, bounces through random boosters between here and Earth. Sometimes indirect but always gets through. I call it a *pager* because that's snappy and retro. If you get in trouble, let us know so we can drink your share of the party booze."

Fergus stepped backward into the compartment, waved to Noura and Kelsie, and then gave Maison a two-fingered salute before Maison slammed the door shut.

It was claustrophobically tight inside, but as soon as he locked the door, it filled with a soft yellow glow and fresh circulating air. When the console powered on, he synced his suit comms with it, buckled himself in upright against the padded back—once he was out of gravity, it would be nice not to rattle around helplessly inside his cupboard—and then connected up his suit and oxygen to the drone's feeds.

"Hello, Mr. Ferguson," a pleasant, matronly voice said.

"I am *Constance*, your droneship system. We are launching in nine minutes. Are you secured?"

"I am, *Constance*," Fergus said. "Thank you."

The connection ended; at class two, *Constance*'s computer probably couldn't manage much beyond that functional exchange. As long as it had all the piloting and navigation skills needed, Fergus could live without conversation. He could also live without the launch. "Constance, please put me to sleep," he said.

"Certainly," the drone answered.

His resistance to the aerosol was just enough that he could feel it start to kick in. "Okay, Earth, ready or not, here I come," he muttered, and closed his eyes.